AMBUSH

ALSO BY PAUL CARSON

Betrayal

Scalpel

Cold Steel

Final Duty

AMBUSH

Paul Carson

St. Martin's Press New York

This novel is a work of fiction. Names and characters are the product of the author's imagination and any resemblance to actual persons, living or dead, is entirely coincidental.

www.stmartins.com

Library of Congress Cataloging-in-Publication Data

Carson, Paul, 1949–
Ambush / Paul Carson.—1st St. Martin's Press ed.
p. cm.
ISBN-13: 978-0-312-36711-4
ISBN-10: 0-312-36711-2
1. Irish Americans—Ireland—Dublin—Fiction. 2. Drug traffic—Ireland—Dublin—Fiction. 3. Undercover operations—Ireland—Dublin—Fiction. I. Title.

PR6053.A719 A43 2008
823'.914—dc22

2008009446

First published in the United Kingdom by William Heinemann

First U.S. Edition: June 2008

10 9 8 7 6 5 4 3 2 1

To Jean

Acknowledgments

Thanks to my agent Darley Anderson and his team at the Darley Anderson Literary Agency.

Thanks also to Susan Sandon and Random House UK for their support and encouragement.

Special thanks to the doctors and nursing staff of the Colman K Byrne Unit, Damiens and Cleary wards, Beaumont Hospital in Dublin.

Since *Ambush* is a novel about bombs, bullets, brothels, drug trafficking and covert police operations my source in these areas has elected to remain anonymous. However, with good behaviour, he should be out in five years.

1

They arrived early, just as the first greyish streaks of daylight broke through a Dublin skyline.

'Shift it.' Sean Kennedy tapped on the driver's side of a black Toyota Corolla and the window slid open. The car was fogged from cheap French cigarettes and Kennedy waited until the air cleared and the two chain-smoking Russians inside stopped coughing. 'I'll cut in front of you at the end of the road. Keep about a five-minute gap between us so I can find a parking space. When I pull out you drive in and wait until I give the word.' Kennedy knew the men only by their first names, Alex and Matthe, and reckoned they were in their mid forties. Alex understood English better so Kennedy spoke mostly to him. 'Stay in constant contact.' Alex translated all this to his partner who was leaning across from the passenger side, his face a mixture of confusion and edginess. His expression didn't change as the instructions were explained.

They were in the driveway of a Georgian house at one end of a quiet road in an affluent south city suburb. Behind its bolted doors a middle-aged bank executive, his wife and three children were bound and gagged, and struggling to get free. But they were roped securely together in a bedroom and out of sight of any windows.

'Does Matthe know exactly what to do?' Kennedy loathed working with outsiders and this duo was worrisome. Their English was poor, they looked shifty and suspicious, and dressed like gypsies. But they were experienced killers and had brought a small arsenal of handguns, smoke bombs and explosive grenades.

Alex leaned his right hand out of the window and flicked a dead cigarette butt on to a sad-looking flowerbed. He fixed on Kennedy and held his gaze, his breath frosting in the chill morning air. 'He understands, Mr Kennedy. I have explained it to him like you said.' The engine was gunned alive and the Toyota edged away from the house, then turned right towards rush hour traffic already gathering on a main road five hundred yards ahead.

Fuck you, thought Kennedy as he limped past a silver Saab coupé, its engine running to thaw ice clinging to the windscreen. The trussed-up banker owned both cars and by giving up the keys without too much of a struggle had protected his youngest daughter from a second lit cigar being ground into her face. Kennedy shivered as the cold penetrated, grabbed at the lapels of his overcoat and dug his chin deep for cover. He stopped at the gateway and looked up and down, then returned to the Saab, satisfied no one was watching.

The street was a mixture of terraced Georgian houses and grand, high, narrow-roofed detached villas. The area reeked of money and style, with electronically controlled gates protecting entrances and CCTV cameras recording all internal movements. There were trees along the pavements;

the gardens were well-groomed and tidy, without debris, unusual in a city notorious for its litter. The residents were mainly well-to-do business types, barristers, surgeons and senior embassy personnel. Lights glowed in bedroom windows as other occupants stirred for the day ahead and already one top-of-the-range black Mercedes had crunched across gravel and out on to the main road before picking up speed and heading towards the city centre. It was five minutes past six on the morning of 10 February and a cold, crisp day, with a hint of snow you could almost smell in the air. The weather bureau had predicted heavy falls along eastern counties of Ireland, with black ice on inland country roads. By now, dark and angry-looking clouds were rolling in from the north, and temperatures were dropping, ice and frost clinging to every surface.

Harry Power, the fifty-eight-year-old Minister for Justice in the Irish government, was already up and dressed in his own spacious town house, halfway along the same street. He was a tall man, six three in his bare feet, with a broad frame and thick, coarse hands. He had cauliflower ears and a crooked nose from his rugby-playing days, yet a ruggedly handsome face despite these imperfections. Power was married to a woman twelve years younger and one inch shorter, making them an eye-catching couple whenever they ventured out on the Dublin social scene, which wasn't often as the government Minister detested small talk and gossip, preferring to be at home with his family or at work doing something useful.

Journalists nicknamed him 'the bruiser' but this had more to do with manner than appearance as he had a reputation of giving tough press briefings. He could scowl correspondents into submission or pull the legs from under them with a well-chosen caustic comment. There was general agreement he'd hardened recently, was now even less tolerant, snapping and snarling and cutting people short when they bored or bothered him with trivial matters.

Alex drove slowly, checking rear-view and side mirrors for any unusual activity, any sign he was being followed. He was tall and bald, with a thick, bushy moustache that covered his flared nostrils. He wore denims and walking boots, with an oversized roll-neck and in between cigarettes chewed gum aggressively, as if frightened his jaws might lock if he stopped.

The traffic crawl on the two-lane artery was steady and the Russians soon cruised past shuttered shops, then a petrol station bustling into activity, with cartons of milk and that day's newspapers piled near the entrance. A youth of Oriental appearance yawned as he struggled to drag gas canisters on to the forecourt. Gradually it became a stop-start journey, with brake lights glowing intermittently along the lines of cars in front. Cyclists in protective headgear zipped past, legs pumping like pistons, dodging and weaving between vehicles. Alex negotiated a particularly dangerous roundabout, then cut through to the single city-bound intersection and another tailback. His mind began to drift until a sudden dig in his ribs focused his attention. Ahead a silver Saab coupé was stopped in a park-and-ride slipway, its sidelights flashing. 'Yeah, that's him,' he grunted and flicked the Toyota indicator, edging the car closer to the right. Now he could see Sean Kennedy, his head craned to check who was following. As the Saab moved out, Alex turned into the vacant spot and killed the engine. He glanced at his sidekick, noticing he was sweating despite the cold. '*Bud gatovi* [Get ready],' he said, then grabbed a hand reaching into a side pocket. '*Ja chatu videt* [No cigarettes. I want to be able to see].' He wetted his moustache with the tip of his tongue and unwrapped a fresh packet of Wrigley's, looking around to familiarise himself with the area.

To his right was a park surrounded by black railings and thick hedging. To his left, on the other side of the road, was an untidy group of shops including a dry-cleaners and pharmacy. There was little activity, with only an occasional pedestrian hurrying against the cold. 'This is good,' he muttered, 'very good.' Matthe nodded as he too checked the locale. Matthe was small and swarthy, with an untidy mop of dark hair, long side locks and twisting hairs coiled in both ears. He was an uneasy man, brown eyes darting nervously from side to side, fingers fidgeting without a cigarette to occupy them.

Eighteen months previously Justice Minister Harry Power's only son Michael, a sixteen-year-old boy with a bright future, had been found dead in a filthy downtown toilet, a syringe sticking out of a vein in his left arm. By the time the door was kicked in rigor mortis had locked the boy's frame and he had to be eased out of the cubicle and transported to the city morgue as discovered. And the tousle-haired Michael was still in that same half-bent, crouched position when his father came to identify the body lying on a white marble autopsy table surrounded by police officers who didn't know where to look. Harry Power stood over his son and wept. He grasped a cold and waxen hand, and tried desperately to straighten the curled-up fingers. Then he squatted on his hunkers and stared into the lifeless eyes of the boy who happily had said 'cheerio' some twenty-four hours earlier, claiming he'd be back soon, that he was only going into town for a few hours. Yet somewhere along that final journey Michael had scored enough heroin to kill himself. No one knew who the dealer was and none of Michael's friends would admit any knowledge of his secret life or where he got money to buy drugs, or who had led him into that underbelly of society. Weeks later and Power was no wiser, breaking his heart even more. He could grieve, and did so openly and emotionally, but could get no understanding of his son's death. What was missing in his life that he needed heroin? He was young and talented, a straight As student, popular among his peers and a keen sportsman.

Sean Kennedy drove the silver coupé to the next set of traffic lights, then turned right and cruised for half a mile before swinging right again. He was on open road and against the flow of traffic, and put his good foot to the accelerator, pushing to fifty in a thirty-speed zone. All he could see was frosted rooftops, icy pavements and lights glowing in windows. No one was on the street. Fifteen minutes later he made another right and criss-crossed three narrow sidetracks until he was back in the driveway at the top end of the quiet road with its red-brick Georgian terraced houses and expensive detached villas. He checked his watch. Six thirty-five. Close, but still on time. Twenty-nine-year-old Kennedy was a native Dubliner and originally from a respectable middle-class suburb close to the city centre. He was six two, with blond hair pulled back in a ponytail, ice-blue eyes and tight, narrow lips. His left leg dragged, the result of an old knife injury that had severed a major nerve.

Harry Power's crusade began ten weeks after he buried his son. He was now a man driven by anger and revenge, determined to make an impact on the country's growing narcotics trade. He forced a series of measures through the Irish

Parliament, including the decriminalisation of soft drugs such as cannabis, while possession of hard drugs such as heroin or cocaine carried a fifteen-year prison term.

Trading in or selling any compound, soft or hard, was increased to a mandatory twenty-year-without-parole sentence. However, Power's main targets were the criminal gangs who controlled the importation and supply routes. Using anti-terrorist legislation, the word of a senior police officer under oath was enough to convict traffickers and guarantee a life stretch. And life meant life, with no hope of release except in a coffin. Power later defended his policy at press briefings. 'These scum will be treated like the terrorists they've become. The burden of proof has shifted and they will no longer intimidate or threaten witnesses, or hire expensive lawyers for protection. They will no longer hold whole communities to ransom.'

Ireland's police force, the Garda Siochana, was galvanised into action. For years they'd been constrained by insufficient evidence to clinch convictions against known drug barons. Witnesses would often retract statements at the last minute, or not turn up for court cases, or simply disappear off the face of the earth. Now, dawn raids became a common occurrence, with petty criminals and their associates lifted for questioning. Intelligence gathering showed five main groups involved in narcotics and within weeks many were either under arrest or had fled the country.

Sean Kennedy spoke briefly with Alex by cellphone, double checking position and readiness. His Russian henchmen were still parked in the slipway of a double-lane, one-way city-bound road. However, one track was strictly for taxis and buses, forcing other traffic into a narrow line. His Saab parked in the front driveway of the banker's house, Kennedy kept the engine running with the heater on and opened a briefcase that lay on the passenger seat beside him. It was full of paperwork and pens, and a pocket calculator with figures on its display. He played idly with the keypad. With his ponytail tucked firmly underneath the lapels of his camel-hair overcoat he looked just another business type starting his work as soon as he'd closed the front door. Underneath the pages rested a Heckler & Koch handgun, its safety catch off. At his feet lay two AN-M8 smoke grenades and a spare magazine of 9mm bullets. He loosened his shirt collar and ran a finger round his neck for comfort, then flicked the car heater to his feet where he felt the chill penetrate. Dark clouds now covered the city and any early morning brightness was turning to gloom.

Harry Power kissed his wife lightly on the cheek as she fussed around the kitchen table, preparing breakfast for their twin ten-year-old daughters moving about upstairs. She was red-haired, with high cheekbones and full lips, at that hour of the morning still in her night attire and wearing floppy slippers. 'Jane, I'll try to get home early,' he said, snatching at a bread roll and nibbling the corner before stopping as crumbs flaked on to his suit. Jane brushed the front of his jacket, straightened his tie and leaned up to peck his lips. Then she held his gaze severely. 'The girls are expecting you at the concert. Don't disappoint them, please.' Power slapped his brow and grimaced. He knew how important such events were to the twins, knew how much Jane was working to restore a normal family life. His wife had been a rock after their son's death, keeping everyone occupied and maintaining daily routines. Now he noticed her face tighten angrily. 'I'll cancel the last press conference and be back no later than six,' he promised. Jane's expression changed to a warning frown. 'You better be here or there'll be hell to pay later.' Power ran through the day ahead in his mind.

There was a Cabinet briefing at eight where he would present interim results of his anti-drug campaign. Later he would offer the same data to the press corps, then the rest of his diary was full with meetings, conferences and a planned visit to the courts mid afternoon for a photo call and TV interview with Sky news. His campaign had caught the world's attention and other police forces were watching developments with keen interest, quietly wondering how they might incorporate some of the controversial Irish legislation into their own criminal laws. 'I'll make it,' he promised, fleeing an even more threatening glare. He picked up a phone in the hallway and punched a ten-digit code. 'I'm ready.' His usual gravelly voice sounded hoarse and he cleared his throat.

Sean Kennedy edged the Saab slightly out of the gateway and stopped. He watched as an unmarked police car pulled up outside the Justice Minister's house and counted two passengers plus driver; each of whom he knew to be armed. Power's anti-drug war had made him enemies and a target for retribution. So every day before he opened his front door he contacted his bodyguards for clearance before leaving. There were also armed detectives on duty throughout the night. While the family slept, two shadowy figures patrolled the downstairs and garden.

Kennedy checked his watch: 6.45 a.m. Bang on time, changeover. He flicked the car heater full to windscreen and a light mist disappeared. Now he had a clear view of the frosted road and all that moved. 'They should be leaving within the next few minutes.' Kennedy spoke slowly and quietly into his cellphone. There was no reply and he glanced at the handset in case the battery was dead. But there was no warning light and this time he barked into the mouthpiece, 'Can you hear me? Where the fuck are you?' He felt his heart race.

Then a thick drawl eased his fears. 'I hear every word, Mr Kennedy. We are waiting.'

Now Kennedy noticed one of the detectives walking up and down the pavement, his gaze taking in the surroundings, then settling on the Saab. He was in a long open trench coat with a beige scarf draped round his neck and his hand reached inside the coat. Kennedy froze as he watched him dial on his mobile phone and felt underneath the pages in the briefcase until he touched the comforting steel of his handgun. Then he leaned back in his seat, cellphone to right ear as if in conversation. The bodyguard still stared in his direction, then suddenly turned round. Kennedy couldn't see what was happening and shifted forward in his seat, eyes darting nervously. Now the large frame of Harry Power bustled into view, carrying a briefcase in one hand and a heavy coat in the other. Kennedy slowly let out a deep breath as he watched the detective put his mobile away. In the cold morning air the exhaust from the police car blocked his vision but he heard doors slam and the vehicle pulled out, heading towards the main artery ahead. 'They're in a blue Ford Mondeo with dark tinted glass and two aerials on the roof. The registration is 03 98192736. There are four inside and our target is sitting behind the driver.'

Harry Power was in ebullient mood. 'Did you see the match last night?' As he shifted around for comfort a bundle of

Cabinet paperwork resting on his knees threatened to spill out of his briefcase. An armed detective in navy tracksuit and woollen cap sat beside him, eyes scanning the roads and sidewalks. He grunted an inaudible reply, implying lack of interest. Any conversation would be one-sided until the Justice Minister was safely offloaded at government buildings, some three miles and about fifty minutes' driving time ahead. 'United were rubbish, absolute rubbish.' Power scanned the most immediate document half-heartedly, then shoved it to one side. 'Giggs missed two sitters. I mean, he had an almost open goal and blasted over the bar each time. You should have seen Ferguson's face, he was livid.' But there was no response from his entourage and he reluctantly switched his attention to the pages in front of him. At one stage he checked his watch and looked outside to see how far they'd progressed. He recognised a small newsagent, its lights glowing in the increasing gloom, a single customer at the counter. They'd gained no more than half a mile and inbound city traffic was banked up some considerable distance ahead. A soft flurry of snow whorled in the wind, not heavy or lying, but steady.

Sean Kennedy broke two red lights and overtook dangerously to close in on the Ford Mondeo. He ignored angry horns and flashing lights, keeping up a running commentary on his cellphone with Alex. 'I've passed the Texaco garage on Collins Road.' Then, 'Now about eight cars ahead but everything's at a crawl. I reckon we're ten minutes away from you.' He was in a wide two-way carriageway fringed by office blocks on both sides, lights glowing and figures moving as another working day began. At one stage he swerved into a bus-only lane and gained three spaces before forcing the Saab back into line. More angry hoots and shaking fists, more lights flashed. He touched base with Alex again. 'I'm five cars behind and coming up to the traffic lights at Hawkins roundabout.'

They had scouted the area closely the previous day and this time Alex came back immediately, his voice clear and zinging with anticipation. 'You are getting close, Mr Kennedy.'

The driver of the police car was a careful man called Liam Grimes, with ten years' experience in surveillance and protection duty. The Ford Mondeo Grimes drove was modified, with a high-powered engine offering extra thrust for a quick retreat in emergencies, but as he edged forward at crawl pace in the rush hour he knew this was the most vulnerable part of the journey. He glanced at the digital clock on the dash. It was seven fourteen and he remembered the Justice Minister had to be in government buildings by eight at the latest. Come on, he urged silently. Move, move. He flicked the windscreen wipers and cleared a light dusting of snow. 'That looks a bitter day out there,' he offered to break the monotony. There was only one half-hearted reply and when he squinted in the rear-vision mirror he noticed Power's head bent over paperwork. Outside the snow was falling more heavily, now settling on pavements. Umbrellas were snapping into action and Grimes silently wondered whether all this would slow them further. Then in his side mirror he spotted a silver Saab edge out from the row of vehicles behind and swerve back. The single line eased again and he touched off the accelerator gently. He considered pulling into the bus lane and cutting forward but knew the Minister would disapprove. And the media would have a field day if they found out: JUSTICE CHIEF CAN'T KEEP HIS OWN LAWS. So for a moment he idly inspected a small crowd milling around a bus stop, some huddled into their coats and jackets and stomping their feet, while others sullenly studied faces in the cars going past. Another forward move and Grimes recognised they were nearing Hawkins roundabout, a wide circular belt where traffic usually broke up. He glanced again in his side mirror. Whoever's in that Saab is in one helluva hurry.

Kennedy was four vehicles behind the Ford Mondeo when the line hit Hawkins roundabout. Here traffic could divert to different areas of Dublin's outer suburbs. Two roads led to the west and a motorway that circled the city, while another led to the eastern seaboard. The fourth cut into a major industrial estate and the final intersection carried remaining cars, vans and lorries towards the city centre. Kennedy knew Power's bodyguards always took the same route at this point. But getting access to the roundabout was a nightmare with vehicles careering at high speeds, often cutting across lanes and ignoring rights of way. It was here he made his move, first diverting to the inside bus corridor, then accelerating ahead of the Ford Mondeo. He sliced through oncoming traffic and cornered tightly and hard until he was within seconds of the city centre turn-off, then pressed his foot to the board. The Saab was forced through a congested tailback, then surged into the correct interchange, producing more angry blasts and shaking fists. But now Kennedy was where he wanted to be and barked into his cellphone, 'I'm there. Start looking.' He reached inside his overcoat and dragged out a balaclava, resting it on his knee. The Heckler & Koch was shoved firmly into his waistband and he began counting into the cellphone: 'One, two three . . .' The windscreen wipers swished furiously at the whiteness ahead.

The Russians stopped chewing. Both had slipped on black leather jackets; zipped tight to the neckline. Each had a hand grenade in one side with a smoke grenade in the other and spare bullet clips bulged their trousers. Kennedy's instructions allowed for a count to twenty over the cellphone and by now Alex could hear him call eleven. He nodded to his partner and they both dragged balaclavas over their heads, adjusting the eye slits. Matthe turned awkwardly so that he was kneeling on the passenger seat, head bouncing off the roof. He eased the safety catch off his pistol and opened the side door slightly, suddenly feeling ice-cold wind around his feet. He checked the street, watching someone huddled deep into an overcoat struggle with the shutters of the pharmacy. Further along, lights flickered in the dry-cleaning shop. The suburb was stirring and there were more pedestrians sheltering in doorways, waiting for their bus into town. Then, out the corner of an eye, he noticed one horrified face stare at him as a car ghosted past.

Liam Grimes, Power's driver, was suspicious. He'd only caught a glimpse of the silver coupé as it scorched past on the inside bus lane and hadn't time to follow its progress as he concentrated on negotiating traffic around the infamous Hawkins roundabout. But as the Ford Mondeo finally swerved into the city-bound road he felt sure it was ahead and still being driven erratically. His vision was further obscured by falling snow. Now he was in yet another one-way tailback running along an inside bus corridor. 'Sharpen up, everyone,' he snapped as he jammed on the brakes just in time to prevent the rear-ending of a VW Beetle in front. Inside, the three bodyguards stiffened and automatically reached for their handguns. Power's head shot up from his note taking. 'Anything wrong?'

* * *

'Eighteen, nineteen.' Kennedy forced the brakes on his Saab and waited for the inevitable crunch as the car behind crashed into his bumper. 'Twenty, go for it!' Thirty yards further back the police car again jerked to a halt as city-bound traffic ground to a sudden stop. Grimes spotted the passenger door of a black Toyota Corolla burst open and immediately tried reversing.

'Go, go,' screamed Alex as he kicked out the driver's door. He threw a smoke grenade directly in front of the spinning blue Ford Mondeo and within seconds there was a soft thump, then thick white smoke spewed into the air.

Ahead, Kennedy jumped from his Saab, balaclava on and ice-blue eyes darting wildly. There was at least a half-mile before the next intersection and no traffic coming against him on the one-way street. He was in total control and trained his handgun at a startled young woman in a Datsun Primera who was half out of the car. 'Make another fucking move and your head's full of holes.' He hurried over, dragging his dead leg, and kicked the door closed, ignoring the screams from inside. Behind that again, another driver, this time a middle-aged man in shirt and slacks, was standing beside his Honda CRV, a look of bewilderment all over his face. Kennedy first shot out his windscreen, then tossed a smoke grenade along the ground. It rolled for about thirty feet, then came another thump, followed by a belching thick white cloud that obscured all view. And still the snow fell, covering surfaces with a soft whiteness.

Inside the Ford Mondeo, Power was being forced down between back and front seats under the body of an armed detective. He could hear muffled angry shouts, then gunfire.

Now came violent curses and screams, and another salvo of shots. He closed his eyes and waited.

Matthe was small but quick. While white smoke billowed around the police car he blasted away the driver's side window and took out the frantic Grimes with a single headshot. Alex was at his side, shooting into the air to frighten off passers-by, but there wasn't a face to be seen as people hid behind cars or hunkered down in doorways to escape the ambush. Then two hand grenades were tossed through the shattered window of the Ford Mondeo and the Russians ran for cover. The explosions came almost immediately, within seconds of each other and now the car was unrecognisable, its metal twisted and tortured. From somewhere inside came a short, high-pitched scream. As the heat of the blasts reached the petrol tank there was an explosive fireball, and the air filled with flames and the smell of burning petrol.

Kennedy hopped from foot to foot, controlling all activity between his Saab and the blazing police car. Through the smoke and falling snow he could see vague shapes, hear screams of terror and bursts of gunfire, then another discharge followed by confused shouting. He spotted a movement about three cars behind and fired two rounds into the air. The movement stopped.

Alex and Matthe were finished. The Ford Mondeo was unrecognisable and burning out of control, the car behind it scorched and blackened. The two occupants had fled when the shooting started and were still running. 'Go, go,' Alex shouted and backed away quickly towards the front of the snarled line of cars. Matthe was dodging and weaving between vehicles, checking for heroes who might intervene. He saw Kennedy ahead, urging him forward, and turned to run. Suddenly, from a short distance behind, there was a burst of automatic gunfire and Matthe spun to see Alex twist in a full circle and fall heavily to the ground. Then two crouching hooded figures appeared out of the smoke and snow, Uzi sub-machine guns at their sides. One ran towards the writhing and bloodied Alex and there was another salvo of automatic gunfire.

Ahead, Kennedy, hidden from view, watched without emotion. He'd seen the shadowy figures scuttle along the side of the line of cars and shouted a warning to the Russians. Then he'd heard the unmistakable spit of an Uzi sub-machine gun and watched Alex slump in a hail of bullets. And now Matthe, the small, swarthy Russian with the rotting teeth and little English, was running towards him. He was about ten yards from the Saab coupé, balaclava off, face contorted with flight and fear. Coming hard after him, and gaining, were two hooded figures, now brandishing pistols. Matthe's black leather jacket was catching snow as he stumbled closer and Kennedy heard him shout something frantic but unintelligible. Kennedy wiped at the snow that was sticking to his cheeks and delayed until Matthe was almost upon him. Then he took out his hired Russian assassin with four quick rounds to head and chest.

2

Scott Nolan killed the clock alarm before it sounded and adjusted the volume to hear the seven o'clock news headlines.

A suicide bomber blew himself up last night in a crowded Tel Aviv restaurant, killing twelve and leaving over thirty injured . . . in Belfast two men were arrested at a police checkpoint after the body of a woman was found in the boot of their car. Apparently the victim had been shot in the head . . . two masked and armed raiders fired shots during an attempted supermarket robbery before midnight in one of Cork's northern suburbs . . . police arrested a gang of six youths after a fracas outside a Dublin nightclub left one teenager with critical head injuries and another with serious stab wounds.

Scott reached out, snapped off the radio and slumped back in bed, staring at the ceiling. Might as well have stayed in Detroit. He turned slightly, trying hard not to disturb, then felt a hand tug at the waistband of his boxer shorts. 'Where do you think you're going?' He rolled back and cuddled up to his wife, Laura, stroking her back under her cotton top. 'Well, I do have to get to work some time today and thought I'd run the shower.' Soft fingertips tiptoed underneath his shorts and a tingle of excitement ran up his spine. 'Although I could go in a bit late.'

Laura laughed teasingly and rolled away. 'You can forget that. I'm due in the office at nine sharp and if we start anything it could go on a very long time.' She leaned across and kissed her husband lightly on the lips, then kicked the duvet aside. 'You make breakfast, I'll have a shower first.' And I'll watch, thought Scott. He never tired of admiring the delicate curves and inviting bumps of his twenty-seven-year-old wife and waited until he heard the spray running, then grabbed his glasses and sneaked into the bathroom. He sat on the toilet seat and ogled, but steam quickly misted up his lenses. 'Pervert.' Laura finally spotted him.

'Tease,' he shot back. 'I've never known a woman take so much time soaping herself as you do when you know I'm watching.'

A wet hand reached out for a towel and Scott picked up his bathrobe and held it at arm's length. 'And just how many young women have you leered at while they showered?'

He grinned. Caught there, better back off. 'Let me rub you down,' he offered, trying to deflect the question. Laura stood in front of him, naked and dripping, though through hazy spectacles Scott was having difficulty getting a clear image. She was five eight, with short black hair she now dragged back with her fingers, and dancing blue eyes that mocked and taunted. As Scott wrapped his bathrobe round her and held her close, he knew why he'd moved to Ireland. Laura was beautiful, intelligent and independent, with a mischievous sense of humour. She made him laugh more than any woman he'd ever met and in bed she made his head spin. Enough, he thought at that moment, to make this full-blooded, short-sighted doctor cross the Atlantic.

'Did you catch the headlines?' Scott was in the shower, Laura drying between her toes.

'The usual,' he shouted above the noise of the power jet, 'bombings in Israel, a murder in Belfast, another robbery and shooting in Cork, and gang warfare outside some city night-club. Your regular dose of reporting in modern Ireland.' He squirted shampoo into his hair and worked it into a lather.

He sensed the shower door ease open and through suds could just about make out Laura's face, blurred but creased in concern. 'And I bet you're thinking, why didn't I stay in Detroit?' she said. Scott was two inches taller than his wife, with a lean frame Laura kept threatening to fatten. He had an awkward stoop from constantly squinting into the middle distance and a nervous habit of resettling his glasses round his ears. Not long into their relationship Laura told him she'd admired his dark eyebrows and eyelashes, grey eyes, strong face and dimpled chin. 'But certainly not your hair,' she added impishly, 'it looks like a wheat field after a tornado.'

Scott was the sort of man women fell for, believing him shy and needing protecting from the world. While it wasn't a ploy he deliberately worked on, over the years this sensitive and vulnerable look hadn't done his love life any harm.

Now he let the spray wash soap out of his eyes and turned towards his wife. 'I wouldn't care if this were the hell-hole of Siberia as long as you were with me.'

Laura's eyes narrowed to questioning slits as she closed the shower door. 'Good answer, cowboy.' Cowboy was her favourite tease word. When they'd first met, Scott had been wearing a Stetson as a joke at a party and she'd not forgotten the image. On bad days, if they were arguing, she might add the derogatory nickname, John Wayne.

They fought over the toaster and threw orange peel at each other before settling down to eat at the small breakfast counter. The Nolans lived on the top floor of a five-storey accommodation block in the red-brick suburb of Sandymount, about two miles from Dublin city centre. It was a typical newly built apartment with tight corridors, two narrow bedrooms, a kitchenette rather than a kitchen, and a half-decent living area with sofa, television and hi-fi sound system. There was an elevator to each level from an enclosed basement garage, with security cameras surveying all corners of the complex. Scott worked at Dublin's north side City Hospital as a paediatrician with special interest in liver disease; Laura was in PR and cycled to work daily. A radio was on in the background, mainly for traffic information. The city's gridlock and tailbacks were becoming as bad as Rome, Paris or London.

'So what's happening today?' Laura was now in tight denims and white silk blouse, and as Scott peered across he thought she looked good enough to eat.

'Grand teaching rounds at nine thirty, then case conference at eleven.' His transatlantic brogue reflected his origins, Irish-American. Thirty-year-old Scott was the second son of an Irish medical family who'd emigrated to the US in the sixties. His parents had moved around, seeking better job opportunities, finally settling in Chicago where his father secured a university post and his mother worked part-time in anaesthetics at North Shore Hospital.

'Why the late start, don't those grand rounds begin early?' Laura was sipping freshly squeezed juice.

'The transplant team won't allow access to the wards until they've moved two patients. I had to reschedule.' Scott had studied medicine, as had his parents before him, and was pursuing a career in paediatrics in Detroit before his move to Dublin.

'What's with the rest of the time?' Laura drained her glass and opened the dishwasher, deliberately flaunting her bottom as she bent over. Scott adjusted his spectacles for a better look.

'I'm meeting the Justice Minister for a press conference and later we've a joint interview with Sky News.'

'Oo,' mocked Laura, 'who's the big and important man, then? Mingling in government circles, TV interviews. Where's it all going to end? Maybe a Hollywood movie.' She paced the small kitchen, eyes dancing with mischief. Her hands drew an imaginary banner headline. 'Scott Nolan stars in *Gangs of Detroit*, the downmarket sequel to *Gangs of New York*.'

Scott grinned and bit into a slice of buttered toast. Silently he wondered about the press conference. He was an integral part of Justice Minister Harry Power's anti-drug campaign, snatched from obscurity because of previous US network experience. Each weekday night, for five minutes during prime-time television, Scott explained the medical background to drug abuse. The addiction, the cravings, the diseases, the cost to the community of caring for just one HIV or hepatitis C victim. With his awkward looks, nervous tics and transatlantic accent he was becoming the centre of curious attention. Who is this guy? He looks a cross between the nutty professor and George Clooney on a bad day. But one shot in particular had hooked his audience. Scott was in Dublin's Rotunda Hospital, the city's oldest maternity unit, holding a newborn. The infant's high-pitched screeches almost drowned his commentary. 'This baby is two hours old and already a drug addict. His mother injected heroin throughout pregnancy and now her child must be weaned off the narcotic like a street addict.' The image was riveting, the wriggling little bundle with its scrunched-up, pain-contorted face brutally captured the horrors of drug dependency.

Other segments caught the thirty-year-old doctor in a different setting. One was at the bedside where he held a wasted and bony hand, his intense grey eyes staring down at the patient. Another clip and he was in a clinic, a row of edgy and shifty strung-out junkies awaiting their turn for treatment. Usually the patients were male but an increasing number of shots captured female addicts, their plight more desperate to the viewers with frequent and very personal tales of selling their bodies to buy drugs. These five-minute clips soon became compulsive viewing and made Scott Nolan a household name. Next week he was arranging to take a crew into Mountjoy Gaol, Dublin's main penal complex. Here drug use was rampant – indeed, almost out of control – and he wanted an in-your-face image of addicts behind bars talking openly about their problems as inmates. The depression, the suicides, the appalling conditions and narcotic-related violence. He'd already cleared this with Harry Power and the prison authorities, the Justice Minister praising this initiative and the TV appearances so far. 'You bring substance and credibility to this campaign,' the big man had boomed at their last meeting three days previously. 'We need more of you and less of me on the airways. I can't do the caring doctor look but it comes naturally to you.' Scott now sipped a freshly brewed mug of coffee, as he planned how to handle the Sky News interview.

'Hey, it's snowing.' Laura was in the bedroom, touching up her eyelashes. 'Looks pretty heavy, too.'

Scott squinted past the blinds across the kitchen window. Large, fluffy flakes of snow drifted silently past and as he shifted for a better view he could see the ground covered in white, with powder lines peppering bushes and branches. Cars were edging nervously forward, their exhausts billowing in the freezing air. There were few pedestrians and those walking were slightly hunched, sheltering under umbrellas. There was a wonderful stillness to the scene, unlike the usual depressing mud and grey and damp setting he looked out on. This is when I really like Dublin, he thought. You can't see the litter, traffic crawls rather than races and it's so cold even the junkies stay off the streets.

'Could you give me a lift to work?' Laura wrapped her arms round her husband and for a moment they admired the snowstorm. 'Looks real cold out there and too dangerous for cycling.'

Scott kissed her lightly on the back of the head, savouring the scents of shampoo and perfume. Then he checked the time on the wall clock, noting it was coming up to eight, and factored the conditions into his cross-city journey. 'We'd need to leave very soon. Is that OK by you?'

'Sure. If I get in early I can clear paperwork before the phones start hopping.' Laura turned the radio up louder for traffic updates and immediately caught a breaking news story.

Reports are coming in of a shooting on the south side of Dublin. While details are sketchy it appears that a number of masked and armed men attacked an unmarked police car on the outskirts of Blackrock, about three miles south of the city centre. One eyewitness said two men in balaclavas forced the police car to a halt, then fired a number of shots directly into the vehicle. There are unconfirmed reports of hand grenades being used.

The female newsreader's voice lifted an octave, as if she were taken aback with the information.

There are a number of casualties, and emergency services are on their way to the scene. The route has been sealed off and motorists are being diverted away from the Blackrock and Monkstown areas. As soon as we have any more information we'll bring it to you immediately.

There was a short pause as paper was shuffled.

In other news, farm leaders say they will picket government buildings . . .

Scott turned the volume down and grimaced towards his wife. She turned away, her expression suddenly hard and tense. Dublin was becoming as violent as many other European capitals and not far off similar sized centres in North America. Scott hated violence, detested environments that bred hatred and hostility, and had been glad to leave Detroit for that very reason. But there were times since he'd crossed the Atlantic two years ago that he felt he was still ducking bullets. And this was a running sore between him and Laura. She was Irish through and through, born and raised in a small town land in County Kildare, a pretty rural area with a world reputation for horse breeding. And she wouldn't hear an unkind word about her country. 'Don't say anything, Scott Nolan,' Laura snapped. 'I know exactly what you're thinking and I'm not getting into another argument about where's the safest place on earth to raise a family.' Her voice, usually light and cheerful, was as tense as her features.

Scott sat at the kitchen table and swirled the dregs in his coffee mug. Where *is* the safest place to raise a family? Not Detroit, not Chicago, even though it's a beautiful town and OK if you know the safe areas. Not New York, definitely not after 9/11. LA? Never, that's a jungle. He thought of a number of other US centres but couldn't convince himself they'd be any better than Dublin. Yet Dublin disturbed him. Maybe it was his involvement with Harry Power's anti-drug campaign, for certainly he was seeing lowlife most people only read about in crime reports. And with his TV research he'd been confronted with the underbelly of Irish society. He couldn't put his finger on it exactly but he knew he was unsettled in the capital, uneasy, insecure and vulnerable. He couldn't get his head round raising children here, and how he longed to start a family. 'Let's just drop it, Laura. It's snowing, we're both running late, you can't cycle in to work and it'll be hell crossing the city.' Laura had her back to him, arms crossed, a posture of defiance. 'You put on something warm and let's get going.'

'OK, no shoot-out until sundown.'

Scott wrapped his arms round his wife from behind and squeezed her gently. Laura let her head rest on his shoulder and reached to stroke his hair. He grasped the hand momentarily, squinting at the engagement ring he'd bought in New York, then the gold band he'd slipped on Laura's wedding finger six months later. 'There'll be no shoot-out at sundown,' he whispered. 'I love you too much.'

For a long, lingering moment they held each other, consoling themselves in their own emotions. 'We'd better move,' Scott murmured, 'or cut our losses and go to bed.'

Laura turned round, now smiling again. 'It's very tempting, but what would your students say?'

'I could tell them I got held up in traffic.' Scott kissed his wife's eyes shut. 'Or smashed my lenses and couldn't get out of the apartment without tripping.'

They kissed, long and lovingly, wet and hungrily. Finally Laura broke away. 'Tonight, I promise. You won't know what's hit you.'

Then the phone rang.

'Yes?' Scott was trying to calm his ardour. On the other end of the line a colleague in the City Hospital was advising of yet another change in scheduling. 'Right, gotcha.' Scott checked his watch. 'It's five past eight. Allowing for traffic and snow I could be there by eight forty-five.' He hung up and caught Laura's teasing grin. 'I'll make you pay for this later. Right, now we'd better be on our way.'

Scott inspected himself in the mirror, adjusting his tie and making sure his fly was done up. His light-brown hair was a mess as usual and he quickly ran a comb through it, hoping Laura would be too rushed to notice. He slipped on a navy jacket, which contrasted nicely with his beige slacks, and closed the middle button. After some rummaging he finally found his briefcase and checked its contents, then dragged a rain jacket and scarf from the bedroom wardrobe.

Down the hallway came a plaintive moan. 'I've left my sheepskin at the office. Now how could I have done that?'

Scott grabbed another coat, one he wore frequently when out walking. It was a green-on-red half-length fleece and he knew it would reach Laura's knees at least. 'Take this,' he shouted and added one of his scarves, holding both out until

Laura was snugly wrapped. 'You drive and I'll get through some dictation until we're close enough to your offices.'

At the front door Laura snatched Scott's only baseball hat and pulled it down firmly above her eyes. 'I'm your chauffeur for the day, Dr Nolan.'

In the basement garge Laura climbed into the driver's seat while Scott shuffled into the back and began sifting through paperwork. He found his dictaphone just as the garage doors rolled up and their blue Volvo 850 edged towards daylight and falling snow. 'Dear Dr Harper,' Scott began in his slow and distinct dictation voice, 'thank you for referring this child for evaluation of his persisting raised liver enzymes.'

'Hey, this looks just great.' Laura sounded excited as the first flakes hit the windscreen and she flicked on the wipers.

Scott didn't look up; he was poring over pathology results attached to his referral letter. 'Take it easy,' he murmured, 'and stay in first gear until you're on level ground. I grew up in Chicago and snow drifts there are as high as houses.'

'So now you're a weather expert.'

Then the Volvo lurched forward, jolting Scott and spilling pages over the back seat. 'For God's sake, Laur—' Suddenly the side window shattered and the car jerked in a stop-start forward motion. 'No, no, please, nooooo,' Laura was screaming. Then Scott heard four rapid gunshots and felt his face splatter with warm, sticky fluid. A bright-red smudge filled his right lens. The Volvo slid slightly back along the incline from the basement garage and Scott scrambled desperately towards the front, yelling and fighting for the seat release. He heard Laura moan, then gasp, her windpipe bubbling. The wipers swished noisily, now dragging on the dry glass, and suddenly a shadowy figure appeared less than ten feet away. There was a handgun pointing downwards and

Scott squinted, then ducked as the windscreen shattered and a bullet whizzed past his right ear. Another pinged off the side panelling and he curled into a ball. 'Laura, Laura,' he shouted frantically as he dragged his wife's slumped body towards him, 'get down, get down.'

3

'That wasn't exactly a great success, Sean, was it? In fact, I'd call it a fuck-up on a massive scale.'

Sean Kennedy sat in the passenger seat of a ten-year-old Land Rover so covered in muck and splashes it was hard to make out its original bottle-green colour. There were dents on the front and sides, scratches along the paintwork and dirt sticking to wheels and registration plates. Beside him was a small, red-faced fifty-year-old called Joe McKeever. He wore a blue boiler suit over muddy boots and a cloth cap pulled down over his ears. Kennedy stared out through the grimy front window, smoking a cheap cigar and huddling into his overcoat for warmth. His face was fixed in a mixture of loathing and discomfort.

'And you can' blame me, Sean, me boyo. I provided the hardware and brought those two Ruskies over here myself.' McKeever's accent was straight Belfast, harsh and whingeing. 'I admit they were no great shakes with the language and looked a bit rough, but they were tough bastards and highly recommended. I'm goin' to have a helluva job buyin' off my supplier.' He shifted in his seat so he had his back to the driver's door and his suspicious brown eyes had a better view of Kennedy. 'Now *that* won' come cheap.' The engine was running to keep the heater powered and exhaust fumes billowed behind. They were parked along a lonely narrow country road in the Wicklow Hills south of Dublin, in a gravel lay-by in front of a pine forest with walking trails. The area was popular with ramblers and country joggers but now deserted, the inclement conditions deterring even the hardiest of hikers.

It was around midday on 12 February, two days after the heavy snowstorm that had swept across the eastern counties of Ireland, and a thaw was setting in. Southerly winds were lifting temperatures to around twelve centigrade, swelling mountain rivers and forcing fast-running streams along ditches and drains. Most roads were now passable and where Kennedy and McKeever made their rendezvous only patches of slush still clung to grasslands.

'I'll pay,' Kennedy finally spoke.

'Damn sure you'll pay, Sean. I'm not goin' out of pocket on those two.' McKeever leaned across, so close Kennedy could smell whiskey off his breath. 'And you took one of them out yerself.' The whinge rose with incredulity. 'I rent a couple of hard hitters, and you shoot one of them in the face and leave him in a heap to die.'

Kennedy edged back from the intimidating glare. 'He knew too much. He was a risk.' His voice was monotone, devoid of emotion.

'Risk, my arse,' snapped McKeever. 'He couldn' speak a word of English, he didn' even know yer name, didn' know who he was shootin', barely knew what country he was in.'

Kennedy stubbed the cigar into the overflowing ashtray and shoved both hands into his pockets. He studied the trees in front, then followed a grey squirrel as it darted and dodged along the ground, stopping and sniffing the air. 'I had to make a call and I decided he was better dead than alive.'

'Good to know that, Sean.' McKeever's voice was full of contempt. 'I'm absolutely delighted to learn how you decided one of my men was better dead than alive. Considerin' you missed Harry Power altogether and blew up two of his bodyguards instead, that makes it easier to understand. Now we have four unnecessary corpses litterin' the fancy streets of south Dublin. Two unknown Ruskies and two well-known policemen. Bullets whistlin' in the air, smoke grenades and hand grenades flyin' like sparrows.' He shifted angrily in his seat and rubbed his hands together briskly for heat. 'Half of the city brought to a standstill and all you can offer me is he knew too much.'

'What do you want me to do, Joe? I can cry if you want, I can send flowers and Mass cards. I could write a letter if that'd make you happy.' Kennedy's angry brogue was a stark contrast to the other man's northern twang.

McKeever wasn't amused. 'How did the doctor fit into yer plans? And how did you manage to screw that one up too?' The sniping had deepened into a suspicious and probing snarl. 'The papers are full of details of the same gun bein' used in both attacks.'

Kennedy dragged the lapels of his overcoat closer round his throat. 'The doctor was an important part of the Power campaign. They all needed to be taught a lesson.'

'And the wee girl? She needed a lesson as well?'

Kennedy faced his tormentor, eyes flaring with rage. 'She was wearing his coat, right? I followed both of them for a month and knew everything about them. How was I to know it would snow when I went for the kill? How was I to know she'd wear his clothes, that she'd drive him to work? The bitch usually cycled but that day they changed routine.' Kennedy slumped in his seat, his anger spent. 'Now back off, McKeever. This is bad enough without you giving me a hard time. I've got a lot of explaining to do elsewhere and I don't need more grief.'

McKeever ignored him. 'What were you thinkin' of, tryin' to kill Harry Power? Nobody's done political assassinations since the civil war days, Christ knows how long ago.' His expression hardened. 'Hittin' policemen's serious business and everybody's up in arms lookin' for you. But goin' for a Cabinet Minister, that's pure madness.' He pulled a pile of crumpled newspapers from a side pocket of the driver's door. 'Have you seen the papers?' McKeever chose the most dramatic banner headline. 'HUNT IS ON FOR THE JACKAL,' he crowed.

Kennedy flicked at his ponytail, ignoring McKeever. Outside, the squirrel was engrossed in a tuft of grass, head bobbing up and down, checking the air for danger. From out of the forest a fox appeared, nose to the ground, sniffing for a trail. Its coat was rust with bald patches on the fur, its tail long and white-tipped. It looked lean and mean, and Kennedy watched on with a simple fascination, almost missing McKeever's next whine.

'You'll have to get the hell out of the country, Sean. I don' know how you do it but just disappear. I'm goin' to have to do a lot of explainin' to a lot of very tough men and they're goin' to want to find out who was behind this.'

Kennedy hid the slight smile that flickered. Joe McKeever had been a one-time Provisional IRA arms dealer. Whatever the volunteers wanted, Joe would make the appropriate enquiries until he knew where to buy the hardware. He had contacts in Libya, Russia, ETA in Spain and some of the meanest weapons traders in the US. Want a surface-to-air missile? Ask Joe McKeever; he'll get it for you. How about armour-piercing rounds? No problem, Joe's got boxes of that buried in the hills outside Belfast, all in good condition. Semtex, grenades, sniper rifles with night vision, you name it, Joe's got it or knows how to get it. McKeever had built a steady reputation over the years and was amassing considerable profits until the paramilitary ceasefires. Then business dropped off dramatically and he had to look for new markets. The terrorists had abandoned berets and fatigues for smart suits, expensive shirts and ties. They mingled with dignitaries and power-brokers, some were now even in government. So Joe McKeever switched loyalties and began supplying the drug trade. Which is how he met Sean Kennedy.

The Belfast man was complaining again. 'You see, Sean, the Provos keep a close eye on me. They don' want me selling hardware to the opposition or any group they're not on speakin' terms with. Which more or less means everybody. So if they get wind it was me who provided the guns and grenades for yer operation, I'll have to start lookin' for a place in the sun.' McKeever's ruddy face twisted as if he'd bitten into something bitter. 'And I don' like the sun, Sean. It brings me out in hives and I get all itchy.'

Kennedy was following the fox as it padded stealthily closer to the squirrel. Wily and careful, ears pricked and shrunken belly brushing off the ground, the beast circled its unsuspecting prey. 'Nobody needs to know.'

McKeever snorted. 'Easy for you to say. You'll be back in Amsterdam and it'll be me answerin' the questions along some wee lane in south Armagh.'

Kennedy cut in firmly, 'Keep your head down and nobody

can pin anything on you. Act normal, go about your business as usual. Don't do anything out of the ordinary. We'll put it out it was a Tony Duffy operation.' Tony Duffy was an ageing drug baron who ran a gang of thugs in west Dublin. There were four in the group and so far they had escaped Harry Power's crusade. They were also heavily armed and ruthless, and likely contenders as cold-blooded assassins.

McKeever didn't speak for a minute, all the time staring intently at Kennedy. 'Who's "we", Sean? I always thought you worked alone. I was told you didn't trust anyone.'

Outside, the fox was within six feet of the squirrel, slumped in a clump of wet grass. The squirrel had darted to one side and was now gnawing at something held between its front paws. The small head swivelled ninety degrees, then back to the meal. The fox slithered forward another inch.

McKeever's left hand reached behind the driver's seat and his fingers curled round a net separating the front of the Land Rover from the back. A deep-throated growl startled Kennedy and he spun to find two angry eyes, narrowed to slits.

'Easy, Major,' McKeever cooed, 'easy, boy, it's OK. We're goin' for a walk soon.'

Behind the netting a large black and grey flecked Alsatian stood upright and shook itself, then scratched its snout on the side panelling, drool dripping from its open jaws. Kennedy didn't take his eyes off the dog. 'I never saw that big bastard,' he said slowly and quietly, not wanting to provoke the animal. 'I wondered where the smell was coming from.'

Suddenly, the Alsatian began barking loudly, sensing the conflict. Outside, the squirrel suddenly stopped gnawing and darted zigzag towards the safety of a pine tree. The fox was now down on its hunkers, slinking uneasily away.

'Who else is in on this, Sean?' McKeever's fingers splayed

out and the Alsatian began licking at the tips. His eyes bored into Kennedy. 'Is somebody payin' yer wages?'

Kennedy sighed deeply, as though he were dealing with a difficult child. He flicked at his ponytail and massaged the old wound where once a knife had been plunged so deeply it scraped off bone. In the cold and damp conditions he felt it ache. 'Joe,' he said and paused, searching for the right words. 'I don't ask about your business, do I? If I want hardware I make a call and place an order. I have never quizzed you where you get the stuff, or how much it costs, or how much profit you make. That's your concern only. And if I ever poked my nose into your interests you'd be the first to tell me to fuck off.' He wound down the side window and took a deep breath of the clear country air. He could still see the squirrel, now hiding on the branch of a pine tree. The fox had disappeared. 'So back off. For your own sake learn when to stop asking too many questions.'

There was a strained silence, Kennedy still staring out and wondering where the fox had gone. It had looked mean and hungry, yet sensed danger in the air when the Alsatian barked. It knew when to back off. It might have missed the squirrel and a decent meal but it had an intuitive sense of self-preservation. Hunger could wait; there'd be other and smaller animals to feast on. But instinct dulled by starvation or greed was another matter. Mistakes could be made.

'Where's the money?' McKeever was focused directly on Kennedy.

'In three red holdalls in the back seat over there.' Kennedy motioned towards his latest acquisition, a stolen blue BMW, now skewed awkwardly up on a grassy bank.

McKeever's gaze didn't waver. 'Why'd you leave the car so far away?'

Kennedy looked across, puzzled. 'So no one would connect us. What if some snoop came driving past and both of us were parked on top of one another? Wouldn't that look like a meeting? This way we could be ramblers out for the day.'

McKeever mulled this over and it seemed to pass his suspicion filter. 'How much?'

'One million US dollars equivalent as agreed. Half in sterling, a quarter in Euros and a quarter in dollars, and all in used notes, mainly small bills.'

'I'll need more, another million.'

Kennedy sat frozen-faced in the passenger seat. He wrapped both hands round himself for warmth and kicked his bad leg with his good foot to restore circulation. 'It'll take time,' he said finally. 'A month, maybe two. I'm not coming back here for some time so I'll have to work out how to move that amount of cash.'

McKeever managed a half-smile. 'That's more like it, more businesslike.' He jerked at the door handle and kicked the driver's side open. Outside he stomped his feet, flaking mud from his boots, stretched and adjusted his cloth cap so it covered his eyebrows. The back door was pulled open, and the Alsatian jumped out and immediately bounded into the forest. McKeever waited for a few minutes, then gave a low whistle and the dog ambled back, sniffing at the ground, pawing at interesting tufts of grass. Kennedy watched on, his body now shaking with rage. No one had ever pulled such a line on him before.

'Here, boy, c'me here, Major, that's a boy,' McKeever crooned at his pet until it was jumping up at him, all teeth and drool. He slipped a lead on to its collar and forced it to heel. 'Where'd you say those holdalls are?' He held Kennedy's angry gaze, unimpressed with the glare.

'Don't fuck with me, Joe. You know bloody well what I said.'

'Where's the car keys?'

'It's not locked.'

McKeever reached inside the cab and snatched at the ignition. The engine died and the heater stopped humming. 'Maybe ye'd leave that door open, Sean. I like to keep an eye on you.'

The sound of a vehicle approaching stopped McKeever in his tracks and he played with the Alsatian, letting it run free again for a few minutes. The dog scampered among the pine trees, barking and snapping, sniffing and drooling, its black and grey flecked coat disappearing, then reappearing. It shuffled back just as a Toyota van eased slowly past. McKeever took off his cloth cap and waved at the unseen driver, smiling all the time like some simpleton. Kennedy continued to seethe and stare straight ahead. Now McKeever was walking round the blue BMW, where it was skewed up on a grassy bank some thirty yards away. He squinted inside, then under the bodywork, spending considerable time inspecting the darker recesses. Apparently satisfied, he opened the boot lock but didn't push it up. 'Anythin' in here I should be worried about?' he shouted.

Kennedy turned and shook his head. 'Check for yourself.'

'It pays to be suspicious, Sean,' shouted McKeever, dragging his cloth cap back down tightly over his ears. There was now a lift to his voice, as if he was enjoying himself. 'You get to stay alive longer if yer suspicious. Ye'd know that yerself.' The Alsatian was sniffing around the panelling and exhaust of the BMW, dragging McKeever at the end of its leash. 'Easy, boy, easy, now.' Suddenly McKeever caught hold of the edge of the boot and swung it open, diving for cover as the hinges strained. Kennedy looked on, shivering as a gust of cold wind cut through the Land Rover cab. McKeever stood about six feet from the open boot and squinted inside, then moved closer. 'Nothin' in here, anyway.' He laughed and the Alsatian barked with excitement.

Fuck you, Kennedy mumbled silently. Outside, the pine trees swayed as another strong breeze passed.

Now McKeever had one hand on the passenger side rear door and disengaged the lock. From a pocket of his blue boiler suit he produced a roll of thin rope and looped it round the outer rim of the door, then coiled it tight into a sliding knot. He unravelled the rope and stepped slowly backwards until he was about twenty feet from the car. He started drawing on the line to make it taut, then increased the tension until the door opened fully. Now he could see clearly the three red canvas holdalls, pushed tightly into the middle of the rear seats. 'Go get, Major, go, boy. Bring them here.'

The Alsatian sniffed at the ground, then looked up at McKeever. 'The car, boy. Get the bags, Major.' He was gesticulating towards the BMW. 'Go, boy, now. Go on, get the bags.' Finally the dog bounded towards the open door and within seconds was inside. There was a lot of barking and snuffling but eventually the Alsatian's hind legs reached the edge of the seat, then dropped down to the grassy bank. 'Good boy, Major,' cooed McKeever, one eye on the dog and the other on the inside of the Land Rover. Suddenly the dog started barking loudly, almost in frustration, and slid out of the back seat. It stood at the open door, growling and drooling, shifting its attention from a red holdall towards McKeever. The first bag had become jammed in the door frame, an end tight against the edge of the seat, the other caught in the hinge. McKeever inspected the problem from different angles, all the time keeping the Land Rover cab in his peripheral vision. 'Sean, maybe ye'd pull that bag out for me.'

Kennedy swore silently, then shouted, 'I'm frozen waiting here. Would you get on with it and take the fucking bags and let's split.'

McKeever tugged his cloth cap up slightly so he could see better. 'I'm a bit nervous here, Sean. We'd all get away quicker if you took that holdall and opened it here in front of me. And then the other two.'

Kennedy kicked open the passenger door and jumped down from the Land Rover, wincing slightly as his bad leg hit the ground. He stomped both feet until he felt the tingle of warm blood rush through, then limped past McKeever to the BMW. With two hands he grabbed the leather straps and pulled the first red holdall out on to the gravel. It hit the ground with a dull thud. His fingers were so cold he had difficulty grasping the zip end but finally managed to open the bag fully. He stood back several paces. 'Check it yourself.' The wind was gathering strength and tumbling leaves in its path as he yanked at the two other holdalls.

Joe McKeever took the leash off his Alsatian but held him by the collar with his left hand. The dog immediately strained to break free but McKeever held tight. 'Easy, boy, easy, now. Just another minute and you can run all you want.' He rummaged through the top of the open holdall with his free hand, turning over tied bundles of notes. His brown eyes darted nervously from the cash to Kennedy. 'It's all here?'

Kennedy was shrunken into his overcoat, checking up and down the lonely country road for signs of traffic. 'Every pound, Euro and dollar. You can spend all day counting it but this part of the deal's over and I'm quitting.' He slammed closed the rear door and boot of the BMW, opened the driver's side and climbed inside. The engine was gunned alive and he reversed the powerful car slowly from its awkward position up on the grassy bank, careful not to sink into the waterlogged ground. He waited for a few minutes until the numbness had left his fingers, then swerved in a tight angle until he had a straight position. He switched again to reverse and backed the BMW slowly, watching through the front window with quick glances in the rear-vision mirror to keep his line. Now in front of him and about fifty feet away, Joe McKeever was still hunched over the first red holdall, laying bundles of cash on the gravel track. The Alsatian had broken free and was off through the trees again in search of adventure. Kennedy switched the engine to drive mode, then pressed a button on the gear stick activating sport acceleration. He released the handbrake and shoved his good foot hard on the accelerator, the sudden surge jolting him violently as the BMW scorched forward. Joe McKeever's body left a deep and bloody hollow on the bonnet.

4

'We are gathered here this morning, not to mourn the tragic death of Laura Nolan but to celebrate her life.'

Scott Nolan sat alone in the front right-hand-side pew of the small Church of Ireland building in the town land of Killinure in County Kildare about thirty miles south-west of Dublin. He was in his best suit, a navy pinstripe, with white shirt and borrowed black tie, and against the cold he carried a heavy grey overcoat. His hair, as usual, was dishevelled. Behind and to the side he could hear the noises of the congregation, muffled sobs and snuffling, coughing and rustling of the Service of Remembrance pages. Somewhere in the middle of the hall a small child was being shushed as he asked awkward questions out loud. In the narrow aisle beside Scott, resting on two inverted V-shaped struts, lay a polished oak coffin with brass handles. He knew where he was, yet somehow didn't know where he was, still in shock and reliving the murderous tragedy that had befallen him three days previously. '*Laura, Laura, speak to me, keep talking.*

Don't give up, please, Keep breathing.' He could remember cradling his dying wife, the images as vivid as the moments it happened, feeling her warm blood on his hands and face, hearing her bubbling and laboured breathing as she struggled for life. '*Don't die, Laura. Please don't die.*' The first at the scene found him like that, confused, crying, disbelieving and heavily bloodstained. By then Laura was dead.

At Dublin's city morgue, where Laura's body was laid on a cold white marble slab, Scott had to be restrained by police officers and dragged away when an elderly and tired-looking pathologist arrived in green fatigues and long green plastic apron. '*Don't you touch her, don't lay a hand on her, you bastard.*' He was a doctor and had attended many autopsies in the past. He knew what dissection was planned, what brutal inspection had to be done. But not to his wife. Good God, not to Laura. His deranged shouts and agitated screams echoed around the tiled walls of the unit until finally the forensic investigator could take no more. 'Get him out of here.' Four burly detectives subdued Scott until another three could drag him away. He wasn't a strong man and carried little weight, but his struggles were violent, driven by anger and despair and hopelessness. Much later and still wearing the same blood-spattered clothes, he was interrogated in the bowels of the local police station. Only then did the full significance of all that had happened that day begin to sink in. Someone had come looking for Ireland's Minister for Justice and killed his bodyguards instead. Someone had come looking for Scott Nolan and murdered his wife instead.

'I had the honour of being the celebrant when Laura and Scott married in this very church less than eighteen months ago.' The rector was a tall, thin man with a shock of grey hair and lined features as dark and sombre as the occasion. He was dressed in a black cassock fringed with purple and addressed the congregation from the first step leading to the altar, hands clasped together at the front. The church was over two hundred years old, built in Wicklow granite and finished inside with a traditional whitewash. Below the building's original stained-glass window the grey-flecked altar was small and plain, without carvings. The only modern compromises to comfort were wall heaters, strategically camouflaged behind side pews. The structure had been consecrated in the mid 1800s and had survived Ireland's turbulent history of religious bigotry and division. Over the years many non-Catholic buildings in the area had been vandalised or burned to the ground, but not in Killinure. Like its dwindling congregation, the church stood steadfast and defiant in a glade of oak and elm trees and moss-covered tombstones. That morning the nave was divided along family lines. Those to the right came to pay their respects and sympathise with Scott but there was only a handful of mainly hospital colleagues and a heavily bandaged Harry Power with his wife Jane, shadowed by bodyguards. Scott had no family in Ireland and had warned his parents not to attempt the long journey. Chicago was in the grip of a winter whiteout with traffic gridlock and blocked roads and he did not want them making a potentially hazardous trip. 'Stay where you are, I have to see this through myself,' Scott pleaded when he finally collected his thoughts the day after Laura's murder. 'You've got Mary to consider.' The third Nolan child, after Scott, was mentally retarded, born with a rare brain disorder where mental faculties could not develop. She was now twenty-five but behaved and thought like a twelve-year-old. 'I've already spoken with Bob. He wanted to be with me but this is a heavy load and I don't want to share it. It's my responsibility.'

The front left-hand-side pew and all the seats behind to the very back were filled with Laura's family and friends. On the aisle side sat her only brother, Mark, in dark suit and tie under a black leather coat. He was six four and muscular, with jet-black hair swept back. When Scott first met him he squinted for some time, trying to connect the two. He could distinguish Laura's eyes and hair, maybe also her mouth and mischievous smile, but little else. Not that Mark had smiled much anyway, inspecting Scott as if he were some unusual and unpleasant specimen of humanity. Scott knew little about his prospective brother-in-law, only that he was thirty-seven, married, with two children, and a senior member of the Garda Siochana, Ireland's unarmed police force. Laura hinted Mark worked mainly undercover on covert missions. 'If I tell you everything I'll have to kill you afterwards,' she'd said at the time and laughed. Scott's relationship with Mark Higgins had always been distant and cold, the detective making no attempt to hide his obvious dislike for the strange doctor with the glasses and slight stoop. His body language said it all: you could have done a lot better, Laura. And now Mark's favourite sibling was dead, brutally murdered by someone who was really out to get her husband. Beside Mark was Laura's older sister who'd flown in from London that morning, still asking when and how and why my sister? She was being comforted by her parents, a worn and frail couple in their seventies who looked distraught and bewildered by all that was happening around them.

'I can remember her radiant smile, her delight in the joy of marrying the man she'd chosen as her partner in life.' The rector's words brought a fresh burst of sobbing from the left side of the congregation and Scott desperately tried to suppress the picture, squeezing his eyes so tight he felt the muscles ache. 'Finally got yah, cowboy,' Laura had teased while they signed the marriage register. She'd looked radiant, a woman glowing with love and happiness. She'd picked a simple white dress, traditional wedding style but without the frills, and white veil held by a flower band was clipped at the front of her hair. Scott was in morning suit, white shirt and grey tie. Later, when they pored over the wedding photographs both agreed they made a handsome couple. And now, as he sat beside the polished oak coffin in which the body of his wife lay, he struggled for composure. I was in this exact seat once before, he thought. On my wedding day, waiting for Laura to walk to me along this same aisle. He froze all images out of his mind. I have to get through this, I must see this through. His lenses misted and he wiped them with a handkerchief. Sit up, no stooping, he could almost hear Laura chide. Can't you do anything with your hair? It's all over the place. He forced himself ramrod straight and half-heartedly brushed at his fringe.

Laura's brother Mark made the funeral arrangements. Scott was almost catatonic when he was finally taken back to his apartment the night of the murder. For most of the next day he sat at the edge of the bed and tried to cry. But he couldn't. Who are the tears for? You? Laura? This hell-hole of a country? His hands bunched in fists, his jaw was tight and clenched. Only his eyes moved.

When he left the room it was to make calls, the rest of the time the phone was off the hook. He was aware the apartment was surrounded by media and police, that there were two armed detectives guarding his front door. He knew this because communication with the outside world was through one of them. He did not listen to the radio or watch the TV circus surrounding the assassinations; he did not want to know. He even rejected a personal call from the Minister for Justice, Harry Power. 'Not now, please. I just want to be left alone.' He felt the most forlorn and helpless man on earth. It should have been me, not Laura.

'Evil men came that morning, men hiding in the cloaks of wickedness and sin.' The rector's baritone voice was strong and piercing, his own anger bursting through. He shifted on the step, his hands now flailing as if grappling with the devil. 'In an act of cruel and mindless savagery they cut down a young woman who had not yet known the fullness of life.' Somewhere near the rear of the church fresh sobs could be heard but Scott kept his stare firmly ahead. He rested his left hand on the top of the oak casket and swept the tips of his fingers sideways along its smooth surface. Where are you, Laura? That's not you in there, that's only your body. Where have *you* gone? 'And I say to you all' – the rector was less edgy now and staring towards the front right-pew where Scott cut a lost and pathetic figure – 'let us support Scott in his hour of loss. Let us pray he may find it in his heart to forgive these killers.' He paused, then added pointedly, 'For as we know so tragically from our own history, hatred only begets hatred.'

Oh, no, Scott almost screamed. Don't anyone search my soul for mercy, don't anyone plead with me to forgive. Murder is murder is murder and some psychopathic executioner has destroyed my life. In his mind he saw again the shadowy figure standing at the incline from the basement garage of their apartment. '*No, no, please, nooooo*,' Laura had screamed in fear. Four gunshots rang out, one after the other in rapid succession, and Scott's face was splattered with blood, his glasses smudged in red. What was going through your mind, you madman? How can you sleep at night, knowing what you've done?

Scott never heard the eulogies from two of Laura's friends, nor the final hymn, so distraught was he.

'Scott, Scott. For Christ's sake pay attention.' Scott was shaken from his reverie by the angry hiss of Mark Higgins. The tall, dark-haired man was scowling at him and when Scott looked around he could only vaguely see the gathering. He quickly wiped at the lens of his glasses and fiddled with the earpiece until he was sure the spectacles were secure. Now everything came into sharp focus. The rector was at the left-hand side of the church, shaking hands and whispering words of sympathy to Laura's parents. Most of the congregation was following the confusion at the front pew, eyes averting as Scott looked across. Then two young men he'd never seen before came forward, both sizing him up, as if he were unstable. 'You take the front right-hand side,' Higgins snapped. 'I'll take the front left. These lads are Laura's cousins and they're going to take the rear. Now move.'

When he'd lifted Laura before she was always light as a feather. Scott was no muscle man but had average power and in playful moments in better times he could swing his young bride and carry her like real men did. But as he shouldered her coffin that cold February morning he wondered would he even have the strength to walk the length of the aisle. 'One step at a time,' he heard Higgins order and the four slowly paced their way between the pews. Scott looked neither to left nor right but sensed blurred faces and intense grief on either side. Someone threw a red rose and it rested on top of the casket. Then the doors of the church were opened and daylight streamed in. Outside it was bright and Scott could see branches move in the wind. He stumbled momentarily and had to grasp the end of a pew for support. 'Are you all right?' he heard Higgins whisper and he managed a croaked 'yes' in return.

The clay was brown and wet, and stuck to Scott's shoes. He stood upright as the rector intoned the final prayers, drawing himself deeper into his overcoat for warmth and trying to stop his teeth chattering. Then he grabbed one end of a wide cloth strap and helped lower the oak coffin into the freshly dug grave. He was aware of Laura's parents and brother and sister, could hear their distraught cries and sobs, but he was drained of emotion and stared stony-faced into the distance. As the earth was shovelled back into the pit it hit the wood with a soft thump. Before the casket disappeared for ever Scott kissed the red rose and dropped it into the depths.

Higgins was beside him, a lit cigarette cupped in his hand, the lapels of his black leather coat up round his neck. 'Scott, there's a lot of family and friends waiting to pay their respects to you. Please don't keep them waiting in the cold.' Overhead the drone of a helicopter caught Scott's attention and he looked up, squinting against the weak sun. Higgins took a deep drag, following Scott's movement. 'That's one of ours, security.'

Scott looked round, now noticing the mourners gathering together at the front of the church, some huddling in the doorway for protection. There was only a light breeze but it was a wintry day and the chill penetrated. Then he gradually became aware of masked and armed men moving like shadows between the trees or squatting beside ancient and tilting tombstones. 'My God, what's going on?' His voice was cracking; his hands shaking so much he thrust them into his pockets.

'They're ours too.' Higgins stood closer. 'I called them up. They're from my division and camouflaged so no one can see their faces.' He looked around the small graveyard, nodding to one of his squad. 'This is your life, Dr Nolan.' His voice was now hard and bitter and full of anger. 'As long as you stay in this country you're under constant police protection.'

5

Thirty miles away, as the final spadefuls of heavy clay were being shovelled on to Laura Nolan's coffin, her killer shivered on a park bench in Dublin's Fitzroy Square, staring intently at a terraced house fifty yards to his right. Sean Kennedy lit a cheap cigar, tilted his head and blew the smoke into the air. He ignored the jaundiced looks of a female jogger and slumped further into the seat, focusing on the front windows and door of number thirty-four. His left leg ached in the cold and he massaged it briskly to get some heat into the flesh. A light breeze scattered leaves and litter, keeping the wind chill factor low, while overhead swirling grey clouds threatened rain.

Fitzroy was a fashionable square close to Dublin centre, four rows of terraced, three-storey red-brick houses protected by black railings. Each dwelling had an imposing granite stairwell, which lead to a narrow gate way and the road running alongside. The terraces surrounded a half-acre oasis of gardens with jogging trails and walking paths. Fitzroy was class, Fitzroy was style. Fitzroy was old money: lawyers, doctors, bankers and corporate accountants. No brash young IT millionaire had yet managed to get a foothold on the respectability ladder of the area. But Fitzroy was also no more than a mile away from one of the city's notorious Corporation tenements, now totally occupied by crack heads, heroin addicts and small-time drug dealers. When these residents needed cash for their habits they often targeted the wealth of Fitzroy and district. So the locale was regularly patrolled by police and had a vigilant neighbourhood watch scheme. Strangers were regarded with immediate suspicion until proven innocent, which was why Kennedy didn't plan on lingering.

He smoked the cigar to halfway and flicked the stump into a bush behind him. A young mother pushing a buggy with a toddler traipsing unsteadily beside her rounded a bend and came close. Kennedy stood up, stretched and made off in the opposite direction. His long blond hair was now shaven to a tight crew cut and he wore a close-fitting navy woollen beret against the cold. He was in black tracksuit and white trainers, and looked no different from any of the other joggers pounding the winding paths through the park. But it was winter and there was little foliage for protection so Kennedy kept on the move.

He had looped the square twice when he spotted movement at number thirty-four. A tall, distinguished-looking grey-haired man in his sixties was standing at the front door, engrossed in conversation with a younger woman about six inches smaller. The man wore a thick knit sweater over grey trousers; the woman was in an overcoat with scarf. In her right arm she cradled a small dog. Kennedy smiled slightly. Not another fucking dog. How many do I have to strangle before she gets the message? From the distance he couldn't decide what breed the animal was but he guessed Pekinese or dachshund or poodle or something similar. His sister had a passion for small dogs; they were easy to manage and didn't give much trouble. Unlike her younger brother. She'd had to plunge a steak knife into his left leg one evening many years ago during a furious family row. Sean had both hands round his father's throat, and the older man was blue and almost unconscious when the knife sliced through skin, muscle and finally severed a nerve. That night Sean Kennedy fled the family home and never returned, even though he was barely sixteen.

Now he left the square and made off towards Leeson Street, past its Georgian offices and basement lap dance clubs before flagging a taxi. Soon he was in a queue, waiting for scrutiny by armed officers. With so many traffic snarls it seemed the city had ground to a halt and there was a sense of heightened tension in the air. The buzz on everyone's lips was the assassination attempt on the Minister for Justice and the hunt for the gang leader. Kennedy sat in the back seat, bored and unresponsive to the driver's attempts to engage him in conversation. His eyes took in the street activity but his mind was elsewhere. Finally the taxi was waved through.

The Zodiac bar was north of the River Liffey, the main waterway that cut through the heart of Dublin before spilling into the Irish Sea. A steady drizzle was driving into Kennedy's face as he limped along a cobblestone pathway, past another line of vehicles waiting at yet another security spot check. He kept his head down, ignoring the glowering and irate drivers staring out of their dry cocoons, occasionally blaring their horns in frustration. Apart from Kennedy there were few pedestrians as the area had a reputation for muggings and bag snatching. Barges were tied up along the quays but in the cold wet weather little moved on or off the boats. The air smelt of salt and diesel fumes, the background a cacophony of revving engines and squawking seagulls.

Without looking up, Kennedy pushed open the Zodiac swing doors and stepped inside. Despite the hour, just after noon, the pub was doing brisk business. Foaming pints of Guinness were being traded with empties as staff struggled to keep up with demand. The clientele was mainly dockers, some coming off night duty, others having an early liquid lunch, and there was a loud babble of animated conversation. Slouched on one stool was the usual dipso found in such establishments, probably drinking his social welfare cheque, child benefit allowance or anything else he could trade for cash. He was red-haired and shabbily dressed, sitting on his own and staring into the middle distance, cigarette burning into his fingers.

In one recessed dark corner at the far end of the room three men huddled around a small table, apparently engrossed in each other's company. But their eyes were shifty, taking in every movement, inspecting every new face. Kennedy spotted them at the same time they noticed him.

'Glass of Heineken.' Kennedy stuffed his damp woollen beret into a side pocket and waited for his drink, running a hand over his unfamiliar spikes of hair. He looked neither left nor right but observed all activity in a long wall mirror behind the barman's head. He suddenly realised his face and clothes were covered in mist, and took off his tracksuit top and shook it. Underneath he wore a white T-shirt, which he checked for damp. Then, in between logos for Jameson whiskey, he sized up his contact. The main man, Derek McCann, was heavy-set with receding black hair. He was in a grey jacket over a white roll-neck and looked quite respectable compared with the rest in the room. He had thick lips, which he now pursed as his eyes caught Kennedy's stare in the glass. His cronies were younger, one a thin and wiry youth who seemed no more than twenty, the other a small, tubby man in denims with a nervous shrug of his left shoulder. Kennedy guessed he was in his thirties. He took a sip of his beer, slipped a five Euro note across the counter and waited for the change. In the mirror he noticed McCann whisper to his companions and the two stood up, looked directly at Kennedy, then sat at an empty table about ten yards away. They shuffled their chairs to keep a clear view of the newcomer and nursed their drinks.

'Foul day out there, Derek.' Kennedy set down his glass of Heineken and fumbled in his pocket for a cigar. He lit up and another puff entered the already thick, smoky atmosphere.

Derek McCann pursed his lips again, folded both hands over his paunch and fixed on Kennedy. 'Bad week, Sean. All sorts of fucking crazy things going on.' An eyebrow was raised quizzically. 'You wouldn't happen to know anything?' His accent was straight Dublin, inner city and harsh. McCann was officially a successful businessman who owned a string of small supermarkets and off-licences throughout the state. Unofficially he was one of the major players in the narcotics trade and used his legitimate enterprises to launder the massive profits he skimmed from selling drugs.

Kennedy ran a finger round the rim of his glass. 'Nothing, Derek. That was not my operation and not my style.'

McCann leaned across the table so his face was less than six inches away. 'This is *very* bad for business. The cops are all over the place; dealers are being lifted left, right and centre. Customers are scared shitless. They want their fix but they don't want to swing for an ounce of heroin or a line of cocaine.'

McCann's voice was hard and angry. 'Whoever pulled this stunt has set us back years. Just when we were beginning to find a way around Harry Power's dragnet. He glanced up suddenly as another customer entered the bar and nodded to one of his henchmen. Keep an eye out. Then he was back in Kennedy's face. 'You have a very bad reputation, Sean. Nobody's ever crossed you and stayed upright for long. And the fella everyone's looking for sounds a right tough bastard to me. The sort who takes no prisoners.'

Kennedy took a sip of his beer, then swivelled his chair so he had his back to the wall and a full view of the bar. Through the fog of smoke it was difficult to make out if anyone of significance had entered. McCann's minders stared at him but he ignored their sullen faces. At the front someone must have cracked a particularly good joke as a sudden burst of raucous laughter echoed off the low ceiling. Kennedy noticed one of the barmen leaning across the counter, an ear cocked to catch the next line. 'Derek, you're not really listening.' Kennedy's ice-blue eyes now locked on McCann. 'I was not involved in that operation, full fucking stop.' He rapped a knuckle on the table to emphasise the point but McCann looked unimpressed. 'Stop lecturing me about how hard done by you are, or who's plotting the revolution. This is not my agenda.'

McCann shifted in his seat slightly. 'Would you happen to have any ideas who might have been involved? I mean, we're talking big stuff here, Sean. A well-planned operation on a senior government Minister, heavy guns and grenades used. Outside hit men. This was no ordinary snuff job, this was a fucking invasion.'

Kennedy allowed himself a slight smile. *A fucking invasion*. That was a good description. 'I'm not sure and don't quote me on this but my sources say it was Tony Duffy.'

McCann mulled this over. 'If it was then Tony's gonna rot in hell for some time. The cops are turning the city over looking for him.'

Kennedy feigned surprise and shock, then shrugged his shoulders and took another sip of his beer. 'That'll be one more out of the picture then, Derek. Tony's been pushing his weight around for a long time, trying to carve out more territory. If he's taken out of the loop it means those prepared to stick around can make a bigger killing.' He ground his cigar into an ashtray, leaving trails of wispy smoke snaking into the air.

McCann waved to one of his lookouts and immediately the thin, wiry youth was at his side. 'Get me a pint of stout.' When the kid was out of earshot McCann leaned back across the table. 'Sean, let's clear the air here. I'm gonna take your word you had no hand, act or part in that crazy plot to shoot up Harry Power. And if whoever done it causes Tony Duffy to be taken out of circulation, that's no bad thing. I can't stand the bastard and he's had it coming for some time. Maybe gaol is better than a hole in the back of his head.'

Kennedy nodded as he took another small sip of Heineken.

'But Sean, whoever was involved has screwed up my dealing big time. I've got a small fortune in . . .'

Kennedy cut across. 'Forget about the attack on Power, that's yesterday's news. Sure there's going to be big waves from the top, sure dealers are going to get pulled in. That's no bad thing, there's too many small fish on the streets already. A clear-out leaves those with balls of steel to keep things moving.' He waited as McCann's pint of Guinness was placed on the table and the lookout had returned to his table. For a moment both men watched the stout settle in the glass and a white creamy head form at the top. McCann took a long, deep draught and wiped his lips. Kennedy knocked back the dregs of his beer and glanced around the bar. 'Tell your minders to fuck off, they're beginning to annoy me. You and I have some serious talking to do.'

6

'Don't do this to me, Tony. We've got your family and every shitty gofer you use to move your drugs around and they're singing louder than a choir.' Mark Higgins was taking a direct interest in hunting down the killer who'd shot his sister in cold blood. It was eight in the evening of 15 February, five days after Laura's death. 'Don't insult my intelligence with that hangdog look of innocence. We know you were in on this, we just need to know what the hell you thought you were going to achieve by shooting up half of Dublin.' The venom in his voice was skin-slicing.

Sitting impassively on a chair at a narrow table in a small room in the bowels of one of Dublin's police stations was sixty-eight-year-old Antonio Duffini. Antonio was better known as Tony Duffy, drug baron of the Westside. At the same time, in different locations, his immediate family and henchmen were also getting the third degree. Duffy stared into the middle distance, mouth moving as he shifted his dentures nervously while Higgins paced the floor before him, drawing deeply on his fifth cigarette inside an hour and deliberately blowing the smoke into Duffy's face. He was the third detective to work on the gangster, the first two giving up after four hours' intensive grilling produced nothing more than an occasional 'fuck off'.

'And I can tell you, Tony, we're getting some very interesting information on you. Stuff we didn't know about before.'

Duffy's expression didn't change.

Higgins nodded towards a two-way mirror behind his target and seconds later a uniformed officer entered the small room and passed over a folder. Duffy watched out of the corner of one eye. 'Two bank accounts in Jersey, one under the name Fludar Enterprises with assets of two and a half million sterling' – he flicked to a separate page – 'and Gondo Corporation, holding over one million US dollars.' Higgins spotted Duffy's eyes widen momentarily and close down again like shutters. 'Stella told us about those.' He sat down and faced the older man across the table. For a moment he studied him closely, wondering if he'd crack. Duffy had been in more interrogation rooms and had been barked at by more detectives than most criminals his age. He wouldn't give up easily. His pock-marked face was thick with stubble, greased with sweat and grime. Despite his sixty-eight years he still had a good head of tight grey hair, now dishevelled and sticking out in all directions. Black hairs coiled out of both nostrils. His skin was sallow and sagging and unattractive, with thick turkey folds at the neck. He was in denims that barely covered his paunch and a white T-shirt with sweat stains at the armpits. He'd been picked up in the loft of a Southside brothel, 'inspecting the plumbing', after an intensive search of his usual habitats.

Tony Duffy was Italian-Irish stock, his grandparents hard-working migrants who'd slaved all the hours God gave them to batter and cook fish and chips for the working classes of Dublin's inner city. They'd arrived in Ireland as Duffini but a generation later the 'ini' was dropped and a 'y' added to take the heat out of the racist taunts levelled at their children. Antonio was sent to school as Tony and told to kick the head off any kid who tried to use the old name. So Tony Duffy grew up expecting a fight at every corner and very often got one. It wasn't long before he drifted into petty crime, shoplifting, burglary, handbag snatching.

By age twenty-one he'd been in juvenile remand centres and gaol seven times, and was considered beyond reform. In the early seventies he became bagman for one of Dublin's first drug kings, when the city was only beginning to understand the scourge of heroin. Tony soon recognised the profit margins and decided narcotics was the business of the future. In an act of treachery still talked of among the underworld, Tony the bagman took over the empire by blowing out his boss's brains at the back of his mother's fish and chip shop. According to the story, Tony sat on the dead man's body for an hour, eating freshly cooked plaice and counting that day's takings.

Now he sat rigidly in his chair, studiously avoiding the angry glare of Mark Higgins. 'Stella's been very helpful.' Stella was Duffy's second daughter, a thirty-six-year-old dark-haired beauty who ran a nightclub in Dublin's Temple Bar, supposedly the cultural heart of the city but in reality no more than a debauched collection of pubs, fancy restaurants and expensive whorehouses. 'She asked us to keep her kids out of the investigation in return for information. And we've swung that deal for her even though we know her sixteen-year-old son sells Es on the streets.'

'Stella's not a well woman,' Duffy blurted unexpectedly, his deep inherited burr ruined by too many years of mixing with Dublin lowlife. 'She's on anti-depressants and tranquillisers. You ask her doctor. He'll tell you how fucked up her brain is. So don't try and sell the "Stella spilling her guts" line, it won't stand up in court.'

Higgins kept his poker face but gave a silent sigh of relief. Duffy had finally spoken.

'I want my solicitor. I'm entitled to call my solicitor and have him here before I answer any questions.'

Duffy's sudden defiance cut no ice and Higgins leaned across the table, straight into his face. 'Listen, you greaseball dago, all constitutional rights have been scrapped since these killings. For once we get to do whatever we like without some slick lawyer standing over our shoulders constantly interrupting. We play by our rules, which in your case, Antonio, means no rules at all.'

Duffy mulled this over. 'My name's Anthony but I'll let you use Tony. Don't ever call me Antonio again.' The threat in his voice was as menacing as a gun pointed at Higgins's head.

'OK, Anthony, who did you use to pull this team of killers together? Which one of your cronies hired in the thugs and supplied them with guns and grenades?'

'I'm pleading the fifth amendment.'

'You watch too many *Godfather* movies, Tony. We don't have the fifth amendment.'

'Then I'm pleading whatever fucking amendment you do have cos I am not opening my mouth. You can question me from now to Christmas but I ain't sayin' nothing, except I wasn't involved in that operation. That was an outside job and you well know it. You're just hitting off me cos you got nothing else to go on.' Duffy shifted his dentures angrily, his eyes now blazing. 'Fuck off and play at being a policeman some other time. I've been interrogated by better shop assistants than you.'

Higgins lit another cigarette and paced the small space on the other side of the table. His shirt was sticking to his skin and he opened the top three buttons for ventilation. The combatants were in stark contrast, Higgins tall and muscular with dark hair swept back, eyes dancing with rage, while Duffy was old and stooped and worn but stubbornly defiant. 'The word on the street', said Higgins, slowly and quietly, 'is that this *was* your operation. The word is you've lost a lot of money since the Minister ordered his crackdown. And now we know about your lap dance clubs with all those Eastern European girls brought in on false work permits. Seems to me you could have made a lot of new friends.' Tony Duffy was back to his staring into the middle distance mode, dentures grinding. 'And we've raided your warehouse along the docks.'

Duffy's eyes came into sharp focus.

'And what a little Aladdin's cave we found there. Bags and bags of Es, still haven't counted how many yet. And a big bag of the white stuff, Tony. Now that alone will send you down for the rest of your natural. You're too old for gaol, Tony, aren't you? Jesus, you've spent more time inside than out, you should be planning your retirement, not thinking of some hell-hole in Mountjoy.'

Duffy snorted. 'You're talking out your arse. I don't have no warehouse at the docks.'

'That's not what Stella's been saying, Tony. I don't know what you did to that girl to make her so angry but she's telling us all about your business ventures. I reckon she feels you're going down one way or the other and has decided the wise thing is to protect her family. You're an old man, you should have got out of this business a long time ago and headed for the sun. You should be growing grapes and drinking wine in the hills above Milan, not shovelling drugs around this city.'

Duffy pulled up his T-shirt and wiped a trickle of sweat from his brow. Higgins lit another cigarette and stared at the ceiling, blowing smoke rings into the air. The small room was becoming oppressively warm and stuffy with no air circulating. Higgins felt at a radiator behind his back, then twisted the 'off' button fully.

'You smoke too much, y'know that?'

'Worried about my health, Tony?'

'Yeah, you've been chain smoking since you came in here. That's not good for your heart. And I bet you haven't had your blood pressure or your cholesterol checked for years. That's the problem with young cops; you think you're fucking invincible. Then one day you're gettin' yourself all worked up asking stupid questions of an innocent pensioner like me and *wham*, your electrics fuse. This is just a friendly warning from someone who cares. Cut out the fags, cut out grease and eat more fish and vegetables. Get out and walk and smell the roses before it's too late.'

'I'm touched by your interest.' Higgins was now standing, rocking on the balls of his feet. He was tired and frustrated, and sensed Duffy wasn't going to open up much more. Maybe another night in the cells and an early morning call might begin to wear the old bastard down.

'I'm always interested in health issues.' Duffy was now fixed on Higgins, his eyes narrowed and threatening. 'I look after my family and take care of their health. That's why it hurts me to hear you've been annoying my Stella. She's not a well woman and guys like you shouldn't come down heavy on the sick. It'll do you no good in the long term.'

Higgins shuffled pages into order. 'I'll bear that in mind.'

'It was your sister that got hit instead of that doctor, wasn't it?'

Higgins glanced down at Duffy, his concentration suddenly heightened. 'Yes, it was.'

'Well, I'm real sorry to hear that cos no innocent civilian should get caught up in all this shit. So, detective, let me offer you one more piece of health advice.'

Higgins sat down and ran his hand through his hair, then flicked an empty carton of Silk Cut into a trashcan. 'What's that, Tony?'

'Don't mess about with me or my family. I've been around the block a lot longer than you and know how to handle myself. I've been in stinking police cells and interrogation rooms since I was fourteen, and right now I'm getting pretty pissed off with you trying to pin these murders on me and my family and employees. We're just honest fish and chip shop owners.'

Higgins's lip curled in a cynical sneer. 'Tony, you're the biggest drug pusher in the west of the city. You and your cronies are linked to at least seven gangland killings and now I find out you've diversified into prostitution and pornography. You've been laundering money through your shops and other outlets for years. I know all this, Tony. But what I really want to know is who pulled off that operation five days ago? We've lifted every scumbag and pimp and pusher off the streets, and they are all singing from the same hymn sheet. This was a Tony Duffy operation. Had to be, only Duffy has that sort of clout, only Duffy is mean enough to shoot innocent civilians.'

Duffy went back to trance mode. 'Like I said,' he muttered, 'I'm an innocent pensioner who earns his living selling fish and chips.'

Higgins motioned behind Duffy's back and the venetian blinds on the two-way mirror were opened. Now Higgins could see a dark-haired woman sobbing uncontrollably into a bunch of tissues. Beside her were two female detectives. 'Have a look behind you, Tony. Stella has something to say.'

Duffy looked up at Higgins, surprise and anger creasing his face. He slowly turned round and stopped, transfixed with the silent image. The blinds were turned closed again.

'Maybe she's too upset at the moment, Tony. Maybe after both of you have another night in the cells you'll feel more like talking tomorrow.'

Tony Duffy clicked at his dentures until they were in place. 'Detective, be very careful what you do to my Stella.' His features had hardened, his eyes were menacing. He clenched and unclenched both fists. 'You've already lost a sister. You wouldn't want to lose your wife and kids too.'

It took three burly officers to drag Higgins off Duffy, but not before he'd broken the pensioner's nose.

'This is as much up-to-the-minute information as I have.' Ireland's senior police officer, Commissioner Peter Cunningham, sat at a wide circular table in a conference room at HQ in Dublin's Phoenix Park. To his left, face scrunched with intense concentration, was Harry Power, the lucky-to-be-alive Minister for Justice. Power's hair was singed at the back, his neck still peeling from the burns he'd received during the assassination attempt. Both hands were heavily bandaged from other burns sustained after he was dragged on to the pavement and pushed away before the grenade exploded inside his car. He'd curled himself into such a tight ball that his winter clothes and the weight of his police bodyguard protected him from further injuries. Only exposed flesh had scorched when the petrol tank exploded. To the Commissioner's right were Scott Nolan and Mark Higgins, both at the briefing because of their close family ties with Laura Nolan.

'Two men travelling on Russian passports arrived at Dublin airport from Rome late on 7 February, three days before the assassination attempts. Interpol has tracked their movements through Frankfurt, then back to Moscow, which was probably their point of origin. Both were using false IDs and had return tickets, apparently due to fly out again on 12 February. This was a smokescreen as there is no way they could have fled the country undetected on any commercial flight after what happened. Every port and border crossing was sealed within hours. I doubt they would even have got near freedom. I believe they were going to be killed one way or another.' Cunningham pressed a recessed button on the desk and on to a projection screen at the back of the dimly lit room separate head and chest photographs of Alex and Matthe flashed. No one in the room turned away, even though the images were of the men lying on autopsy tables, their torsos blackened and distorted by gunshot wounds. 'Nobody knows who these men are. We've had full co-operation from police forces throughout Europe and beyond but they are, as yet, unidentified.' Cunningham's eyes moved quickly from face to face. 'However, eyewitness reports of their expertise suggest they were professional hit men and not terrorists. There are any number of cheap guns for hire in Eastern Europe nowadays.'

'What about the one who escaped?' Power's expression

had changed. The intense concentration was now total revulsion.

The Commissioner pressed the recessed button again and the images of Alex and Matthe disappeared to be followed by a grainy still from a CCTV camera. It showed a blurred shape standing at the head of a long line of stalled cars. A bright flare glowed intensely from a barely recognisable vehicle in the middle of the queue. The figure in control had both hands extended and clasped together at the front, pointing in the direction of the fire. 'He more than likely organised and controlled the whole operation. He was shrewd enough to use outsiders, then ruthless enough to kill one of them rather than compromise the operation. And he was determined to press ahead with the attack on Dr Nolan knowing the risks involved. There were police cars swarming that area within minutes of the first shot being fired.'

Higgins swivelled in his chair, fumbled in his pocket for a cigarette, then remembered where he was and stopped. 'He must be local. He knew the area like the back of his hand, knew short cuts and one-way streets, knew the quickest route from where he attacked the Minister to Dr Nolan's apartment. No outside could have pulled that off and escaped.' Higgins was in T-shirt and denims, black hair slicked back severely, broad chest heaving.

Power turned to the Police Commissioner. 'What's your opinion?'

Cunningham rested both palms on the table in front of him and paused momentarily. He was in shirtsleeves and navy trousers, with a crease you could cut yourself on. In the gloom his bushy grey hair and eyebrows made his gaunt face sickly pale. 'I agree. The problem is we're not getting any intelligence. The gaols are bursting with dealers and crack heads, all spilling their guts and offering material we've never even guessed at before. But no hard information is coming out. We've got them so tight they're ratting on anyone to save their skin but there's not one whiff about this operation.'

Scott Nolan cut through. 'Isn't there even a photofit to work on? Didn't anyone notice anything about him?' Both Power and Higgins turned towards the doctor. Scott was sitting ramrod straight, his glasses fixed and his neck muscles taut as ropes.

The Police Commissioner flicked open a thick file and began sifting through paperwork. 'Let's start at the beginning.' He found the pages he wanted and scanned them quickly. 'At ten minutes past five that morning three men took over the end house along the road where the Minister lives. The property is rented by a Mr Hans Gunter, a forty-three-year-old Austrian banker attached to Commerzbank Europe. Mr Gunter was asleep in bed with his wife on the middle floor, his two daughters aged twelve and eight had separate rooms on the top level. The girls were lifted from their beds, bound and gagged almost before they realised this was for real and not a bad dream. Then Mr Gunter was dragged at gunpoint to the top floor landing, shown his daughters and also gagged and bound. His wife was beside him in minutes.' Cunningham paused only briefly to emphasise the next point. 'Not one word was spoken by any of the three, every order a threatening gesture with a gun. They wore balaclavas and gloves, and kept out of vision. All commands after that were scrawled felt-tip writing on blank pages. GET INTO THAT ROOM; WHERE ARE YOUR MOBILE PHONES? WHERE ARE THE CAR KEYS? When Mr Gunter refused to co-operate, one of the men lit a cigar, took about three deep drags and ground the lit end into the eight-year-old girl's forehead.'

'Which one?' Scott was now focused totally on the Police Commissioner.

'Our mystery man. The one who got away.'

'Could Mr Gunter give you any sort of description, even the slightest detail?'

'The three stayed out of sight throughout the time they spent in that house. There was no conversation in front of Gunter or his family, though he did hear muffled voices downstairs as they were leaving. He could offer nothing on accent, just dress code.'

'Were they speaking in English?' Scott probed again.

'He couldn't be sure. You must remember this man and his family were taken by surprise and Gunter's only thought was survival. When he was finally released he babbled incoherently for more than an hour and it took almost a day before he and his wife got their thoughts clear. Then he demanded to be put on the first flight out of the country.'

Power sighed as he rubbed at a peeling patch of skin on his neck. 'Can't say I blame him.'

'However,' the Commissioner continued, 'there is one recurring observation about the mystery assassin. Mrs Gunter noticed it and three other people reported it during the shoot-out. He limps.'

'Which leg?' Scott was in like a flash, leaning forward on the table.

'Consensus is he dragged his left leg. Now, I don't know if this was deliberate and faked but . . .'

'Can't be.' The doctor was like a man possessed, eyes flaring behind his lenses, fingernails digging into the table surface. 'You can fake injuries or limps or bad necks or whatever game you want to play. But in the heat of battle you forget to keep up the charade. He couldn't have kept a bogus limp dragging during that shoot-out on the street.'

'Bully for the doc.' Higgins brought him back to reality. He was leaning back in his chair. 'It's good to have an expert medical witness in on this investigation.'

Scott ignored the jibe. 'Do we have anything else? Fingerprints, other CCTV footage? Surely this man couldn't have planned and executed this sort of operation without someone seeing something suspicious.'

Higgins was about to make another comment but a withering look from Cunningham cut him dead. 'I understand your frustration, Dr Nolan. And we are doing house-to-house enquiries, checking for fingerprints and discarded cigar butts, sifting through photographs of top suspects. Everything that's possible. But what's worrying in this case is the lack of firm intelligence we're getting back. For such a high-profile assassination, and with intense international interest, I'd have expected some scrap of information to have leaked by now.'

'You mean you have absolutely nothing to go on?' Scott pushed his glasses back on to the bridge of his nose, his neck muscles now tightened to snap tension. 'Not a thing?'

'Cool it, doc,' snapped Higgins. 'Stick to your stethoscope and quit playing detective.'

Scott rounded on his tormentor angrily. 'Back off, Mark. I've as much right as anyone in this room to know what's going on. I lost my wife that morning.'

'And I lost my sister,' Higgins countered. 'It's her should be walking the streets right now, not you. She took those bullets for you.'

The room went suddenly quiet, the tension like static electricity. The Police Commissioner spoke next, his voice tired and strained. 'Listen up, everyone. All of us in this room have lost something. Two of my most experienced officers died at the hands of this gang. Dr Nolan lost wife and Mark' – he glanced towards the seething figure staring at the wood grain on the table – 'you lost your sister. Minister Power has already lost his son and now he and his family are constantly looking over their shoulders, wondering could this happen again? Nobody has come out of this unscathed. Cut out the aggro and focus on the problem.' His words hung on the air like a heavy fog and Power's head dropped, the demeanour of a man totally crushed. Scott Nolan and Mark Higgins looked like caged lions ready to rip one another's throats if released.

The Commissioner flicked another slide on to the screen. The image was so different it refocused all attention, defusing hostilities. 'This', explained Cunningham, 'is the opening to a popular walking trail in the Wicklow Hills. The area is thick forestry with the occasional open field. As you can see, there's a narrow road and to the left of that shot but out of view an old Land Rover is parked. Look carefully at the top right-hand corner and you'll see the shape of a body.' Another slide flashed up, this time a close-up of a man lying awkwardly up against a ditch. The face was squashed against dirt and grass, and unrecognisable. 'That's a well-known arms dealer called Joe McKeever, knocked eight feet along the ground from the impact of a car driven at some speed. He was originally from Belfast but had been living in a farm south of the border for the past six years. Now, McKeever's reputation reaches well beyond these shores. He's had contacts with Basque separatists, senior Libyan government sources, weapons dealers in the US and the Provisional IRA. McKeever never got his hands dirty, he just supplied the hardware. However, two days after the assassination Joe McKeever met with someone at that spot in Wicklow and came out the worse of the encounter. There is one eyewitness report from a local farmer who drove past around twelve thirty and is sure it was McKeever he saw standing at the side of the road. There was another car swung up on a grass verge but the farmer didn't notice anyone else around. He came back that same route about an hour later and found the body.

'You think this is connected?' Power's slumped shoulders had straightened.

'Joe McKeever', explained the Commissioner, 'only dealt with the top men in any organisation. Provos, Basque separatists, drug dealers or whatever, he never mixed with middlemen. McKeever had the hardware or knew where to get it and was on everyone's wanted list. But he never put a foot wrong. Also, he was big time in the criminal underworld, untouchable and unapproachable, and I can't believe his death, two days after the assassination attempts, is coincidence. I'm guessing McKeever provided the guns and grenades, probably even brought in the Russians. I'm guessing he met with our mystery man for payment and that something went wrong. Maybe McKeever was angry he was unwittingly involved in such a high-profile operation, or maybe he wanted more money. Maybe he just said the wrong thing at the wrong time. It could be anything, I don't know.' The Commissioner looked up at the slide and studied the image briefly. 'What I do know, and this is purely instinct, is that he was somehow involved in this operation. And if I'm right then our mystery man becomes a much bigger player than we thought.' Cunningham glanced towards Higgins. 'Local, I agree. But not so local he lives here. I'd say it's one the bigger fish who fled the country a long time ago.' The Commissioner paused, drilling his fingers against the desk, head slightly bent. Then he straightened and looked at each face in turn. 'Now this is my last hunch, and no one's going to like to hear me say it.' He now had everyone's attention. 'If I'm correct this could be a very long and difficult hunt.'

The small group broke up and out the corner of his eye Scott Nolan noticed the Commissioner beckon Mark Higgins angrily towards him. Harry Power joined them and the three hurried out of the room, leaving Scott to his own thoughts. For a moment he stared at the table, his brain a whirlwind of mixed emotions. Mark is right; it is Laura who should be walking the streets, not me. But can you turn back the clock? Can you undo what's done? He rebuked himself at the self-torment but guilt continued to force through. Everyone knows those bullets were meant for you, not Laura. Why did you let her drive, what were you thinking that morning? The charges and recriminations continued in his mind until his brain could take it no more. He looked around, almost in a daze, and realised he was alone. From somewhere in the near distance he could hear angry voices, the Commissioner and Mark Higgins probably having a stand-up row, he decided. Can't blame him for what he said, I'd feel the same. He found the recessed button on the table and on to the screen at the back of the room flashed the image from the CCTV. The mystery man with the weak leg, holding a row of traffic at gunpoint, gripped his attention. He sharp focused and the image became larger. Now he could just about make out a figure in the second car, a woman he guessed, holding her head in her hands. The woman's mouth was open in a silent scream.

* * *

Five miles away, in the fashionable Fitzroy Square of central Dublin, thirty-two-year-old Anna Kennedy was screaming. She held her head in both hands and tried to shield her eyes. The bloodied stump of the head of her pet poodle was impaled on the railings of the front gate.

7

It was minus ten degrees in Amsterdam when Sean Kennedy hobbled along Nieuwmarkt. He dodged errant cyclists, their heads bent against the bitter cold, breathing like dragons. Nieuwmarkt was a small market place close to the old town centre and between the canals of Kloveniersburgwal and Geldersekade, now frozen over and locking in the colourful houseboats and small craft moored there. The hum of traffic and jingling of bicycle bells followed Kennedy everywhere, interrupted only by blaring car horns. Close by, a long line of delivery vans and trucks was stuck along a narrow canal side road, edging forward at snail's pace. The cold was so intense few lingered on the sidewalks and most had layers of scarves round their faces for protection as they hurried along the streets and icy sidewalks.

He took Zeedijk, a familiar territory of high gabled terraced houses, delicate frescoes and wide bay windows. He pushed his pace faster, glancing at his watch. It was eleven thirty in the morning of 18 February and he had a rendezvous at noon in a café on Voorburgwal. He cut through narrow and seedy backstreets with gaudy front doors and glowing lights, then past porno houses and sex shops with girls in windows pouting and wiggling their wares. Even in the wintry conditions there was the usual collection of giggling sightseers, all heavily wrapped yet still taking photographs, while the more serious punters looked determined, usually scouting their target a few times before ducking inside. Kennedy knew all about Amsterdam's red light district, he'd been living in the heart of it for the past three years. In a small penthouse loft reached by four flights of rickety stairs, he hid away from the world and planned his life. On street level a blonde called Candy took in clients and offered a variety of sexual favours for ridiculously high prices. The second floor was a porno shop and the third level a storeroom.

Candy (Kennedy never asked what her real name was and wouldn't have expected an honest answer if he did) was twenty-eight, as tall as the tenant on the top floor, and oozed sensuality. She had high cheekbones, deep, almost sad blue eyes under fluttering long black lashes and was blessed with full, luscious lips, which she used to full effect when luring customers inside. Candy was a German country girl who'd fled a dreary existence on a farm fifty miles from Munich and headed north to Amsterdam and anonymity. After a year working as a barmaid, then a hotel chambermaid, she decided to screw her way into some decent money. She had the looks; she had the body and knew how to use her assets. She and Kennedy moved into the same back alley building within a month of one another. A small man called Evan van Bronken, who called for the rent every week, owned the property. He was thin as a whippet, with tightly shaven head and rings in both ears. Kennedy put him in his early forties and thought he was probably a pimp. He kept away from van Bronken as much as possible, leaving his rent with Candy to be paid when he wasn't around. He trusted Candy and she trusted him, and the two relied on one another. If Candy was having trouble with one of her clients, she knew she could call on Kennedy for help. Equally, if the girl was behind with her rent, Kennedy helped out, never looking for the money back. The hooker had a gambling and cocaine habit, tastes that often outstripped her income. In return she was Kennedy's eyes and ears, primed to warm if anyone suspicious or unfamiliar came looking for him. As yet, no one had. Candy had long since stopped asking what Kennedy did for a living; now she just accepted him at the top of the house, her shadowy protector.

Once, the previous August on an especially hot and sultry night, an English thug, all beer belly, shaven head and tattoos, tried to force his attentions on the girl. Kennedy heard her protests shrill right to the top of the house and came down to check. 'Come on, come on. I'll pay ye, don' worry.' Kennedy recognised a Midlands accent and when he glanced outside he spotted a party prowling the street, six or seven in their mid twenties or thirties, boozed and horny and looking for action. They looked like a group celebrating someone's stag night, a last fling before respectability. One or two shouted catcalls and wolf whistles at any window offering services. But none of them was Candy's type. She could do tricks that would spin heads but was selective in her choice. And the particular piss artist now annoying her was definitely not on her wish list. She was pushing the door closed and shouting at him in a string of German obscenities but he was stronger and fuelled with alcohol. The door was quarter open and he grabbed at Candy's sweating hands where they slipped on the frame. 'C'me on, luv, you might even like it.' The slurred speech and beer smells only added to his disgusting appearance.

Kennedy quietly closed the front door, clicked the lock and then felled the yob with one solid punch to the side of the neck. The man buckled, screaming with pain and shock, then half turned to see what had hit him. Kennedy's knee smashed into his face, breaking bone, teeth and cartilage. Five minutes later the lout was lying in a bloodied heap in the gutter one block away, his mates still staggering around the streets looking for him.

Candy shut up shop for the night and Kennedy took her to his loft to calm her down. The girl was shaking and agitated and sobbing, and it took Kennedy some time to reassure her she was safe and no one would come after her. In the sweltering heat both were perspiring heavily and he opened a six-pack of Heineken and rolled a particularly strong joint. They smoked and talked the night through, she telling him all about her dreary existence in rural Bavaria and why she'd fled for the bright lights and city life of Amsterdam. Kennedy told her nothing. 'Come on,' she teased at one point, 'there must be a reason why you live in a tiny loft above a whorehouse? And why do I have to warn you about strangers? Who's chasing you?'

But Kennedy just inhaled deeply, grinned stupidly and opened another beer. 'Some day, when I'm ready, I'll tell you. But not right now.' Candy curled up in his arms and soon fell asleep. In the morning she mounted Kennedy and the two discovered a mutual animal passion that surprised them both. After that incident, Kennedy became the unofficial protector for a small group of Candy's friends working the alley. In return he got laid for free whenever he wanted, a deal he considered more than fair. He liked getting laid and he liked smashing people's faces.

The coffee-cum-hashish shop was in Oudezijds Voorburgwal, close to the Amsterdam Chinese church and directly above a sex cinema. Kennedy pushed his way through the crowded room to a table at the far corner, sweating from the long walk in his heavy overcoat and thermal clothes. A bored-looking waitress was beside him in seconds, black denims and white top proclaiming RED LIGHT DISTRICT. 'Double espresso, please.' He glanced around, noticing a group of teenagers giggling manically as they shared a joint. The smell of coffee mixed with marijuana filled the room and Kennedy stretched out his long legs and began to relax. This was his kind of city. He could get stoned and lie in a stupor for as long and often as he wished. He was his own man and a free agent. Amsterdam suited him nicely. The coffee arrived just as Davis sat down beside him, waving the waitress away.

'Howya, Sean?'

'Good, Jay. Feeling real good.'

'When'd you get in?'

'Last night. Took a train to Belfast, then on to Larne along the Antrim coast. Grabbed a ferry to Stranraer, another train to Manchester and the next flight out to Schiphol. Piece of cake, really.'

'What was security like?'

'Very tight at the border, then another spot check before boarding the ferry.'

'They weren't looking for a baldy-looking bastard like you.' Davis laughed. He reached across and ran the palm of his hand along Kennedy's spiky haircut. 'Jaysus, you change your styles quicker than David Beckham.'

Kennedy sipped his espresso and grinned. 'Gotta keep on the move, gotta keep changing your looks. Especially when the whole country is looking for you.'

Davis waved to the waitress and ordered coffee and a plate of cheese. He was a tall, slim and handsome man in his mid forties. His hair was thinning at the front but he had thick locks that covered his ears. His tan was from Marbella where he lived in some splendour with a string of different girls he picked up at bars and nightclubs.

'Bloody right they're looking for you. Our little operation went more or less as expected. I've never seen such a fucking commotion.' Jay Davis was a Dubliner who'd worked for fifteen years in the Irish police force, the last five in the Drug Squad. He'd quit unexpectedly, citing he couldn't take the flak and hassle any longer, and said he was going to try his luck running a bar in the south of Spain. He even bought one, near the seafront in Puerto Banus, about thirty miles along the coast from Marbella. But Davis's main motive was to move in on the lucrative drug trade he'd seen at first hand in Ireland. He knew all the contacts, had arrested most of them and interrogated others. He left with a grand plan to carve out the biggest piece of action the country would ever see. And the first part of that strategy had been completed.

'We expected that.' Kennedy leaned across the small table, glancing around to make sure no one was eavesdropping. They had the corner to themselves, the rest engrossed in newspapers or wrapped up in their own conversations. The waitress was busy keeping the group of stoned students topped up with nibbles. Smoke filled the air as another joint was passed round. 'Can't go blowing up government Ministers and shooting policemen without somebody complaining.'

When Kennedy had finished talking, Davis sat back in his

seat, nibbling a slice of cheese. His right leg jiggled under the table, a habit Kennedy recognised when the other man got excited or worked up about something.

'So we still have the guts of that million?'

Kennedy nodded.

'Did you talk to McCann?' Davis had finished the plate of cheese and was swirling the dregs of his coffee.

'Derek's shit scared. He's seen five different gangs busted in less than forty-eight hours and he's nervous he could be next. Nobody knows what's coming out with everyone squealing to save their skins. He's worried someone will use him as an ace card to get off the hook.'

'It's good for him to sweat for a while,' said Davis. 'It'll make our move so much more important when the time comes. I've been following every development closely. Tony Duffy and his gang are now out of action, as well as that crowd of misfits on the Northside, the Flanagans. What Power didn't drag away with the first wave of his campaign is being snared now. The place is being cleaned up big time and pretty soon there won't be a coke head with a supplier. The junkies are already going crazy. From what I hear there hasn't been a shipment of horse for weeks.'

The two lapsed into silence, each to his own thoughts as they considered the situation. 'What happened was enough to really shake the bastards up.' Davis finally spoke. 'Pity about the young woman, though, that was the only casualty I didn't like.'

Kennedy shrugged. 'Collateral damage, isn't that what the Americans call it? You don't see them crying into their Budweiser when one of their smart bombs blows up a hospital instead of an arms dump two miles away. She got in the way and had to be wasted, simple as that.'

Davis's right leg began jiggling again under the table. He swivelled in his chair to inspect the coffee house, waved for another cup, then turned back. 'Papers are full of the guy now. Break your heart stuff about a young man with high ideals and lofty ambitions coming to Dublin to marry his sweetheart, only to find the city worse than anything he'd experienced back home.'

Kennedy wiped a mock tear from his eye. 'Look at me, Jay. I'm broken-hearted.'

Davis grinned. 'No doubt about it, Sean. You're one mean bastard.'

'And you worked in Calcutta with Mother Teresa?'

'Fuck off.' The rebuke was good-humoured. Davis's coffee arrived and he sipped it, then wiped milk froth from his lips. 'Did you look in on Fitzroy Square?'

'For a while.' Kennedy sat back in his seat and fixed on Davis. Now his demeanour had switched to defensive.

'And did you do anything?'

'Not much.'

Davis groaned. 'I warned you to stay away from there. What's the point in us breaking our balls to pull off the biggest heist ever if you're going to screw it up with this fucking vendetta.' His voice wasn't raised but the anger was razor sharp.

'He murdered my mother.'

'Look, I've heard all this before. What's the point in going over old ground? Where's that going to lead you? Nowhere and you know it.'

Kennedy leaned straight across the table until he was inches from Davis. 'He murdered my mother. Then made her out to be a drink- and tranquilliser-junkie who wasn't responsible for her actions. It was me found her at the bottom of the stairs, it was me tried to resuscitate her. And her body already cold and stiff. I know she didn't fall, she was much too careful for that. She knew what was going on; I heard all the shouts and arguments months before. I just know that old bastard pushed her.'

Davis turned away to escape the torrent of vitriol. He noticed one of the other patrons staring at them and flashed a warning *shut up* to Kennedy. He dropped a twenty Euro note on the table, grabbed his coat and motioned across the table. 'Let's go. This place is too stuffy.'

Outside the icy cold took their breath away and Davis dragged the collar of his overcoat higher up on his face, then pulled a woollen beret tight down on his head. 'Jaysus, this place is freezing. Why don't you move down to Spain and get some heat in your bones? I couldn't spend a whole winter here, it'd wear me down.'

Kennedy looked around him, savouring the sights and sounds of the city: the manic cyclists, the gaudy shopfronts, even the frozen canals with houseboats and small craft iced to where they rested. Amsterdam was a buzz town, liberated from petty laws and constantly on the go. 'I like it here. Nobody knows me and nobody bothers me. I do what I like.'

'Still living in that poky loft?'

'Yeah. And getting laid by real pros. Can't beat that.'

Davis sighed. 'Just don't catch something from them other than a head cold.'

They walked in silence along a maze of side streets, Davis slowing to allow for Kennedy's limp. A weak winter sun struggled to be seen through low cloud cover as they passed the Tattoo Museum on Oudezijds Achterburgwal, then the Hasj Marijuana Hemp Museum, a small crowd gathering at the front door straight off a tourist mini-coach. The canal beside was being freed by an ice-breaker, the cracking of frozen water ricocheting in the air. The two watched for a moment, then Davis turned to Kennedy. 'What about our plan? Are we still on target?'

Kennedy leaned on an iron railing and arched his back. He lit up a cigar and blew smoke rings into the freezing air. 'Yeah. I know McCann's nervous as hell but I think he'll keep his head above water. And he's just bought out a courier company that distributes around the city and provinces. Ideal for moving his goods. Now that the well's dried up for a lot of users he knows he's got an almost open market. When things have died down I know he'll want to do business.'

Davis stomped his feet and thrust both hands deep into his side pockets. There was a light wind whipping off the canal and his tanned features were turning purple. 'Why wait? Nobody's going to be shifting much with the cops on the warpath. Now is the time to kick start our operation.'

Davis started walking and Kennedy followed. They crossed the road, dodging a slew of cyclists and warning bells, and paused briefly to inspect paintings on display in a shop window. Davis checked no one was taking an unhealthy interest in them. 'Sean, our contacts won't wait for ever. They've got their own timetables, other customers. I'll do Miami if you take Bangkok. But let's do it now, this week.'

8

Less than a thousand miles away, in the small cemetery of the Church of Ireland in Killinure in County Kildare, Scott Nolan stared down at the simple white cross at the head of his wife's grave. LAURA NOLAN. RIP. The narrow rectangle of ground was still in a wet clay mound, the earth not yet settled from the digging and interring, and recent heavy rains. A strong wind moaned through the copse, swaying the cypress trees lining the gravel path to the church and rustling the naked branches of trees in the glade beside it. In the almost deserted graveyard one could find peace. But not Scott Nolan. He couldn't hold back his tears and let them run shamelessly, shoulders heaving as each sob racked his body. Sheltering in the doorway of the old church, his armed bodyguard turned his back to allow him to grieve in privacy. The only observers of this distress were two stonemasons; erecting a headstone on another new plot about thirty yards away. They averted their eyes and continued cutting and hewing, only too used to seeing anguished relatives walk trance-like around the lonely sanctuary, as if hoping to see their loved ones arise and become flesh again. The masons' faces were red from effort and the bite of the wind, and they finally stopped and rested, glancing occasionally at the solitary mourner.

Through the blurring of tears Scott inspected other headstones, trying to distract himself from his misery. But when he looked, each departed soul had at least lived to a decent age, sixty or seventy, even a few eighties and he counted five who had passed their ninetieth birthdays. About twenty paces to his right he came across the poignant marker of a child who had died in his third month of life ('at peace with the angels') and he was ashamed to feel relief that at least Laura was not the youngest resting in Killinure.

For a confusing moment Scott thought he could hear Laura's rebuking voice and he spun round, as if expecting to see her skip through the headstones, dark hair bouncing off her shoulders, her smile mocking him. But the only movement was one of the stonemasons, a tall bald-headed and heavy-set man, with coarse weather-beaten features and hands like shovels. He was edging nervously towards Scott, wiping his palms against the front of his denim work suit. A cloth cap poked out of a side pocket. 'I'm very sorry for your troubles,' he finally said in a faltering thick country accent. 'I know it's yer wife that was shot last week and ye must think we're all savages in this bloody country.' He looked down at Laura's grave and pressed a muddy boot heavily on a patch of turf sticking up. 'But we're not. There's not wan of us not broken-hearted with what yer having to go through. I didn't want to disturb ye but I just had to say that. It's the least I could do.'

He turned to go but Scott reached out and managed to grab a sleeve. The mason looked round, startled. 'Thank you,' said Scott. 'Thank you so much for those words. You have no idea how much they mean to me.' He shook the man's hand, his knuckles cracking in the stronger grip. 'Will you cut a headstone for her? Nothing too big or ornate, Laura wouldn't have wanted that. She was never one for showing off or boasting. Make it simple but strong, I don't want it to stand out from the others but I want people to be able to read the inscription if they do come upon it.'

The mason's face creased in thought. 'I've a good idea what ye want. Leave it with me; I'll do a grand job. It'll take a few weeks, mind, for this'll be a special order. The granite I'll choose myself and then polish the surface for lettering. What would ye like inscribed?'

Scott didn't hesitate. 'Laura Nolan. RIP. Murdered 10 February 2006. That's all.'

The mason looked at Scott, inspecting his face and gazing deep into his eyes. Then he shook his head. 'And it's only the truth.' The sadness in his voice was like a heavy weight as he turned away. 'Sure it's the God's only truth.' He walked back towards his companion, head still shaking.

Scott called after him. 'Make sure you send me the bill.'

The mason turned, dragging his cloth cap firmly down on to his bald head. 'There'll be no bill. Let this be from the people in Killinure. At least in this parish we care about our own.'

The journey back to Dublin took two hours in heavy traffic and stair-rod rain. The darkening skies had been driven eastwards by strengthening winds and eventually a torrent was unleashed. Raindrops drilled off the motorway in front of their car and pounded the windscreen, defying the wipers to clear. Scott hadn't the enthusiasm to strike up a conversation with his bodyguard and the two stayed in sombre silence until they reached the Sandymount apartment complex where a different squad car waited to take up surveillance duty. Scott gathered up yet another large collection of fresh flowers lying against the front door, cards of sympathy stuck to their wrapping. His living room was becoming more like a florist's shop with wreaths and bouquets. Total strangers were driving from different parts of the city just to leave a tribute and in his bedroom there were six mail bags of sympathy cards, letters and notes from Ireland and abroad. He'd been swamped with compassion, overwhelmed by a national outpouring of outrage and grief at Laura's death. Somehow it didn't make him feel any better.

It was now six in the evening, the rain had eased to a steady drizzle but it was dark and cold, with gusts of wind blowing litter along the pavements. People were hurrying to catch their trains to the southern suburbs or pick up cars from long-term parking lots. People were alive and living, but Scott felt he might as well be dead his soul was so empty, his heart so broken. He was the loneliest and saddest man in the world. Not especially hungry, he ordered in a pizza to keep up his strength, only to be embarrassed as an armed officer frisked the delivery boy on the stairwell. Unfortunately his next-door neighbour arrived at the same time and looked on open-mouthed and shocked before scurrying to the safety of her apartment. Scott heard dead bolts and locks being forced home as soon as the door closed. He'd noticed an unusual amount of activity from security companies since Laura's murder in the underground car park, the residents deciding Scott was still high risk. No one wanted to get caught up in any second-wave attack. It was getting to him, and there were too many bitter memories here. He'd give Dublin another six months and then look for a position elsewhere.

He went back to work at the City Hospital the next morning, slipping through a side entrance just before six thirty.

'Good to see you again, Dr Nolan,' the matron of ward seven greeted him as soon as he made his way to the nurses' station. 'I can't tell you how sorry we all are . . .'

Scott held up a hand to shush her. 'Just update me on the patients, sister. I'm finding this difficult enough and if everyone keeps saying sorry I'll not be able to finish the day.' So the matron, a portly and red-faced woman in her mid fifties with tinted grey hair, held her reserve and went through the list of children still officially under Scott's care. Since the shootings his caseload had been shared with colleagues and his second in command. But Scott knew the facility was understaffed and under-resourced, and his absence would have put intense pressure on the others. It's time to get stuck in again, he decided. It'll be as much therapy as necessity.

One by one his team drifted in, surprised to see their boss standing at the end of a bed, white coat on and stethoscope slung round his neck, wearing blue shirt and striped tie, freshly pressed slacks. He was evaluating each child's condition, treatments and progress, and by nine o'clock was up to scratch. By five past nine his squad knew he was back in action.

'I want LFTs and FBC on this boy.' A chart was passed across to the most junior doctor, a baby-faced Malaysian girl who'd overslept. 'I need the results in an hour so get the phlebotomist on to this immediately. Also book him in for an ultrasound scan of the upper abdomen.' The sleep sticking to the Malaysian's eyes was wiped away as she hurried to the phone. 'Now' – Scott turned to his second in command, a tall man in his thirties with rugby-squashed nose and tight red hair – 'we'll have a conference at ten thirty sharp so you can brief me on any problems and new admissions. We have a full outpatients' clinic this afternoon and I'd like to feel I'm on top of what's going on in the wards before we decide who can be discharged and who needs admission.' The registrar started grabbing at files and pathology reports, nodding at the other two in the team, both young men, to get their acts together. Whatever pace they'd worked at over the previous eight days was now obviously being upped by the Detroit whirlwind. Soon the buzz of activity along the wards, even the constant smell of antiseptic, began to filter into Scott's senses and he felt his tensions ease, his spirits lift. This is your life now, he told himself as he scribbled notes on an observation chart. Focus on your work and live for your patients. They deserve your expertise.

He was examining a ten-year-old girl with liver damage from hepatitis when his pager sounded. He took the call on a wall phone close to a scrub room. 'Hi, Dr Nolan here.'

'Dr Nolan, it's Harold Winters, the hospital chief executive.'

Scott's brow furrowed. What the hell does he want? 'Yes?'

'Could I have a quick word with you right away? You've caught me off guard this morning, I didn't realise you'd be back so soon.'

'Is there a problem, Mr Winters? Was I supposed to give you notice?' Scott was beginning to get peeved.

'Not really,' Winters assured him, 'just some protocol we need to sort out, that's all.'

Scott wasn't convinced by the other man's tone. 'Can't it wait until some other time? I'm trying to catch up on work.'

'Dr Nolan, I'd like to get this issue out of the way pretty much immediately.'

Alarm bells rang in Scott's head. Issue? What issue? 'Can you give me an idea what you're talking about here, Mr

Winters? I don't like walking in on someone else's agenda unprepared.'

'Dr Nolan, how about you call into my office right now and let's sort this out.' The executive's tone had changed from 'please' to 'do it'.

Scott glanced at his watch. His conference was fifteen minutes away. It would take him at least five minutes to get to the administration suite on the top floor, the same to return. 'Will this take more than five minutes? I've got a clinical meeting at ten thirty.'

'Five minutes should be more than enough.'

He pounded the stairs rather than take the lift, immediately recognisable with his dishevelled hair, unfashionable lenses and slight stoop. Out the corner of an eye he noticed heads turn as staff tried to say something, but he kept his gaze rooted to the floor and pressed ahead. He knew there'd be nothing but 'I'm so sorry', or 'Scott, I don't know what to say', or 'if there's anything I can do, please shout'. But he didn't want sympathy or consoling words, he couldn't take one more 'sorry for your troubles' or other well-meaning and sincere gesture. He was determined to move on, to throw himself back into his work and immerse his mind in the ill children under his care. The time for self-indulgent remorse was over. Maybe another six months in Dublin, he'd decided the night before, then look for a position elsewhere. Dublin would always carry too many bitter memories.

Harold Winters's office was on a corner site with magnificent views of the city from two picture windows. He sat behind a kidney-shaped desk in a tall swivel chair, a clutter of paperwork in front and to the side and even littering the floor. Even though it was only mid morning he looked like a man under pressure, shirt collar open and tie dragged down to the third button. 'Thanks for coming so promptly, Dr Nolan.'

Scott shrugged. 'You called, I answered.'

'You see,' Winters started explaining, 'I wasn't sure when you'd be back on the wards. In fact, none of us was sure you'd ever come back after everything that happened. And can I say right now how . . .'

'Please,' Scott cut through, 'no condolences. I'm swimming in them at the moment and could drown from overload. Don't take this personally but I'd like to get to the point of our meeting.' He glanced at his watch. 'I'm running late already.'

Winters stood up, lifted files and loose pages from a chair and pushed it towards Scott. 'Sit down, Dr Nolan. Let's not rush anything.'

'Look, I've got a clinical meeting', Scott protested, angrily stabbing an index finger at his watch, 'in less than . . .'

Winters sat at the other side of his desk and rested his chin on clasped hands. 'Forget the clinical meeting. I rang your registrar and told him to go on ahead, that you might be a bit late.' His wrinkles seemed to melt into one deep fault line, his forehead creased into high wave crests.

'You rang my registrar?' Scott wasn't sure he was hearing Winters clearly. An administrator interfering in clinical matters wasn't usual in the City Hospital. 'What the hell . . .'

Both Winters's hands went up in the air for calm. 'Relax, I know how important your work is to you and to the whole institution.'

'I don't think you actually do, Mr Winters, or you wouldn't be messing me around like this.' Scott was halfway on to his feet, forcing his glasses back on his nose, gripping the chair sides to control his hands. Right then he wanted to wrap them around Winters's neck.

'Then let me get straight to the point,' snapped Winters unexpectedly, 'so you'll grasp how significant this discussion is to me and you and everyone who works in this hospital or even visits it as a patient.' The executive's voice had hardened to a 'let's cut the crap and get down to business' tone. He leaned into his swivel chair and held Scott's hostile stare. 'For the past three days we've had armed policemen and plain-clothes detectives swarming over all departments here. I've had to hand over every single file on every employee, full or part-time, even casual labour. All for security clearance. No less than twenty-seven staff have been forced to leave because they have criminal records. I *knew* that when I hired them, it was part of their rehabilitation programme and most of them were damned good workers, so I was less than pleased to let them go. And they were very angry at being forced out of employment, complaining bitterly at being classified as security risks.' Winters spun slightly in his chair, as if to let his words sink in. His eyes never left Scott. 'And now I'm advised by the Police Commissioner that undercover officers will shadow you from the moment you cross the threshold here until you drive out of the car park later. If you go for a leak, some guy with a handgun will check the cubicles first. When you walk the wards or corridors, somebody dressed in surgical scrubs and carrying a loaded Smith & Wesson will follow.'

Scott's heart sank. Now he understood why Winters had called him as soon as he'd returned to duties. He slumped in his chair, his legs stretched out in front. He took off his glasses and polished them with a corner of his white coat, as much to clear his head as his vision. Winters was off again. 'The Commissioner has also told me his men will have the power to stop and search anyone they feel might be acting suspiciously, or where they perceive a real and imminent threat to your safety.' He sighed loudly and muttered under his breath, 'It's like something out of a bloody Tom Clancy novel.'

Scott was pole-axed, unsure how to react. 'Who else knows about this?' he asked finally.

'The board of management. There was an extraordinary general meeting held last night to discuss the issue.'

'And what was the mood?'

Winters shrugged. 'Astonished, perplexed, anxious. What else can I say? This is not your usual hospital incident. I mean, we've handled doctors drunk on duty, doctors stealing drugs, even doctors screwing the patients or having a quickie in the sluice room with one of the nurses. But this is new territory. We've never before had an employee who needs armed protection while on duty.'

Scott adjusted his glasses at his ears, trying desperately to get his thoughts in order. He was having real difficulty grasping the full significance of what he'd heard. 'Maybe I'm not following you correctly' – he stumbled over the words – 'but are you suggesting I'm a liability to the hospital? Is that it?'

'That's your take, Dr Nolan, not necessarily mine. But I'd have to say that the board is having great difficulty coming to terms with these security orders. I rang the Police Commissioner first thing this morning for clarification and half an hour later had a most abusive call from Harry Power, our Minister for Justice.'

Scott groaned. 'Oh no. What did he say?'

'I'm not going to repeat what he said. I know the Minister has had a dreadful time recently, losing his son and then that attack where he was lucky to get out alive. But we all have to get on with our lives, we can't create fortress Ireland, a police state on constant high alert.' Winters stood up and gazed out of the picture window, hitching at his trousers and tucking in his loose shirt. Outside, low cloud covered the city and spats of rain ran down the glass. 'Dublin is becoming a nightmare, I know that. Our Emergency Room is full every evening with drug addicts and drunks and thugs kicking the head off one another. Over the past six months I've taken on eight new security men for the night shift alone. Wages paid to hire men to protect the staff when that money should be directed to patient care. And then the government has the gall to rant about our costs overrunning. How the hell can I balance the books in a war zone?'

Scott listened uneasily. 'What did Harry Power say?' he repeated.

Winters turned round, leaned on the desk and fixed on Scott. 'He told me that if necessary he'd call in the army to patrol the corridors. Your safety is paramount.'

Scott's brain went into overdrive. He recalled Mark Higgins's words at the graveside the day Laura was buried. '*This is your life, Dr Nolan. As long as you stay in this country you're under constant police protection.*' Scott hadn't really grasped the significance of the comment then, severe emotional distress clouding his thinking. But he was already finding the continual police bodyguard around the apartment complex oppressive. He had secretly thought this would be kept up for a few weeks, then discreetly wound down. Now he was learning he'd called the situation all wrong. For Christ's sake he was a doctor, not the US president. What physician needs twenty-four-hour armed protection? What was being suggested was absurd, total overreaction by Harry Power.

'And what do you think of all this, Mr Winters? What's your take on the situation?'

Winters sat down and ran the palms of his hands along the desk surface, as if feeling for a pin. Finally he looked up, his Mount Rushmore features seeming very troubled. 'To be honest, Dr Nolan, I spent all last night thinking about this. Hardly slept a wink.'

'Sorry to hear that.'

Winters ignored the comment. 'And I have to tell you my main concern is not *your* safety, despite what Harry Power says. My concern and responsibility is the safety of all the staff here. If the police consider you to be in constant danger, I can only assume they're working from intelligence information I'm not privy to. And if you are under continuous threat of attack, can I in all conscience ask doctors and nurses to work with you, knowing they could get caught up in a shooting match? We could have a bloodbath in the corridors if someone opens up with an automatic weapon. Or what if some poor bugger decides to play a joke and pulls a plastic gun? Is it shoot first, ask questions later?'

The room went silent, the only noise coming from voices in the outside corridor and the drilling of rain on the picture windows. Harold Winters was spinning in his swivel chair, but avoiding Scott's stare.

'There's a bottom line here, Mr Winters, isn't there?' Scott caught Winters mid swivel. 'This meeting is more than just to let off steam and acquaint me with the problem. I am the problem, isn't that right?'

Winters nodded slightly. 'That's one way of looking at it, I agree.'

'Then what you really want is this' – Scott sought the right word – 'this *issue*, as you described it earlier. You want this *issue* resolved quickly, don't you?'

Winters stayed silent, but his eyes narrowed.

Scott looked down at his watch. It was eleven o'clock and he knew his case conference would be over, his team wondering what the hell was going on, the nursing staff waiting for his orders for those children still in the wards. He was so behind in his work, so out of touch with his own squad of doctors.

When Winters spoke again his voice was razor sharp and the words sliced through Scott like a scalpel through flesh. 'I think, Dr Nolan, it would be much better if you sought another position in another hospital. And preferably in another country.'

After his conversation with Harold Winters, chief executive of the City Hospital, Scott returned to the wards in a daze. His team had finished the case conference and was yet again working from orders from the second in command. Scott began flicking aimlessly through charts, half-heartedly reading lab reports and X-ray printouts. He glanced down at his patients, children in various states of ill health. Some were lively and boisterous and tried making jokes, others were subdued, their eyes sunken and listless, their bodies too weak for activity. IV lines and drainage bags restricted their movements further and they lay burrowed into their pillows, forlorn and dejected. Usually Scott would sit at each bedside and engage the young patient in conversation, trying to assess progress or lift any flagging spirits. 'How's this young man today, feeling any better?' or 'Hey kiddo, you're looking brighter this week. Like to go home soon?' But right then he was so deflated by Winters's comments he couldn't enthuse himself to speak to anyone. *I think, Dr Nolan, it would be much better if you sought another position in another hospital. And preferably in another country.* You're not wanted here. You're no longer the great asset everyone hailed when you first arrived, the US specialist who would fast forward liver disease treatment in Ireland by at least five years. The American plucked from the ranks of the City Hospital by the government to spearhead the medical information campaign in Harry Power's anti-drug war. Oh, how the hospital board had basked in reflected glory then, how delighted the staff were that one of their own would represent the institution in such a positive light. But by God, how quickly attitudes change. Dr Scott Nolan the talent was now Nolan the risky millstone. Time to move on, Dr Nolan. I hear there's a good post in Antarctica for someone with your skills. Assassins should have difficulty tracking you there.

Finally he could take it no longer and hurried from the unit, ignoring the puzzled glances and questioning looks. What *is* going on with that man? He could sense bewilderment as he skipped down the stairwells, head held high and pretending to be oblivious to everyone around him, even though he couldn't but notice their confused half-takes. On ground level he skirted a stricken family group listening intently to a young doctor talking earnestly to them. Someone else is having a bad day, he thought as he hurried past. Still in white coat, still with stethoscope swung round neck, he left the main building through the public entrance and flagged a taxi.

'Where to?' The cabbie was a small bald man in leather jacket over blue crew neck. Stuck on the dashboard were his ID, a green air freshener and a small plastic statue of the Blessed Virgin. He gunned the engine alive and inspected his fare through the rear-vision mirror.

'Sandymount, please,' Scott mumbled, his face forced towards the side window.

'Sure.' The taxi eased away from the rank. 'You just get off duty or something?'

'No, not really.' Scott was still in a faze and ill prepared for questions. 'Well, maybe yes, you could say that. I am getting off duty.'

The cabbie kept glancing in his rear-vision, negotiating hospital traffic and patients, then up a long ramp to a side street. 'Funny time to be quitting. Most of the staff I carry leave around seven in the morning or eight at night. Not lunchtime.'

Scott looked out at the blurred streets as they flashed by. On the sidewalks people were trying to keep umbrellas from being blown inside out, or sheltering in doorways as another heavy shower crossed the city. 'I got sent home early for bad behaviour,' he said bitterly.

The phone buzzed at ten o'clock exactly. Scott let it ring out to the answering machine, as he'd been doing for days. 'Scott, it's Bob here. There's a full-page article about you in today's *New York Times*. When you get a chance call me . . .'

Scott killed the answering mode and cut through. 'Bob, hi. It's Scott here.'

'Jesus, Scott, I've been ringing you all week. What the hell's going on over there? I haven't heard from you, the folks say they haven't heard from you. How are you coping? Are you OK? Give us some news, Mom and Dad are real worried.'

Right at that moment Scott felt he could do without another interrogation, especially from his older brother. But he had noted the calls from Chicago and New York, had recognised his family back home were trying to get through. 'I'm sorry, Bob, I've been to hell and back and I'm finding it very difficult to talk with anyone. I'll call the folks as soon as we hang up.'

'Do that, they'd appreciate hearing your voice. The old man said he'd fly to Dublin if he didn't make contact in the next forty-eight hours.'

'I'll call, don't worry. Just as soon as we're through.'

'You sound pretty down to me, Scott. Maybe you should see a therapist. Or how about Prozac for a while? It worked wonders for me last year when the markets crashed and I lost a bundle.'

Scott couldn't help but smile. His older brother taking Prozac, now that's a first. 'I'll think about that, Bob. It's certainly an option.'

There was a strained pause before Bob came back again, his strong drawl zinging clearly across the line. 'Well, come on, Scott. How are you getting on? Are you gonna stay in that hell-hole of a city or come back to civilisation? A guy like you would be snapped up in any of the big hospitals along the east coast. You'd earn some decent money, too.'

'I'm considering all options right now,' Scott lied. If he told Bob about his conversation with the City Hospital's chief executive there'd be a torrent of scorn.

'Ah, Jesus, that's a politician's answer. You're my kid brother so don't sell me horseshit. Tell it like it is.'

'You tell me, Bob. What's the *New York Times* saying?'

'That's why I called again so soon. I'm looking at page five right now. Big headlines: SECURITY NIGHTMARE FOR CHICAGO DOCTOR. It's an exclusive from their European correspondent reporting from Dublin. Dr Scott Nolan, a Chicago-born paediatrician blah, blah, blah. There's a bit of background, then he gets to the meat of the story. According to inside sources the Irish government considers Scott Nolan a security headache. With round-the-clock surveillance by armed detectives and an emergency response unit at the ready should any further attack be attempted, Nolan is fast becoming the most expensive doctor in the Irish health system.

'A government spokesman said there is no rift between Dr Nolan and Ireland's Justice Minister Harry Power who was also attacked on 10 February. But close sources have confirmed Nolan has not returned Power's many calls and the two have only met once since the assassination attempts. Then there's a side bar about the hunt for the mastermind behind the murders and the lack of progress on that front. Short snippet about Interpol and the FBI offering every assistance. That's the gist of it. Photo of you and a separate shot of a car on fire, then a shadowy photofit of the murderer, which looks pretty useless as it could be anybody. Still, it's big stuff for the *Times* to give it so much space.'

Scott listened with mounting fury. If the *New York Times* report was only half true, Harold Winters was voicing more than his own opinion when he'd advised Scott to seek another position, preferably in another country. The City Hospital staff was obviously coming to the same conclusion and probably secretly harbouring the same thoughts. Certainly his neighbours in the apartment complex had already taken extra precautions, common sense suggested anyone associated with him might be equally nervous.

'I'll read it on the Internet,' Scott said, trying to control his breathing. He didn't want Bob to sense his simmering emotions. My biggest problem is with Laura's family. They've barely spoken to me since the funeral. I just know they blame me for her death.'

'Scott' – Bob sounded at his most bullish – 'I never liked the idea of you going to that asshole of a country in the first place. What has it ever given the world but Guinness,

Riverdance and terrorists? It's a backwater. The only place to advance your career is in the good old US of A.'

'It wasn't Ireland I came for especially,' Scott snapped. 'I found a woman I loved and wanted to spend the rest of my life with.'

'Yeah, so did I.' The cynicism across the line almost dripped on to the floor beside Scott. 'Three times and still counting. And each one has cost me a fortune in alimony payments.'

'Bob, we're going nowhere with this conversation. Thanks for calling and for all your advice. Maybe see you soon.'

'Don't forget to talk to the old man. He's really worried about you and when he hears about this *Times* piece it'll upset him even more.'

'As soon as we hang up.'

Scott spent the next half-hour reassuring the rest of his family in Chicago that everything was all right, that he was looking after himself and steadily coming to terms with the loss of his wife. He talked for fifteen minutes to Mary. Conversation with her was always a joy to Scott, she reminded him so much of the kids he looked after and he delighted in her childlike mannerisms. By contrast, for older brother Bob any contact with his sister was like pulling teeth without an anaesthetic and he barely lasted more than five minutes before remembering something he just *had* to do.

Then he booted up his PC and searched on the Internet for the *New York Times* piece, reading it through carefully before printing the full page. He stared at the photofit of the man who had changed his life for ever. It was a grainy image even on the PC screen and didn't print much clearer but it suggested a narrow-faced, tall and youngish-looking male. Late twenties or early thirties was the offered age bracket.

The eyes were indistinct and hooded by over emphasis on eyebrows. The lips were thin and tightly closed, the ears set well back and covered by long hair that was drawn into a ponytail at the back. Scott fixed on the likeness for almost ten minutes, unblinking despite the tiredness and depression he felt sweep through his body. Who are you?

He rang Mark Higgins just before eleven.

They met the next afternoon, at two o'clock exactly, in the car park of a big Catholic church opposite St Vincent's Hospital three miles to the south of Dublin city centre. Scott walked the twenty-minute journey from his nearby apartment complex, aware all the time that he was being shadowed by an unmarked police car. The skies were clear, with unseasonably bright sunshine and a hint of spring in the air. The weathermen hoped temperatures might reach fifteen but warned of a cold front threatening from the north. Used to the vagaries of the Irish climate, Scott wore denims and roll-neck sweater but carried an overcoat. He strode purposefully past the Sandymount red-brick mansions in sneakers that gave each step an easy lift. Along the main Rock Road facing south he was oblivious of the long lines of traffic, the building works at the hospital or the post-lunchtime stragglers drifting out of the Merrion Inn, a popular pub restaurant in the area. Mobile phones were pressed to ears, cheerios called as companions broke up and reluctantly headed back to work.

He was wiping perspiration mist from his glasses when he spotted Mark Higgins's car swerve into the almost deserted lot, a dark-blue Saab 95 with tinted windows. He'd been inside its leather-upholstered interior only once before, the day his brother-in-law drove him back to Dublin after Laura's funeral. As he reached for the passenger door handle, Scott couldn't but think of how much his and Higgins's lives had changed inside ten days.

'I've got about an hour,' Higgins greeted him sourly, eyes fixed straight ahead. 'What do you want?'

'And nice to see you too,' Scott came back sarcastically.

'Fuck you, Nolan. I don't like you, never did. Never knew what Laura saw in you, but she'd made her choice and I had to live with it.' He turned in his seat and glared at Scott. 'And look where it got her.'

Scott took deep breaths to control his temper. 'Are we going to waste an hour spitting insults at one another?'

'It's up to you, doc. I've got quite a selection I'd like to offload.' Higgins slipped his jacket off, he was wearing a navy blazer over beige slacks. He undid the top button on his shirt and loosened his tie, then opened his side window to halfway. Car horns and pneumatic drills filtered in from across the road.

Scott felt for the door handle. This is a mistake; I should never have arranged this meeting. There's too much anger here, too many layers of bitterness and grief. Then he relaxed his grip. If I walk out now I'll never get what I came for. 'How much do you really know about me?' He tried to lock the attention of his tormentor but Higgins focused straight ahead.

'Not much and I'm not that interested. Laura told me just the basics, family, job, career prospects. She offered more but I didn't have time for a full CV.'

Scott waited a minute before speaking again. 'Do you always keep this tough-man attitude? I mean if you're paying for a pack of cigarettes do you go out of your way to glare at the tobacconist? Do you eat your food or chew it to pulp? Do you sleep with your eyes open or can you even bear to let them shut?'

Higgins turned slowly in his seat and looked at Scott, his eyes darting angrily as he sized up his brother-in-law. He rested one hand on the dash and leaned the side of his face on to an open palm. 'What are you rambling on about? I've been looking for any excuse to lift your head off at the shoulders and here you are presenting me with the ideal opportunity. Are you on a suicide mission?' He gestured with a thumb out of the window. 'Your bodyguards wouldn't have time to save your skin I'd be so quick.'

Scott's shadowy protectors had pulled up to within twenty feet of the Saab and he could see one of the duo talking on his cellphone, probably checking registration and ownership. He glanced at his watch. 'I've been sitting here five minutes and we haven't said a civil word to one another. You promised me an hour and I'm going to take that full sixty minutes to talk this out. Now you can be as bullish and full of anger as you wish, I don't blame you. But it's getting us both nowhere and I don't want to waste this opportunity.'

Higgins flicked open the top of a pack of Silk Cut and lit a cigarette. He ran his fingers through his hair and eased himself into a more comfortable position. He glanced over at Scott, took a deep drag and admired the glowing tip, then flicked the first ash burnings out of the window. 'What's on your mind?'

Scott pushed his glasses up on his nose. 'I want to find the man who killed Laura.'

Higgins almost burned himself on the tip of his cigarette with surprise. 'You want to find him? The whole country wants to find this bastard. What makes you so special?'

'How can everyone be so sure he's not going to return to finish off the job?'

Higgins's upper lip curled into an ill-disguised sneer. 'Playing detective again? Being a doctor too boring, not enough excitement in your life?'

Scott ignored the taunt, determined to press ahead. 'Just answer the question,' he said, 'why do *you* think he won't try again?'

'Because it would be too dangerous.' Higgins was looking out of the side window at worshippers exiting the church. There was a small gathering of elderly citizens gossiping among themselves, edging towards a minibus. 'Harry Power is surrounded by armed bodyguards, so is his family. They can't scratch their arses without feeling cold steel. This guy was good but not kamikaze, he'll not risk his neck trying to finish off a job unless there's a massive pay-off. And there's no money good enough to land you in a funeral home.'

Outside, the minibus had filled up and the prayer group was being driven off slowly in the direction of the city. The wooden doors of the church were dragged shut and soon the car park was quiet again.

'So, you're scared.' Higgins lit another Silk Cut. 'Why not cut your losses and go back to the States? It's not as if you have any ties here now.'

Scott stiffened in anger and had to hold his breath rather than risk another furious outburst. 'You just don't get it, do you? Your brain won't allow possibilities other than what you want to believe. You are so narrow-minded; can't you get it into your head I actually loved your sister?' Scott's voice was spilling with emotion. 'Laura was the most precious thing in my life, I would have followed her to the ends of the earth rather than be without her.' Higgins dragged on his cigarette and listened impassively. He kept his gaze fixed on the middle distance ahead, not a flicker of an eye betraying his thoughts. 'We were as one, Mark' – Scott struggled to control himself – 'in as close a relationship as I've ever experienced. We were planning our future. We'd saved enough to put a deposit on a town house close to her work and she was window-shopping for furniture and colour schemes. We'd even talked about starting a family next year. And now I've lost everything. I've lost my wife and my future with the only woman I've ever fallen in love with. Now I can never have children with that beautiful free spirit. For me, life has lost all meaning.' He stopped, exhausted by his outpouring of anguish. Higgins shifted uncomfortably in his seat and finally turned to look at his brother-in-law. Before he could speak, Scott spat out his final say. 'I want to find the bastard who killed Laura.'

'Nice speech. That would go down well with the local Rotary Club but it cuts no ice with me.' Higgins jabbed at Scott with his index finger. 'So you listen to me for a change.' Outside there was a sudden blaring of car horns and screeching of brakes, then angry voices. Higgins ignored the distraction and leaned towards his passenger so they were no more than a foot apart. For the first time ever Scott was staring into Higgins's eyes at close quarters and he felt distinctly uneasy. He was wary of what he sensed behind the dark pupils. 'You only knew Laura for a few years, I've known her since she was a baby. I worshipped that girl; she was my kid sister, my best friend and my confidante. We shared everything, kept nothing from one another. I knew about her first boyfriend, her first serious date and her first break-up. And she advised me on everything from girls to food to clothes to career choice. We were limpet close and it broke my heart when she went to the States to work. Then it got worse, she rings and tells me she's found someone special and wants to marry him. I must admit I was actually jealous. I resented someone – anyone, I suppose, but especially a male – coming between her and me. If I'm really honest I would have preferred she'd stayed single all her life so I had her companionship and attention when I wanted. So my dislike for you isn't that personal, it just happened to be you she fell for.' He stopped, then snorted in disgust. 'Christ knows why, but then she was far from home and probably lonely.' He turned away and Scott immediately felt a charge of relief, free from the intensity of the other man's fiery stare. Higgins started tapping his fingers on the steering column, his head bowed. 'So your loss counts for nothing compared with what I'm going through.' Scott could have sworn he heard a sob catch in the other man's throat, but then Higgins was off again, as angry as ever. 'And having you sitting in my car, knowing you can walk and talk and eat and breathe. Boy, that sticks in my craw.' He punched the steering wheel viciously. 'Why couldn't you have driven your own fucking car that day?'

The venom in the voice was like a slap across the face and Scott slumped in his seat, crushed and demoralised. We're going nowhere here. This man's distress is as painful as my own, neither of us can think straight. He looked at his watch, noting it was now ten minutes past three. Outside, dusk was falling and street lights were glowing. Car headlights lit up the main road and the traffic roar grumbled steadily, like a machine grinding on constant mode. Yellow JCBs, with their bright amber hazard lights, moved around the building works in the hospital grounds across the road while pedestrians dodged in and out of the lines of cars, hurrying to catch the blue-and-white buses that ploughed their routes each way. There were more people exiting the Merrion Inn than going in, the usual lull before the post-work scramble. Only the big church with its magnificent stained-glass windows and large car park did little business. Modern Ireland, thought Scott bitterly. They've sold their souls to BMW and Mercedes Benz. He broke the strained silence. 'The City Hospital has told me to find another job, preferably in another country.'

Higgins looked across, confusion all over his face. 'What the hell are you talking about? I thought you were their biggest catch in years.'

So Scott told of his discussion with Harold Winters that morning, of his own reaction and anger. For once Higgins listened without looking indifferent. 'The bastard,' was his only comment at the end. He clicked his cellphone into action and spoke briefly with someone, advising of a delay. Then he turned to Scott. 'So that's it, I suppose. You'll head back to Detroit, or wherever the hell you came from, and pick up the pieces again.'

'No.' Scott cut this line of thinking short. 'I'm going nowhere. Whoever killed Laura has destroyed my life and I want to get even.' He dared look into Higgins's questioning gaze. 'Like I said at the beginning, I want to find this man and I won't stop until I do.'

Higgins inspected Scott as if he had two heads. His brow furrowed, his eyebrows almost folded over his eyes. 'How?' he asked finally.

Five minutes later Higgins burst open his driver's side door and practically leapt out of the car. 'That is the stupidest fucking idea I have ever heard in my fucking life.' He was shouting so loudly that passers-by turned to look. Scott sat in the passenger seat, heart sinking. This was not the reaction he wanted. Higgins leaned his head inside the door frame, face contorted with contempt. 'You have lost the plot completely. I knew you were upset but I didn't think you were funny-farm material. Doc, if I were you I'd take Mr Winters's advice to get the hell out of this country. You are a health hazard big time.' The rage in his voice carried to Scott's bodyguards and one was out of the car in a flash, handgun drawn. Scott climbed out of the Saab wearily and waved to the man that he was OK. No sooner had he closed the door than Higgins was back inside, gunning the engine alive and scorching off as if fleeing the fires of hell. Scott dragged his overcoat over his shoulder and shuffled towards the unmarked police car. He ran a hand through his dishevelled hair and grimaced at his minders, his embarrassment obvious. 'Could you give me a lift home?'

They drove back in silence and stopped outside the apartment, for once free from floral tributes. Then one of the detectives, a tall, thin man with a thick, bushy moustache, leaned towards the back seat. In the late afternoon gloom Scott couldn't make out his facial features clearly. 'Be careful of Higgins, he has a certain reputation in the force.' The soft brogue held a hint of menace. 'Suspects in his care have jumped out of windows and died from their injuries. One drug dealer was found in the river after a chase and nobody knows whether he jumped or was pushed. I don't know what you two were talking about back there that annoyed him so much, but if I were you I wouldn't bring it up again. He's a vicious, mean bastard.' The detective got out and opened the back door for Scott. 'And that's *on* the record,' he added firmly.

9

On 24 February Sean Kennedy touched down at Bangkok International Airport after a long and difficult flight. Over the previous two days Arctic conditions had swept across the south of England, dumping six inches of snow on London and adjoining counties. The affected areas were brought to a standstill, with towns and villages cut off by drifts and unstable banks of white powder. There was traffic chaos as long trailer transport lorries jackknifed on motorways, effectively closing all lanes. Trains were cancelled, buses stayed in their garages and the only safe transport was by foot. Kennedy, and dozens like him, simmered in a motel close to Heathrow, waiting for airline clearance and cursing the quality of daytime television. Using a false passport and fictitious Dublin address, Kennedy chose London as it offered direct access to the Far East and was the most logical outward departure point for Irish travellers. However, the three major airports around the capital were diverting incoming flights to Manchester and Birmingham, even as far north as

Glasgow. All outbound movement was cancelled. By the twenty-third Heathrow was open to about fifty per cent capacity, in and out, and by the twenty-fourth Kennedy was at last able to confirm he had a seat on a Thai Airways 747, non-stop to Bangkok.

However, the plane was two hours late taking off, further souring tempers all round. And the flight was full, with no spare seats in economy class, adding little to improve the assassin's foul mood. His weak leg was aching in the bitter northern European winter, more so than he could ever remember before, and it didn't let up throughout the trip, especially as he had few opportunities to stretch. He spent ten hours wedged beside a family of four with the two children below five years old and the kids screamed and fought and whined almost the whole time. Kennedy gritted his teeth and tried to endure the misery by drinking neat brandies and watching every frame of the in-flight movies. 'Always go steerage,' Jay Davis had advised a long time before, when their partnership was becoming solid. 'First class and business attract attention. People fuss and wonder how you can afford to travel that way. They remember faces and names. In economy nobody gives a fuck, you could be dying and they'd still ignore you.'

As the 747 finally jolted to a halt and the whine from its giant engines cut to a hum, Kennedy unbuckled his seat belt and stood up to find his briefcase in the overhead locker, wondering what class Jay Davis was travelling en route to Miami. I'll bet that bastard sipped champagne and had his feet up at the front the whole flight. He looked around, noting the litter-strewn aisles and worn-out faces in the economy rows. No bloody way am I coming back steerage. If we're going to make a fortune I'm spending some of it now.

The sudden heat of a Bangkok evening beaded sweat at his shaven hairline as he edged his way uncomfortably down the aircraft steps to a waiting bus. Shouldn't have drunk so much brandy, he reproached himself as he grabbed at a side rail for support. And my mouth's parched. The local temperature was twenty-eight degrees, with humidity in the eighties and he momentarily basked in the warmth, noticing the ache in his leg was easing. As he shuffled along the tarmac he held up both hands to protect his ears from the high-pitched turbo drone of a passing Quantas jet. The smell of Avgas swamped the air and halogen lights glared down as he and his exhausted fellow passengers were driven to the relative calm and cool of the arrivals building. WELCOME TO BANGKOK INTERNATIONAL AIRPORT was written in Thai and English and a number of other languages, with separate menacing warnings about the punishment for drug trafficking, including the death penalty. He glanced behind him, noticing a British Airways jet rumbling along a strip after a jeep with amber light flashing. The concourse was a buzz of activity, with policemen in blue serge uniforms inspecting every incomer, while beautiful young women in traditional Thai costumes and hairstyles handed out fresh orchids. Towards each passenger they placed both palms together near the forehead and offered a courteous *wai*. Nothing's changed, thought Kennedy as he gripped his briefcase tightly and slipped into line at passport control. Eventually a small, sallow-skinned official with tight crew cut politely inspected his documents. He noted the visas and stamps of arrival/departure that suggested he was dealing with a Mr Ronald O'Leary, born Dublin, nationality Irish. Mr O'Leary was obviously a regular traveller with a US immigration entry via Miami, then South Africa via Johannesburg,

Malta via Valetta, one for Barbados and finally Vietnam via Saigon. 'Have you been to this country before, Mr O'Leary?'

Kennedy almost missed his false name and there was a moment's pause before he forced a smile and said, 'No, this is my first visit.' The maroon passport was handed back and Kennedy slipped it into side pocket. He picked up his brief-case to move through the control barrier.

'But you have been to the East, yes?' The official was staring at him intently and Kennedy was again caught off guard.

He looked around, as if someone behind were going to answer, then found his tongue. 'Yeah, eh, I was in Vietnam about a year ago.' The words tumbled uncertainly, as if he'd forgotten about that particular trip.

'Next please.' Before Kennedy could get his head round the unexpected questioning he was dismissed and the official turned his attention to a young couple holding a sobbing tod-dler. They both looked shattered and at their wits' end, and Kennedy used the distraction to grab his bag and move away. What the fuck was he on about? He could feel his heart race and had to wipe his brow as more sweat gathered.

At the carousel, waiting for his one in-hold suitcase, he tried to calm his fears. That was probably a throw-away line and meant nothing. He took out his forged passport and studied the pages carefully, checking he'd memorised every entry. It was a 'to order' document, crafted by a Lithuanian Jew master forger living in Paris at the top of a tall, narrow-fronted building a few minutes' walk from boulevard de Montparnasse. Jackob Helst was a small, wizened man of indeterminate age, with darting blue eyes and gnarled fin-gers that still managed to move with the grace of a concert pianist. He wore a pince-nez and smoked cheroots, always speaking out of the corner of his mouth. Nicotine stained his lips and face, making his features even more aged. His accent was mid-European and hard to understand, especially as he coughed and chewed as much as he spoke. Helst charged big money to create IDs, driving licences, passports and other travel documents, and had been introduced to Kennedy by Jay Davis. And it was the master forger who suggested the various visas and arrival/departure stamps for authenticity. Kennedy had ordered six different aliases using six different hairstyles for separate passports, driving licences and ID cards. 'This guy is one of the tops in the business,' Davis explained later as they chatted on the outside terrace of a café at Place de l'Etoile. 'He has a close group of middlemen who supply him with stolen passports, credit cards and the like. From these he can create a whole new identity, and back it up with business cards and notepaper to match. For another thousand US dollars he'll throw in your choice of credit card.' That had been eight months previously; around the time he and Davis first began teasing out their master plan.

Paris, that June, was showing the first signs of summer, with temperatures in the mid twenties and sidewalk cafés busy with patrons sipping coffee and eyeing the passers-by. Young girls flaunted themselves in skimpy cottons and silks, and car windows were down with wolf whistles and lewd shouts the order of the day. Jay Davis loved Paris and was dressed appropriately for the high-fashion city in a loose linen suit, dark-blue shirt open at the neck, highly polished brogues. With his Marbella tan he stood out among the pale-faced natives. Sean Kennedy had stayed the winter in Amsterdam and didn't much like the sun. He was in denims, white T-shirt and sneakers, and almost looked like he might be Davis's oldest son. 'I heard of him when I lifted an ex-IRA terrorist turned drug dealer called Tommy Boyle. Three of us pulled Boyle's house apart and under the floorboards in the attic I found a selection of passports, driving licences, IDs, even a frigging laminated photo and pass for the Bank of Ireland so he could walk around like he owned the place. They were all high-class items, impossible to distinguish from the real thing unless you took them away and had them checked. Certainly good enough for border crossings and casual police stops.' Kennedy listened closely, for these occasional moments when Davis talked freely gave him an insight into the man he was dealing with and his familiarity with the criminal underworld. 'So I carefully put the floorboards back, told the other two in the search team I'd found nothing and left Tommy sitting open-mouthed, not believing his luck. But I returned an hour later, all the time keeping an eye on the house. Sure enough there he was, working away with hammer and flat chisel, lifting board after board. He had up to ten thousand pounds in sterling and another ten grand in US dollars. Plus six bags of coke and all those travel documents. Tommy, I said, tell me who makes your forgeries and I'll ignore everything else. So that's how I heard about Helst.'

Kennedy thought about this for a while, then asked the obvious: 'So how did Helst take to you arriving at his front door wanting to do business?'

Davis smiled and eased himself back in his chair, glancing around to make sure no one could overhear. 'He was fucking livid and refused to deal with me until he knew who'd spilled his name and whereabouts.'

'Did you tell him?' Kennedy was engrossed in the story by now.

'Of course,' Davis crowed, 'I needed Helst more than I needed Boyle. And now that Helst knew who had grassed on him, Tommy was unlikely to do business with him again.'

'So what happened?'

Davis leaned across the table, almost into Kennedy's face. 'A week later Tommy Boyle's head was delivered to Helst, packed in ice in an overnight freight from Dublin. Next day I rang and placed my order, and the paperwork and passports were ready within a month. And Helst didn't charge me, saying I'd done him a big favour. Considering his fee is five thousand US dollars for a single passport I reckon I came out of that deal very well.'

Kennedy sat back in his seat and studied Davis. The ex-policeman was grinning from ear to ear, his white teeth flashing against his deep-tanned features. 'Who did the cutting?'

'Not me,' Davis assured him, hands raised in self-defence. 'I never get involved in the dirty stuff. When Helst named his price I put it about in certain circles that Tommy Boyle was a grass, a highly paid police informer. And I made sure I knew exactly who got this information. My only problem was finding Tommy's head, for this gang's favourite punishment was leaving headless torsos outside police stations. Anyway, the head came my way and the body ended up floating in a canal.'

That image of a headless torso drifting in the still waters of a Dublin canal flashed through Sean Kennedy's mind as he studied his passport again. It looked perfect, and had already passed scrutiny at a number of checkpoints in London, Dublin and Amsterdam. And even though he knew a master forger had created it, Kennedy was still uneasy, the first official's unexpected questioning unnerving him. He looked around at the tired and frustrated crowd waiting for their baggage. Some sat on the floor, slumped and dishevelled, others jostled to be closest to the front of the carousel and claim their cases as soon as they emerged. He scanned the faces closely, noting most looked European with a scattering of Asian and African faces. And most were in groups of two plus. At a rough estimate he was one of about twenty male Caucasian solo passengers. Did that put him under immediate suspicion? Sex tourist, maybe? He'd read somewhere that Thai police were under government orders to crack down on the international sex trade, especially single white males with possible paedophile tendencies. The carousel jumped into life and Kennedy stood back and waited for the unseemly scramble to commence. Thirty minutes later he was wheeling his single bag towards customs.

'Sir, please stop, sir,' a voice called from behind a long desk. Kennedy was halfway through the small search unit and sure he was in the clear when he was summoned to a sudden halt.

'Step this way, please.'

Kennedy stood motionless for a moment, trying to control his racing heart and sudden sensation of dread. 'Yes?' he finally managed to croak.

A Thai customs official in short-sleeved brown fatigues was staring straight at him. The man was about five eight in height and paunchy, with a moon face and thick-lens glasses. He had chubby hands, which he clasped together over his belly. 'Please place your bags on the table and show me your travel and immigration documents.' The English was perfect but with a local tone. Sean Kennedy lifted his suitcase up on to the counter and slowly began unfastening the straps. 'Stop.' The sudden command jolted the Irishman and he looked up, puzzled. The customs official signalled to a younger man standing to attention behind and began issuing instructions in Thai. 'Stand back, please.' Kennedy stepped to one side, noticing the stares of his fellow passengers as they trooped past him unchallenged. The younger officer produced a set of small keys, selected one and tried it on the suitcase. The lock didn't turn and the man began sifting through the rest of the bunch.

Kennedy rummaged through the pockets of his lightweight fleece. 'I have the keys here if you like.'

A podgy hand was thrust forward signalling no intervention and Kennedy watched impatiently until the locks finally gave and his case was sprung open. Again the younger officer was given instructions in Thai and immediately began laying all the clothes and shoes on the table. Each one was inspected carefully, and then felt along the sleeve and collar. Kennedy glanced around with a forced bored and irritated expression. 'Passport please.' Now the briefcase was snapped open and the senior official very slowly and deliberately took out each piece of paper and document, and laid them on the counter side by side. By now all Kennedy's clothes, underwear and soft shoes were spread out, as if for sale. As he looked on he noticed the sides of his suitcase being checked, then turned over and inspected underneath. Finally the empty bag was taken to some scales jammed into a corner and weighed. Seemingly satisfied with the result, the younger officer threw the bag back on to the counter. Sweat began dripping down Kennedy's face and he dabbed at it quickly rather than show how frightened he was. The pain in his leg was forgotten, the long and arduous journey a distant memory. Right then Kennedy was feeling the worst sense of panic he'd ever experienced as he watched the moon-faced official flick through his passport. Jackob Helst, I hope you've done a good job or I'm totally fucked. His business cards were being inspected.

'You are from Ireland, Mr O'Leary?'

'Yes. Dublin, I live in Dublin.' Kennedy was surprised how calm his voice sounded considering his insides were churning.

'And what do you work at?' The question sounded innocent enough but Kennedy sensed there was more than a casual interest in his offered profession.

'I'm in the furniture business. I export teak products from Thailand and Malaysia and Vietnam. The quality is good and the costs very competitive.'

Moon-face was reading from a business card. 'You have offices at this address? Number sixteen Mountjoy Lane, Dublin four district?'

'Yes, that's where all orders come from.' Kennedy knew there was an office in his company name at sixteen Mountjoy Lane in the Dublin four area. He and Jay Davis used it and a number of other answering services throughout the city. It was no more than a large, high-ceilinged room with a desk and swivel chair, manned by a secretary surrounded by a bank of phones, fax machines and computers. Her job was to answer with whatever business the phone, fax or e-mail communicated was rented in. She took messages and passed them on, nothing else. For painting her nails and waxing her legs and occasionally doing some work, this facility paid handsomely.

'But I have a warehouse five miles outside Dublin where we store incoming goods and check for transit damage.' He was pleased how easily the lies flowed.

Moon-face listened impassively, then passed one of the business cards to his assistant who inspected it, shrugged his shoulders and handed it back. The card was placed inside the briefcase again, exactly where it had been found.

'And who is your contact here in Thailand?'

Kennedy smiled awkwardly and reached inside a hip pocket, producing another business card. 'I'm sorry but I can't pronounce the name correctly. I think it's Preecha Thipthong.' He looked up for approval and two heads nodded. 'He has an office in Sukhumvit near the Samithiwej Hospital, that's the nearest landmark he offered.' The Thai pronunciations were just as faltering as might be expected from a *farang* and Kennedy showed the card to the customs official who gave it no more than a casual glance before handing it back.

'And is this your first trip to Thailand, Mr' – the passport was opened again and the pages flicked to the ID – 'O'Leary?'

'Yes,' lied Kennedy.

'How long do you plan to stay?'

'About a week. I was planning a few days of business in Bangkok, then maybe a break in Phuket.'

'And will you be travelling alone?'

Kennedy sensed this was a loaded question and couldn't make up his mind what way to answer. 'Yes.' He decided this was safer than creating any fictitious partner.

Moon-face started putting all the paperwork and documents back in the briefcase. He nodded and his assistant began shoving clothes and shoes into the open suitcase. 'I hope you have a pleasant trip, Mr O'Leary.' Kennedy's heart skipped a beat. Is that it, just a routine security check? Jesus Christ, I was sure he was on to me. He silently kissed the Lithuanian Jew who'd created his passport and driving licence and business cards and headed stationery. The locks were snapped on his cases and he reached to drag them off the bench. There was a lift to his step as he turned towards the arrivals terminal. Through a half-partition he could see people milling about, some with name plaques held up waiting to collect arriving passengers. There was a babble of noise and loudspeaker announcements, the usual clamour of airport terminals. 'Let me out of here,' he whispered under his breath.

'Dublin seems to be a dangerous city, Mr O'Leary.' Moon-face had shifted along the bench and was now level with Kennedy again. The Thai official had one hand thrust into a side pocket, the other clutching a walkie-talkie. Kennedy stopped, a puzzled expression flooding his face yet again. 'There was an attempt on the life of one of your government ministers recently.' For split second Kennedy almost lost control but he managed to keep his face impassive, his concern suddenly heightened at this new line of questioning. Where's this leading? Moon-face was inspecting Kennedy from head to toe. 'Every major airport has an alert for anyone fitting the description of the man behind the assassination attempt.'

Now Kennedy felt his insides were dropping and fresh beads of sweat trickled down the back of his neck. 'Yeah, I guess so,' was as much as he could offer. The customs officer was paying close attention to Kennedy's left leg. 'And the suspect carries a limp, just like you, Mr O'Leary.'

Kennedy's brain went into overdrive, the implications of the comment so grave he knew he had to defuse the line of questioning or be detained. 'Well,' he began boldly, 'I actually don't have a limp, I have cramp after that flight from London. I spent ten hours in economy class without as much as an inch to stretch my legs. When we landed I was worried I had a clot in my leg as my ankles were swollen.' He deliberately inspected his watch. 'It's around mid afternoon in Dublin now. If you contact my office they'll confirm I was away on business the day that dreadful attack took place.' He forced an air of disgust into the reply, shook his left leg for effect and summoned up every ounce of strength as he walked towards the customs exit. He didn't drag his weak leg once, even though the effort exhausted him.

He struggled through the crowds without looking behind, though the temptation to check whether he was being followed was almost too much to resist. A young woman in tracksuit and knapsack knocked against him heavily, making him jump. He was edgy, uptight and frightened; emotions he hadn't experienced for years. Outside the terminal he waited in line while the airport control desk flagged a cab, handing him an ID number to tally with the driver. He climbed into the back seat, absolutely drained. 'Grand Hyatt Erawan,' he half shouted to the driver, 'four nine four Thanon Ratchadamri.' The cabbie pulled out from the rank and drove for about a hundred yards, then suddenly stopped. Kennedy's already heightened senses went back into overdrive and he quickly looked around to see what was going on.

The driver was a skinny man with pock-marked skin and rotting teeth. He held out what seemed like a deck of cards tied together with string so they could be dropped concertina-like. 'You like one of these?' Kennedy couldn't believe what was going on, he'd just come through the most nervous and potentially dangerous grilling he'd ever experienced at any border crossing and now his cab driver was showing him a deck of cards. As he squinted closer he realised this was no ordinary deck, each card showed an image of sexual activity ranging from the most orthodox to the plain disgusting. 'You like a girl? Two girls for price of one? One hundred US dollars now and I bring them to your room. Good clean girls, no disease.'

Kennedy leaned across the seat and faced the driver, his eyes burning like red-hot coals. He was about to unleash a string of obscenities but bit his tongue and waved the images away. 'No, no. Just the hotel.' He sprawled into his seat, by now drenched in perspiration.

They took the elevated expressway, the driver cutting in front of and past Mercedeses and BMWs and Japanese four-by-fours and other taxis carrying *farangs*. At the second slip road past the brothels of the Nana district the taxi was eased into the chaos of the downtown traffic, the cabbie blasting the horn and waving angrily to anyone who blocked his way. The city lights glowed brightly and the streets were crowded with night revellers. Bangkok was alive and buzzing, but Kennedy wasn't up to exploring its delicacies. Within half an hour of checking into his hotel he lay soaking in a deep and long marble bathtub, smoking the first of the Cuban cigars he'd bought on the flight. Am I under surveillance? But he was too tired to care and eventually slumped into bed and fell asleep.

Kennedy stood at a bank of house phones in the lobby of the Grand Hyatt and dialled from a number he'd scribbled on a scrap of paper. The ringing tone continued for about two minutes, then someone at the other end answered with a greeting in Thai the Irishman didn't understand. 'Toby Wurschanda.' Kennedy said the name in what he considered clear and distinct local dialect. 'Can you pass a message to Toby Wurschanda?'

There was an immediate silence. Finally: 'Who is speaking?'

'Sean Kennedy is here and wants to meet as arranged.'

Despite his best attempt this message obviously confused the listener. 'What name again, please?'

Kennedy quickly glanced around the opulent surroundings of the five-star hotel. The atrium was cool, with rich marble flooring and occasional lounge chairs, and he spotted a group of business types relaxing with coffee and newspapers, brief-cases at their feet and mobile phones pressed to their ears. Two elderly female cleaners in dark fatigues were shining brasses and brushing at non-existent cobwebs while at reception a polite queue of Japanese males, all glasses and suits, waited for check-out, talking only among themselves. In a distant corner a teenage girl with long plaited hair prayed at a Buddha shrine, lighting an incense stick for luck. No one in the foyer was showing the slightest interest in the tall, shaven-headed, pale-faced man dressed in knee-length denim shorts and white short-sleeved cotton shirt. 'Sean Kennedy,' he said again, turning in towards the wall with chin on chest to shield his voice. This time he spoke even slower and with clearer diction. 'From Ireland. Do you understand me?'

There was a sharp intake of breath over the line. 'Ah, *Kennedy*. We have been expecting you. I will call Wurschanda.'

Kennedy heaved a sigh of relief. For a worrying moment he'd thought his rendezvous might collapse. 'Good,' he said, 'I will see him where we arranged.'

The mouthpiece at the other end was cupped for a few seconds and Kennedy could just about make out a babble of shouts in Thai. 'You will meet Mr Wurschanda, yes?' Kennedy held his patience. The conversation was going fine, if a little slowly, but he recognised this might be a deliberate ploy, his contact probably checking details with someone else. Toby Wurschanda didn't see just anyone, and especially not *farangs* calling on a landline number known to very few.

Wrap-around shades in place and carrying only a waist-grip security bag, Kennedy left the hotel, ignoring the swarm of taxi cab drivers loitering around the forecourt, and headed on to the main road, walking past the Peninsula Plaza and Regent Bangkok Hotels. His weak leg had stiffened during the night and he hoped that some exercise might loosen up the tight muscles. The traffic was chaotic, with cars and small vans vying for space with tuk-tuks, funky motorised rickshaws whose drivers cut across lanes with klaxons on full blast. Tourist buses and container lorries barged their way through the congestion, and the smell of diesel hung in the air. Light smog barely filtered the intense sunlight and Kennedy shaded his eyes against the glare as he darted across the thoroughfare. It was hot – in the hotel lobby he'd noticed the outside temperature was thirty degrees, with humidity at eighty per cent and after five minutes' walking he found himself perspiring heavily. And the pollution was getting to his breathing, making him feel unduly breathless. He checked the time, twelve thirty, and decided to speed things up and flagged a taxi, relieved to feel the comfort of air-conditioning again. They drove along Thanon Ratchadamri past the Royal Bangkok Sport Club, then swung right on to the even busier and more congested Thanon Rama IV, horns blaring and motorcyclists scything through traffic gaps. The streets teemed with people and Kennedy, who had lived in Bangkok for two years in his early twenties, sensed a new-found wealth and self-confidence in the passers-by since he'd left. Held up in an angry line of vehicles, he inspected a group of young women wearing Westernised clothes, gossiping and laughing outside the lobby of yet another skyscraper. The traditional Thai costumes he remembered seemed much less usual than before. The city has definitely changed, he decided as he counted three recent high-rise developments, all glass and steel glinting in the early afternoon sun. Then, like a tooth missing in a perfect row, there was a pile of rubble with a half-hearted attempt at hoarding from the street. The building boom of the late nineties that went bust had left great shells of half-finished structures, now mostly inhabited by squatters and down-and-outs.

About a mile before the river he asked the cabbie to pull over and stepped out into a blast of humid heat. He stood for about five minutes attempting to orientate himself, identifying old landmarks and trying to reconcile them with the latest sights. He studied his downtown tourist map closely, stepping on to the roadside at one point to avoid being knocked over in the street rush. Finally he decided to swing left and walked along sidetracks, ignoring the hucksters and hawkers, and keeping his head high so as not to make eye contact. From experience he knew it was easier to avoid conversation than get into an angry exchange with touts. In the shaded alleyways and narrow lanes coffee bars and fruit juice stalls were doing a roaring trade while in small open-fronted eating houses lunchtime diners squatted over steaming bowls of rice and grilled meats on a stick. The smells of spice and smoked fish filled the air as Kennedy pushed through the crowds, both hands firmly gripping his money belt. He skipped past stalls selling rip-off designer handbags, T-shirts, jeans and swimwear. Here the stretch was run by deaf mutes communicating in sign language, offering silent bargains in illegal CDs, DVDs, videos and tapes. Kennedy soon realised he was the only *farang* venturing so far off the main tourist trails and put an extra pace to his steps.

At Soi Chulalongkorn number five he found the exact Bangkok Bank branch he wanted to do business with. Inside its cool interior a Mr Ikont Chuwan, as identified by his name tag, greeted the sweating Irishman. Mr Chuwan was a small, middle-aged Thai in beige short-sleeved shirt over perfectly creased navy slacks. He offered a courteous *wai* and showed his new customer to a small cubicle where he inspected his passport, IDs and business cards. Then, with a broad smile and another bow, he produced a number of banking forms and asked Kennedy to fill them in, sign and wait for a few minutes. 'I will check whether your money transfer has arrived.' The efficient Mr Chuwan slipped out of the cubicle, stopped one of his female staff and whispered something to her. Within minutes a tray with bottled water, glass with sterile seal and small silver ice bucket arrived. A beautiful young Thai woman bowed and backed away, leaving Sean Kennedy, the world's most sought-after assassin, alone with his thoughts. This, he decided as he poured Perrier water over three thick ice cubes, is the life for me. The thought of the deal he and Jay Davis were working on pumped fresh adrenalin into his jet-lagged body. We'll be set up for life. Jesus, what I won't do with some of that money when it rolls in. An image of himself and Candy frolicking naked in bed and throwing hundred dollar bills in the air momentarily aroused him and he had to readjust his clothing and focus on the day ahead. He stretched out both legs, suddenly realising his weak limb was no longer aching and this gave him an extra boost. Jay could be right; maybe I should head for a warmer climate.

He watched idly as two male customers entered the bank, one holding back while the other spoke with a teller at the main counter. Kennedy spotted the bulge of a handgun in the minder's waist belt, poorly disguised by a thin cotton jacket, and for a horrible moment thought he was involved in a robbery but was relieved when the first man left with a leather bag chained to his right wrist, closely followed by his armed shadow. The doors of the bank rarely stayed closed as a steady stream of customers conducted their business and made their way back to the hot and buzzing streets outside. Silently he congratulated Jay Davis. Good choice, Jay, busy bank in a busy neighbourhood. Everyone anxious to please and get the customers in and out quickly. No time to linger and wonder about total strangers, local or from overseas.

Mr Chuwan was back in the cubicle again, his smile even broader. 'There was a Western Union money transfer to you for twenty thousand US dollars three days ago, Mr O'Leary.'

'I'd like to draw down five thousand dollars in local currency, please.'

Mr Chuwan stood slightly to one side. 'After you, Mr O'Leary. If you present yourself at checker number four and show her your passport I will make the arrangements.'

Ten minutes later the Irishman was out in the teeming streets, his money pouch bulging with thousands of baht. Even though perspiration dripped down his face and neck, his sweating hands never left his waistband until he was inside the first cab he could flag down. The driver scorched to a halt, almost causing a pile-up, then calmly waited until his fare was settled into the rear seat. Horns blared and fists waved but the cabbie was oblivious to the frenzy and then pulled out as if he had a clear road ahead, causing two tuk-tuks to career wildly out of the way. More fists were shaken, more Thai expletives filled the polluted air and Kennedy kept his head down, silently wondering how the city didn't grind to a halt with such anarchy on the highways.

Outside the Oriental Hotel, on the bank of the great River Chao Praya, he peeled off three twenty-baht notes and passed them to his driver, politely declining his offer of a cheap tour of the city's fleshspots. He made his way through the Oriental's magnificent lobby, past a collection of some of the city's beautiful people being interviewed by a local TV crew, and found a table on the terrace with spectacular river views. Jet lag was beginning to catch up and he tried to calculate what time his body thought it was but gave up and ordered coffee and Yum, a spicy salad with noodles and squid. It was now one forty-five and Kennedy eased himself into his chair and enjoyed the view. In front of him the swirling waters of the snaking Chao Praya were as hectic as the streets he'd just left. Tubby ferries chugged in looped arcs, wallowing uneasily between the boats moving up and downstream. Longtails, with their bright vivid colours and narrow prows, overtook express boats and tourist cruisers, leaving a foam of dirty water in their wakes. The thud of heavy steamers was drowned by the cacophony of rocket-like engines and Kennedy looked on with wonder, fascinated by a river life that was as much part of Bangkok as saffron-robed monks and Buddhist temples.

He was still eating when he felt a gentle tap on his right shoulder and looked up to see a narrow-faced man staring down at him. 'Mr Kennedy?' Kennedy wiped his lips with a napkin and turned slightly to get a better look at the contact. He was thin, with deep-set brown eyes and jet-black hair in an untidy mess. Dark eyebrows and broad nose, a cigarette dangling from the corner of his small mouth. He was in a short-sleeved shirt, which showed off tattoos on both arms, one looked to be a dragon, the other a long coiling snake. 'I am Preecha Thipthong. You contacted my office in Sukhumvit this morning.' Kennedy made to stand but Thipthong dragged a chair from the next table and sat down. The cigarette never left the corner of his mouth, the smoke drifting into his eyes and making him blink repeatedly. 'Have you finished eating?'

Kennedy's plate was still half full and his hunger was far from satisfied, yet he knew his meal was over. 'Yes.' He fiddled in his money bag and left three hundred baht under his coffee cup on the table.

Preecha Thipthong was already on his feet and Kennedy hurried after him through the hotel, quickly aware he couldn't keep up. But Thipthong paused at a shop in the lobby and inspected a rack of expensive sunglasses. There was an interchange of views in Thai and finally a pair of Ray-Bans was exchanged for a wad of crumpled local currency. Then Thipthong bit off the price tag with one savage swipe across his side teeth and slipped them on. 'The sun is very strong today' was the only explanation for the sudden diversion, though Kennedy immediately interpreted it as a sign to some unseen minder. Contact has been made with the Irish *farang*. Now they were off again, out through the main entrance and striding quickly towards a pier where a selection of craft waited to be hired.

Thipthong choose a longboat, bright red with yellow stripes and blue fins painted on the front, and haggled with the owner, an angry-looking youth in a dirty loose cotton vest and football shorts with Nike motif. Kennedy watched on as the two bartered, amazed that his contact never once lost his cigarette despite the animated conversation. Finally, after an ill-tempered waving of hands and scowling, the youth beckoned Kennedy on to the boat and he and Thipthong sat one behind the other unsteadily in the middle while their driver gunned the engine alive and edged the boat out into the river.

It was not a sightseeing trip. The longtail zipped and bounced along the dirty waters, cutting past tugboats and pleasure cruisers full of tourists with their cameras and videos trying to capture the flying water taxi. Spray misted Kennedy's face and eventually dampened Thipthong's cigarette. He spat it out overboard and immediately lit up another, cupping his hands against the breeze. Not one word was spoken as the craft passed the magnificent temple of the Wat Muangkhae, its shaven-headed monks at prayer close to the river bank. They swept underneath the Phra Pok-Klao Bridge, narrowly avoiding an express boat caught up in the foaming wake of a passenger ferry. There was another angry exchange from driver to driver but Thipthong paid no attention and continued to stare impassively ahead. Five minutes later he leaned forward and shouted something in Thai, and the sullen-faced youth snarled a reply. The longboat was edged across the great river and guided to a side canal. Now the engine revs slowed as the water traffic became more congested and the longboat dodged and weaved past local craft.

Kennedy felt the smells had changed along this stretch. On the great river a cooling breeze and the speed of the boat had cleared his head and freshened his jaded senses. Here, along the narrower canal, he could almost taste the food as spiced rice dishes were being prepared at the front of stilt dwellings fringing the waterway. People stared at the passing traffic, often from behind clothes hanging out to dry on makeshift lines. Some children on wooden ladders were washing themselves and rinsing the suds in the dark waters. There was a slight thud against the side of the longboat and Kennedy looked behind to see the bloated corpse of a dead dog being dragged by the current. Suddenly Thipthong was half standing, one hand on the driver's shoulder, speaking quietly in Thai. The youth cut the engine and let the longboat drift for about fifty yards, then gave a fresh boost, carrying the trio another short distance. Thipthong was pointing agitatedly at one particular house on stilts and the longboat finally bumped against its thick wooden poles. The youth reached across and grabbed a steel handgrip; steadying his boat and allowing him finally to inspect his pale-faced passenger.

'Here,' barked Thipthong, lighting yet another Marlboro Red and facing Kennedy. 'You get out here and wait inside. Stay one hour only.' He pointed at his watch to emphasise the point and Kennedy checked the time. It was coming up to three o'clock. 'If no one comes after one hour then you leave.' Thipthong motioned to the driver and he began turning the longboat round for the return journey.

Kennedy grabbed Thipthong's shoulder. 'How?' He pulled his sunglasses on to his forehead to make sure Thipthong could see him clearly. 'How do I get back if no one shows up?'

The driver muttered something and Thipthong suddenly burst out laughing, almost losing his Marlboro. He turned towards Kennedy, grinning like a hyena with poor dental hygiene. 'Swim.'

On the opposite side of the narrow canal, standing well back inside a stilted house so he could not be seen, Toby Wurschanda looked on as Sean Kennedy reached the top of the ladder. Wurschanda lifted a pair of binoculars and inspected the Irishman close up, a slight smile flickering as he watched him squint hesitantly into the darkness of the dwelling he'd been dumped at. Wurschanda was six foot two, broad-chested, with tattoos running down both arms. His eyes were Oriental, deep-brown pupils set against dark eyebrows and lashes, but there was a Caucasian softening of both orbits. He was in linen trousers and navy silk shirt open at the top, and wore canvas shoes. His dark hair was swept tightly into a long braid at the back where it touched his neck. The braid was held together in a gold clasp. Two smaller men stood beside him, both with revolvers tucked into their waistbands. The three stood in silence, watching every movement on the other side, until Kennedy disappeared into the gloom. Then Wurschanda spoke quickly in Thai and one of his henchmen grunted and disappeared out of the back of the wooden dwelling.

Sean Kennedy was perplexed. Inside the open-fronted stilt house was a thin-framed, hollow-cheeked elderly man lying flat out at the rear fast asleep. He was wearing a dirty, sweat-stained white long cotton robe and rested on the bare boards of the floor, with his head propped up on a folded yellow shirt. The man was bald, rather than shaven-headed, and open-mouthed, his breathing so light that for a moment Kennedy wondered whether he was alive. But apart from this unexpected companion the wooden shack was bare, with no furniture or lighting or cooking equipment. The Irishman was on his own, somewhere in Bangkok with the guts of five thousand US dollars in local currency strapped to his waist and by any standards he knew this was risky. He edged himself into a dark corner and sat down gently, careful not to disturb the sleeper. Outside he could hear the engines of longtails and express boats, the shouts and babble of nearby conversation, the smell of cooking. The heat began to stifle him and sweat dripped down his shirt, staining the cotton and making it stick to his skin. He rocked his legs from side to side for exercise, all the time listening for any unexplained noise. He'd sensed a rustling along the ladder and heard childlike giggles, but they'd stopped. He stared into the distance, wondering was this one of Toby Wurschanda's elaborate schemes to protect his whereabouts, or had he been abandoned? Then an impish face with deep-brown eyes squinted at him from the front and he shooed the child away, hearing a loud laugh, then a splash and the threshing of water as the kid swam to safety. And still his sleeping companion continued his rest, oblivious to every shout or engine roar along the waterway.

By three forty Kennedy was becoming uneasy. For the Irishman this was a nightmare scenario. He was out on a limb with no back-up and no clear idea how he'd deal with any hostile attack. He never felt comfortable without some form of protection, preferably a handgun with full magazine. And from his years in Bangkok he knew how *farangs* were considered soft targets by the criminal underclass, even by opportunist touts. One ill thought-out move and he could be following the dead dog down the Chao Praya river, yet another statistic in the city's many DOAs. He stood up slowly, peering at the old man who still seemed to be fast asleep. In the gloom Kennedy saw the outline of a door at the very back and tiptoed towards it. As he got closer he noticed the old man's left leg was turned in such a way that it effectively blocked the door from being opened. Kennedy considered the situation, wondering how best to get out without disturbing him. He decided to drag the door slowly, gently easing the sleeper's leg until he had enough room to squeeze past. He was just leaning across when he felt something cold brush against his ankle, startling him so much he jumped back.

The old man was now wide awake and holding a handgun, pointed straight at him. 'Sit and wait.'

Kennedy held up both hands and backed away. 'OK, OK,' he said softly, 'I'll sit and wait.'

The old man rolled on to his side and rested his head on an open palm, all the time keeping the pistol trained on Kennedy. 'Mr Wurschanda will send for you when Mr Wurschanda is ready.' Then he pulled out a fat spliff from underneath the yellow shirt, lit up and immediately the air filled with the tang of *ganja*. The old man smiled at Kennedy and the Irishman forced a smile in return. But he was sweating as he hadn't sweated for many years.

At four fifteen Kennedy heard feet on wood close by, moving with an urgency he hadn't sensed before. The old man's glazed eyes blinked slowly and he drew his legs upwards and away from the exit. The footsteps were now at the rear entrance and the wooden frame shook as the door burst open and a wiry youth with a shock of black hair pointed towards Kennedy. 'Quickly' – he waved agitatedly – 'follow me.'

Forty minutes later Kennedy was on the pillion seat of a 200cc Suzuki being driven at dangerously high speeds along the seedy alleys and backstreets of the Patpong area of Bangkok, its infamous sex strip. He held his knees in tight as the driver cut through narrow tracks, missing walls and parked cars by inches. They flashed by gaudy signs offering 'lady massage' and overdressed touts outside brothel doors trying to drum up business. Kennedy shut his eyes and prayed for a speedy end to the nightmare ride, his nerves by now stretched to breaking point. Then, with a screech of tyres and the smell of burning rubber, the driver scorched to a halt outside a bar called Club 19/21 on Silom Soi number four. 'Inside, go inside,' he shouted before speeding off. Kennedy's inner thighs ached; his shirt was soaked with sweat and his heart pounded with a mixture of fear and apprehension. Where the hell am I? He rested his back against a wall and took deep breaths to calm his anxiety and control his shaking hands.

'Handsome man, you like massage? I want to go with yooo,' a tart in shorts and tight see-through blouse crooned from a first-floor balcony. The street was alive with white men and brown girls, *farangs* with bulging bellies clinging to young women no bigger than their legs. Americans leered while Germans shouted *ja, ja* excitedly as they sensed their luck was in. There were East Europeans and Russians; the men had come to buy and the women to sell. The Soi oozed sex, the trade in your face and uncontrolled.

Then the smell of a Marlboro Red flared his nostrils and he looked round to see Preecha Thipthong standing at the club entrance. 'You didn't have to swim, no?' He laughed, another cigarette dangling from the corner of his mouth. If I ever get the opportunity, thought Kennedy as he forced a grin, I'll rip your fucking throat out.

Club 19/21 promised its clients that no girl was younger then nineteen or older than twenty-one and inside a group of about twenty gossiped and preened themselves from tiered benches behind a two-way mirror in a room about thirty foot square. On each chest was stuck a number, an identity disc so to speak. The girls were dressed provocatively, some in schoolgirl uniforms, others in nurses' outfits, and a few in tight black leather that showed off their extravagant assets. Their lips were deep red with lipstick and slits along skirts exposed enough flesh to tantalise even the most jaded sex drive. A circular cocktail bar to one side allowed prospective customers to sit on a stool and sip an overpriced drink while they decided which girl to choose. Decision made, the number was passed to the *mamasan*, the middle-aged madam of the house dressed in a green-and-gold neck-to-toe sarong. She sat close by on a deep red velvet couch, cooling herself with a small battery fan and keeping an eye on her girls and their clients. Kennedy followed Preecha Thipthong past the bar where a couple of teenagers with Australian accents were trying to make up their minds on the delicacy of the day. Beside them a more serious-minded middle-aged and balding American jiggled his legs in anticipation as he scribbled down his choice for the afternoon. Kennedy smirked at the teenagers, remembering how many hours he'd spent in similar massage parlours during his Bangkok days. But the older man he had doubts about. Back in Amsterdam, Candy told him this type were usually frustrated perverts looking for the type of action many girls hated. But in Club 19/21, if the money was good anything and everything was up for grabs. And there were panic buttons and telephones in case things got out of hand. Kennedy knew that somewhere upstairs, beside the narrow massage cubicles, a handful of heavyweights were on standby for difficult clients.

In a large air-conditioned room at the very top of the four-storey house, Toby Wurschanda sat behind a wide steel-and-wood desk. There was minimal furnishing, a high-backed swivel chair on one side and four office chairs on the other side of the desk, plus a grey couch in one corner with a small coffee table beside it. Wire-strengthened windows on two sides allowed in plenty of natural light, with security bars on the outside. On one wall hung a framed portrait of the king and in a corner a small shrine, its Buddha standing with one palm up, the other pointing to the earth, a position known as '*restraining the waters*'. But the first thing Kennedy noticed as the door closed behind him was its deep thud. Soundproof, he decided immediately. Is this an interrogation or dealing room? He quickly scanned the decor, noting no obvious chips or stains suggesting someone's blood or brains had splashed the walls and flooring.

'Good to see you again, Sean.' Toby Wurschanda pushed

himself from side to side in the swivel chair, his deep-brown eyes fixed on the Irishman. He was still in linen trousers and navy shirt, his dress code a stark contrast to the Irishman's denim shorts and sweat- and grime-stained short-sleeved shirt. The motorbike excursion had left his head and face wet and flecked with dirt.

Kennedy inspected the dealer he'd travelled so many miles to meet. 'You've put on a bit of weight, Toby.' He squinted closer. 'And more tattoos. I didn't think you had any clear skin left.' It was eight years since he'd last seen Wurschanda, when Kennedy was barely twenty-one and Wurschanda touching thirty. They'd met at the seaside playground of Phuket, where Western and Eastern tourists gathered to drink and frolic, and usually screw themselves to exhaustion. Kennedy was working as a barman and bouncer at a seafront club, Wurschanda supplying the local demand for heroin, cannabis and amphetamines. After a particularly ugly argument with a group of American backpackers, Wurschanda hired Kennedy to shadow him and sort out troublemakers. He soon found the Irishman had a natural aptitude for the job; indeed, the drug dealer often had to cool Kennedy's aggression, especially after he kicked one young Japanese student into a coma. Both men had to flee the resort and lie low in Bangkok for six months until the local police finally closed the case for lack of information.

Wurschanda stopped swivelling and leaned on the desk, chin resting on tattooed knuckles. 'And you haven't changed. Did I read recently something about a mystery assassin attacking an Irish government Minister in broad daylight? And didn't the mystery man have a limp?' There was a distinct English accent burrowed deep in the Thai's dialect. 'Soon as I saw that bit I said to myself, that's my friend Sean Kennedy.'

Kennedy shrugged, his expression giving nothing away. 'From the descriptions I reckon it could be anybody.'

Wurschanda grinned. 'Not anybody, somebody special, very daring and dangerous. Someone confident with firearms and prepared to take risks. I'm sticking to my own conclusion.'

'No big deal, Toby. This is your territory. If you say it was me I can live with that.'

'And it's such a clever way to sort the opposition, isn't it? Instead of starting a turf war you stir up a hornet's nest and let the police clear the shit off the streets, leaving you in control of the market place?' He didn't wait for Kennedy's response. 'It reminds me of a similar scam you and I pulled off in Phuket before you left. Wonderful idea, wasn't it? Since then I've taken control of nearly all the islands and territory as far north as Chiang Mai. I own a string of massage parlours here and in Phuket where I can launder the drug money that rolls in. And on the payroll are two influential politicians and a dozen police from the Crime Suppression Division. They don't come cheap, two hundred thousand baht every month goes into their pockets. And they use our facilities downstairs free when they like. Which is often and regularly.' Wurschanda had a smug grin on his face. 'If you'd stayed with me you'd be a wealthy man now.'

Kennedy eased himself deeper into his chair, his long legs stretched out fully for comfort. His thighs still ached from the nightmare motorbike ride that had carried him halfway round the inner Bangkok loop. 'I had things to attend to back home,' he said, avoiding Wurschanda's self-satisfied smirk.

There was a snort of disgust from the other man. 'Like carrying on that vendetta against your family. I hope you've got that out of your system by now. That sort of shit only destroys you in the end.'

Kennedy eyeballed Wurschanda. 'Toby, you've settled your own scores over the years. And from what I remember nobody was still standing at the end.'

Wurschanda was the only child of a union between a tall and distinguished English silk trader and a beautiful middle-class Bangkok schoolteacher. Toby was called after his father, Tobias Winston from London, a man who lived a double life hopping between separate families in England and Bangkok. Toby grew up in a decent-sized apartment in the north of the city and had a happy childhood with nanny and home tutor. He was loved by both his father (when he was in the city) and his mother. But when Toby reached twelve, Tobias Winston took off for London again, only this time he never returned. His mother waited six months before making a fruitless trip to England in search of the man she thought was her husband and her husband only. But the Winston family (UK division) had left Britain and moved to Toronto with no forwarding address available to the grief-stricken Thai lady. She returned to Bangkok, sold the apartment even though at the time the property market was weak, and moved herself and Toby to the northern city of Chiang Mai. The surname Winston was dropped and the maiden name Wurschanda became the family title. Toby grew up with his father's physique and mother's Oriental features. But the move to Chiang Mai was not a happy one and Mrs Wurschanda found she could not live in any comfort with her now meagre earnings and dwindling savings. The growing boy needed new clothes, new shoes and had a healthy but voracious appetite. To supplement her income, in desperation Mrs Wurschanda carried heroin and opium from a factory deep in the forest near Chiang Rai, in the Golden Triangle along the Thai–Laos–Burma borders. Twice a week she ferried parcels to a dealer in Bangkok who paid her five per cent of the sale.

One morning the bandit running the factory burst into the small town house near the Thaphae Gate where Toby and his mother lived. He was a small, wiry man with scars on his face and arms barely hidden by tattoos, and he carried a handgum and long-bladed knife. Round his head he wore a bright-orange rag that covered his receding hairline and ears. Toby was eighteen at the time, tall and already powerfully built. He heard the shouting and angry curses from his room and went to investigate. In the small living room where he studied and his mother sewed his ragged clothes, he found the bandit clubbing the woman with both fists and accusing her of skimming off the top and running her own sales and delivery. Five minutes later the attacker lay dead, his neck broken and his face purple from strangulation. Toby Wurschanda the teenager grew up that day, his life changed for ever in five minutes' violent rage.

Now the man faced Sean Kennedy across a table on the top floor of a Bangkok brothel. 'We've both had to adjust, Sean. We might have gone different ways if we'd had better chances. I might have become an accountant with some city bank, maybe even using this whorehouse after work.' He ran his hands through his long hair and checked that his gold clasp was in place. 'What do you think you would have done if things had been different?'

Kennedy came back immediately. 'Things are as they are, Toby, and there's no point in going over the "what ifs". You and I have made the best of the cards we've been dealt. I like what I do and take care of anybody who gets in my way or threatens my lifestyle. Those who know me know better than to try to cross me.'

Wurschanda nodded. 'I remember that clearly. And that's why I had you closely watched today. I had to be sure you were on your own and not being followed. You're a dangerous man, Sean, out on your own. You *like* killing and that always worried me. I just wanted to make money and enjoy myself but you needed that something extra. The smell of blood.'

Kennedy's lower lip twisted, his cynicism obvious. 'This is like being lectured by Attila the Hun. I've seen you pulp faces and slit throats. I was there when you blew up that heroin factory across the border in Burma. You prayed to Buddha for a week before and burnt incense every day. Then you got me to plant the explosives while you lit the fuse. Fifteen killed as far as I remember, some of them as young as ten.' He drew his legs back slightly, feeling a cramp in his damaged thigh. 'This isn't a competition, neither of us is an angel and we're not likely to change. I can't see you shaving your head, wearing saffron robes and becoming an abbot any more than I'm likely to become pope. Let's cut the crap and talk business.'

Wurschanda ran the tips of his fingers along the top of the table, as though he were playing the piano. 'Business it is then, Sean. What can I do for you?'

'I want to buy twenty million US dollars' worth of teak furniture.'

Wurschanda's eyes widened. 'That's a lot of wood.'

'Forget about the wood, what I want to know is what you can pack into it? I need heroin and amphetamines.'

'How do I get paid?' Wurschanda stopped swivelling and his eyes narrowed to suspicious slits.

'Half in ten days, half on delivery. I want ten million in heroin, the rest in amphetamines.'

Wurschanda's features softened. This was business with a

capital B and the figures being bandied were top league. Each knew the profit margin, at least eight million US dollars after costs and pay-offs to middlemen. 'Where do you want the furniture delivered?'

'Rotterdam.' Kennedy did a quick mental calculation. It was nearly the end of February and he knew Jay Davis was anxious to move in on the Irish market as soon as possible, certainly before someone else took advantage of the vacuum they'd created. 'Ideally by the beginning of April.'

For the first time Wurschanda frowned. 'That's tight, Sean. What's the hurry?'

'Like you said, Toby, the market's open. Time to shift the goods.'

There was a pause, both men assessing the situation. Wurschanda spoke next. 'I may move this through Laos and Cambodia, and that will cost. What if the second half of the payment never reaches me?' He was running a finger along pursed lips, his eyebrows arched in misgivings.

Kennedy wiped his face with the corner of the sleeve he could reach. 'And what if I pay you half up front and only get teak furniture in Rotterdam?' Now he faced his one-time friend as if he were a new and dangerous enemy. 'Because, Toby, if you double cross me I'll come after you and you know that. I don't care how many minders you have or how many safe houses you use, I'll track you down and shoot you like a dog.' The business banter was over, now this was hard and venomous bargaining.

'I believe you, Sean. I'm sure you would.' Wurschanda studied the angry and twisted mouth opposite, the darting blue eyes and the hardened features. 'So we'd better not screw up. Whoever blinks first stands to lose a lot more than ten million dollars.'

'You've got it in one.'

Wurschanda was beside Kennedy now, towering over him by a couple of inches. He threw an arm round the Irishman's shoulder and squeezed him affectionately. 'It's good to see you again, Sean. And good to see you haven't changed, always looking for a fight, always trying to settle old scores.'

'Can't afford to let your guard down, Toby. You know that. If anyone sees you weaken they try to take advantage.'

'Forget all that. We've agreed a deal that's bigger than any I've moved for some time. The goods will be with you when you want.' Wurschanda was now in a relaxed and generous mood, all smiles and reassuring body language. 'Let's celeb-rate. There's a good Italian nearby we can eat at without being bothered. Then we come back here, smoke a little *ganja* and get laid. I'll pick my best girls. They don't work the floor, I keep them for special guests like you.'

For the first time since he'd entered the room, Kennedy actually smiled.

It was past midnight, local time, when Sean Kennedy lit up his first joint and settled into a deep soapy bath. He had dined well with Toby Wurschanda, enjoying the best Italian food he'd ever eaten. Then Wurschanda drove back to Club 19/21 and ushered him through a side entrance, 'for VIPs'. On the third floor three young women awaited him in a sound-proofed room with circular bed and ceiling mirror. On one wall a wide screen plasma TV carried images of some porno movie, while to the side a small cabinet held the neces-sities of erotic massage: scented oils, Johnson's baby powder and five bottles of Listerine mouthwash. One of Kennedy's masseurs was an olive-skinned Filipino beauty with dark-brown eyes and provocative flickering eyelashes, the next was Burmese with long legs, long hair and full lips. The third was a local Thai girl with delicate features and even more delicate hands. In a side cubicle the trio washed and soaped the Irishman's body, cooing and whimpering and admiring his muscles and stroking his chest. Then, as he shared the joint round, they dried him and laid him naked on the bed, tying his hands to a railing with silk scarves. He was relaxed, stoned and helpless, and stared at the ceiling mirror as the girls slowly greased his body, then stroked and rubbed with the delicate touch of professionals. As they helped him smoke, he watched while they disrobed and oiled their own bodies, then each in turn rolled over his chest and face and back and buttocks. As the hashish kicked in the images in the ceiling mirror became more blurred, the sensations rippling along his body more exquisite. The girls giggled and crooned and fondled and caressed for over an hour until Sean Kennedy's body finally gave up.

10

While assassin Sean Kennedy slept in drug and post-orgasmic bliss in the heat of Bangkok, back in Dublin four men left their homes in different parts of the city to meet in a basement room at government headquarters. Last to arrive was Scott Nolan who finally shook off his surveillance duo just after seven local time. He'd earlier sneaked away from his Southside apartment through a service door and hailed a taxi to the downtown area. But the detective shadow caught up with him in Grafton Street, one of the city's premier shopping precincts. There he led them on a fast-paced trip around stores and pubs before finally giving them the slip out of a side exit of Brown Thomas, a busy and expensive fashion house. Heart pumping from an adrenalin surge, he mingled with the late night shopping crowds, half stooped to keep his head down, before quickly edging his way along side alleys and back roads towards the rendezvous. It was a bitterly cold evening with temperatures struggling to stay above zero and Scott huddled into his overcoat to keep warm as he zigzagged through traffic congestion on Kildare Street. He entered the five-star Shelbourne Hotel on St Stephens Green from a side street, then ducked and weaved his way through its bars and lobby. The hotel was buzzing, its facilities filled by delegates at a convention of international rugby enthusiasts. Big men with red faces and thick necks clutched foaming pints of lager and huddled in boisterous groups. Peals of laughter echoed off the rafters as jokes and anecdotes flowed as freely as the beer pumps. Bored-looking wives and partners, dressed for better occasions, stood or sat politely, trying to find the same enthusiasm for the conversations. What I wouldn't give to be as carefree and jovial as them, thought Scott bitterly as he pushed his way through the revolving front door and entered the night chill again. Fifteen minutes later he was being led along a maze of corridors and stairwells by a security guard who marched in front until they reached a door in a windowless and dimly lit passageway somewhere in the depths of an administration complex.

The room inside was sparsely furnished with a tight-pile beige carpet, circular desk and six chairs. The overhead fluorescent lighting was harsh and its glare picked up every nook, exaggerating even the smallest decor defects. Tucked into one corner was a glass and wooden-topped cabinet with telephone and fax facility, plus swing light and stacked filing trays. Resting near the edge was a single mug with a collection of pens and pencils, and a small silver-plated tray with water jug and glasses. The jug was empty, the glasses upturned. When Nolan entered he found Justice Minister Harry Power, Police Commissioner Peter Cunningham and Mark Higgins already waiting. They merely glanced towards the door, as if gathered at a wake and collectively too sad to speak. He acknowledged each face with a brief 'hi' and quickly grabbed a chair to the right of Higgins, keeping him to the left of the Commissioner and almost directly opposite Power. He noticed everyone had a copy of his submission and could tell by the well-thumbed edges that the pages had been turned repeatedly. At least they've read it, he thought. After Higgins's initial reaction Scott was approaching this encounter with grave misgivings, worried he was going to suffer a final rebuff. But he was determined to try every angle to get his way, convinced that doing nothing only handed the initiative to the opposition. He needed to persuade at least two of the three men to his point of view.

Police Commissioner Cunningham spoke first. 'Before we go any further, I want it clearly understood this meeting is not actually taking place. What we are about to talk about is dynamite, even if it never gets beyond discussion stage. If the media got the slightest whiff of the contents of this document . . .' – here Scott Nolan's proposal was momentarily waved in the air – 'there would be hell to pay.' Cunningham looked pointedly at Power. 'And if I may say so, Minister, your head and mine would roll. There is no way we could stay in office if this leaks, no matter what the circumstances.'

Power acknowledged Cunningham's comments with a silent wave of a bandaged hand. Higgins grunted a 'yea', while Scott nodded sombrely. Cunningham was dressed in a white crew neck over grey slacks, his hair slightly dishevelled as if he'd been running a hand through it continuously. His gaunt face was highlighted under the fluoro rays, exaggerating its fine lines and wrinkles. Scott studied the Commissioner out of the corner of an eye, feeling the man had aged since they'd last spoken less than nine days previously. His once fine and upright physique now sagged; the strong voice that had admonished Higgins was tired. It was as if Cunningham were half afraid to continue, fearful what might come out from this gathering. 'Can I assume you've read Dr Nolan's plan?' Power and Higgins nodded.

The later was leaning into his seat, a black leather jacket hung over the back. He was in open-neck shirt over denims, hands twitching as if he needed a cigarette badly. Across the table, Power was also in shirtsleeves, his face furrowed in concentration as he watched and listened. The first page of the document lay open in his big hands and a pair of half-moon glasses rested on the end of his crooked nose. But his eyes were fixed firmly on the Police Commissioner.

'Right,' continued Cunningham, 'let me give you my reaction first as I believe I'm actually the last to know of this idea.'

'That was not intentional,' Scott apologised immediately. 'I'm an outsider in this world and wasn't sure whom to approach first.'

Cunningham dismissed the explanation with a wave of a hand. 'It's not important. What is important is our joint response, and here I'm very mindful of all that has happened and what everyone in this room, including me, has suffered recently. None of us has come through these events unscathed, we have all been to hell and back.' Then he flicked at the pages now lying on the table in front of him. 'But I'm not sure we should go back to hell just to feel the heat again. And I'm afraid that's what I believe will happen if we implement this strategy.'

Scott's heart sank. That's it, dead and good as buried. The Commissioner was his only hope after the rebuttal from Higgins and he couldn't stop his disappointment and frustration breaking through. 'We can't give up,' he pleaded, his voice charged with anger. 'I know this is a gamble and a highly controversial one at that. But at least we're doing something.'

'With respect, Commissioner,' Power unexpectedly cut through, 'I'm coming round to Scott's way of thinking on this.' The room went silent and Scott almost thumped his head to make sure he'd heard correctly. 'This *is* high risk, it *is* controversial and it exposes those involved to great danger. I have never heard of such a covert operation, especially one that involves a civilian.'

'Nor have I,' the Commissioner snapped.

Power dismissed the aside with a dart of his eyes. 'I must confess I am re-examining my position.'

Scott's heart was racing. Maybe everything is not lost; maybe there is a possible breakthrough. He tried keeping one eye on the Commissioner as he listened to Power, knowing Cunningham was the most important player in the room. Even if Power and Higgins came round, the head of law enforcement could still kill the idea. Essentially the proposal was a security matter and strictly his territory only. Scott prayed Power's words would make an impression.

'My family is living a nightmare,' Power began. 'Our house is protected by six armed guards, we even have two others who patrol the downstairs level from dusk to dawn. Like Scott, each of us cannot go anywhere without being shadowed and that includes our twin daughters. Again, like Scott, those living near us now look on us as a risk and shun our company. The twins cannot visit their friends, stay overnight or even go to the cinema without an armed escort.' He sighed deeply, a troubled man finally able to unburden his soul. 'Jesus Christ, we're talking ten-year-old girls here, not some high-ranking government minister.' Power adjusted the bandage on his right hand where it was threatening to come undone. 'My wife has lost so much weight from worry she's no more than skin and bones and relies on tranquillisers to steady her nerves.' He paused briefly to ask this disclosure be kept in confidence and there was an immediate murmur of agreement. 'I brought this on our heads with my anger and desire for revenge after my son died from a heroin overdose. But my anti-drug crusade has backfired horribly, so much that my family live a nightmare existence. So we're saying to ourselves, what's there for us here? I'm lucky to be alive but very aware two men lost their lives protecting me. And others could die in the line of duty some time in the future if this bastard decides to strike again. The initiative lies completely in his hands.

'OK, maybe he was a hit man on a one-off mission, but who knows? *Maybe* that was a single attack, a never to be repeated retaliatory offensive in our war against drug cartels. But what if we call it wrong? What if we're dealing with a vicious and determined enemy who decides to finish off the job he botched? Can we wait for him to make up his mind where and when he's going to come back? And in the meantime my life, my family's lives and Scott Nolan's life are on hold. We're on tenterhooks, waiting to be attacked. We're counting down the days to our own funerals and in the meantime alive but not living, if you can understand what I'm trying to say.' Power's voice was clear and unemotional, as if he were reading from a prepared speech. And it was the lack of passion that made his words all the more compelling. At last, thought Scott, someone else is vocalising my own thoughts. Maybe this is the tipping point. With Harry Power behind me my plan has a greater chance of being effected. He glanced at the Police Commissioner, noting the sombre look on the man's face. Then out of the corner of an eye he squinted at Mark Higgins, noting his brother-in-law grip and ungrip clasped fists. He's wound up like a caged lion. What's he thinking?

Peter Cunningham drummed his fingertips on the table, shrugged his shoulders and turned to his Justice Minister. 'Am I to assume from this you feel Dr Nolan's plan could be implemented?'

Scott held his breath. Go for it, Harry, we've nothing to lose.

'Yes.' Power was emphatic. 'Let's go after the bastard.'

Scott had to hold in his sigh of relief, contain his excitement. One down, two to go. He kept his eyes on the table, now not wanting to seem overanxious. He sensed a switch of mood in the room, from resigned rejection to a potentially nervous acceptance.

Mark Higgins adjusted himself in his chair so he was slightly away from Scott Nolan and spoke. 'I'm going to put my own ideas into this melting pot.' Power pushed himself back slightly and rested his chin on bandaged knuckles.

The Police Commissioner ran a hand through his hair, making it stick up. 'You're the covert expert,' he said. 'I think we all should know your thoughts.'

Now Scott's insides did somersaults again. His brother-in-law hated him, had openly declared his desire to take his head off at the shoulders and had also rejected his proposal outright using choice language at the time. Was he going to use his police skills as a final weapon against Scott? What he couldn't do by force because of possible repercussions might now be achieved through spite. He waited for the onslaught.

'This plan proposes an undercover operation using no more than two men, one of them a civilian, and that's dangerous in itself. I've been involved the best part of ten years in covert police work and it is not something you just step into. All the men I've worked with have been serving officers with many years' experience. I've never heard of a rookie policeman going undercover, let alone an untrained civilian.'

You bastard, thought Scott. This is where you put the knife in, then twist it somewhat. He dropped his head into both hands and stared at the table, only half listening to what Higgins was saying. In his peripheral vision he could see Cunnigham's face lighten up. Scott could understand this was the sort of common sense the Commissioner wanted spoken out loud and clear: real cops talking cop language and tactics.

'On the other hand,' – Higgins's argument took an unexpected turn – 'there is logic and courage in the basic concept. I know exactly where Dr Nolan and Mr Power are coming from, their lives are under a constant shadow. Also, what is more unsettling is our lack of intelligence gathering. Nobody seems to know who did pull the final trigger that day and that's almost unheard of in modern police work. We may not always be able to prove who did what, but sure as hell we usually have a firm idea of the main suspect. But not this time and that should concern us all. For my part I've spent every waking hour since my sister's death trying to uncover this mystery man's identity. And I know from colleagues closely involved in the investigation we are nowhere near a breakthrough.'

Now Higgins shifted again so Scott could see him clearly. The mean and angry face he'd had to deal with was softer, more compassionate. He's grieving like an adult now, thought Scott. The hard-man façade has gone and he has a softer side, even if he's probably loath to show it. This is the man Laura worshipped and doted on as a sister, the man she couldn't wait for me to meet. He treated me like dirt from the beginning but at last he's coming up trumps. For a moment Scott Nolan began to like Mark Higgins.

'From all of this,' Higgins continued, 'I can only conclude

we are never going to bring this man to justice by routine police methods. And if that is correct, we are almost obliged to throw away the rule book and sink to his level. To find this scum we must become like scum ourselves. We must go rock bottom and work upwards, as the proposal outlines.' Higgins turned towards Scott and for the first time acknowledged his presence in any meaningful way. 'I'm giving your plan my endorsement, Scott.' Scott opened his mouth to speak but was cut short by a sudden and dramatic change in the other man's demeanour. The softness had vanished, the thug had returned. 'But there is no way you can be involved.'

There was a sudden stunned silence in the room before Scott Nolan erupted. 'You bastard, Higgins, you absolute . . .' He was on his feet, spectacles almost flying off his nose as he reached for his tormentor's throat.

Fortunately the Commissioner must have anticipated such a move and jumped across to intervene. 'Oh, for Christ's sake, grow up you two. If you want to settle your personal grievances do it outside on the streets like the other hooligans.' He had both arms around Scott's upper body, restraining all movement.

A flickering sneer of contempt crossed Higgins's lips. 'See what I mean,' he crowed. 'One insult and he blows his top. How could anyone work with him?'

There was a loud and angry thump on the table as Harry Power stood to his full six feet plus height and glowered across. The irritation and discomfort of the effort on his burns was obvious but the big man didn't flinch. 'This is the most ridiculous outburst I've ever seen from two supposed responsible adults. Pull yourself together, Scott; can't you see Higgins is deliberately trying to bait you? For such an intelligent man you do lack street credibility. I knew Higgins was going to try to take over this proposal once he agreed to back it. And he has every right to make a sound case for not involving you. Now if you're so goddamn hot, tell us why you must be involved.'

Scott shrugged himself free from the bear-like grip of Cunningham and sat down, ignoring Higgins. He pushed his glasses back up on his nose, ran a hand through his untidy mop of hair and drew breath. 'I was expecting to be rebuffed totally, but not stabbed in the back. So you'd all better listen up because this plan either runs with me or doesn't run at all.' His voice was hard as steel and his face taut, the tensions of the confrontation showing.

'Why,' snapped Higgins? 'Make me understand why you're such a pivotal cog in the wheel.'

Scott sat forward in his chair, made an arch with his fingers and stared at the structure. When he spoke it was as if he were addressing himself. 'This strategy depends on brawn and brains. There can only be two involved, one an experienced undercover agent, the other a medically qualified and suitably trained doctor. The policeman must have street knowledge of the drug scene here in Ireland and abroad, and be prepared to take huge personal safety risks. The doctor must be as involved but doesn't need to have such background knowledge. But he too is going to be gambling with his life, perhaps even more so as he's entering totally alien territory. Both men should have a strong vested interest in tracking down and finding this killer, otherwise I foresee a less than enthusiastic approach if the going gets tough. When you think about every detail in the proposal and add in what you know of us all in this room, you can only come to one conclusion. There is only one combination that fits these criteria: myself and Higgins.' There was a snort of disgust to his left but he pressed ahead, determined he would not respond to further taunts. 'The plan either runs with us as a unit or dies a death right here tonight. Take it from me, you're never going to find a medic with skills and training and commitment who'd take on this job. And if you did I'd seriously question his mental health. Now I could work with another police officer, but believe it or not, would prefer not to. Mark Higgins hates my guts, that's plain to see and he has the honesty not even to try to disguise his feelings. He believes his sister should be alive and that I should be dead. And he's right. But that's what makes my role in this so pivotal. I can never be at peace as long as I know that somewhere her killer still walks the streets.'

The room went quiet again. All four men were avoiding looking at one another, each consumed in his own counsel. Finally Police Commissioner Cunningham took a deep and audible breath, then let it out slowly. 'Can I tell you what I think?' Three heads looked across. This was the final say and from the most important man in the room. Whatever had gone before meant little if Cunningham vetoed the idea. 'I waited to hear what the general mood was going to be like before saying yes or no to Dr Nolan's proposal. And now that I know what each of you feels I must say I'm impressed by the honesty and courage shown. The outline as written in the document is carefully thought through, well argued and devoid of emotion. That's important, as we can't let our hearts rule our heads. At the start I expressed the worry that if we ran with this we'd be entering the gates of hell. I still believe that but those words were meant to draw out the discussion, make each one fight his corner, though I didn't think it would actually lead to fisticuffs.' He smirked and the mood immediately lightened.

'So here's my assessment. The idea is dangerous, with definite chances of loss of life. But it's bold and audacious, and takes us into territory this police force has never gone before. Maybe the FBI or MI5 run clandestine operations like this but certainly not the Garda Siochana. We do have special units who monitor subversives and terrorist cells, and who also put their lives on the line; indeed, in this area we may have more experience than many other law enforcement agencies. But still we're heading into uncharted waters with a two-man unit who want to kick each other stupid, which is not exactly the most auspicious start to such a risky plan. But I knew about this ill feeling before we met here this evening, especially after Dr Nolan's and Higgins's recent meeting in a church car park.' Beside him, Scott felt sure his brother-in-law was blushing but he hid his delight, keeping close attention to the Commissioner's words. 'And it didn't exactly encourage me to feel that the two of you could work together. But I have to agree with Dr Nolan on the fundamentals of who's in if we give him the go ahead. No one other than you two has the experience and knowledge and, more important, the hunger to follow this through. And I'm not going looking for any other combination. So if you want me to sanction this request then I do so on the basis that Dr Nolan and Higgins shelve their differences for the common good and go after this man.'

Scott was torn between elation and fear. His plan could go ahead, but would Higgins co-operate? Would hatred override his desire to find Laura's killer?

'What do you say, Mark?' The Commissioner was staring straight at one of his best detectives. 'Could you work with Dr Nolan to track down the assassin who murdered your sister and two of your colleagues?'

Higgins leaned back in his chair, eyes to the roof and one hand fiddling in his pocket. 'Mind if I smoke?' he asked the audience.

'Actually, I do,' Power snapped, 'cut the delaying tactics and tell us straight. If you won't agree to this, spit it out now.'

'OK,' Higgins came back just as aggressively, 'I think better when I'm smoking, it's no big deal.' He sat forward in his chair and opened another button on his shirt. The room was actually quite cold but the intensity of the discussion was making everyone feel hot under the collar. 'My sister meant more to me than any of you will ever know and my anger and bitterness towards Dr Nolan, however difficult for you all to accept, is based on the simple premise that the killer took out the wrong person. Laura should be alive, not Dr Nolan. But we have to move on and live with the realities of what happened on 10 February. That assassin has destroyed so many lives and families he cannot be allowed to escape. If we don't go after him the consequences will have wider repercussions than Mr Power and Dr Nolan losing their lives. Our force is coming under intense scrutiny with other agencies watching how we handle this, paying close attention to our tactics. In truth we are on the world's stage with a very critical audience paying top dollar to see the show. To do nothing is folly, which means we must do something. And the proposal in these pages' – here Scott Nolan's document was pushed into the centre of the table – 'while risky, is the only plan I've seen that could bring results.' Higgins faced his boss. 'Sir, if catching the man who snuffed out my sister's life means working with Dr Nolan then I'll have to live with that.'

'No.' Cunningham shook his head. 'You do not have to

live with it, Higgins. You have to bloody well do it and shut up about how hard done by you feel. This self-pitying shit doesn't impress me one bit. I know you, Higgins, I studied your file before coming here tonight. You're a loner and don't like working with anyone because you often use less than orthodox tactics to get results. In fact, that profile alone makes you an ideal candidate for this assignment. The problem is not whether you can put up with Dr Nolan, rather could he put up with you.'

Scott decided the conversation was drifting into a cul-de-sac of police procedures and prior use of shady tactics. He decided to settle the issue once and for all. 'Commissioner, I've worked with doctors whose personalities and manners would make Mark Higgins seem like an angel. I've slogged through night shifts with drunken surgeons, cocaine-high anaesthetists and spaced-out psychiatrists. And do you know what? I still managed to do my job and save lives. Higgins is no big deal to me; he's just one more very angry man I'll have to work with. But work with him I will, because he's the second linchpin to success. We'll catch the killer together, but not alone. We both have strong vested interests in this operation and I know we'll find our way around one another. So why don't we quit talking and start moving on this?'

Higgins had an unlit cigarette in his mouth, chewing frantically on the tobacco for relief. 'I agree. We could spend all night trying to make this a perfect marriage and it wouldn't work. Let's just call it a temporary little arrangement for special circumstances.'

Power finally seemed able to smile. 'I've heard that phrase used unwisely in political circles so maybe we'll think of some other description.' He looked towards Scott. 'How do we shift this up a gear?'

Scott reached into a side pocket and produced another sheaf of paperwork, which he passed across to Cunningham, who scanned the immediate pages, eyes widening as he grasped the significance of each paragraph. He slipped two sheets to Power who started reading, a flicker of a smile touching his mouth. Finally the Commissioner looked across to Scott. 'Where the hell am I going to get all this stuff? I'm in law enforcement, not hospital supplies.'

Scott grinned, his sense of relief that the ordeal was over with a positive result showing in his body language. His hair stuck up like a cornfield after a tornado and his glasses were wet from perspiration but he was practically beaming by now. 'That I'll explain later, it's the easy bit. Guns and special materials I'll have difficulty obtaining but I'm sure you can organise the hardware. The special items will come from a source who owes me big time.'

Power was almost laughing as he came to the end of the new paperwork. 'More important, Peter' – he was talking to his chief of police – 'is how do you put this through Garda expenditure? Since when do they use anaesthetic trolleys in your department?' Cunningham's groan was the only light-hearted moment of that evening.

In Bangkok, Sean Kennedy turned in his sleep but found his right hand was being restrained. Still half groggy from the earlier drugs and sexual high jinks, the Irishman briefly thought his masseurs had tied him up again for later activities and smiled to himself. Then he realised what was gripping his wrist was hard metal, not soft silk and he tried to drag himself upright in the massive circular bed.

'Did you enjoy yourself with my girls?' Toby Wurschanda stood at the bottom of the bed, a handgun gripped firmly in his right hand, its barrel pointing straight at Kennedy. 'They said it took an hour before you gave up. That's good, for they are real experts and usually get a result sooner. They're impressed. And a lot richer.' There was no banter in Wurschanda's voice, only menace, and Kennedy blinked repeatedly to get his eyes focused. When he finally could take in his surroundings his heart jumped and his mouth dried immediately. Standing on either side of Wurschanda were two uniformed policemen, truncheons hanging from their leather-belted hips, guns in holsters. They stared impassively at the Irishman, expressionless and silent.

'What's with the escort, Toby?'

Wurschanda smiled slightly, but it offered no relief to Kennedy. It was the smile of a man who liked seeing people die and had arrived in time for a public execution. 'These are friends from the Royal Thai Police. I look after their interests and they look after mine.' Wurschanda looked from one officer to the other but neither as much as blinked, continuing to focus on the naked body in the bed, his lower half barely covered by a black silk sheet. 'And they came to me with information. Something you might be interested to hear.'

Kennedy tried to haul himself into a more dignified position but was restrained by the handcuffs. And the silk sheet was slipping. He glanced around and caught sight of himself in the ceiling mirror. Where hours earlier he'd watched with aroused fascination as three naked women took turns on him, now the reflection was of a man manacled and struggling for composure. He wasn't sure whether to try an act of bravado and brazen the situation out, or be meek and compliant. He had no idea what Wurschanda was planning, but with a handgun pointed at his chest he quickly decided this was not a casual conversation.

'Have I committed a crime since my arrival?'

'No, Sean. No crime here, but big stuff in Ireland. The city police assigned these men to a four-unit squad to track you down. They've already taken all your personal belongings and cases from your hotel room and are making long-distance calls. They're running with the idea you could be the assassin who caused chaos in Dublin recently.'

Now Kennedy really began to sweat. It was one thing trying to work out what Wurschanda's motives were, but with two policemen standing over him and law enforcement on alert for his detention, this was trouble big time. 'You know I had nothing to do with that, Toby. I told you so already.' Kennedy forced a smile, as if this were some ridiculous case of mistaken identity. He tried desperately to recall what exactly he had said to Wurschanda but his brain was still fogged with hashish and he couldn't remember. 'I was out of the country at the time and can prove it,' he offered, knowing the excuse sounded as lame as it was false.

Wurschanda moved closer and sat on the side of the bed, gun still trained on Kennedy's chest. His dark hair was now braided to each side of his head and the plaits bounced as he spoke. 'I'm not interested in that, Sean. Really, I'm not. My friends here passed the facts on because you'd been seen in my company and they were worried I might be hauled in with you. That's the sort of background support you need in this business, isn't it?'

Kennedy tried to focus on Wurschanda's eyes but there was still a blur to his vision. He offered a weak 'absolutely'.

The handgun was forced against Kennedy's skin, hard enough to cause pain but the Irishman gritted his teeth and kept control. Something's going to happen now, he decided. And there's fuck all I can do about it.

'You remember Preecha Thipthong, don't you? The man whose head you wanted to take off at the shoulders.' The gun was shifted viciously, dragging huge welts on Kennedy's skin. The pain was sudden and intense but he didn't flinch.

'That was just a comment made in the heat of the moment. You told me he's an excellent furniture maker and we need skilled craftsmen.'

'Fuck off, Kennedy.' The English lilt to Wurschanda's Thai accent came through, but vicious and ugly. 'You'd slit his throat soon as look at him. I know you and I remember how you work. Right now Preecha's getting heavy interrogation at central HQ while the CSD decide if he's involved with you in any way.'

Kennedy's guts immediately knotted. This was getting heavier by the minute. Am I going to sweat it out in some Bangkok hell-hole prison for the rest of my life?

Wurschanda was off again, his voice becoming more and more angry. 'Now that's going to cost me a lot of money. Preecha's a good man and very loyal. Comes from Chiang Mai, where I lived years ago. I know his family and they know me. And they're screaming at me to do something, anything, to get him out of custody before he says something stupid.' Behind him one of the Bangkok officers was whispering something into his colleague's ear and through his fog Kennedy could sense they were also getting nasty.

'So what do I do, Sean? Hand you over, saying these men tracked you to Club 19/21? They'd get big promotions, make the TV channels and maybe even get a decoration. We'd insist Preecha was an unwitting and unsuspecting businessman caught up in your web of international terrorism. Maybe we'd suggest you are an IRA man on the run, trying to buy arms and gather recruits from other terrorist groups. Then even I'd be a hero, I'd get the TV coverage and decorations.'

Kennedy played his only card. He knew Wurschanda was quite capable of doing what he said. It would make him and his police informants national, even international, heroes. It might even offer Toby Wurschanda, well-known brothel keeper and drug dealer, the chance to become respectable in the Thai community. And he knew how important that was culturally in his country. 'Toby, if you turn me in I'll sing like a bird. Whatever you think you'll gain I'll make sure you'll lose with a very loose tongue.' His vision was unclouded now and he could see his opponent's eyes clearly. Here were two tough and dangerous men playing roulette with each other's lives. 'And if you decide to turn me in and something serious happens to me before I talk then, Toby my friend, your life would be as good as over. For every Sean Kennedy who comes knocking on your door for business there are ten others waiting to settle old scores if things go wrong. So why don't you cut the shit talk and buy your friend out of gaol? If the police really are looking for me, get your stooges here to drive me to the airport where I'm sure someone on your payroll at passport control will let me through on the next flight to Amsterdam.' Despite the shackles, Kennedy leaned forward and whispered. 'Don't forget, Toby. In ten days you are due a significant lodgement into your Swiss account. And when Preecha is back at his furniture business another big payment will be on its way. That's a lot to pass up for short-lived local glory. You'll never be a pillar of society, Toby. I know everything about you, we're cut from the same stone. We prefer the shithouses and brothels to cocktails at the ambassador's residence. We choose the thrill of the chase and the lure of money over listening to some socialite's pathetic bleating.'

Toby Wurschanda's face twisted in fury and he swung the pistol hard against Kennedy's face, hitting him on the side of the head as he swerved to avoid it. Then he babbled instructions in Thai to the policemen and they quickly unlocked the handcuffs. Kennedy wiped blood away from his ear where the skin had broken, his eyes never leaving Wurschanda. Now the brothel keeper was pacing the room furiously, smoking and muttering to himself. Finally he marched back and pushed his face against the Irishman's nose. 'Get the fuck out of here. This is our last deal, understand? I'll make sure you get your poison and you make sure I get paid. But you've become too hot to handle. Some day the police are going to find you and I don't want to be around when that happens. I'll read about it in the papers.'

Kennedy massaged the twist burns on his wrist and stood up, letting the silk sheet drop away. He noticed the Bangkok officers studying his genitals. 'Toby, if the police ever catch up with me I guarantee it won't be Sean Kennedy who'll come out in a coffin.'

Wurschanda spun on his heel and stormed out of the door, calling out in English as he disappeared, 'Get him out of here.'

Fourteen hours later Kennedy was on a KLM flight to Amsterdam, travelling business class on a back-up forged passport he carried for emergencies. He was wearing new clothes, linen slacks, shirt and soft leather loafers. And he was drinking champagne, wondering if Wurschanda had sprung his furniture maker yet. Hope not, he considered idly, I hope they make the bastard sweat. He smiled at the pretty hostess assigned to him and asked for the dinner menu, delighted to see a chicken dish as a main course. He scanned the wine list and ordered Premier Cru Chablis, then settled back to enjoy the trip. I hope Candy's not too tired when I get home. I want to tell her about a few new tricks we could do that I learned here.

'Would you like another drink, sir?' the hostess asked, smiling sweetly at her charge.

Kennedy looked up at her, his mind still buzzing with images from the night before. 'No, thank you, I'll wait until dinner is served.'

What a pleasant man, the hostess thought. I wish they were all as easy to deal with as him.

As Kennedy lay back in his recliner he kicked off his new loafers and slipped on a pair of cabin slippers, feeling more comfortable immediately. He glanced around at his fellow passengers, all four of them male and each with that touch of style and flair only money can bring. Silver-grey hair swept back to an inch of perfection, carefully tailored suits, silk shirts and expensive-looking ties. There wasn't even a hint of denim or cotton anywhere. Well, Sean, he thought to himself. How did you get to this stage, travelling business class and negotiating twenty million US dollar deals? And taking on Toby Wurschanda and still surviving. How you've moved on from the night you staggered out of thirty-four Fitzroy Square, bleeding and screaming in pain. He let his thoughts drift back over the years.

That night he'd ended up in St Vincent's Hospital on Dublin's Southside, taken there by ambulance after being discovered in a collapsed state on the street. Surgeons operated and saved his leg but could not repair the severed nerve. 'When you're in better shape we'll go back in and pull that tissue together,' they promised when he'd finally surfaced from the anaesthetic. Like fuck you will, thought the young Kennedy.

I'm getting out of here. He gave a false name and address, something he was to become familiar with for ever after, and calmly limped out of the ward three days later wearing stolen clothes and carrying one of the doctors' wallets. That same afternoon, when he was sure both his father and Anna would be out of the house, he used his emergency key to collect a bagful of personal belongings, passport and ATM card for the few thousand pounds his late mother had secretly passed on to him some months earlier.

For two years he lived in a single bedsit in Fulham, west London, working at anything that came his way. Labourer, barman, bouncer, dishwasher and waiter were some of the jobs he played at, wondering how he was going to make some real money and find a life. In the meantime he learned that word being offered from thirty-four Fitzroy Square was that Sean had taken off round the world on his own, too devastated by his mother's tragic death to stay on in Dublin. What a shame, and such a sensitive boy. Neither Norman Kennedy nor his daughter Anna knew when he'd be back, but they were in constant touch.

The first man he killed was almost by accident. Lingering over a beer in a trendy bar off Sloane Square, a middle-aged man in a sober suit, shirt and tie engaged him in conversation. It turned out the gentleman was a banker and involved in major overseas trading out of an office along Canary Wharf, and Sean soon cottoned on that his new friend was gay and looking for an overnight stand. Almost out of curiosity Kennedy allowed himself to be driven back to an expensive pad in Kensington in an open-topped Mercedes. And inside, while Kennedy admired the extravagant decor and splendour of the large apartment, his partner put on background music, handed Sean a glass of champagne and danced with him, cheek to cheek. And, fool that he was, the poor man then offered to give Sean Kennedy a foam bath and rub-down. Fifteen minutes later he was lying face down in eight inches of water, his Liberty silk tie wrapped tightly round his neck. Kennedy left with the dead man's wallet, a collection of gold and platinum credit cards and an open-topped Mercedes. He switched registration plates from another car and drove in style for a week before deciding it was too risky to continue.

By then he had reached Amsterdam where he spent the next two years as bagman for a city centre drug dealer. But it was small beer, nothing more than corner sales to spaced-out teenagers and tourist deadbeats. The profit margins were low and Kennedy soon became bored beating up debtors younger than himself. At the age of twenty he took off for Thailand and Patong, a beautiful hill-ringed crescent bay ruined by running sewage, spilled rubbish and a population of touts and prostitutes. Kennedy settled into the area immediately and soon involved himself in its nightlife, bars and clubs. He developed a reputation as a tough and vicious trouble-maker, and his name came to the attention of a Toby Wurschanda, then a fledgling trafficker looking to improve his share of spoils in the 'anything goes' strip. And it was under Wurschanda's careful tutelage that Kennedy became an experienced killer, learning to use guns, big and small, taught how to handle explosives and make bombs. By the age of twenty-five Kennedy was a seasoned executioner, as feared as his master but more dangerous. Some time around then the two men became distant, Wurschanda trying to put space between his increasingly lucrative drug dealing and his Irish second in command's lust for gore. But it was a chance encounter on the island with another Irish holidaymaker called Jay Davis that triggered Kennedy's decision to return to Europe. Over countless beers and even more joints, Davis, an ex-detective in the Irish narcotics squad, explained his master plan to take over the chaotic drug scene in Ireland. Three months later Kennedy quit Thailand and headed for Amsterdam from where he and Davis gradually became the most dangerous and reliable traffickers in the business.

Throughout these years the official version from Fitzroy Square suggested Sean was still on his world tour, one year sheep shearing in Australia, then a spell cattle farming in Argentina before moving northwards and a long stint as a beach bum in California. Norman Kennedy even came up with the gem that Sean had progressed in life and was now a building contractor in the Midwest, running his own company. And yes, Sean kept in regular contact and hopefully would come home one day with all that grief out of his system.

One year later Kennedy casually mentioned to Davis a plot he and Toby Wurschanda had schemed to eliminate opposition without getting too close to the action. It involved assassinating a high-ranking Bangkok CSD detective who was in charge of narcotic control along the tourist trails on the Andaman coast. The resulting crackdown cleared out a rash of Australian beatnik and Malaysian small-time dealers, leaving the market open for Wurschanda and his thug henchman. Jay Davis listened to the story open-mouthed, stunned at its simplicity, delighted at its success and convinced it could be repeated. And Ireland's Justice Minister Harry Power, with his personal vendetta against local drug barons, offered the ideal opportunity to run the same plan, this time with Kennedy in control and Davis as back-up. Allowing for a few hiccups, both men considered the plan was running to schedule.

So while Kennedy enjoyed Chicken Kiev with baby carrots and asparagus tips, and savoured his expensive wine, he sensed he was coming to the end of a very long journey.

'Is everything OK for you, sir?' the pretty hostess was at his side again, all pouting lips and concerned face. Kennedy shuffled his backside to a more comfortable position, stretched out his long legs and passed over his food tray. 'Wonderful, thank you.' Then he searched for the in-flight movie guide but couldn't find it. 'What's on view after dinner?'

The hostess frowned. '*Prairie Dogs*. I'm told it's a bit violent; I hope that won't bother you.'

Kennedy thought for a moment, then said, 'I'll close my eyes at the nasty bits.'

11

Scott Nolan's hunt for his wife's killer began on 1 March, two days after the murderer arrived back in Amsterdam. NOLAN QUITS ran a banner headline in one of the Irish tabloids that day. TOP DOC FLEES IRISH HELL suggested another. DRUG BARONS WIN AS HERO LEAVES was a more exaggerated caption while the quality broadsheet *Irish Times* summed up the story a little more accurately: SCOTT NOLAN DECIDES TO PUT IRISH NIGHTMARE BEHIND HIM.

The newspaper carried a single photo on page one showing Scott at the departure terminal of Dublin airport, his lean frame and windswept hairstyle barely identifiable behind a strong presence of six bodyguards. Then on three inside pages, accompanying an in-depth analysis of the US doctor's departure, more shots captured Scott leaving his apartment, again armed detectives obvious in the background, one even carrying his luggage. Further on Scott was shaking hands and saying farewell to Harry Power at government buildings and finally Scott handing over his travel documents at an Aer

Lingus check-in desk. Two extra file clips showed Scott in better days, one during a press conference announcing the anti-drug campaign, then a TV still from one of the promotional slots. The *Irish Times* reporter could not get a direct quote from Scott, though Justice Minister Harry Power went on record openly decrying the state of a nation where such a talented and courageous doctor felt he had to leave rather than live under the shadow of violence. The Police Commissioner added his tuppenceworth with comments about gun law and there was a side bar containing cynical and hypocritical bleatings of regret from a spokesperson at Dublin's City Hospital: 'We're losing not only a very talented physician and compassionate doctor, but also a true friend. Scott Nolan was a popular and highly regarded colleague whose very presence lifted the standards of this old and proud institution. His young patients and everyone at the City Hospital will miss him, and all of us wish him well wherever he settles.' TV crews followed the proceedings and the high-profile departure made all the Irish news channels that evening, the story travelling as far as Sky News, BBC and ITV in Britain.

Chicago was still in the grip of a winter whiteout as Scott touched down at O'Hare Airport after an eight-hour flight. It was midday local time when sixty-seven-year-old Jim Nolan greeted his son at the arrivals terminal; the retired university lecturer huddled into an overcoat against the cold. Unlike the commotion at Dublin airport surrounding his departure, Scott was relieved to see no cameramen or TV crews ready to hound him as he cleared customs. 'Hi, Dad,' he said, immediately catching an intense sadness and sense of loss in his father's eyes. Jim Nolan was six two but quite stooped, with wisps of grey hair at both temples. His face was red raw from the elements and a drip clung defiantly to the end of his nose despite him repeatedly wiping at it with a handkerchief. He was in long coat and earmuffs, with a tartan scarf tucked under his chin.

When he spoke it was with a brogue that hadn't hardened despite all his years in North America. 'How are you, son? Your mother and I have been sick worrying about you. We've had little communication despite calling many, many times.'

Scott dragged on his overcoat and wiped his glasses, as much to adjust to the temperature change as to think. Around him the concourse was busy with a swarm of passengers coming off transatlantic flights and there was much meeting and greeting, shouts of joy and cries of recognition. Under the watchful eyes of airport police, trolleys full of luggage were being pushed with little respect for personal space and no one's ankles were safe. As the sudden cold hit, coats were dragged on and gloves and scarves removed from side pockets or carry bags. The bank of telephones to the left of the main exit was occupied and heads nodded or shook as arrangements were confirmed, hotels booked, onward connections discussed. O'Hare in midwinter, even when surrounded by snow, always kept going and as Scott looked around he began to remember the buzz of the city he'd grown up in and forgotten. But his father's immediate and anxious concern made him feel guilty. So much had happened in such a short time, and so much more was planned that he was momentarily at a loss to know how to handle the questioning. There's going to be an official version here, Dad, he thought, and the truth. And no way are you're going to learn the whole truth. 'I'll tell you when we get home,' he offered by way of diversion and putting off the lies. 'No point repeating myself over and over.'

Jim Nolan gave him a baleful look and shrugged. 'Come on,' he said, 'the car's in the short-term lot. Let me give you a hand with that luggage.'

The city skyline loomed into view within fifty minutes, the freeway running reasonably clear despite banks of hardened snow on either side. The traffic, thought Scott as he stared out of the side window, moves easier than Dublin despite the sharper weather and poor lane sense. And the streets are cleaner. They drove in silence until Nolan senior's Lincoln crossed the Chicago river and entered the downtown area. 'It's good to be home,' Scott finally muttered as he admired skyscrapers soaring into a cloudless sky: Sears Tower, the Prudential Building and the Tribune Tower, some of the major landmarks in a metropolis renowned for its stylish architecture. Dirty slush tracks lined the inner city routes but their fellow travellers moved with reasonable ease, cops with whistles and scowling faces helping out where intersection lights threatened to lose the battle between man and machine. They drove north along the Magnificent Mile, its wide sidewalks bustling with shoppers muffled against the elements but still determined to get that fashion statement or bargain basement special. Breath frosted in the sub-zero temperatures and all movement was slower than usual with patches of ice underfoot. The Lincoln paused at a stop red beside the Hancock Tower, icicles clinging to its black marble and tinted windows façade all the way to the top. After two loops and one diversion because of roadworks, they finally arrived outside their high-rise apartment complex on East Walton overlooking a now deserted Oak Street beach and the still waters of an equally quiet Lake Michigan.

Ellen Nolan was sixty-six but looked younger, and her face beamed as soon as Scott pushed open the front door and gathered his mother in his arms. 'It's good to see you, son.' Ellen stood back to take stock of her second boy, then shook her head in disappointment. 'You've lost weight. I'd say a stone at least and you can ill afford to drop that much.'

Scott was at least able to grin, feeling like a child all over again, his mother forever trying to fatten him up. 'I'm only admitting ten pounds, even though my clothes are hanging off me.'

Ellen took a closer look and tut-tutted, teeth showing as her lips flared. 'It took me years to get ten pounds on you, Scott. Bob I never had trouble with, if anything it was the opposite, he ate like a horse and never did enough exercise. Last time we saw him he was bursting out of his clothes.'

Scott grinned when he heard this. 'And chewing his nails?' he asked mischievously.

'To the quick,' responded Ellen tartly, 'I've never seen such poor manicure, and him meeting daily with New York's top bankers and investment brokers.'

'He works too hard and worries too much,' he offered by way of a sop.

But his mother wasn't having any of this. 'And you don't? Isn't it enough you carry out the work you do without looking over your shoulder for some gunman to start shooting? What sort of a country has Ireland become, Scott? It was never like that when your father and I were growing up. How could anyone kill that beautiful young woman?' At that moment the happy welcome ended and the grieving resurfaced. 'She was such a free spirit,' Ellen continued, her voice choked with emotion, 'I loved her like she was my own.'

Scott took his mother in his arms again, feeling her body shudder as the tears flowed. He smelt her hair and it was just as he remembered years before as a child when she'd set him on her lap to read a book or comfort some hurt. And as the memories flooded his reserve almost crumbled and he had to dig deep to keep his composure. Jim Nolan looked on, helpless and distressed, unsure what he could say or do that might ease the grief he was witnessing. 'She was one of our own,' Scott finally mumbled as he fought for control, 'she was my wife and your daughter-in-law. We've all lost someone very special.' They separated, Ellen going off in search of tissues while Jim Nolan helped Scott off with his coat.

'Where's Mary?' Scott wanted to distract himself and his parents from more anguish. He'd been in so much pain for so long recently that he was desperate not to sink into that mire again. Time with his younger sister usually lifted his spirits.

'She's at remedial school until three,' said Jim, fussing with the buttons on his cardigan, 'and excited as hell you're coming home. Ellen had to drag her out of the door to get there in time.' Scott looked around the apartment, interested to see had there been any changes since his last visit. The single-level unit was large by any standards, with three bedrooms and bathrooms, fifty square feet of living room with picture windows and lake views, a kitchen-cum-dining area and separate laundry. The Nolans had moved into the city from a timber and brick dwelling on a half-acre plot in Highland Park, an exclusive neighbourhood some miles further north. As their children grew up and left, the ageing parents needed compact living quarters, extra amenities and the special schooling for Mary, which was only conveniently available in the downtown area. So while their older son Bob took his career and nail-biting habits to New York and second boy Scott moved along various hospital posts, Jim and Ellen

Nolan focused on caring for their last child. They sold up the family home, with its rose beds and American native trees set in manicured lawns, double garage and snaking driveway, to live in an expensive lake-front complex with concierge and underground parking.

Now the three sat in the lounge, the decor a drag roll of pastel colours, the carpet a dark blue contrasting nicely with soft-peach furnishings. On the walls hung oils and water-colours, all Irish rural and mountain scenes, with one a charcoal-and-ink sketch of Dublin's Trinity College, where both parents had studied medicine in the fifties. On a highly polished antique sideboard sat silver-framed photographs of the family in happier times. There was a group shot of Bob and Scott and Mary, the ages rolling from twenty through twelve down to five. They were squashed together on a dry-stone wall looking into the distance, in the background an Irish finger-pointing black-on-white signpost advising the sea-side town of Dingle was thirty miles away. It was the last time the Nolan family had visited Ireland as a unit; after that Bob said he'd had enough of being forced down memory lane when he could be looking for a job in Wall Street. Two years later he married a stockbroker's daughter with a heavy chest and thick legs. The union lasted eighteen months, Bob deciding he could move up the financial food chain faster with a prettier wife. As Scott inspected the faces in the photo he suddenly realised that the next time he was to leave North America to visit Ireland was with Laura and he quickly switched attention to another silver frame of him at gradu-ation, then one of Bob with his latest wife and finally a recent shot of Mary holding a scroll. 'What's that?' he asked, picking up the picture and studying his younger sister. Mary was like her mother, about five six in height with short auburn hair, elf-like features and impish eyes. In the shot she was wearing a pretty cotton dress, a below knee-length plain blue with flecks of white and on her head was an academic mortar with tassels to one side.

'That's graduation last autumn,' said Ellen. She was standing beside Scott, her head resting on her son's shoulder, and admiring the image. 'We were so proud of her that day, weren't we, Jim?' Over on the couch Jim Nolan smiled, but his expression suggested more loss than gain. Scott kissed his mother on the forehead and took her by the hand back to the sofa, and for a moment the three smiled awkwardly at one another, no one quite sure where to take the conversation.

Finally Jim Nolan spoke: 'What are your plans, Scott? Would you consider working here in Chicago? I spoke to the chief of paediatrics at University Hospital and he'd be delighted to take you on board. His name's Joss Hernandez, a swarthy individual with stocky build, so I suspect he's got Mexican blood in him somewhere.'

Now that's a classic Jim Nolan comment, thought Scott, with his typical Irish-American attitude. It's not what you can do but where you came from that matters. 'And what'd he say,' he asked politely, stifling the urge to correct his father's racist attitudes. He felt he had to go through the motions; he couldn't give them an inkling what his real plans were.

'Hernandez said you had an international reputation and since the hospital wants to increase its profile in liver disease treatments he'd be keen to discuss a research post with you. Might be a good idea, take your mind off things for a while.' Jim Nolan tucked up his trousers at the knees and looked across.

'Thanks for that, Dad. I've heard of Hernandez and Mexican blood or not, he's crash hot.' This was a subtle rebuke to his father and Jim Nolan dropped his head slightly, smiling as he grasped what had been said. 'But I have something else in mind.'

His mother leaned forward in her seat. 'What? Has someone headhunted you already?'

Scott shook his head and shoved his glasses back on his nose. 'No, it's nothing to do with medicine, strictly speaking. A little unfinished business I have to attend to.' The words hung in the air and Scott noticed his parents exchange puzzled glances. He wondered how to take the explanation further, total lies, half-truths or the real facts? If he came out with his plan he felt sure Jim and Ellen would be shocked, and they'd had more than enough upsets recently. Certainly they'd spend hours trying to dissuade him, recognising how dangerous the venture was. But equally if the scheme that was already in motion back in Ireland went belly-up and he was killed or injured, they would be stunned initially, then feel bitterly betrayed by his deceit. He'd rehearsed his explanation throughout the long flight from Dublin, yet as he prepared to open up he knew it was wrong to lie. They were family and now, with Laura dead, his only family. Could he treat them with the disrespect of dishonesty? In the end he decided on a middle course, leaving them with some idea of his plans but not enough to keep them in a constant sense of dread, fearful of the telephone call that might bring bad news. He took a deep breath, looked from face to face and began, 'I'm going back to Ireland to find the man who murdered Laura.'

If he'd said he was renouncing medicine to take up a career in second-hand car dealing he couldn't have got a more bewildered reaction. 'You're going back to Ireland?' Ellen's voice was a mixture of surprise and incredulity.

'You want to find the man who killed Laura?' blurted Jim. 'What the hell do you know about police work, you're a doctor for Chrissake? Have you taken leave of your senses? Maybe you haven't got over the shock of that day yet, Scott. I think you need time out. Why don't you stay here with your mother and me for a few months, just until you get your head clear?'

Ellen came in hard on her husband's heels. 'Your father's right, Scott. You look shaken, you've lost a lot of weight, your clothes don't even fit and your hair's a mess as usual. At least Laura kept an eye on grooming and sent you to work each day dressed like a doctor. But right now, Scott Nolan, you look malnourished and addled. Are you sure you're thinking straight?'

Scott sighed, having half expected this sort of response. He recalled Mark Higgins's and Harry Power's first reactions, and realised he was silly to await anything different from his parents, particularly since they were his flesh and blood. He stood up and walked to the picture window, then half turned so he could keep one eye on the couch. Outside, about quarter of a mile into Lake Michigan a large pleasure cruiser moved slowly through the icy waters like a ghost ship, while five hundred yards or so below on Oak Street beach a bunch of kids were making a snowman, their brightly coloured coats highlighted against the background whiteout. 'There's more to this story than what I've told you or what you've read in the papers,' Scott began. 'Things have been happening behind the scenes in Dublin that I'm involved in and I have to return there to be an active part of the final solution.'

'What sort of things?' Jim Nolan was watching his son closely while Ellen nervously rolled and unrolled a paper handkerchief until it began to flake on to the carpet.

'To be honest, Dad, I can't tell you too much.'

'Scott.' Jim Nolan had his head resting in both hands, staring at the carpet. 'What you're telling us is that this battle is far from over, am I right?'

'Absolutely.'

'And that whatever plans are being hatched back in Dublin involve you?'

'Yes.' Outside, the kids on Oak Street beach disappeared behind a clapboard hut, their snowman kicked and punched to pieces.

'But you don't want us to know too much as it might compromise everything?'

'It would be better if you were only aware of the broad canvas but not the fine strokes.'

Jim Nolan snorted his disgust. 'That's as evasive an answer as I've heard in some time. Even your brother Bob comes up with better lines than that.'

Scott took off his glasses and polished them, thinking furiously. How do I explain this? He was about to launch into his back-up account when the doorbell rang and one minute later he was hugging his younger sister.

'Scotty,' she screamed with delight, 'how are you? Oh, I've missed you so much.' She broke away and began jumping up and down in the hallway. 'Are you going to stay with us now? You can have your old room back, I only use it for leaving my clothes and things but they can all go somewhere else. Come on, Scotty, promise you'll stay.' Mary was in a long coat, Mickey Mouse earmuffs and thick woollen gloves. Her pixie face was blue from the cold and Scott had to brush frost from her eyebrows. While her voice was adult the mannerisms were pathetically childlike.

'Why don't you come into the heat and warm up,' said Scott. 'Mom and Dad are waiting.'

Ellen fussed over her daughter immediately, getting her out of her winter heavies and into a long jumper that stretched to mid thigh over a pair of denims. Then her feet were eased into sheepskin slippers and five minutes later a pot of coffee and some croissants were on the table. For the time being Scott's hesitant discussion with his parents was shelved as Mary told about her day at school and how her teacher had given her such great praise. She showed off a drawing she'd done especially for her brother's homecoming and everyone gathered round to admire it, oohing and aahing at the accuracy of the lines and curves and colours. Mary was glowing with happiness, her face beaming with a smile that almost lit up the whole room. She was home from school, she'd had a good day there and now her favourite brother was back in the family fold. But childlike inquisitiveness soon took over and the hard and penetrating questions began. She curled up beside Scott on a couch facing their parents and he hung an arm over her shoulder, kissing her lightly on the cheek.

'You're my girl,' he whispered and Mary giggled.

But there was less than a minute's comfort before the young woman began firing questions. 'Scotty, do you still miss Laura?' Ellen immediately tried to shush her but Scott waved a hand not to interrupt. He knew how important this reasoning was for Mary, no matter how difficult the grilling might be.

'Yes, I do, Mary. Very much.'

'Were you really in love with her, like you said at the wedding?'

'Yes, I was. Big time.'

'More than me?'

The pixie face was forced into a semi-hurt pose and Scott made a mock effort of searching for an answer. 'Hmm, not more than you. Differently maybe, but not more.'

Mary wet the tip of a finger on her tongue and picked crumbs up from her plate. 'And did you actually see the man who shot her?'

'Not really, it all happened so quickly I wasn't sure what was going on. All I saw was the vague shadow of a man holding a gun pointed at me.'

'The newspapers said he was trying to kill you and not Laura.' Mary turned towards her brother. 'Is that really true?'

There was a deep and exasperated sigh from Ellen Nolan but Scott ignored the attempt to switch direction. 'Yes, unfortunately it is true. It should have been me who was shot that day, not Laura.'

Mary's expression suddenly changed and Scott could sense that in her mind she was trying to understand what she'd just heard. 'But why you, Scotty? You're a doctor. You help people.'

Sitting on the opposite couch, Jim Nolan's eyebrows arched severely. 'Out of the mouths of babes,' he muttered.

Mary rounded on him angrily. 'I'm not a baby, I'm twenty-five and a half and I wish you'd stop treating me like a child.'

Scott cut through to defuse the situation. 'Dad didn't mean you were a baby, Mary. He was just using a phrase that means young people sometimes say things that are very accurate, which older people might be too afraid to say out loud.'

But Mary was still smarting and she pouted at her brother until he made a funny face that changed her mood again. 'How long are you going to stay with us, Scotty? Make it a year, please.'

Scott leaned back in the couch, jet lag grabbing at his body and brain. It was five o'clock in Chicago and early morning in Dublin, so his system was crying out for sleep. 'Right now' – he yawned – 'if I hit the pillow I think I'd sleep for a year.'

Mary turned to her mother. 'Mom, get Scotty a pillow quickly. Then we'll have him here for a long time.'

The innocent comment at least made them laugh, even if the amusement was forced. As so often had happened in the past, Mary's simplicity could penetrate and cut to the bone, then seconds later lift everyone's mood. But as Scott studied his parents he saw nothing but fear and apprehension on their faces. I've brought my problem to their front door. I've unhinged the edgy stability by which they lead their lives. They thought they only had Mary to worry about, that their boys were grown up and independent. But now the favourite son is back in the firing line.

Jim Nolan spoke next, his voice full of suspicion. 'Stan Roth called this morning.'

Scott's fatigue eased immediately and he sat forward on the couch, eyes alert. 'Oh, yeah? And what'd he say?'

'Left a number for you to call back. I have it in my room.'

Scott nodded, his mind elsewhere.

'Isn't he in the army or the CIA or something?' The guarded tone had deepened.

'The army,' said Scott. 'He's involved in research at a facility outside Washington.'

Now Scott's father's whole demeanour changed, the mistrust obvious. 'So how come he said he'd meet you when you're ready? What's so important he couldn't deal with it on the phone? When I asked, he claimed he was heading this way anyhow, but I know that's horsesh—'

A disapproving frown from Ellen stopped Jim Nolan finishing. 'Please don't use that sort of language in front of Mary,' she scolded.

'Horseshit.' Mary giggled. 'Horseshit, horseshit. I know words much worse than that.'

'Well, we sure don't want to hear them, young lady.' Ellen Nolan began clearing away the coffee cups and plates. 'And I hope your father doesn't allow you to say anything naughty when I'm not listening.'

'No, Mom.' But Mary was having difficulty controlling herself and her body shook with mirth.

Jim Nolan scowled at his daughter but she only put out her tongue at him. He returned his attention to Scott. 'So why is this army man flying all the way from Washington in weather like this?'

An old phrase Laura had thrown at him a long time ago suddenly forced itself to the front of his brain and Scott couldn't stop the words spilling. 'If I tell you everything, Dad, I'll have to kill you afterwards.'

It was Mary's reaction that summed up everyone's: 'That's total horseshit.'

Before he crashed into bed for an hour's sleep, Scott made the call to Washington.

'Well, it's the man in the news,' answered a Southern drawl after numerous redirections along a switchboard. 'How are you, Scott?'

'Getting there, Stan. Just getting there.'

'That's what I heard. I'm not going to offer my condolences or spew the usual pity. My sources tell me you're swimming in that stuff and want a break.'

'You've got it in one,' said Scott, his relief obvious. 'All I want is a time and a place for us to put our heads together.'

'My brief allows me discretion on where, when and how, so why don't we meet noon tomorrow in the lobby of the Hyatt Regency?'

'I'll be there.'

'Also,' Stan Roth finished the short conversation, 'for the record, this is off the record, both this call and our meeting. As far as the army is concerned Dr Scott Nolan is a private citizen with no military connections whatsoever.'

12

Scott Nolan finally surfaced at eight thirty the next morning after a night of troubled sleep. He'd woken some time in the early hours, disorientated and confused. Where the hell am I? In total darkness he felt around the bed, gradually realising it wasn't the familiar double he and Laura had shared in Dublin, but the rather less spacious single mattress of his room in the Chicago apartment. Then, for what seemed like hours, he tossed and turned, going over in his mind the offered half-truths and concealment, and his parents' reactions during the conversation the previous afternoon.

Then the doubts set in, as they had so often over the past forty-eight hours. Swaying the Dublin government and police to his side had been a success, but no sooner had he celebrated than uncertainty niggled. Is this a good idea? What in God's name are you thinking of, chasing an unknown and ruthless criminal mastermind who wouldn't think twice before putting a bullet in your brain? This is real life, not some Hollywood-scripted sideshow, and detectives do get hurt in murder investigations, even killed. Are there going to be more bodies littering the streets of Dublin and will you be one of the victims? What about Mark Higgins, your reluctant buddy? What if he gets killed? How could his widow and children ever understand the driving force and personal motivations that carried such a bizarre partnership on a secret and perilous mission? Would they ever forgive if Mark got killed, and you survived and the target was never caught? No, they wouldn't, he concluded as his brain swirled with images of guns and blood and bodies falling. They'd say it was you who should be dead, not Mark.

'*And I lost my sister. It's her should be walking the streets right now, not you. She took those bullets for you.*' Higgins's biting rebuke flashed like a bolt of lightning and the imaginary repercussions followed like an expected clap of thunder. '*It's Mark who should be walking the streets, not you. He took those bullets for you, waging your war, just like his sister. Do you ever fight your own battles, Dr Nolan?*' Mercifully sleep eventually swamped his tortured senses, relieving him of the misery of dreamlike recriminations and blame. '*Let's go after the bastard.*' Harry Power's forceful words carried him into oblivion until he was wakened by hushed voices outside his door.

Minutes later Mary sneaked in and planted a wet kiss on his cheek. 'Hi, Scotty,' she whispered. 'I've gotta go to school. See you when I get home.'

He reached out and grabbed his sister before she could escape and dragged her on to the bed, tickling her until she screamed. 'That'll teach you', he joked, 'to wake me up.' Mary wriggled and giggled until she could break free, then hurried out of the room before her mother could reprimand her for waking the favourite son.

By ten o'clock on the following morning Scott had put aside all the previous night's anxieties and fretting. He was fired up and ready to take on the world, but first there were a few cosmetic changes he wanted to introduce.

Water Tower Place along Chicago's Michigan Avenue was a high-rise mall of offices and shops, a vertical shopping development with an artificial cascade of free-flowing water coursing down its centre in stepped marble waterfalls. It was here on level four that Scott located a one-hour optician. 'I want to change my image,' he announced to a bespectacled young woman behind the counter.

Through his scratched and well-worn lenses Scott could see a pretty blonde, her hair cut and styled to emphasise her facial features. A name tag let customers know they were dealing with Lisa and at that moment Lisa was giving Scott a rather intense head-to-toe assessment. 'I think that's a good idea,' she said firmly, 'and where better to begin than here?' Twenty minutes later and after an updated sight test he selected a pair of Yves St Laurent narrow-lens designer eyepieces with carbon steel frames. Lisa murmured her approval as he added another pair for good measure, agreeing to call back at eleven thirty to collect.

One level higher Scott discovered CUTS, a hair salon with style and attitude. He looked in through the plate-glass window, noting all the clients at the basins or in front of mirrors were female. What the hell, he decided, I don't have that much time and I don't give a damn what people think. He presented himself at reception where a tall, ebony-skinned girl with studs in her nose and lower lip was on the phone discussing her love life while flicking through an appointment book. As the conversation came to a close Scott noticed he was being scrutinised yet again. 'I need a haircut,' he started, 'and I need it now.'

The receptionist stood back from the chest-high counter and dragged at her plaited hair. 'You sound like an alcoholic. Are you sure you're in the right place?' Before Scott could answer the girl frowned, then sucked at the stud on her lower lip. She was studying the tornado-swept wheat field that was his hairstyle. 'No, on second thoughts you are in the right place.' She scanned that day's appointments, muttering to herself and glancing towards the activity at the mirrors. 'You're in luck.'

Thirty minutes on an almost bald Scott Nolan patrolled the aisles of Lord and Taylor men's wear section, running the palm of his right hand along the soft fuzz that covered his pate and checking his reflection in mirrors and tinted windows. How am I going to explain this when I go home? Then he found the exact unit he was looking for and began filling up: three pairs of fleece-lined tracksuit bottoms, all black; fleece-lined crew-neck T-shirts, all black. Two rows along he collected five tracksuit tops with zipper side pockets, again all in black. Finally he badgered a sales assistant until the young man tracked down six woollen ski hats and four pairs of Nike trainers, again in black. As Scott paid, the assistant eyed him suspiciously. 'We do have other colours, sir. That's a lot of black you're taking out.'

Scott watched as his credit card was processed, head down and mentally trying to speed things up. It was eleven forty and time was getting tight. 'It's a nightclub special,' he offered by way of explanation, 'they only let you in if you wear black.' The credit machine clicked and whirred, and finally

Scott's details were verified and the transaction accepted. In an empty cubicle he tore off the sales tags and hurriedly slipped into one set of his new uniform, then grabbed his bulging shopping bag and loped his way out.

Lisa, the optician, was waiting. 'Lord, what did you do to yourself?' she gasped.

'Changed my image,' Scott offered as he waited for his new Yves St Laurent spectacles.

The Hyatt Regency on East Wacker was a giant convention hotel with views over the Chicago river. At twelve fifteen Scott was dropped on to its wide forecourt by a cabbie wearing a turban. The zone was busy with cars and taxis collecting and delivering, and uniformed valets hovering around with trolley-loads of luggage. The biting wind off the river cut short most conversations and few lingered on the tarmac. On a protective awning over the wide front doors icicles had formed in long tapers. Scott pushed through one of the swing doors into a lobby flooded with people and noise. A large flashing sign welcomed delegates from Overeaters Anonymous, Franklin Park High School '96 Class Year Reunion and US National Orthodontists Annual Conference. The only group to stand out in this throng were some of the overeaters, a bunch of grossly obese adults and children who were sitting around the central restaurant keeping the waiters busy. Extra large helpings of food were being carried on trays to their tables and Scott idly wondered how the kitchens would cope with the demand. In the centre of the expanse a new model Toyota was parked on a raised dais, coloured lights dancing off its metallic paintwork. Car buffs walked round it, admiring its sleek lines and whistling at the offered price tag. The atrium was open space and overlooked by a balcony on the first floor, and Scott noticed a group staring down, one he thought taking an especial interest in him. He dismissed the idea as fanciful and stood on tiptoe, scanning the crowd for his contact. Finally he spotted Stan Roth sitting in a corner near the bar, a coffee cup in front of him and the *Chicago Tribune* opened at the sports page.

Roth was around the same age as Scott, in his early thirties, but with a central wide bald patch that he was trying to hide by letting the rest of his hair grow thick. He had a sallow complexion, broad nose and bushy black eyebrows, which bobbed with surprise as Scott sat down opposite. 'I heard you'd taken this badly,' he began by way of greeting, 'but I didn't think it was this extreme. You working for a funeral home?' Scott grinned and pulled off his woollen cap, revealing his new hairstyle. Roth's mouth dropped open. 'Now you've become ridiculous. Like this you wouldn't even get a job in a funeral home.'

'New image,' Scott explained, 'I'm going undercover.'

'You watch too many movies.' Roth folded the *Tribune* in two and set it to one side. 'Secret agents try to blend into their surroundings, not stick out like some roadside pole.' The accent was a New Orleans drawl, hardened by years of working on the east coast. 'But I'm not here to give you advice, just pass the goods.'

Scott flagged a waitress and ordered coffee. When he was confident they were far enough away from anyone who might be able to listen in, he leaned across the table. 'Did you bring them?'

Roth nodded. 'First, let's get the ground rules clear. As we speak, on the first floor balcony, which as you can see overlooks us, there are four army agents watching every move. Don't bother trying to pick them out.' He smiled sardonically at Scott. 'They are undercover and dressed appropriately. Depending on prearranged signals they'll either allow me to hand over a silver-coloured steel-strengthened briefcase or surround this table and take you out to a waiting limo with restraints and tranquilliser darts.'

'You don't trust me, Stan, is that it?'

'You've got it in one.' Roth swirled the dregs in his cup and stared hard at Scott. 'I read the briefing report from the Irish police, then the Washington FBI comments.'

Scott's coffee arrived and both men waited until the waitress had moved on to another customer. 'What'd the feds say?' Scott took a sip and waited.

'Consensus was the scheme is seriously flawed, controversial and dangerous. The field chief said he'd never authorise such an operation because of the risks involved.'

'We know all that,' Scott countered, 'it's not as if Dublin didn't consider every angle before sanctioning.'

'I'm only the messenger, Scott. You asked what the feds thought and I'm telling you.' From somewhere nearby came shouts of recognition and both looked towards the far end of the lobby where a group of men in suits had emerged from elevators and obviously discovered one another. Hands were being pumped, shoulders slapped. 'I think the dentists have arrived,' said Roth and he made a deliberate biting movement. 'Keep your mouth closed or they'll start looking for ways to pay the hotel bill.'

Scott took another sip of his coffee and for a moment watched the gathering. By now the orthodontists had broken up into small groups and there was much gesticulating and animated conversation. The background din was threatening to swamp all conversation and Scott turned an ear to one side to hear better. 'Was there anything positive in that report?'

Roth's forehead creased as he thought this over. 'Yes. There was a summary that concluded the special and peculiar circumstances the Irish authorities find themselves in justify our involvement. Assisting friendly governments in their fight against organised crime and terrorism is now official Washington policy. You might not remember this but two years ago we had an FBI double agent infiltrate the IRA and help convict their leader. There are CIA and FBI agents in dangerous parts of the world all the time working with the local agencies. After the bombings in Indonesia we sent a special anti-terrorist unit to help with the hunt for the extremists involved and Christ knows how many army intelligence and CIA men we have in Iraq at the moment. So when your request came in we first checked with Dublin that it was legitimate, then a squad in Washington assessed the plan and materials demand. Final conclusion: crazy but worth supporting.'

Scott leaned back in his chair and held Roth's gaze. 'Did you support it, Stan?'

Roth sighed and dragged his jacket together at the front. His features looked troubled and when next he spoke his voice was subdued. 'As a friend, Scott, if I'd had any sense I'd have killed your request stone dead. My initial reaction was to protect you. We go back so many years, first as hospital interns, then career doctors moving up the ladder. We covered each other's asses on night shifts, traded insults in bars and seemed to support the same losing team wherever we moved.'

Scott listened without interrupting, remembering how he and Roth had first met as newly qualified doctors, scared stiff to make decisions, yet desperate to gain experience. They'd come to rely on one another, double checking each other's work, both able to sound out problems or check drug doses or read difficult ECG traces or set up IV lines on patients whose veins had collapsed. They were two strangers thrown together by the camaraderie that exists in medicine when young doctors struggle together to earn their status. And such friendships endure for years after; especially since Scott had spotted Roth mistakenly prescribe ten times the recommended dosage of a heart medicine by putting the decimal point in the wrong place. He'd corrected the error and covered Roth's back by ripping out the drug sheet, saving one patient's life and a young doctor's budding career. This was the favour Roth owed, which Scott called on in his hunt for Laura's killer. He had subsequently moved into paediatrics while Roth was headhunted by the military, his interest in anaesthetic drugs catching their attention. Scott had no idea what Roth actually did, but had heard on the grapevine that his friend was in Guantanamo Bay during the interrogation of al-Queda prisoners. And he'd concluded he wasn't there to give anaesthetics.

'However,' Roth was finishing his explanation, 'I know everything that happened that day, it was reported widely over here. And I know how much in love you were with Laura; the last time we were together you hardly took your eyes off her the whole night. But she was a real looker so I was kind of ogling her myself.' He paused for a moment, his eyes now fixed on some spot on the table. 'I said to myself, what if this happened to you? How would you handle the situation? And the more I thought about it the more I came round to your response. So I argued your case long and hard, Scott. The army wanted no hand, act or part in this but I pushed your proposal until I wore them down. Just don't make me ever regret that decision. This isn't some emergency room with poor equipment you've decided to move into.' To the right there was a loud crash as a tray full of food and drinks hit the floor and the air filled with curses in a babble of Latino. A large woman at one of the Overeaters Anonymous tables gazed at the mess wistfully.

Scott brought the discussion back to the moment. 'I know that and thanks for your support. I don't know where this is going to lead me and I don't even know if I'll come out alive. But life is meaningless without Laura and there's no way the bastard who killed her is getting away without a fight.'

Across the table Roth was grinning. 'That's what I like to hear, Scott. You never let a problem beat you in the past, that I do remember. You go after this killer and if you find him don't start reading him his rights. Give him one between the eyes, then add another from me.'

Scott drained his cup and wiped his lips with a napkin. 'Where are the goods?'

'Under lock and key in a limo outside, guarded by two army agents.'

'How do I use them?'

'Full instructions are inside the briefcase. They are clear and precise, and cannot be easily confused. I wrote them myself.'

Scott silently offered a prayer of thanks. From his years of working with Roth he knew how he'd developed as a doctor. No one now could fault his communication skills.

Roth continued, 'There's a list of contraindications and potential side effects, plus administration, dosage and over-dosage protocol. Some of these compounds are no more than old-fashioned anaesthetics, but the rest are strictly in the development stage and not on any drugs formulary in any country. That won't change in our lifetime.'

'Have you used them?' Scott was almost on top of Roth, desperate not to miss a word.

'Their use is strictly confidential, Scott. As far as you're concerned the new products have only been tested in animal experiments. If you like I can give you the results of those studies, but nothing else.'

'Did you use them, Stan?' Scott wasn't going to be put off by Roth's half-hearted attempt at military secrecy.

'On the record, no. Off the record, I not only developed the new compounds but was the first to try them out in Cuba.' Roth had made an arch with his fingers and was resting his chin on them, watching Scott closely. A waitress interrupted, asking did they want refills. Without looking, two heads shook no.

'And how helpful were they?' Scott felt a slight draught on his head and unconsciously ran a hand along the stubble.

Roth pretended to cough to hide his response. 'Depends on which you use. However, we got more information in one hour than if we'd hung them by their toes for a week.'

Scott smiled slightly, his heart speeding as he began to get a feel for what lay ahead. 'Any significant problems?' he asked.

'Each man had a full medical as soon as he arrived in the base. So we knew what we were dealing with in terms of their physical condition. From what I understand of your plan there won't exactly be time for a case history and examination, will there?'

Now Scott could grin, the humour of Roth's comment certainly not wasted. 'No, Stan, I can't see myself using the stethoscope much. Just my brain and medical experience.'

'Two strong assets, Scott. They haven't let you down so far in life. Keep them to the forefront while you're in the heat of battle. You're a doctor, not a homicide cop.'

That phrase haunts even my dreams, Scott thought.

'Some final points.' Roth's face tightened and his eyes narrowed so that his bushy eyebrows almost folded over. 'None of these carry US army markings. If you lose one, or if they are stolen or if somehow they get into anyone else's hands, they cannot be traced back to my department. Understand?' Scott nodded. 'Secondly, some are strictly experimental and therefore unlicensed for use anywhere in the world. You use one and it's your responsibility. Finally, there is a back-up plan should you get killed during this venture.'

This was news to Scott and he dropped his head slightly to drown out all distractions.

'According to documentation drawn up by the Irish government that I've seen, if anything disastrous happens your body will be flown to Chicago ASAP for burial. Your family will be offered an autopsy report showing you suffered a massive heart attack and died instantly.'

'Have you actually seen this autopsy report?'

'Yes, in full.'

'So how do my insides look?'

'Clean as a whistle apart from your brain.'

Scott looked surprised. 'What did the pathologist find wrong with my brain?'

'When he cut into the frontal lobe there was no blood, only anger. And that's really why you died so suddenly. Anger took over your brain and dulled your responses.' Roth placed both palms of his hands on the table and started drumming his fingers. 'When the shooting starts, Scott, keep focused. Think with your head and not your heart.'

Scott said nothing, secretly stunned that back in Dublin provisions for his death had already been made.

'One other little matter I forgot.' Roth had finished drumming and was inspecting his fingernails as if trying to decide on a manicure. 'To transport these compounds to Ireland you need a special permit. Inside the case is all the documentation necessary, should you be challenged at any airport or border crossing in the US. Outside of that they are contraband and likely to be seized and you arrested.'

'That's already been taken care of,' said Scott. 'The Irish Justice Department has arranged to collect the case and have it transferred using diplomatic channels.'

Roth snorted his disgust. 'That breaks all rules of diplomacy. What sort of a government do you have over there?'

Scott leaned back in his chair, his eyes scanning the balcony above. There was one black male with a severe crew cut and smart suit resting his chin on his hand, his gaze fixed on the table he and Roth occupied. As their eyes met, the crew cut began talking into his sleeve. 'You seem to forget that Oliver North used fake Irish passports during some clandestine army venture in the Middle East. Don't pretend to be naïve, Stan; this sort of stuff goes on all the time. Hell, if anything it's worse here than any other jurisdiction.' He stood up slowly and stretched, then leaned on the table. 'Your friends on the balcony are getting bored. Let's say our goodbyes and I'll collect the goods.'

Roth gathered himself together and reached across to take Scott's hand. The grip was firm and commanding, Roth's expression that of a man ill at ease with the situation he found himself in. 'Look after yourself, Scott. It's bad enough losing Laura, but if anything happens to you then this killer you're chasing will have succeeded big time.'

Scott held his gaze. 'Don't worry, Stan. I don't plan on hitting the autopsy tables for a helluva long time.'

Roth gave Scott's hand a final squeeze that almost cracked his knuckles. 'Nobody ever plans to hit the autopsy tables before their time. But when the bullets start flying some people don't duck quick enough.'

* * *

The silver-coloured, steel-strengthened briefcase was eighteen inches long, fourteen inches wide, six inches deep and weighed eight pounds exactly. The handle was recessed and attached to the body in such a way that it could not be detached without significant force and skill. The swivel hinges were also reinforced for protection. The lock was a number combination device and as Scott Nolan laid the case on his bed back in his parents' apartment overlooking Oak Street beach, he rolled out the code as Stan Roth had recited. Left side: 9, 3, 1. Right side: 7, 4, 0. Now, as the locks clicked and he slowly lifted the lid, the doctor's mouth was dry with anticipation. Yes, he silently exclaimed as he saw the first row. Resting on a felt and Perspex lift-out tray were twenty vials, each containing a clear, colourless fluid. Ten vials had an ID, a number beginning with a batch grouping: XP 6390, followed by the individual unit ID starting at 20X01 through to 20X20. XP, Scott decided, stood for *experimental* and the numbers a method of tracking individual units in the event of any adverse reaction. As in hospital critical event investigations, treatment drugs carried batch numbers and specific IDs so that manufactures could be brought to book if their compounds subsequently failed quality control checks. The other ten in this row were basic anaesthetic agents that Scott was already familiar with and had used before during his hospital training days.

Now, hands trembling with excitement, he quickly scanned the attached pages of explanatory text for the unknown compounds, immediately recognising Stan Roth's neat handiwork. The leaflets were clear and unambiguous, with precise instructions. 'Good on you, Stan,' Scott muttered quietly as he read each line, going over the pages twice to make sure he understood all the medical terminology. Anaesthetics wasn't his field and he had some moments of rethinking old lectures and previous operations where he'd been involved in sedating the patient. But after the third sheet he decided this might be less of a task than he'd expected, Roth's directions were so good. He removed the first lift-out row and discovered below an exact replica second group in felt and Perspex, but with different compounds and explanatory leaflets. Fifteen minutes later he moved to the third and final row, checked the contents and again read the directions. Two hours after that his heart was racing with excitement. This could work. He'd inspected the case thoroughly, its contents and accompanying sheets and, as Roth had cautioned, there were no markings suggesting a US army connection. The border crossing documentation was then set to one side to be for ever kept separate. Now the self-doubts and conscience scouring was over. With Roth's help and Scott's medical expertise, his side of the investigative duo was firm and secure.

And he had few doubts about Mark Higgins's commitment, maybe only that he might get overly aggressive if things got too hot. But, he'd decided days before, I'll deal with that if and when it happens. Now is the time to start progressing the hunt for Laura's killer. From a bedside locker Scott fished out the photofit image from the *New York Times* article he'd downloaded off the Internet. He stared again at the picture of a narrow-faced, tall, youngish-looking male in his late twenties or early thirties; the indistinct eye slits, tight and thin lips and the long hair drawn into a ponytail at the back. I'm looking for you, bastard. You don't know it, but the hunt is on to get you. He balled the page and tossed it into a trashcan. And when we catch you, I'm going to kill you.

He dragged on to the bed one of the suitcases he'd carried from Dublin and snapped open its locks. From a depression to one side, disguised with Velcro-lined felt, he pulled out a cell-phone and charged it up. The first call was to Dublin and lasted ten minutes; the second to the British Airways desk at O'Hare Airport where he booked a first-class flight to London, leaving at eight on the evening of 4 March, only two days away. Then he sat at the side of the bed, his heart heavy as he tried to find the words to explain to his parents, and especially his sister Mary, that he was leaving. And not just quitting Chicago for a hospital position in another city; rather he was heading off into the unknown, maybe never to return alive.

Conversation that evening was tense and subdued. As soon as Jim and Ellen Nolan saw their son's image change they were shocked. At least Scott had the good sense to get out of his undertaker black casuals but his haircut couldn't be hidden. 'My God, Scott,' Ellen exclaimed, 'what has come over you? That shaven look I only see coming out of run-down projects. You look like some underfed drug dealer.'

Jim Nolan said little, his body language shouting louder than a megaphone. 'How did your meeting with Dr Roth go? Did he offer you a position with the army by any chance?' The sarcasm was layered in spades and Scott ignored the issue.

Mary Nolan couldn't stop laughing when she spotted her brother coming out of his room shortly after she arrived home from school. 'Scotty,' she squealed, 'did the Indians take your scalp? Woo, woo, woo, Big Chief Hair Cut takes white man's curls.' At least her humour brought a few smiles to the strained atmosphere, but all that quickly dissipated when Scott passed on his travel plans during dinner.

His parents just quietly acknowledged the information and continued eating, but Mary was crushed. 'Scotty, are you going after the man who killed Laura?'

At this Jim Nolan threw his cutlery on his plate, wiped his lips on a napkin and stood up. His face was red with contained anger as he turned towards his son. 'Scott, it's not fair to be so evasive to any of us, least of all Mary. We deserve better than the half-truths and vague grunts you've been offering us this past twenty-four hours. If you don't want to tell us whatever it is that you're involved in, that's fine. We find it hard to accept but can live with it. However, you should at least put your mother's and sister's minds at ease by reassuring them it's nothing so dangerous we're going to be living off our nerves from now on.'

Scott pushed his plate aside and looked first towards his mother, then Mary. His sister was staring at him, wide-eyed and frightened, a trickle of tears coursing towards her chin. Scott knew his father had never addressed any of his children in such a tone after they had passed eighteen years of age. Jim Nolan's outburst was undermining Mary's already fragile world and Scott felt like a lowlife as he searched for the right words to say. Finally he looked straight up at his father, where he still stood, waiting for an answer. 'I'm sorry, Dad, but I can't put anyone's mind at ease, least of all my own. I really don't know where I'm going and I can't be sure I'll ever come back.'

Mary's distraught sobbing echoed in his head for the next forty-eight hours.

13

'Derek McCann's giving me a lot of grief. He now knows you were behind the attacks and says he can't trust a word that comes out of our mouths after the way you lied to him in Dublin.'

In a small bar on the seafront in Marbella in the south of Spain, Jay Davis and Sean Kennedy were moving their heist ahead, both anxious to keep the pace of developments steady. Davis's trip to Miami had been hugely successful, the ex-cop clinching a twenty million US dollar cocaine order with a Colombian middleman, the total to be delivered by container to Rotterdam.

It was 5 March and the usually sunny resort was clouded over, with drizzly rain misting the harbour views and keeping most residents indoors. After returning from Bangkok, Kennedy had flown in from Amsterdam to be with Davis. For the first day he and Davis spent hours debriefing one another, Kennedy explaining in detail every move of his visit to the Far East. Davis's eyes had widened with surprise as he listened to Kennedy's account of being hunted by the Bangkok police and only escaping with Toby Wurschanda's bribed help. This set him back and for a while the two argued over moves and counter moves. Davis was worried Kennedy had become a liability since he was probably number one on the most wanted criminal list in Europe. But Kennedy wasn't prepared to take a secondary role in the joint venture and fought his corner aggressively, so much so that after hours of bitter exchanges Davis reluctantly caved in and agreed to the original set-up. But the discord soured their previously sound relationship and an air of mutual distrust began to creep in.

Kennedy suspected Davis was snorting some of the white powder they were shipping to Ireland; certainly the other man's behaviour was becoming more paranoid. Davis never sat anywhere unless he had his back to a wall and full view of entrances and exits. He had an increasingly strong habit of looking over his shoulder wherever he went, his blood-shot eyes scanning faces and cars with strange intensity. The cocaine was in storage for their Dublin contact, Derek McCann, who was buying in small quantities on a weekly basis to maintain his customers and secure his position in the market place. But McCann was also preparing for the big shipment and badgering Davis for a delivery date. A lot of money rested on the cargo transfer, the profits so substantial that Davis and Kennedy could split them and spend the rest of their days in the sun. And, in Ireland, Derek McCann was very focused on becoming the main player in the narcotics supply chain. Like Davis and Kennedy, he was setting up offshore accounts and preparing a hideaway, for him a hillside villa on the Costa del Sol.

'We agreed McCann would be involved on a need-to-know

only basis,' countered Kennedy. 'He was shit scared back then and if I'd owned up he'd have pulled. He's best kept in the dark. What he doesn't know he can't tell.'

'He's taken on a partner, Nick Ferguson, a Liverpool dealer with Irish connections who wants in on the act.' Davis was pushing his empty coffee cup in wide circles, leaving a dark trail on the table. 'Ferguson will put up half the costs if McCann gives him a cut in the goods.'

Kennedy ground out the cheap cigar he was smoking and thought this over. 'What do you know about Ferguson?'

'Not much. But he must have enough assets to muscle McCann on this deal, even though it makes sense to spread the risk.'

'Do you think Mc Cann has told anyone about me?' Kennedy brought the topic back to his role in the February assassinations. He didn't want his name out in the open so soon. What happened after the heist he couldn't care less about, by then he'd be long settled in some safe haven.

'No, I warned him to stay shut.' Davis shifted his chair for the fifth time, always moving to keep a different view of the small room. The bar was almost empty, with only a few seasoned alcoholics watching Sky Sports on a corner TV, but to the drug pusher every face represented a potential threat, a suspect eavesdropper. 'Derek, I said, you keep your thoughts to yourself. Who ambushed Harry Power is yesterday's news. The next big thing is our shipment and if you go around snivelling about being lied to, you're out of the loop. Sean Kennedy only kept you in the dark to protect your interests. You can either bury your worries or bail out. We've got other clients who'd give their eye-teeth to get a piece of this action.'

'What'd he say?'

'He'd shut it, but he warned if there was the slightest hint of him being double crossed he'd follow us to the ends of the earth and personally blow our brains out.'

Kennedy mulled this over. In Bangkok the bartering was accompanied by threats and counter threats, but he knew Toby Wurschanda from old and also knew how seriously to treat his warnings. But Derek McCann was a piece of shit in Kennedy's estimation, a small-time dealer who'd only moved up the food chain after he and Davis cleared the opposition. For him to start issuing threats was almost an insult and Kennedy didn't much care for insults. Mentally he added McCann to his list of people to sort out before he finally quit Europe. 'Forget McCann, he's really only a bit player suddenly hitting the big time. Once he's knee deep in dope and the money starts rolling in he'll be on his knees for another deal.'

Davis adjusted his jacket and flicked at his hair. His tan had faded slightly after a spell of indifferent weather along the Spanish coast but he still looked sharp and sexy. 'I told him about the mix on offer. Coke for the suits making too much money, scag for the scum to give their miserable lives a lift and uppers for kids at the discos. I told him we'd cover the market completely, teens to oldies. He liked that and it seemed to keep him quiet.'

Kennedy shifted forward in his seat and stretched his legs out fully. He was back in his favourite attire: denims and T-shirt and sneakers. His shaven hair was growing and now looked an untidy mess, not long enough to comb and too short to shape. 'So when do we move the goods? I need a date to work towards, I've got exit plans.'

Davis grinned at his co-conspirator. 'Heading off somewhere?'

'Mebbe.'

'Somewhere warm, I hope. Holland gets too cold in the winter.'

'Yeah, possibly somewhere warm. South America seems far enough.'

Davis's eyebrows arched. 'South America? What the hell would you do in South America? Lay every woman from Argentina to Mexico?'

'That would help pass the time.'

'And clear your pockets. Let me tell you something about women, Sean. They're great in bed and on the beach in string bikinis. But put them in a department store with hot money and they'll leave you broke in no time. Love them and lay them, but keep them at a distance.'

At the bar one of the dipsos suddenly started cheering and when Kennedy looked over he noticed Sky Sports was showing a local Spanish derby. On the screen an angry-looking goalkeeper was fishing the ball from the back of his net, gesticulating wildly at his defence. There was an action replay and in slow motion the goalie was seen to dive the wrong way as the ball spun in a curl from a free kick just outside the penalty area. The dipso shouted his support again and ordered another beer. Shaky hands flicked open a packet of cigarettes and soon another cancer stick glowed. Kennedy turned back. 'A date, Jay. I need a date.'

Davis flicked through a dog-eared diary until he came to a page already heavily lined in red. 'The goods arrive in Rotterdam on 6 April. It'll take us a day to reorganise the containers into one shipment. I've checked with P&O containers and we can get a delivery on to the docks in Dublin arriving 8 April.' He glanced over at Kennedy. 'How does that sound?'

Almost as if savouring the words, Kennedy repeated slowly,

'8 April. That's fine. Gives me plenty of time.' To collect the money, settle a few old scores, get the hell out of Europe. 'Let's run with it.'

As the two men sauntered along Marbella's wet side streets, in the chill of a London morning a certain Dr Scott Nolan was making arrangements to travel by train and ferry to Dublin. While his passport photograph matched the man's face, give or take a few pounds' weight loss, his travelling attire of all black did not reflect the usual dress code of a member of the medical profession. That apart, the customs check was cursory at Heathrow Airport and soon he was travelling first class by train to the ferry port of Holyhead on the Welsh coast. As Scott gazed out of the window at the wet and misty countryside flashing past he made two quick calls on his cellphone. One was to Garda HQ in Dublin's Phoenix Park to confirm his special delivery briefcase had arrived safely and was now under lock and key in a secure vault. The second lasted less than thirty seconds and was to his brother-in-law, Mark Higgins. The exchange was short and to the point. 'I'm on the way to the ferry and should arrive at eight thirty.'

There was only a second's delay in the response: 'I'll be waiting.'

Around the same time in the town land of Clonart in County Meath, about one hour's drive from Dublin city centre, Derek McCann was counting out a bundle of used notes to the value of ten thousand Euros. Finally satisfied, he handed the total over to a small, ruddy-faced man in an ill-fitting tweed suit. 'Are ye sure ye don't want to hang on to it for another few months? Sure if business picks up ye'd need good storage space like this.' The two men were standing in front of a large warehouse in a remote rural part of the county, the building accessed only by a narrow dirt track almost destroyed by deep water-filled potholes. On all sides thick forest protected the site, making it invisible from the nearest main road about half a mile to the east. Well-worn lettering spelled out the original use of the store: CLONART FERTILISER SUPPLIES. But the front and sides of the structure suggested it hadn't been used for some time, with flaking paint, guttering hanging loose and wood rotting on the main doors. McCann turned to his new business partner. 'I'm going to see how the first shipment goes. It's a new range of furniture to Ireland and I don't want to get my fingers burnt. I'll hold on to it until the end of June and give you a shout then, and we'll see if I'll take another six months' option.'

Tweed suit was already stuffing the Euro notes into a recess in the boot of his mud-stained Honda Civic. 'Fair enough, I'll wait till I hear from ye.' Derek McCann let the Honda disappear from sight along the dirt track before he clicked his mobile phone into action. 'Get a handful of the lads down over here tomorrow. I want new doors and strong locks, and a bloody big watch dog.' He killed the call and walked around the clearing for the next ten minutes, surveying the site and buildings. Perfect, he thought. Fucking perfect. Close to the motorway and yet so hidden away. I might hang on to it for a while longer right enough. Things are definitely looking up.

At Garda HQ, Police Commissioner Peter Cunningham read again the report from CSD, Bangkok. Suspected sighting of a man wanted for questioning in relation to a political assassination attempt in Dublin on 10 February 2006. International arrest warrant still outstanding. There was a detailed description of a white male local CSD officers had observed. Indeed, thought Cunningham, that does fit our photofit release. Also, he was travelling on a false passport and disappeared without collecting the luggage at his hotel. Yet as he stared at the pile of two hundred plus other filed sightings of 'the jackal', he realised this could be another false alarm. Still, he sent a request for follow-up and further details to his colleagues in Bangkok, thanking them for their time and interest in the case. Before he turned off the lights in his office and made his way to the staff car park, Cunningham cursed the mystery assassin for the millionth time. We'll get you, you bastard.

14

'This is a nine-millimetre Beretta automatic. It weighs about two and a half pounds, total length nine inches, and has a fifteen-round magazine.' Mark Higgins was preparing Scott Nolan for his new role as homicide investigator. 'I talked this over with one of our instructors and he suggested it as the best weapon for a rookie. It's light, not too bulky, carries enough bullets for any shoot-out and is easily concealed. What do you think?' The two men were in rough terrain in a remote forest area north of Dublin accessed only by a four-wheel drive that Higgins had requisitioned from the police HQ range of off-road vehicles. The unmarked grime-covered and dirt-splattered jeep was parked about five hundred yards away, partly hidden by foliage. Both were in combat fatigues and near where they stood Higgins had stuck a target sheet on the thick trunk of a sycamore tree, a cardboard outline of a body holding a gun directed forward. Circles in ever decreasing circumference closed in on the target's chest, the bull's-eye of practice shooting. Scott stared at the Beretta, noting its black steel frame and barrel, its grooves and notches. This was alien territory to the doctor and he wasn't sure how to respond. 'Go on, handle it,' Higgins snapped, 'you have to get used to this part. If we're going into enemy territory you'll need more than a stethoscope and prescription pad.'

Scott scowled at his reluctant partner. 'That's not very funny.' He took the Beretta and felt its weight in his right hand, transferred it to his left, then back to his right. Slowly and almost painfully his grip closed on the handle and he allowed his forefinger to ease its way round the trigger. He'd never held a gun before, though he'd seen many in action during his years as an emergency room doctor. Once, in LA, he'd looked on in horror as armed security guards had a shoot-out with gang members attacking the ER Scott was working in. Lying on an emergency trolley was one of their members, handcuffed and already under arrest. Bullets filled the air, skimming patients and medical staff alike until finally two of the thugs lay dying on the now bloodstained floor. Scott remembered vividly kicking away a handgun still gripped in the twitching fingers of a large black youth in case his trigger finger had one last squeeze left. Then, as he turned to deal with the gunshot injuries, he thought how absurd and dangerous US gun laws were. He had two patients with head wounds from which they'd never survive, and another holding his belly and moaning as the colour of his face drained from pink to deathly white. Ever since, he'd had a loathing of guns and gunmen, an abhorrence that was reinforced after the brutal murder of his young wife. Yet now he was in the middle of isolated woodland, holding a loaded Beretta and about to start firearms training. How my life has changed, he thought, not for the first time. Doctor to detective, stethoscope to pistol.

Higgins took the Beretta from Scott and quickly unloaded and reloaded, showing his student the intricacies of the hardware and how to use it safely. Scott looked on with a mixture of fascination and apprehension as live ammunition was clicked into place so casually. Suddenly, and without warning, the detective spun on his heel and fired four quick rounds, the loud reports echoing throughout the damp forestry and sending crows squawking into the air. Scott's ears were ringing and he shook his head to try to restore normality. 'Did you have to do that?'

Higgins was scowling as he returned from the target tree. 'You don't have to shout,' he snorted, 'I can hear you.' Scott didn't realise the gunfire had affected his hearing so much he couldn't recognise the strength of his own voice. 'And I missed the bloody thing altogether,' Higgins complained as he eased another four rounds into the Beretta. 'Must be getting out of practice.' He handed the gun back to Scott and forced him into standard firing position: legs slightly splayed, body straight forward, both hands in front gripping the gun. One grasped the handle and trigger while the other covered and supported the shooting hand.

'Shouldn't we have ear muffs?' Scott complained. 'I'd like to be able to know what people are saying when we leave here.'

Higgins was obviously delighting in his brother-in-law's discomfiture. This was his territory and he was milking every minute of it. 'Where we're going no one uses protectors, so we have to prepare for field action. Just do it,' he snarled. Again the stillness of the rural countryside was filled with another ugly burst of gunfire and for the first time in his life Scott Nolan felt the recoil of a weapon, noticing his hands jump slightly as each round discharged.

Higgins scanned the target markings. 'Not bad,' he muttered, 'but not good enough. Let me give you a few tips.' He took the Beretta and opened up the magazine. 'Treat this gun like a delicate instrument, it's made by craftsmen and easily ruined by rookies. Keep your ammunition safe and dry, and don't let it get overheated or too cold. Keep the bullets clean. If you drop a round clean it before use, otherwise dirt can get in the firing mechanism or along the barrel and the gun can jam. When shooting take it slowly and deliberately, squeeze the trigger gently and give yourself about two seconds before pulling again. Keep control, that's vital. When handling use the cup and saucer grip.' Scott Nolan's expression reflected his puzzlement. Cup and saucer? Higgins began to explain, his demeanour that of a man suffering the presence of his brother-in-law, yet concerned and anxious Scott should familiarise himself with the firearm. 'The cup hand holds the gun handle with your index finger on the trigger. The saucer hand sits underneath the magazine feed, holding and steadying. Have you got that?' Scott nodded, mouth dry and heart racing as the significance of each instruction sank in.

'Always go for the trunk, heads can duck but it's more difficult to get your body out of the way when the bullets start flying. If your target has his back to you shoot him there and then. Two quick rounds to the chest area, then one to the head when he hits the floor. If he's coming at you keep your gun by your side to the last second, then shout real loud to distract him and open up with two bullets to the heart. Don't anticipate the noise, it's going to happen and if you're in a confined space it'll deafen, which is good. But if you're waiting for the bang it'll put you off and make you aim down and sideways. Once you've used your weapon for a while you'll get a feel for it, know how it pulls and learn how to correct for any drag. It's vital for both of us that you don't go around treating it as if it's dog dirt, something you can barely tolerate to have on your person.' Higgins was watching Scott's reactions and his comment cut straight to the truth. 'If the going gets tough you'll be damned glad to have the comfort of that steel in your hand.'

Scott's insides were churning as he took in Higgins's words, knowing how important they were. As he gradually became used to the Beretta and its mechanisms he realised he was preparing for a final confrontation. If I do come face to face with Laura's killer, will I have the guts to use this gun? *Think with your head and not your heart.* He recalled Stan Roth's warning just before they parted in Chicago. *Look after yourself, Scott. It's bad enough losing Laura, but if anything happens to you then this killer will have succeeded big time.*

Get real, he finally admonished himself. This is not a game, this is live ammunition we're using and if you don't come to terms with your life change then somebody's going to get hurt in battle. So for the next two hours Scott put aside his mantle of healer and carer to assume the responsibility of a gunman working on behalf of Irish law enforcement. He let loose over two hundred rounds of ammunition, at one point stopping to let the gunmental cool from overuse. In between, Higgins coaxed and cajoled, corrected and encouraged, advised how he was going off target, cautioned about handling and using the safety catch. Dusk was falling as the two men finished collecting the spent cartridges scattered around their feet and finally climbed into the mud-splattered jeep to make their way to police HQ. There was little conversation during the hour-long journey, each preoccupied with his own thoughts. Higgins drove, headlights flashing and using the service lane of the main motorway back into Dublin. The heavy queues of traffic beside them flashed by as the jeep sped past the airport roundabout and on to the M50 ring road that circled the city. Higgins took a turn-off and began rat-running through various housing developments until they reached the Phoenix Park, just north of the River Liffey and central base of the Irish police force. As the jeep edged under the security barrier and into the front quadrangle, a steady rain began to fall, creating miniature rainbows under glowing Georgian lamps in front of the main granite buildings.

'What type of hardware do you use?' Scott finally broke the long silence. They were parked at the back of the police HQ in an area reserved for forensic training. Under the pretext of renovation this zone was now off limits to staff and had been secretly turned into an interrogation complex. Scott had supervised equipment loading and positioning, then spent the best part of twelve hours checking every piece of apparatus. Nicknamed 'the chamber' by Scott, these rooms were now ready for use.

Higgins shifted in his seat, feeling in a side pocket for a pack of cigarettes. When he'd lit up and taken his first deep drag he looked across at Scott. 'I use a nine millimetre Walther. It has a full eight-round magazine and is easily carried. But because of the shitheads we're likely to come up against I may use a back-up Uzi. It can fire nine hundred and fifty rounds in a minute if necessary. If you can get your head round this whole weapons issue, I think we're as prepared as we'll ever be. You can be damned sure the opposition are used to guns and ammunition. They won't think twice about raining lead on us if cornered.'

As Scott wound down his window to escape the cigarette fumes he felt the bulge of his Beretta, strapped and holstered across his chest. 'I'm ready. I hate violence and would usually run a mile rather than get involved in something like this but I've crossed that bridge and there's no going back until we've seen this through.'

Higgins ground out his cigarette and opened the side door. 'That's good. We're on the same side at last. Now show me this box of tricks you're so excited about.'

The chamber was a thirty-foot square area inside an annexe of four interconnecting rooms. The floor was tiled, the walls bare and all lighting was from glaring fluorescent tubes. Jammed into one corner two racked stainless steel trolleys on wheels held a collection of emergency medical drugs, boxes of syringes, needles and sterilising wipes. Beside them was a security safe, heavy-duty with combination movement. In the middle of the room, anchored firmly to the floor, was a standard hospital issue anaesthetic table with side arms and padded headrest. Immediately to one side was a portable anaesthetic machine with cylinders of gases, masks, tubing and delivery apparatus. There was also a smaller unit connected by stainless-steel clamps, a monitor for blood pressure, heart rate and blood oxygen levels. Colour-coded wires allowed these gauges to be attached directly to anyone lying on the trolley. Underneath was a suction apparatus with pump, tubing and stainless-steel head. To anyone who might have strayed into the room by mistake it looked like an operating theatre but without the usual cutting instruments and overhead halogen lights.

Higgins walked slowly round the set-up, his eyes taking in every detail. He reached for another cigarette but Scott stopped him immediately. 'Can't allow that, sorry. I'm trying to keep this as sterile an environment as possible. It isn't hospital clean but as good as I can produce and I don't want you filling the air with noxious fumes.'

Higgins shrugged and stuffed the packet back into his fatigues. He began sifting through the boxes on the steel trolleys but suddenly seemed to recoil and backed off. 'What about the special delivery case you picked up in Chicago?' he mumbled. 'What's inside that?' Scott squinted at him, slightly puzzled. The swagger and firm footsteps had disappeared and Higgins now looked edgy.

Scott dismissed this and squatted down at the safe, playing with the combination until the door came free. From inside he produced his own very personal hardware, Stan Roth's present from the US army. He lifted the silver case on to the anaesthetic trolley, entered the security code and snapped the locks. With a grand flourish he opened the lid and stood back. 'There they are,' he announced triumphantly, 'better than any Beretta or Uzi. No bullets or blood, nobody gets hurt and we don't have to beat the pulp out of anyone for information.' He noticed Higgins was lurking in the background, only half looking. 'Come closer. You'll need to know how to use these.'

Higgins took a crablike step nearer, clearing at his throat repeatedly. 'OK, what've you got?'

Scott had removed each of the Perspex racks and was inspecting his new toys. He didn't notice his brother-in-law wipe furiously at sweat collecting on his brow. 'These are auto-injectors,' he explained, 'and work as if you're pressing a ballpoint pen into action.' He held up one of the units to demonstrate, a four-inch narrow-barrel plastic tube with black top on one end and open at the other. 'Inside this open end' – he pointed – 'is a recessed half-inch fine-point needle. When you pull off the black top' – he indicated this with his thumb

– 'you'll see a red button underneath. One firm press on this and the needle shoots out. The drug is inside the tube in a precisely calibrated dose. If you hold this against someone's leg, or arm, or any soft tissue, the needle penetrates to an exact point and automatically injects the drug. Then it kicks in pretty much immediately. Ingenious, isn't it?' Scott turned to the heavy breathing behind him and noticed Higgins perspiring profusely, his face ashen white and hands trembling. 'What the hell's wrong, Mark?' He reached out and grabbed Higgins, immediately realising he was close to fainting.

'I can't stand needles,' croaked the detective, his knees buckling as he slid towards the ground, his large frame protected by Scott's frantic grasp.

'Jesus Christ,' groaned Scott. He was now almost on top of Higgins's prostrate body. 'This I was not banking on. You give me grief about guns and I'm scared stiff watching you throw live ammunition around like jellybeans. But show you a simple injection needle and you're putty. What sort of a partner have I landed myself with?'

Higgins managed to force his head forward from his position flat on the ground. 'If you tell anyone about this, Scott Nolan, I swear I'll kill you.'

It was eight o'clock that same evening, and Scott and Higgins sat in the snug of a smoky, noisy, busy pub along Dublin's north quay. Higgins had recovered from his fainting episode, although his embarrassment was still obvious. Scott had difficulty keeping a grin from his face as the image of his tough-guy partner sprawled and sweating kept forcing itself to the front of his brain. He ordered a Budweiser and sipped it to distract himself. Higgins had a foaming creamy pint of Guinness half finished with one long draught and froth clung to his upper lip as he finally spoke: 'I have a lead to start on.'

Scott immediately leaned closer; the background din was so loud. Orders were being shouted over the heads of a crowd gathered at the bar and the lounge staff were struggling to keep up with demand. In a corner a television was showing golf from Florida but no one seemed the slightest bit interested. 'What?'

Higgins took another draught of his Guinness and this time wiped the froth from his mouth. He glanced around to satisfy himself they weren't being overheard. 'There's a new boy on the block shifting cocaine. One of our officers bought from him and it's almost one hundred per cent pure.'

'So,' Scott voiced his understanding of the situation, 'if this new dealer is selling the real McCoy he must be getting it from a top supplier?'

'That's right. We're only talking about a kid here, plankton in the food chain. But your plan suggested we start at the bottom and follow the money, and that's what we're going to do. This youngster has never been seen on the streets before and none of our squad has anything on him. So we have someone higher using cannon fodder to shift his goods. I think we should talk to the street pusher and see where it leads us.' Higgins finished his pint, flagged a waiter and ordered another. 'You want one?' He nodded towards Scott, who shook his head.

They waited until the fresh glass was set on the table and Higgins wiped at the overflow with a beer mat. Then he took another long draught, sighed with contentment and set the Guinness back on the table, watching its bubbles settle. Scott knocked back the dregs of his Budweiser and eyeballed Higgins. 'I'm ready. When do we strike?'

Higgins studied his brother-in-law for a minute, his eyes deliberately running from shaven head along stubbled chin and down to black T-shirt. 'It's hard to think you're the same man who married my sister. You look like a bloody underworld hit man. I swear to God you'd scare the shit out of me if I saw you coming in the dark.'

Scott managed a grin. 'That's the idea; no point in letting them think I'm a wimp.'

'And I like the new glasses, much better than those other ones you used to wear. Laura called them your Coca-Cola lenses.'

Scott laughed slightly; the sudden thought of his late wife making fun of him behind his back saddened him. She was such a vixen and so full of life.

'How are you settling in your new living quarters?' Since his return from Chicago Scott now lived in a single-bed unit in an apartment complex one mile from the city centre.

'Fine. It's pretty basic and adequate for my needs, but I wouldn't like to stay there too long.'

'No,' Higgins agreed, 'and I'm not planning on running this operation longer than necessary.'

His comment focused Scott's mind again. 'When do we lift this guy?'

'Tomorrow. Like vampires these dregs don't surface until dark so you and I may have to kick our heels a little. But as soon as he hits the streets we'll grab him.'

15

The youth was small fry and even Scott Nolan could see that. Aged somewhere in his late teens, tight crew cut, rings in both ears and tattoos on neck and hands, the dealer shifted from one foot to the other on the corner of Talbot Street in Dublin's inner city. It was closing in on ten o'clock on a Monday night and the earlier bumper-to-bumper traffic had drifted to an intermittent stream along the narrow streets. Neon lights and gaudy shopfronts reflected off the damp pavements and pedestrians had to move quickly to avoid wheel mist. The pubs, as usual, were doing a roaring trade. Mark Higgins and Scott were parked about a hundred yards away in a newly acquired navy-blue transit van with sliding side panels. The windows were tinted, the number plates false and the interior was fitted with restraints, mattress and anaesthetic drugs. Scott was in his all-black dress code, Higgins in denims and thick woollen crew neck. Both men had guns strapped to their bodies. Scott inspected the youth up close with special night-vision binoculars, noting his eyes darting nervously, his hands thrust firmly into bulging denim side pockets. At irregular intervals individuals or groups of two, but never more than that, approached the dealer. They were mainly male, suspicious and dishevelled and agitated, but occasionally Scott could identify a strung-out, wasted-looking female among the wretched clients. Conversation was brief, hands moved in a blur as small packages were passed across and a clutch of notes pocketed in return. Within a thirty-minute period Scott counted eighteen different transactions, each lasting no more than two minutes, some as little as thirty seconds.

'Do you see that car parked about ten yards behind him?' Higgins directed Scott's binoculars along the street. Initially distracted by a group of revellers spilling out of a nearby pub, finally Scott zoomed in on the dark vehicle, its make indeterminate in the gloom. 'That's a two-man back-up. Anyone tries muscle or starts giving aggro about money and they move in.'

Scott put his designer lenses back on. 'So how are we going to take him out without them noticing?'

'Using a diversion.' Higgins slipped out of the driver's side and disappeared along a back alley. Ten minutes later Scott spotted him further ahead, staring into a shop window, one of about ten people hanging around the pavement. Now he was only feet behind the dealer's support car and Scott caught the glow of a cigarette, then a hand twisting in a circular movement. Seconds later Higgins was casually walking away from the scene and five minutes after that he was back in the driver's seat, sweating from exertion and muttering numbers under his breath. He lit a cigarette, glanced in his rear-vision mirror and continued his counting out loud. When he hit fifty he nudged Scott in the ribs. 'Get ready.'

At sixty the dealers' car alarm suddenly began to shrill, its klaxon so loud and unusual the din stopped everyone in the road, heads turning towards the racket. Higgins gunned the engine of the transit and shifted the gears. 'OK, move. Make as if you're going to score and as soon as you hear the horn take him.'

Scott slipped out of the passenger door, his heart racing. This was his first covert mission along the dark and damp streets of downtown Dublin; finally coming face to face with the city's lowlifes. It was a far cry from white coats, stethoscopes and the sterile environment of the City Hospital. There, he stood out like a beacon while here on Talbot Street he hunched to make himself small. He moved as instructed, straight and without looking left or right, making sure not to draw attention to himself. Glasses pushed firmly back on to his nose, he had both hands in side pockets, his right grasping tightly on to one of Stan Roth's US army auto-injectors. Sweat beaded his brow even though the night temperatures were hovering around a respectable ten centigrade. Now he was less than thirty seconds from his target and through the gloom he noticed the youth give him a questioning stare before turning towards his crew, his body language screaming for support. Scott's breathing was heavy, his legs like lead as he closed in.

'What the fuck do you want?' The kid was jumpy and uneasy; sensing the man in black coming at him wasn't a casual bystander. He looked nervously backwards but found his vision blocked by a transit van.

'I need a hit. Gerry told me I could score with you.' Scott was surprised at how easily the street language tripped off his tongue.

'Who the fuck's Gerry?' Scott was now shoulder to shoulder

and holding out a bundle of twenty Euro notes. The money distracted long enough and the youth's eyes dropped. From the left came a short blast from the transit and instinctively Scott flicked off the black cap of the auto-injector and jammed the plastic barrel against the dealer's leg. 'What the fuck . . .' Scott felt something give and kept the unit rammed tight until he sensed the kid buckle, then he quickly grabbed him. Within seconds Higgins was beside him and both manhandled their first target into the open-sided van and on to the mattress. Scott jumped in after him and bundled the limp body on to one side, pushing it as though it were a dead weight. The transit van then drove slowly along the street past the back-up vehicle and as it swung off the road, through the tinted back window Scott watched with delight as he saw the two-man protection crew dart wildly around, searching desperately for their money man.

By eleven that evening the dealer was in Scott's chamber at police HQ and strapped securely to the anaesthetic trolley. The fluorescents were on, their harsh glare lighting up the room as Scott and Higgins paced the floor, waiting for some movement. All the way to the Garda depot Higgins sang Scott's praises, relishing the ease with which they'd been able to grab the drug pusher from under the noses of his minders. 'They'll go fucking crazy,' he crowed as he negotiated the transit along the wet alleyways and backstreets of the inner city, blasting the horn angrily if traffic threatened to slow progress. 'One minute he's there making big money, the next he's gone. Whoever owns that gang will crucify them.' In the back Scott kept a vigil, making sure his prisoner's breathing wasn't compromised. He was secretly as elated as his partner but concerned about the drug he'd injected. It was the first time any of Stan Roth's products had actually been used in battle and despite all the information on effects and side effects, as a practising doctor Scott knew only too well about unexpected reactions, the nightmare of every physician. However, the transfer from street to HQ had gone smoothly and now the two investigators waited impatiently for the youth to come round.

He opened his eyes at eleven twenty; fifty minutes after the injection had been so unexpectedly jammed into his leg. Higgins sat on a steel chair in one corner, watching and studying every movement. Scott stood over the freckle-faced teenager, checking his vital signs of pulse and blood pressure, neither of which showed any significant variation. The drug, part muscle-paralysing agent and part short-acting tranquilliser, had worked smoothly and Scott expected the pusher to surface with his brain reasonably clear. Under the fluoro tubes the kid's heavily freckled face was like a rash and he blinked repeatedly to shield his eyes from the glare. He tried to get up but found both hands and feet restrained while separately a neck collar restricted head movement to ninety degrees. 'Where the fuck am I?'

Out of view, Scott moved behind his head. 'You're in hell.'

The youth tried to find the voice and fought vainly against his restraints. 'Fuck you, you bastard. You better let me outa here or they'll come after you.'

'Who'll come after me?' Scott's voice was even and emotion-free, in total command.

'Me mates, that's who. I was carrying gear and they're gonna want their cut of the takings.'

'You had ten deals of cocaine and nearly two thousand Euros in cash. If I hand you over to the police you're going to spend years in some stinking hell-hole of a prison cell.'

The kid considered that for less than thirty seconds. 'I'm fucking warning you, let me outa here or your balls are dog meat.' His accent was inner city, streetwise and tough, and obviously hardened to threats.

'I'll let you out when I'm ready. First I need information.'

'Fuck off.'

'I'm not interested in you, your name or where you come from. But who's your supplier?'

'Fuck off.'

'Who's your supplier?'

'Fuck off.'

'Who's your supplier?'

'Fuck off.' The curses began to echo off the walls.

Scott moved into view, in his right hand he held up a syringe and needle, its steel glinting in the strong light. Then, from an ampoule, he began drawing up a clear liquid. In the corner Higgins averted his eyes and began chewing furiously on nicotine gum.

'What the fuck's that?'

Scott slowly and deliberately drew back on the syringe, then forced a tiny drop out of the needle tip and let it drop to the ground.

'What's in that fucking syringe?' Scared.

Now Scott fixed a tourniquet round the pusher's right upper arm and tightened it. He waited a few seconds, then began slapping at the inner crease of the elbow to make the veins stand out. Soon a distinct blue cord-like blood vessel bulged like a ripe berry. 'Good veins,' Scott whispered into the kid's left ear, 'makes my job so much easier.'

'What the fuck are you doing, you bastard? Lemme outa this fucking place.' The screams were now those of a frightened boy, the bravado had disappeared.

'Who's your supplier?'

'I can't tell you that, he'd kill me.' Desperation.

'Who's your supplier?'

'Take the money, take the fucking coke if you wannit. Just let me outa this hell-hole.'

'Who's your supplier?'

'Fuck off.'

The needle tip slipped into the bulging vein, despite terrified shouts and frantic wriggles. Scott drew back on the plunger, grunting with satisfaction as he saw bright-red blood spill into the syringe. He had a perfect hit.

'Who's your supplier?'

'I can't tell you, he'd kill me. What are you doing to me? I'm just a street dealer! Jesus, I only get two hundred for a night's work. Why don't you go after the big men?'

'Who's your supplier?'

'Fuck off, you cunt.' Under the heat of the overhead lights sweat blistered and began trickling down both sides of the hostage's face.

Scott slowly pressed the plunger on the syringe and five millilitres of liquid disappeared into the kid's arm. Within seconds he started yawning and his eyes glazed. 'What's in that syringe? I'm warning you . . .' His voice drifted and the anger and bluster melted. 'Who are you?' Another deep yawn. 'What's your game anyway?' Scott watched carefully, noting reactions and checking pulse rate. Satisfied, he collected three colour-coded leads from the monitor behind the anaesthetic trolley and made a great show of connecting them up.

The teenager strained to lift his head and see what was going on, his eyes rolling in his head. 'What's that for? Where the fuck am I?' Another five millilitres entered his bloodstream and fresh yawns surged. Scott inspected the blue-screened monitor and mentally noted the basic vitals. Then he nodded towards Higgins. He stepped behind and whispered into his prisoner's left ear. 'You should have told me something. I'm not a violent man, but my friend here is.'

Now Higgins was standing over the anaesthetic trolley, a Smith & Wesson revolver in his right hand. He'd chosen this instead of his preferred 9mm Walther for better effect, reckoning the Smith & Wesson looked more intimidating. Despite his rolling eyes and indistinct vision, freckle-face could see there was a gun being pointed at him. 'Ah fuck,' he moaned. 'Ah fuck, ah fuck, ah fuck.'

Scott leaned down again and whispered into his left ear. 'Who's your supplier?'

The kid shook his head from side to side, as if desperately trying to distance himself from the nightmare he found himself in. 'I'm not saying.'

Higgins pressed the barrel against the side of the dealer's head. 'Then goodnight, sunshine.' He squeezed the trigger. *Click*. The hammer hit an empty chamber. 'Oh, tsk, tsk,' muttered Higgins, scolding his mistake, 'I just shot a blank. Let's try again.'

By now the youngster was shaking with fear, his body drenched in sweat. He was half awake, enough to recognise what was going on around him, yet in a dreamlike stupor where it seemed as if everything was happening to someone else.

'Who's your supplier?'

'Is that gun real?'

Higgins pressed the trigger again. *Click*. Another empty chamber. Tsk, tsk.

'Who's your supplier?'

'Fuck off, you wanker. I've had better fights with me kid

brother.' The bravado was returning and Scott nodded to Higgins. Higgins squeezed the snout of the Smith & Wesson right against his forehead so the unsteady eyes underneath could see what was happening. Glazed though they were, an element of terror was obvious.

'Go on,' the half-dazed youth taunted, 'shoot me, you big bollox.'

Bang. The room echoed to the report, the sudden blast startling even Scott.

'Who's your supplier?'

Freckle-face had wet himself, a large pool of urine staining his trousers. His ears were humming, his teeth chattered and his limbs trembled. Higgins engaged the firing mechanism yet again and pressed the gun against his forehead, twisting the skin. 'This time,' he snarled, 'I'm using live ammunition. Who's your fucking supplier?'

'Charlie Fegan, for fuck's sake don't shoot me. It's Charlie Fegan.'

Scott and Mark exchanged satisfied glances. 'And where does Mr Fegan hang out,' whispered Scott into a left ear.

'That's all I'm telling you, you can fuck off and . . .' *BANG*. Another blank round was discharged, the walls ringing with the echo. 'Stop doing that, you're scaring the shit outa me.'

Higgins lifted a box of live ammunition and made a great show of emptying the spent cartridges from the Smith & Wesson before slowly inserting fresh bullets. 'This is for real. No blanks, just lead. One will make a big hole in your head, two will leave you without a face, three and I'm taking your balls off. Now where does Fegan hang out?' He cocked the handgun and pointed it straight at the kid, just as Scott emptied another five millilitres of drug into his vein.

For the next hour the streetwise and toughened drug pusher

sang like a lark. While a tape recorder rolled, he spilled everything about Charlie Fegan, who he was, where he lived, how he operated, where he distributed, how much the kid reckoned he grossed after expenses. Charlie Fegan was turning out to be another new face on the block, not that high in the food chain but probably taking in over three hundred thousand Euros a year. Not bad for a twenty-five-year-old postgraduate chemistry student with a degree from Trinity College, Dublin's oldest and most prestigious university.

'I don't remember hearing drug dealing was included in third-level education.' Higgins was cleaning his handgun, while Scott held an oxygen mask over their prisoner's face, waiting for him to come round. 'What the hell did you give him anyway?' Higgins was shouting to be heard above the ringing in his ears.

'On the street I used one of the US muscle relaxants and tranquilliser combinations,' Scott loudly explained as he inspected the pupils of his reluctant patient. 'Then in the back of the van I gave IV Maxolon to speed up stomach emptying so that he wouldn't vomit.'

'Good idea, don't want the little scumbag ruining our upholstery.'

Scott sighed. 'It wasn't to stop him fouling the van, but to prevent him getting sick and inhaling his own vomit. If he did that we'd be in deep shit as stomach acids destroy the lung lining and cause a slow lingering death. And we're into this on a minimal risk exposure agreement, meaning the targets as well as ourselves.'

Higgins considered this new information for about thirty seconds as he spun the Smith & Wesson chamber. 'Serve the bastard right. He's scum, peddling death on the streets. Dying in his own acid somehow seems OK to me.'

Scott decided to let the comment ride; this was not the time to start an argument. 'Once we had him strapped to the table I used small doses of Pentothal, an anaesthetic agent. You can fine-tune it to the point before sedation when it lowers inhibitions and acts like a truth drug. Most people open up and tell their innermost secrets, often to the pre-med nurses. Then they're too embarrassed to look the same girl in the eye after the operation when they recall what they said.'

'So how are we going to stop him from telling the world what happened tonight?' Voice levels were easing as the humming in both men's ears began to subside.

'That's where xylorprozalamat comes in, another beauty from my bag of tricks. It induces total amnesia for all events over the previous twenty-four hours. As soon as he comes round I'll give him a shot and then he's back to the gutter.'

Higgins drew deeply on the end of an unlit cigarette, his expression a mixture of delight and wonder. 'Maybe I should've gone to college and studied like you bright guys. What sort of a doctor do you think I'd have turned out?'

Scott bottled his immediate response, which was a cross between Hannibal Lecter and Genghis Khan. 'A psychiatrist, yes, that's what I think you'd be good at.'

'No shit, why?'

'Because of your easygoing, good-listening and sympathetic attitude. That and you'd kick the head off any patient who didn't get better quick enough. I bet your success rate would stun the medical community.'

Higgins pointed the Smith & Wesson straight at Scott. 'If I take your head off at the shoulders that'll stun the fucking medical community.'

Scott grinned, then turned his attention to his patient who

was slowly coming round. 'Time to move. I'll give him another few minutes, then jab him.'

Higgins slipped outside to have a cigarette, leaving Scott to his thoughts. He was relieved their first joint mission had gone smoothly and with such immediate results. Only time would tell if the name divulged by their hostage would lead them any closer to the ultimate target, the man who killed Laura. But equally important, Scott sensed a grudging acceptance from Higgins. The detective wasn't pouring scorn on every suggestion he made; rather he was listening attentively and acting under instructions. *Maybe we are becoming a team, two very unlikely and different strangers thrown together by tragic circumstances.* He looked down at the freckle-faced youth who was shaking his head from side to side as he struggled for consciousness. *Brains and brawn, that's quite a useful combination when you think about it.* Then he injected Stan Roth's amnesia drug and rolled his charge on to his side. *Time to go, scumbag.*

Freckle-face's real name was Aaron Murphy, a nineteen-year-old from an inner city run-down flats complex who'd recently been recruited to sell drugs. At dawn on 9 March he was found wandering in a distressed state along the beach close to Killiney, an upmarket suburb fringing the south Dublin coastline. Murphy was first taken to the nearest police station and questioned but could offer no explanation for his confusion and loss of memory. When searched he had eight grubby five Euro notes but nothing else. The Garda in charge noticed fresh needle tracks on his right arm and immediately decided he was a junkie coming down from a fix. He arranged for Murphy's transfer to hospital where the disorientated teenager still managed to escape from his uninterested minder and grab a cab. Through his brain faze he at least remembered where he lived and gave directions. He arrived outside his front door around mid afternoon, only to be greeted by his two street handlers who immediately bundled him into a car and drove to some nearby waste ground. There he was searched, interrogated, then stripped and finally beaten to within an inch of his life with baseball bats. It was a bad twenty-four hours for Aaron Murphy, budding drug pusher in Ireland's post-Harry Power narcotics era.

16

They followed Charlie Fegan for a week. Using unmarked cars and a back-up crew of five drug squad officers, Scott and Higgins tracked the twenty-five-year-old narcotics dealer from his home in Loughlinstown, south Dublin, where he lived with his ageing parents and one younger sister. The house was comfortable and well kept, in a housing estate developed some time in the late eighties. Most of the residents were middle income or retired but there was also a significant congregation of twenties-plus who hadn't yet left home because of the high cost of housing in Dublin and its immediate suburbs.

The undercover unit soon learned Fegan was a careful and cautious man, with no set pattern to his movements. He commuted daily to Trinity College, where he was completing a Ph.D. in biochemistry, but took special care to vary his routine. Sometimes he used public transport, on other occasions he would leave his house, walk about five hundred yards out of sight and be collected by an unidentified white male on a high-powered motorbike. On day four he was spotted driving a red Mazda soft-top sports car, garaged in a group of lock-ups one mile from his home.

By day five Higgins had obtained details of six separate bank accounts in which Fegan held assets to the value of half a million Euros. He also owned an apartment along the quays with spectacular views of the River Liffey. Higgins made a rough guess at its current market value and came up with six hundred thousand Euros. Further searches through title deeds revealed there was no outstanding mortgage on the property. 'This guy', he explained to Scott as the two sat in their transit van sharing an Indian take-away, 'is worth more money at twenty-five than I'll ever gross by retirement. He's some mover.'

Then more information filtered in from sources within the university where Fegan studied. He'd been a regular supplier of soft drugs for years, but only on campus. Mostly he dealt in cannabis and amphetamines, refusing to handle heroin or cocaine. However, following the Irish government's crack-down on the narcotics trade, Fegan went dry for a month, declaring himself no longer involved in the business. But quietly he'd moved his interests outside the university walls, where he had too high a profile, and on to the streets. He employed two heavies and five different pushers, the strongmen ferrying and protecting their younger charges when they worked the city and suburbs. It was a tight operation, well-protected and low-key, with good back-up exit strategies. And Fegan wasn't living the life of a man of considerable assets, instead dressing in casuals, eating at McDonald's, bringing sandwiches and a soft drink to college each day supposedly to save on expenses. Higgins was impressed, Scott disgusted. 'He's a smooth operator,' Higgins declared at the end of their week-long surveillance. 'I'd say he's been on the scene for at least five years and managed to keep his head down. He's not on our list of known dealers and his way of life doesn't reflect their usual pattern. He's salting his money away, making sensible investments and not living a flash lifestyle. Smart cookie.'

'Ruthless bastard,' countered Scott. 'Quite prepared to beat the hell out of that kid we lifted.'

Higgins made a mock face of surprise. 'Goes with the territory. He sent freckle-face out on business and he disappeared with the drugs and the money. No self-respecting dealer is going to let one of his workers get away with that. It would make him look weak, he'd lose face and his clients would start thinking he'd gone soft. Soon there'd be addicts scoring and not paying, or just taking the dope and running. This whole industry thrives on threats and fear and violence. Fegan just happens to be middle-class, well-educated and intelligent. His sort do the thinking and gets others to do the dirty work.'

But Scott reckoned he disliked the Charlie Fegans of this world more than the foot soldiers peddling his wares and spent some time deciding which strategy he'd use to crack the pusher when the opportunity arose.

They took Fegan off the streets on Tuesday, 23 March when they spotted him in a vulnerable position for the first time. The dealer had vanished from everyone's view three days previously and there was immediate concern he'd gone underground or fled the country. Twenty-four hours later the postgraduate student reappeared, first spotted in the corner of a city centre pub with his two-man heavy detail, splitting up bags of cocaine into smaller deals for distribution. Higgins decided Fegan's sudden reappearance and renewed activity suggested he'd collected the goods from a supplier higher in the narcotics food chain so he called off the support crew and prepared Scott for action.

'Hi, I'm kinda lost and was hoping you might direct me to Merrion Square?' Scott stood on the pavement on Dawson Street, close to Trinity College, a city guide in one hand and a 9mm Beretta in the other, but jammed deep in a side pocket of his windcheater. He had a bewildered touristy look and exaggerated his American accent for effect. Twenty yards behind, side doors open, Higgins edged their blue transit van forward. Up close, Charlie Fegan was clean-cut, dark hair neatly parted to one side, designer stubble and good-looking features. He was about six foot in his shabby Nike trainers and wore denims, white T-shirt and red fleece. There was the almost obligatory earring in his right lobe but no other jewellery or visible tattoos. To passers-by he must have seemed like an average student sauntering towards the city's premier seat of learning, textbooks bulging his satchel.

Fegan had alighted from a bus at his usual stop from where Higgins calculated a window of opportunity fifty yards further ahead where the wide gates of an office car park offered little activity. Dawson Street was a particularly busy thoroughfare, with good shops, restaurants and strictly enforced traffic by-laws. While on face value it seemed the least likely place to abduct someone off the sidewalk, Higgins gambled that in the hustle and bustle of daily life no one would pay much attention to their plan if it was handled properly. Which is why he shoved Scott Nolan into the firing line and now the doctor stood on a blustery corner, turning his body against the breeze.

'Sure, man, it's about five hundred yards round the corner.' Fegan was accommodating and polite, his accent south Dublin middle-class. Pretentious. 'Anywhere in particular you want to go?'

Scott smiled and turned the city guide towards his target. 'Yes, I'm looking for the National Art Gallery. It's on my recommended list of places to visit.' Out of the corner of his eye he watched as the transit van levelled beside them, its gaping side panels so inviting. A sudden gust of wind flapped the pages of Scott's directory and he forced it closed under an armpit.

'Yeah, man, it's really good. Make sure you take in the Caravaggio, it's class.'

Now Scott glanced quickly up and down the street, checking no one was taking any particular interest in the conversation. Apart from trucks offloading supplies into a nearby book-shop there was a lull in pedestrian traffic. The blue transit van was blocking the road where it narrowed towards a T junction and car horns blared angrily. Scott pretended to take a sudden concern in this and Fegan followed his puzzled gaze. With one crashing shoulder charge Scott heaved Fegan into the van, jumped in after him and slid the panels shut. The transit sped off, leaving a spew of road rage in its wake.

Initially stunned, Fegan finally dragged himself into a squatting position at the back, his satchel and books scattered beside him. He looked up to find a Beretta pointing at his chest. Scott pulled his woollen cap off and flung it to one corner. 'If you make one stupid move your face is full of holes.' He forced his glasses back on his nose, the gangland vernacular now almost second nature.

Fegan held up both arms in surrender pose. 'I'm sitting tight here, man. I'm no hero.' As his gaze took in the intimidating background of mattress, restraints and anaesthetic drug ampoules his expression swiftly switched from stunned surprise to anxious concern. The van bumped and rolled over roadworks and Scott had to steady himself with one hand, his new prisoner noting every move. 'Who are you, man?'

Scott kept his handgun firmly trained on Fegan's chest, though he wasn't convinced he'd use it if the student came at him. He ignored the question; glancing every now and then out of the rear tinted window to get a feel for how far they'd progressed. From the line of vehicles and background din he decided they were close to Temple Bar, south of the River Liffey and less than twenty minutes from police HQ and his interrogation chamber.

Fegan fixed on some spot straight ahead and Scott could almost see his brain working overtime, trying to decide what was happening. 'You're not the filth, so who the fuck are you?' The polite middle-class accent had now hardened into intimidating menace.

Scott switched the Beretta from one hand to the other and felt around in a side pocket until he found the auto-injector he'd brought. With the flick of a thumb he eased off the black protector cap. 'Shut the fuck up,' he snarled.

Ahead, at a notorious intersection, an articulated lorry pulled across the road and came to a sudden stop as the driver realised he didn't have enough room to turn. Higgins blasted the horn angrily and jammed hard on the brakes, throwing his passengers into one another's arms. Fegan grabbed at Scott's right hand and forced the Beretta up and away, then swung an elbow viciously into his throat, immediately winding the doctor. As Scott momentarily struggled for air, the student grasped the side panel handle and dragged on the door. It was now half open, with Fegan scrambling to get out but Scott managed to jab him in the back of the leg with the second of Stan Roth's auto-injectors. Fegan almost collapsed into the roadway and only Scott's restraining hands prevented the student tumbling into the path of following traffic. As he hauled the quivering body inside he glanced up to find Higgins grinning at him from the driver's seat. 'You're getting the hang of this, doc.'

Fegan came to in the chamber, limbs strapped to the anaesthetic trolley and neck firmly secured underneath a padded collar. For the first two minutes he blinked repeatedly, slowly taking in the surroundings he could see from his restricted position: the glaring fluoro tubes, the anaesthetic machine with bottled gases and colour-coded electrodes, a box of syringes and sterile needles. A selection of ampoules, all neatly laid out in a row on a stainless-steel rack. And now the face of Scott Nolan was leaning over him, massaging his throat where it had caught the full force of a jabbing elbow. Fegan's eyes narrowed, his venom and fury obvious. 'Where am I?'

'That really doesn't matter, sunshine.' From his now favourite seat in the corner of the chamber, Higgins clipped a full magazine on to his Walther pistol. 'You could be anywhere. Dublin, London, Paris, Rome, who cares? All that matters is you're with us and we want to talk to you.'

'Well, you can fuck off. I'm in no mood for conversation.'

Higgins and Scott exchanged weary glances. This could be more difficult than their first success.

'You're not getting out of here until we're ready and I don't care if that takes a day, a week or a month. It's up to you, tell us what we want to know and you'll soon be home with Mum and Dad.' Higgins was now standing over their target, waving his handgun inches from his face, taunting with his words.

Fegan's eyes darted viciously from side to side. 'Fuck off.'

Scott sighed out loud. 'That's what your young friend Murphy kept saying. He was very brave, when I think about it. He put up a helluva fight but cracked in the end. So now we know about your bank accounts, your fancy apartment along the quays, your flash sports car. Quite the entrepreneur, aren't you?'

Fegan stared ahead, his face fixed in a mask of fury and defiance. 'I don't know who you bastards are but you'll get nothing out of me.'

Higgins pressed his handgun against Fegan's forehead. 'Who's your supplier?'

'Piss off.'

'One more time, now. Who keeps you in regular coke supplies?'

'Go fuck yourself.'

'This is not going well for you, Charlie. You're a bright kid, a postgraduate student, aren't you? And good looks to go with the brains. You wouldn't want that grey matter splattered on these walls, would you?'

'Holding on to my brains is my business, fuck-face. If I tell you who handles my supplies my brains are as good as gone and you know that. Nobody grasses in this game, it doesn't look good on their CV.'

To the side, Scott was weighing up the situation. Fegan was intelligent enough not to get involved in dirty work, he only pulled the strings. And now he knew his young pusher had turned up alive from whatever ordeal he'd had to endure. Scott suspected that behind the defiance, a sharp brain was calculating the odds, weighing the risks. So, Scott reckoned, Fegan's probably going to tough this out. He's in a no-win situation anyway. If he opens up to us his empire is exposed and his supplier identified. If he holds tight and keeps his mouth shut, the worst that might happen is a severe beating, maybe a bullet in the leg. But he'd have stayed quiet and protected his assets and sources.

'I'm going to ask you one more time, Charlie.' Scott spoke from behind Fegan's head, an intimidating position that made the hostage feel vulnerable. By now Scott was itching to work on Fegan. His sort had been responsible for peddling death to Harry Power's son. 'Who's your supplier?'

'Go jerk yourself.' Fegan was becoming emboldened, either by bluff or rationale. His posture, restricted as it was, suggested he wouldn't cave in easily.

Scott shifted so the narcotics dealer could see his every move. 'Have you ever had a general anaesthetic, Charlie? Maybe had your appendix out or your tonsils removed?' As he spoke he tightened a tourniquet round Fegan's right upper arm and waited for a vein to surface. Soon a deep-blue vessel bulged invitingly and Scott slipped a butterfly needle into place, then secured it to the arm with Micropore tape. Now he had ready access to Fegan's blood supply and could deliver whatever drug he chose with ease.

'So what are you, my personal physician?' Fegan's eyes followed Scott, the defiance not as aggressive as before. Scott drew up an ampoule of Maxolon and injected it, then waited for five minutes. The medication would speed up Fegan's stomach emptying with no effect on consciousness. Which is exactly what Scott wanted, teasing the pusher into a false sense of security. Higgins was back in his corner seat, inspecting the floor. It was becoming a pattern; at the first sign of needles the detective retreated quickly, keeping his eyes averted from the action. Scott checked his watch and decided now was the time to act. 'Last call, Charlie. Who's your supplier?'

'Fuck off.'

Scott stood to one side with a syringe full of clear fluid. 'I'm going to make you very sorry you didn't co-operate.' As the fluid was slowly squeezed into Fegan's body, his neck muscles tightened as he struggled to see what was going on. 'I'll fucking kill you, I will. With my own bare hands I'll strangle the fucking life out . . .' Suddenly the words trailed and on the trolley Fegan's body twitched and quivered as a fine tremor coursed through it.

Higgins glanced over, concerned at the dramatic drop in abuse from their prisoner. 'What's happening?'

'Our friend here is being paralysed,' explained Scott. 'But without sedation. His brain is perfectly clear and alert, and he can hear every word we're saying. But he's slowly losing power and gradually being deprived of oxygen.' Higgins crab-stepped closer, almost half afraid to watch. On the table Charlie Fegan's facial muscles rippled, his fingers jerked, his legs quivered. His eyes screamed for help but could not move. A blue tinge hit his lips first, then spread all over his exposed flesh. 'He can't breathe,' Scott explained as he looked on, apparently unconcerned, 'and while his respiratory drive is on full throttle his muscles can't work so he's unable to draw air into his lungs. Every organ in his body is screaming for oxygen but his chest cannot move up and down to draw it in. In three minutes he'll be brain-dead. In five minutes his internal organs will start to die from oxygen deprivation and in ten minutes' time Charlie will be a corpse.' Scott was following the time on his watch. It was now two minutes since the first ripples had coursed through Fegan, in sixty seconds if he didn't get air every cell in his body would start to disintegrate.

Charlie Fegan was already convinced he was dying. He was totally paralysed, unable to move the smallest finger muscle even though every fibre fought for power. The room around him, so bright when he'd first opened his eyes, was becoming darker. The gloom started at the periphery but was rapidly spreading inwards, while at the same time a strange humming sound filled his ears. He desperately wanted to close his eyes, to escape the frightening shadows swamping his senses, but he couldn't move a lid. The noise in his ears was now like an express train hurtling through a tunnel, becoming louder and louder. The room was totally dark, his dilated pupils seeing nothing. Though his consciousness was slipping fast, through the fog Fegan thought he was entering hell. If he could have opened his mouth his screams would have been heard for miles.

Looking on, Higgins was uneasy. Beneath him on the trolley Fegan's face was almost black from lack of oxygen and his pupils were an unhealthy dusky colour. On the nearby monitor alarm signals shrilled as the pusher's pulse raced and his blood pressure soared. 'Jesus, Scott.' Higgins grabbed at Scott's arm. 'Are you sure you know what you're doing?' He could see their first casualty looming and didn't know how to prevent it. The detective hopped from one foot to the other, his anxious gaze flicking from the black-faced prisoner to his partner. Scott calmly reached behind to the anaesthetic machine and flicked on the oxygen cylinder, then adjusted the gas flow to maximum. He inserted an oro-pharyngeal Perspex tube past Fegan's blue lips, twisting it until he had it positioned correctly. Then he forced an anaesthetic mask over Fegan's mouth and nose, and began artificially ventilating him, deliberately squeezing high levels of oxygen into the man's lungs. Within thirty seconds the deathly bluish-black colour disappeared and a pink blush surged through.

'See,' said Scott calmly as he continued to ventilate their

prisoner, 'there's a fine point between killing this man and just scaring the shit out of him. The drug I injected will wear off in a few minutes, allowing him to breathe on his own again. But Charlie has just been to the gates of hell and knows what colour they are.' He leaned down and shouted, 'Don't you, Charlie? You wouldn't like that darkness enveloping you again, would you?' The muscle relaxant was still active in Fegan's system and he could neither move nor blink an eye but every word was understood and he felt his bladder empty, his legs becoming warm and wet.

'Fuck this,' muttered Higgins as he lit up a cigarette and inhaled deeply, his nerves by now stretched to breaking point. 'I'm out of my depth here.'

Scott continued to squeeze the anaesthetic bag, checking his patient's pupils as they returned to normal. He inspected the monitor, noting a dramatic recovery in pulse and blood pressure, the alarm signals no longer flashing. 'This is where brain might work instead of brawn,' Scott suggested. 'If Charlie has any sense he'll tell us all we need to know, otherwise he goes into the dark again and this time he might not come back.'

Higgins drew deeply on his cigarette and opened a window, sucking on the fresh air for relief from the stuffy and overheated atmosphere of the chamber. 'Jesus,' he kept muttering, 'Jesus, Jesus, Jesus. What kind of a monster have I created?' Outside a cloudburst drilled off black cobblestones and in the distance thunder rumbled through heavy clouds. As Higgins glanced up at the darkening skies, a flash of sheet lightning lit up the gloom.

Charlie Fegan was chewing on the Perspex oro-pharyngeal tube, trying to spit it out of his mouth. Scott was standing behind, wafting the oxygen mask over his face and clearing mucus and spittle from his patient's lips. Fegan's chest heaved convulsively as his body struggled to take a voluntary breath and as the paralysing agent wore off the drug dealer's eyes began to move. Scott had never seen such fear before in all his life. Finally, with a convulsive cough and violent clearing of his throat, Fegan filled his lungs and held it there, before exhaling slowly. He gasped for more air and was able to reduce his oxygen need to short raspy pants. A few minutes later he felt power restored to his legs and arms, could wiggle his fingers and toes. His tongue loosened too. 'You fucking bastard.' He coughed and spluttered. 'You fucking whore of a bastard.' But Scott held up a syringe and waved it in front of the pusher's now bloodshot eyes. 'Like to go down the tunnel again?'

'Oh, Jesus, no.' Fegan's reserve collapsed completely. 'Don't do that again, don't fucking do that again.' Despite his weakened state the student's pleas echoed around the chamber.

17

Charles James Patrick Fegan was committed to a secure unit in a major south Dublin psychiatric hospital on the afternoon of 24 March. Earlier he'd been found wandering the downtown streets in a confused and disturbed state. The twenty-five-year-old student was unkempt, dishevelled and obviously incontinent of urine. His identity was read off a student ID and through university records police soon located his family who hurried to be with their son. But Charlie didn't recognise his parents, couldn't account for his movements over the previous twenty-four hours and seemed terrified. He repeatedly mumbled about a black tunnel and darkness and strangers out to get him, and eventually his distraught father agreed to a formal hospital committal.

In the psychiatric unit the admitting doctor struggled to make sense of Charlie's mental state. According to collateral history from his sister, the postgraduate student had left home in good spirits the previous day to attend college. He was clear and lucid in every way, discussing his plans for the coming weekend and moaning about his academic course workload. This was standard conversation in the Fegan household and certainly nothing out of the ordinary by any means. But then Charlie disappeared off the face of the earth, not answering his mobile phone, not ringing home and not returning that evening as usual. His parents formally notified Gardai and placed a missing person report at nine the next morning, after hours of frantic telephone calls to friends and neighbours and college authorities. Police made contact within the hour, setting their minds immediately at ease. Their son was alive. But when they called to identify him at a city centre station they were shocked by his physical and mental state, and Charlie Fegan was subsequently transferred to hospital around two that afternoon. By three o'clock the psychiatrist in charge had a working diagnosis of drug-induced paranoid schizophrenia, based on the needle tracks in his patient's arm, his delusional and psychotic state and fearful expressions of being under threat. However, the doctor was concerned there might be an organic cause for the student's sudden mental deterioration and ordered a CT scan of his brain. Fortunately this proved negative and Charlie was commenced on antipsychotics and placed in solitary confinement in an observation room. A full toxicology screen to identify the chemical agent involved came back negative, which was worrying. Some new street drug must have come on to the market, the psychiatrist explained to Charlie's parents. Something potent and as yet undetectable by our standard drug abuse testing. The doctor could offer no timescale as to when Charlie might regain his mental health; he was working in the unknown.

Convinced their son had indeed taken some chemical, Mr and Mrs Fegan besieged the authorities at Trinity College, where their beloved Charles studied. They berated the dean, accusing him of doing little to stop the scourge of narcotic abuse in the university and adding they considered him personally responsible for their son's crisis. They left after an hour, spent of vitriol but still angry and vengeful and threatening a lawsuit. The dean, a wise man in his mid fifties who'd heard this and many similar stories, sat back in his worn leather chair and reflected on the world and his role in it. He'd taken an earful of abuse from two well-meaning but totally misguided parents trying to defend their son. But the dean knew all about Charlie Fegan, how long he'd been plying his trade within the university walls, how much he charged and how he protected his illicit industry. As he gazed out on to a cobbled forecourt thronged with students going to and from lectures, he concluded Fegan had been sampling his own goods and lost the plot. Maybe this will be a wake-up call, he silently prayed. Maybe this will take him out of circulation behind these walls. If it doesn't, I certainly will.

At ten o'clock that same evening four men gathered for a second time in an airless room in the depths of government buildings close to Dublin city centre. Justice Minister Harry Power and Police Commissioner Peter Cunningham were there to hear the first briefing from their maverick covert unit. They sat round the same chipped Formica circular desk where one month earlier they'd argued over Scott Nolan's uncertain strategy.

Mark Higgins opened the meeting with a quick overview of their missions and the latest information bulletin. 'His name is Nick Ferguson and he's a significant Liverpool underworld figure who's moved in on the scene here. He bought two city centre public houses within the last nine months and both are known drug dens. The agency handling the sales says he paid over twenty million Euros. Liverpool police have passed on a mountain of background details and I spoke with one of their officers an hour ago. Ferguson is a ruthless thug who's been running heroin, cocaine and Ecstasy through a string of nightclubs for years. He's built up quite an empire and has a core of about ten close helpers who move the goods. Rumour has it Ferguson has at least two high-profile soccer players on his client list and relies on police informers for tip-offs. He's been lifted countless times and questioned but nothing can be linked directly to him. Legal advisers have repeatedly refused to take a weak case to the courts, so they're hanging on until they get a breakthrough.'

Cunningham sighed. 'That might explain why he's moved to this jurisdiction. Maybe things are becoming too hot for him in Liverpool.'

'I agree. But he can't just get off the boat and open up a case full of cocaine and start selling it on the roadside.'

Scott listened as the law enforcement officers interpreted the information he'd helped bring to the table. Charlie Fegan had spilled more information than either he or Higgins had anticipated, naming names, identifying sources and stunning both men with tales of ruthlessness in the market place since Harry Power's anti-drug campaign began. He told of jostling for territory and position as new dealers forced their way to the front in the drive to supply addicts. And behind the scenes there was considerable bloodletting and intimidation as small-time crooks struggled to protect their turf. Already five bodies had been buried in the concrete foundations of a major docklands development project and at least a dozen others had been beaten, kneecapped or threatened. The Dublin underworld was simmering.

'Ferguson offered cut-price cocaine to Fegan in exchange for a list of contacts. According to Fegan, Ferguson wants to expand his empire and he's in deep with at least one other player here. Unfortunately he didn't know a name or anything about him.'

Power leaned across the table, his large frame throwing shadows under the overhead lights. 'Do you think he was holding back?'

At this Higgins and Scott exchanged knowing glances. 'Not a chance,' Scott answered this time, 'I've never seen anyone so scared. I'd say we got as much out of him as he knew.'

The Police Commissioner inspected the two men, his penetrating stare appraising both closely. 'What did you use to loosen his tongue?'

Scott let the question hang in the air for about twenty seconds before replying. 'An anaesthetic muscular relaxant called Scoline. Basically I paralysed him so deeply he couldn't breathe, then lifted him from the brink of death with forced oxygen.'

'Jesus Christ,' muttered Cunningham, 'I wish I hadn't asked.'

'But it worked.' Scott sounded aggrieved, as if his strategy were being challenged all over again. 'Fegan opened up and we learned more in one hour than might otherwise have taken months.'

'OK, OK.' The Commissioner obviously didn't want to hear more details of operational tactics. 'What's the next move?'

Higgins drew himself to his full size and faced his superior. 'We want to take Ferguson out. We need to know who he's teamed up with; that information alone could give us a whole new perspective on the drug scene here.'

'When?'

'As soon as we have an exit strategy. It's one thing tracking him down, now we know his movements, but it's another grabbing him without being seen or caught.'

'Do you feel confident you can do this, or should we just arrest the bastard and interrogate him?' Power's features reflected his concern.

'No.' Scott was emphatic. 'We'll get nothing that way. If Liverpool police can't pin anything on him I can't see us having better luck with standard procedures. I say we continue as planned.' Beside him Higgins nodded.

Cunningham dragged a briefcase on to the table and snapped open the locks. From inside he pulled out paperwork and black-and-white photographs. He slid two across the table, one to Scott and the other to Power. 'Those are stills from a CCTV at Bangkok International Airport,' he explained. 'On 5 March we received a report from local police of a possible sighting of the man we want to interview in connection with the shootings last February.' Across the table three sets of eyes suddenly fixed on the Commissioner. 'I asked for further information and our Thai colleagues sent a ten-page fax of potentially vital details, and couriered CCTV tapes and still photos. A man answering the description of our assassin flew into Bangkok on 24 February. He was stopped and questioned at customs but not detained.'

'Why was he stopped?' Scott was almost on top of the table, his hands gripping the edge, his face muscles rigid.

'There is an international arrest warrant in circulation for our suspect and border control guards in most countries are screening passengers on our behalf, often doing random checks. In Bangkok the customs official felt this particular man was acting suspiciously. He seemed edgy, uneasy. And he had a limp.'

'Jesus Christ,' Power's exclamation echoed everyone's thoughts.

'However, he let him through but made a note of where he

was staying and passed details to police HQ. The next day an armed unit of the CSD took his hotel room apart and searched his personal belongings. They soon found he was travelling on a false passport and using bogus business details. Subsequently they learned he was seen in the company of a man called Toby Wurschanda, a well-known narcotics dealer. Wurschanda owns a string of massage parlours and it's believed he launders most of his drug money through them. No one saw our mystery man again after that and certainly he didn't leave the country using the passport he came in on.'

Scott was inspecting the grainy black-and-white image in front of him, aware that Higgins was craning to see over his shoulder. The man at Bangkok airport was almost bald, whereas the photofit profile suggested a full head of hair pulled back into a ponytail. But that wasn't vital; Scott himself had successfully changed his identity using a similar ploy. But it was the facial features, the narrow profile and the tight lips, that grabbed Scott's attention. He couldn't see the eyes and had to imagine the full body picture. But what he stared at was uncannily close to the man he so desperately sought.

'If he was allowed through customs why did they go after him?' Power's hands were trembling, his eyes darting from the photo to the Commissioner.

Cunningham rocked back and forth in his chair. His hands were folded, his lips pursed. 'The officer challenged him but his story and documents seemed genuine. He was a thirty-one-year-old white male Irish citizen called Ronald O'Leary, there on business to buy teak furniture from a reputable city dealer. When specifically asked about a limb weakness the suspect was able to walk away with no obvious limp. However, when CCTV recordings at baggage control were later reviewed the target could be clearly identified dragging his left leg.'

'Left leg?' Scott's voice was raised, his heart pounding as the jigsaw of the Commissioner's story began to come together.

'Yes, like the man who murdered your wife.'

Power wiped at sweat collecting on his brow. 'Jesus Christ,' he muttered again.

'Now maybe I'm putting two and two together,' Cunningham continued, 'and coming up with ten but there's so much coming out of the woodwork that alarm bells are ringing. Bangkok police say Toby Wurschanda only deals with top players in international narcotics. We now know someone answering the description of our main suspect met up with him a month ago and then disappeared as law enforcement officers closed in. Also, this man had a counterfeit passport and fake documentation. That combination suggests Wurschanda wanted him protected and shipped out of the country as soon as possible. It further suggests they were planning something, possibly a drugs haul from Thailand to Europe. Now tonight I'm hearing about new and significant players entering the local scene, even cocaine offered at low prices to open up the market.' Cunningham stopped rocking and looked deliberately across the table at his rapt audience. 'There's something in the air, I can sense it. There are too many loose ends coming together and I can't help but feel the attacks last February were not revenge or scare tactics. I think the killer was setting us up to clean out the opposition. If so, he succeeded admirably. And my gut instinct is he's coming back to reap his rewards.'

In Amsterdam, Sean Kennedy lay in his loft apartment smoking a joint and sipping beer. And thinking. Money was flowing from country to country at a rapid rate. Derek McCann and his new Liverpool business partner, Nick

Ferguson, had collected advances from a number of dealers down the line, all expecting an imminent and significant inflow of drugs. Days later McCann and Ferguson transferred ten million US dollars from a number of offshore banking accounts to a holding trust Kennedy and Jay Davis traded from in Zurich. Funds from this account in turn had moved to Bangkok, Miami, Lichtenstein and the Cayman Islands. Discreet calls across the globe confirmed that a major consignment of cocaine was en route from South America to Rotterdam. There was also a separate cargo of heroin and amphetamines concealed in teak furniture being ferried through Laos and Cambodia, ready for eventual shipment to the Dutch port. Allowing for weather and delivery timetables, both hauls were scheduled for offloading on 6 April. The master plan Kennedy and Davis had worked on so carefully for so long was finally coming to an end.

In Marbella in the south of Spain, Jay Davis was thinking about the future. He gazed out at a sunless sky from a harbour café in the seaside village of Puerto Banus, thirty miles along the coast from Marbella, sipping an espresso and eyeing a young blonde leaning over protective rails about ten yards away. The more she leaned the more her short skirt rode up at the back and Davis silently pleaded for an extra inch. 'Another coffee, sir?' Davis ignored the waiter, his eyes fixed on the vision in front. In between images of lustful intent, Davis plotted how he would spend his split of he profits once their shipment had landed. But the sight of the edge of a pair of black frilly panties was too much and Davis slipped a ten Euro note under his coffee cup and bustled past other customers to get outside. 'You should be careful,' he cautioned as he placed a hand lightly on the blonde's right arm, 'pickpockets could have snatched your purse while you weren't looking.' The young woman quickly checked her shoulder bag and sighed with relief it hadn't been touched. Davis pointed at one of the luxury yachts berthed along the quayside further along. 'That one came in overnight. Locals say Justin Timberlake was on it.'

The girl's eyes widened with surprise and awe. 'Really? Did you actually see him?'

Davis shook his head, a hand dragging his thick locks into shape. He took the young woman's right arm, steering her along the quayside. 'This place is full of mystery and intrigue. Now, see that cruiser . . .' His free hand brushed against the blonde's bottom, his mind already easing her black panties slowly downwards.

18

It was unusually warm on 26 March on the east coast of Ireland, with temperatures reaching eighteen degrees centigrade, as recorded by the Dublin weather centre. For once the skies were clear, with only fluffy cotton wool clouds rolling lazily overland from the south, blown off course by continental air currents. Daffodils were in bloom, their vivid colours further brightening the sunlit morning and lifting everyone's spirits. Crocuses, battered by weeks of wind and rain, seemed to shake themselves dry and flaunt their displays as if to say winter is over, let spring begin. The feel-good factor was everywhere and the citizens of Dublin relaxed as they strolled in municipal parks and pedestrian thoroughfares. It had been a difficult few months since Christmas. A bitterly cold and uncertain climate had dragged on longer than usual. But now the dark evenings were shortening, the days getting longer, the weather changing. Some reports even suggested it was safe to walk the streets at night but few were prepared to risk that degree of optimism.

Maybe some day, but not just yet. Perhaps when the summer really came.

'It's an ideal spot. You can't see a thing from the road through those trees and you'd need to know where that trail is to get in. No one could stumble down here by mistake.' Derek McCann was showing his Liverpool business partner, Nick Ferguson, the remote storage depot he'd rented.

Ferguson glanced around the clearing, face creased in thought. 'Where the fuck are we anyway?' His accent was Scouse through and through, thick enough to cut with a knife.

McCann waved a hand southwards. 'The main motorway into Dublin is about two miles in that direction. The slip road we came off leads into the town land of Clonart, about five miles away. It's no more than a pub and a post office and a few houses. This is probably the most desolate and isolated spot in all of County Meath.' McCann was smiling, a too-tight sweater stretched over his paunch, his receding hair slicked flat on his head. It was two thirty in the afternoon and apart from a gentle breeze rustling through surrounding woodland the glade was quiet and peaceful. The run-down CLONART FERTILISER SUPPLIES building was now IRISH TEAK FURNITURE TRADERS, repainted in snot-green with the original doors replaced and now securely held closed by strong locks and bolts. At the end of twenty-foot chains, two lean and hungry-looking Alsatians threatened to take a chunk out of any intruders. 'They go on longer leads when there's no one around,' McCann explained helpfully, noticing Ferguson retreat out of harm's way. 'I keep them half starved and put a tablet of speed in each of their feed bowls. It drives them mad, you should see it. They froth at the mouth and race around in circles trying to bite their own arses. Christ knows what would happen if they lit on someone.'

Ferguson was the same height and age as McCann, both an inch or so below six feet and in their late fifties. But Ferguson was a whippet compared with the overweight Irishman. He was dressed in navy corduroy trousers and a white long-sleeved shirt open at the neck. Over one shoulder he held a leather jacket, a pair of sunglasses sticking out of a side pocket. The Liverpool thug had a gaunt, hollow-cheeked face with deep pockmarks and a V-shaped scar to the left of his forehead. With shaven hair, crooked nose and neck tattoo he looked as intimidating as the reputation that preceded him. He skirted his way out of the range of the guard dogs and inspected the locks on the large wooden doors, pulling and dragging at them until he grunted his approval. Then he stood back from the building and squinted at the roof and side walls, before disappearing out of view. One minute later he was back beside McCann. 'There's no fuckin' windows.'

'And we're not putting in any.' McCann was glaring at Ferguson as if he were challenging his manhood. 'What do you want windows for? It'll only encourage burglaries.'

'Yeah, I know that. But how d'ye see inside? There's gonna be a lorra work done in there. We need to get rid of the shitty furniture and then start breakin' up the good stuff into smaller deals. I hate workin' under floodlights, fuckin' hate it.'

McCann resisted the urge to tell Ferguson to bugger off back to Liverpool and play with himself. He needed the Scouse heavyweight for muscle and money, the deal coming through was turning out much bigger than anything he'd handled before. Involving Ferguson gave him extra protection at a time when the Dublin underworld was rippling with change. And the finances helped McCann spread the risk. 'Well, it's too late to start pulling this dump apart.' He turned away to hide his anger. 'We're only three weeks from delivery. Give or take a few days to get the gear unloaded and burn the furniture, I'd say we could be out of here in a month. I'm not risking workmen hanging around putting in windows; there'd be too many questions, too much pub talk.'

Ferguson thought this over. 'Yeah, mebbe yer right. We'll leave it.' Suddenly one of the Alsatians made a lunge, its neck jerked backwards sharply as the leash was strained to its limit. An angry snarl was strangled to a whine and Ferguson almost tumbled over, swinging his leather jacket as a shield and waving it in front of the snapping jaws. His sunglasses fell out and a drooling bite snatched them up, chewed briefly, then they were spat back on to the dirt. 'The fuckin' bastard,' Ferguson swore viciously, 'those shades cost me over a hundred quid. I'll kill that fuckin' mongrel, I will.'

McCann's eyes disappeared towards heaven. What a wanker. 'Leave it, Nick. Let's go before the traffic builds up.' The Alsatians started racing up and down, barking and growling, saliva dripping from their bared fangs. The leashes were at full stretch, and McCann and Ferguson quickly cut their losses and jumped into the Irishman's new metallic-silver Mercedes 500. He drove cautiously away from the clearing over a narrow potholed track until they reached a side road. Then he glanced backwards, shaking his head. 'Great spot though, isn't it?'

Ferguson was fiddling with his seat belt, still cursing the loss of his sunglasses. 'Ye better feed those dogs, Derek. I'm not havin' me arse ripped out every time I go in there.'

McCann put his foot to the board and the powerful car surged forward, rear wheels spinning on grit. 'I'll let you shoot them when we've finished.'

Ferguson looked across, a grin spreading over his ugly face. 'Good idea, Derek my friend. I'd like that. Fuckin' would.'

For the next hour the two threaded their way through the early evening rush hour into Dublin, discussing the deals, their clients and the two men who were going to make them very rich. Ferguson made a passing comment about one of his middlemen, Charlie Fegan, losing his mind but the aside was dismissed. Middlemen were expendable. Near the city centre Ferguson called in to one of his new purchases, the Green Man pub, a criminal underworld haunt with a reputation for drug dealing and bar room brawls. After a quick check on the day's takings, he was back in McCann's silver Mercedes. Neither noticed the navy transit van that pulled out from behind a yellow skip and began to follow them. The Mercedes was pushed through two amber lights and one red at a dangerous junction before McCann eased into a long stretch of carriageway stretching west.

'Who's the fella besides Davis?' Ferguson had found the reclining button and was smoking a cheroot while he studied the roof padding.

McCann had been dreading this question, avoiding all mention of Sean Kennedy. Since he'd decided Kennedy was indeed the main player behind the assassination attempt on Harry Power he realised just how dangerous the young Dubliner was – more than he'd even considered before, which was saying a lot. To McCann, Kennedy was a loose cannon and a psychopath as well. So explosive was this combination that he believed the fewer who knew about him the better. That way they'd both get to stay alive. 'I don't know his real name,' he lied. 'And I wouldn't waste your brain with the number of aliases he's used over the years. He's a loner, very secretive and keeps everything tight to his chest. You only know he's been involved in something when it's over and the money's being counted or the dead are being buried.'

Beside him Ferguson's eyebrows arched. 'Tough tout, is he?'

McCann overtook a delivery lorry and cruised past a crowd gathered in the dusk at a bus shelter. Loitering around the glow from pub doors, thirsty punters took advantage of the warm weather and sipped their drinks, idly watching the crawl of headlights snake by. 'Not to be crossed, Nick. He's the one link in this chain I'm not happy about. If he took the hump he'd start World War Three and not give a fuck. Once we've got the goods and he's paid, good riddance to the bastard.'

They stopped at a red light in the west of the city, McCann with one foot on the brake and itching to put the boot to the board. The shadows were lengthening as street lamps flickered, then spluttered into life, and McCann idly studied the glowing dashboard on his new car, admiring the cockpit-like instrumentation. Ferguson was beginning to irritate him and he wanted to let him off as soon as possible. A navy transit with tinted windows was right behind but he couldn't see the driver- or passenger-side and for a moment he wondered why the van needed tinted windows. The lights changed and he was off again, the transit staying in the same lane, but at a reasonable distance behind.

'What if we don't pay the second instalment?' Ferguson was now staring out of the side window, face furrowed in thought.

McCann nearly rear-ended the car in front. 'What? Are

you out of your mind? You don't now what you're dealing with here. That bastard's evil, he likes killing people. I think it's his bloody limp that has him so fucking sour.'

Ferguson glanced across, cheroot smoke drifting into his eyes. 'Has a limp, has he? Weak leg means weak mind. Mebbe we should put him to the test, Derek my friend.'

Fuck you, Nick my friend, thought McCann as he slowed down outside a well-known pub-cum-brothel in the suburb of Blackcastle. The navy transit skewed past so close it clipped the Mercedes side mirror but McCann paid no attention. He was having second thoughts about the wisdom of inviting his Scouse business partner into his venture. Double crossing Sean Kennedy? Try that on your own, Nick. He let Ferguson out at the brothel entrance and the Scouser skipped up the stairs in an obvious hurry.

'How long do you think he'll be in there?' Scott sipped a McDonald's strawberry milk shake, squinting out through a narrow gap he'd allowed in his side window.

Higgins's mouth was full of hamburger, ketchup stains smearing his upper lip. He continued chewing for a full three minutes, swallowed heavily, then reached for his large Pepsi. He sucked on the straw noisily, chasing the dregs round the bottom of the cardboard beaker. 'How should I know?' he growled. 'How long does it take any man to have a ride? It depends on what mood he's in. Is it a quickie, then a pint and a packet of crisps and watch the soccer downstairs? Or maybe he's into whips and chains, in which case we'll be eating our breakfast out of the back of this van.'

Scott looked around the front of the cab with distaste. Since the transit had become their main form of transport and observation post, most meals and snacks were consumed there. On the floor lay countless empty packets of crisps, chocolate bar wrappers, drink cartons and the odd French fry. Behind, where their hostages were carried, more litter lay scattered. Beer cans, large grease-stained brown bags from Indian and Chinese takeaway food, countless paper cups. 'This place is beginning to stink. I don't think I could spend a whole night here without getting sick.'

Higgins was picking at his teeth with the end of a matchstick. 'This is what covert missions are all about, doc. You have to lie low and rough it out for days until the right opportunity strikes. And with Ferguson we can't afford to take chances, he's too mean a bastard. If we get fed up and rush we could lose everything and get our asses shot.' He charged up his mobile phone and called HQ, passing on registration details of the silver Mercedes 500 and requesting an ID.

Scott half listened in to the exchanges, more concerned with the pub and its first level. They were edged into the darkest corner of a large car park, surrounded by vehicles of every make, ranging from expensive and showroom-clean BMWs to mud-caked Hiace trucks. The pub, called the Blackcastle Arms, was a popular watering hole in west Dublin with three lounges showing English premier league soccer on wide-screen televisions, then two smaller public bars with traditional smoke-stained mahogany counters and stained-glass snugs. Through a separate side entrance a neon sign proclaimed Westside Nite Club and here, via a rickety set of stairs, clients could enjoy a late drink and dance. But behind the façade of a sparsely furnished cocktail room was the equally well known but unmarked Westside brothel, a series of cubicles and narrow beds where young women, usually from Eastern Europe, offered a range of sexual favours for the right price. The first floor was open twenty-four hours a day and produced almost as much profit as the boozy establishment below.

'Right kip, isn't it?' Higgins followed Scott's gaze, squinting against the security lights now flooding the building. He jammed a CD into the disc tray and fiddled with the control panel.

Scott's heart sank. 'This isn't another one of your Country and Western specials?' he groaned. 'I don't think I could take another second of that crap.' His protests were drowned out as the van filled with the gravel-voiced Willie Nelson complaining of lost love in some Midwest township. Higgins turned the volume up slightly, grinning from ear to ear. He drummed his fingers on the steering wheel, then joined in the chorus like a cat being garrotted. Scott buried his head in his hands and wished the night away.

Suddenly the music stopped and Scott glanced over to find Higgins staring at him. 'What music do you like, doc? What movies do you go to, what kind of life do you lead outside hospital?' He eased himself back in the driver's seat, one shoulder resting on the side door so he had a good view of the pub and its upstairs whorehouse. Two burly bouncers dressed in black now guarded the narrow entrance, stopping every client and checking their bona fides. So far only three, including Nick Ferguson, had been allowed upstairs. 'Tell me more about yourself. I'd sure as hell like to know what Laura saw in you.'

Scott wriggled his backside into a more comfortable position and jammed his knees against the dash. What is he getting at? Since when did he start taking a sudden interest in me? I'm only a means to an end in his game, once I gather the intelligence he'll dump me. Scott decided to play Higgins along.

'Bruce Springsteen, the Beatles, Frank Sinatra,' he started.

'Frank Sinatra!' His brother-in-law couldn't hold back his scorn. 'Jesus Christ, what age are you anyway?'

'He's a classic, a legend and a damned sight better than that bloody rubbish you torture me with.'

'We'll agree to disagree on Frankie boy. How about films, what was the last movie you saw?' Higgins was wiping ketchup stains from his lips and inspecting the tissue.

Scott considered the question for a minute, his eyes scrunched as he struggled to remember the most recent visit to a cinema. Then it hit him. It was with Laura, at a multiplex in downtown Dublin, maybe a week before she was murdered. 'Laura liked romantic films, period dramas with lavish costumes and where the Queen's English was spoken as she argued it should be. She adored Jane Austen and Emily Brontë and reread their novels time after time. So the last actual movie I sat through was a modern version of *Wuthering Heights*. I spent half the time asleep but she was totally captivated and snuffled away into her tissues.'

Higgins made a noise that sounded like agreement, a mixture between a grunt and a groan. 'That was my Laura all right. Lived her life like she was born into the wrong century. Couldn't tolerate bad language and gave out to me constantly about my personal habits.' The grunt-cum-groan sounded again. 'Jesus, but I miss her.'

The barely suppressed emotions from his street-hardened brother-in-law caught Scott by surprise but he pretended not to notice. He swallowed hard and fiddled with the side window to disguise his own smarting eyes.

'Do you know why she fell for you?' Higgins was staring intently across the cab, both men shaded by the outside gloom.

Scott angled himself against the side door for comfort but couldn't bring himself to face his partner. What bile is he likely to throw at me now? This can't be a compliment coming up. 'No. Do you?'

Suddenly outside Higgins spotted a car edge out from a row of vehicles close to the side entrance of the Westside Nite Club and he gunned the engine alive. He drove slowly towards the vacant space, eyes fixed ahead, continuing the conversation out of the corner of his mouth. 'The two of you had a big date; she wanted to take you to an exhibition of some French painter . . .'

'Monet.' Scott remembered it immediately.

'Wha'? Money who?' The transit was close to the parking space and Higgins was reversing. The first effort was too close to one side and he swore softly, then moved out for another go.

'Monet. That was the name of the painter. He was an Impressionist.'

'Could be,' agreed Higgins, now aligning the van so there was space on both sides. 'Impressionist, expressionist, depressionist. How the hell would I know? That's not my territory. But she liked him and wanted to educate you in fine arts.'

It all came rushing back. There was a two-week showcase of Monet's years at Giverny in town and Laura insisted she take Scott along, despite his obvious lack of enthusiasm. Hospital work was extremely busy – with so little time out he cherished any free moment, usually taking in a local ball game or hanging loose with his colleagues in a nearby bar. But secretly Laura was trying to decide if he had a more sensitive side. Was there life beyond liver damage, transplants, X-rays and pathology reports? Could she lift his level of conversation above medicine? It was their third meeting and he was already besotted with the young Irishwoman, though unsure if he could hold on to one so lively. Her free spirit and stunning beauty enthralled him, but her attempts to educate caused early friction. Laura dragged him to the theatre (boring), art galleries (waste of good wall space) and even bought him books – Hemingway, Fitzgerald, Joyce – to educate his mind (discarded). He was a doctor and medicine was all consuming, filling up even his spare moments. When he left the wards he couldn't discard the images of children under his care, their illnesses and progression or deterioration followed him everywhere. Occasionally, in the middle of a meal or drink he'd make a feeble excuse just to call in and check his charges, maybe even change their treatment schedule. So Laura Higgins was beginning to grasp what life as the partner of a dedicated medic might be like and she wasn't totally enamoured with the scenario.

Higgins cut the engine and opened his side window, lighting up his sixth cigarette in an hour. Scott wound down his window fully, to escape the fumes. His clothes already stank of smoke and when he showered each night he could almost taste tobacco in his mouth as the shampoo rolled down his face. 'Anyway, she was waiting for you in some coffee bar opposite the hospital.'

'Starbucks.'

'Whatever. Laura sat and drank about six mugs of coffee and read the papers from cover to cover, all the time looking for her date. After an hour she finally decided she'd had enough and you and she were history as far as she was concerned. But she wasn't the sort of girl to get stood up, most men crawled on their knees just to get a chance to say hello. So she took your delay as a personal insult.'

Scott listened without interrupting. He could imagine

Laura crouched against the side window of the coffee house, angrily staring at the main entrance of the hospital opposite, willing him to turn up. And remembering her fiery spirit he knew she'd have been ready to snap his head off if he had appeared, no matter how apologetic.

'So she stomped across the road, called up the nursing station and demanded to know what you were up to. Apparently the sister in charge said you were still on the ward and not to be disturbed. But that didn't stop our Laura, oh no. She had the idea you might have been muttering sweet nothings into some other girl's ears, maybe even having a swiftie behind the curtains.'

Scott groaned and Higgins chuckled at this revelation. But the detective's attention was also fixed on the front door of the Westside Nite Club. The bouncers had split up, one moving through the car park, inspecting car registrations and making notes while the other continued his vigil at the front door. No one else had gone past since Ferguson.

'She pushed through security guards on each level and made her way to the unit you were working on. Now, according to Laura, you were sitting at the bedside of some very sick kid, holding her hand and talking quietly to her, totally oblivious your girlfriend was looking on.'

'The child's parents were there too,' Scott mumbled, as the distant memory now flooded his brain. 'She was celebrating her twelfth birthday on her deathbed and I couldn't do a thing to save her life.'

'Laura kept watch from a distance. One of the nurses even gave her a gown and face mask to help her blend into the background. She told me you stayed with the family for two hours, explaining and coaxing and trying to make that kid's last hours as comfortable as possible. When you got up to leave you were three hours late for your date and looked like a wet rag.'

'And Laura was waiting for me outside when I finally finished. She took me back to her place . . .'

'Now the rest I don't wanna know,' snapped Higgins. 'It's my sister we're talking about here.'

'Nothing happened. That's the whole point. She bought a bottle of wine, made me dinner, ran a bath and told me to go to bed for a rest. I woke up very early some time the next morning and she was fast asleep on the couch. I just sat on my hunkers beside her and stared at her for hours, thinking how beautiful she was.'

'Well, that episode had a major impact on her, doc. Laura told me she'd never seen a man who cared for children as much as you. Sure, you were no movie star and looked like a scarecrow most of the time, but you had something very basic she fell for. She decided you were a good man and wanted her children by you and you only. And she could have had anybody, big shots with lots of money and big houses, driving fancy cars.' He stopped briefly, squinting out of the side window. 'Personally I think it makes you look like a big sissy.'

There was a strained silence, both men stifling their simmering emotions. Then suddenly Higgins opened the driver's side door and edged himself out. 'That's the end of the sob story. In a few minutes you're going to hear a fucking big explosion and somewhere in the corner of this park a car of my choice is going to go up in flames. As soon as that happens you make a run for that entrance and I'll be hot on your heels. I reckon we've got five minutes max to get Ferguson out of that whorehouse before his goons know what's going on.' He slid open the left side panel and fiddled inside a sports bag he carried until he found what he needed. 'Get your gun out and prepare for action. Whether you're God's gift to women and children or not won't count a damn once we go for this Scouse bastard.'

19

It took Mark Higgins less than five seconds to force open the petrol cap of a fancy-looking Audi soft-top coupé he'd had his eye on about fifty yards to his right. Then, using an unwound wire coat hanger, he shoved a strip of rag down the funnel until he sensed he was in the fuel tank. A quick glance sideways and he spotted the bulky shape of the forecourt patrol bouncer, now less than ten feet away and admiring the sleek lines of a red Porsche. In the gloom he could just about make out a hawk-like face and a cluster of ear studs. Higgins flicked a cigarette into his mouth, snapped a lighter and lit up, relaxing against the boot of the Audi like a man out for a quiet smoke. He took two deep drags, then turned the glowing tip towards the now damp rag and there was an immediate flare as it caught fire, followed by a two-second delay as the flames funnelled deeper. Higgins was already on the ground and rolling furiously away when the Audi exploded in a fireball. The Blackcastle Arms car park suddenly lit up with the intensity of the blaze and very soon paintwork on vehicles close to the conflagration blistered. Within minutes tongues of fire were licking around the rubber tyres of a hackney cab and a separate plume of dark smoke began billowing into the night sky. Then the hackney's fuel line overheated and another blaze started. The once dark corner was now an amber glow and Higgins thought he'd never seen a finer sight in all his life.

But he didn't hang around to enjoy the pyrotechnics. Ahead he spotted the hunched figure of Scott Nolan rushing through the narrow doorway of the Westside Nite Club, its one security guard barking into a mobile phone and looking for help in the opposite direction. Higgins sprinted as fast as his cigarette-inflamed lungs would allow and within a minute was halfway up the rickety stairs, balaclava on and handgun drawn. Behind him he heard two more muffled explosions and an increasingly loud babble of agitated shouts.

The small cocktail bar of the Westside Nite Club reflected its function as a front for a brothel. Jammed against adjoining walls two deep semicircular red velvet couches faced the drinks area, itself no more than a narrow counter before an array of bottles in front of long reflective glass. Wall mirrors caught and reflected subdued lighting, making the tight space seem only slightly bigger. Soft music drifted from some corner and the smell of hashish and incense filled the air. Two middle-aged men in suits lay slumped into the couches, one nursing a flute of champagne and drawing hungrily on a reefer while the other nibbled the ear of a dark-haired beauty in a black mesh bodysuit, which did little to cover her considerable physical assets. Behind the counter a bored and busty blonde smoked a cigarette, looking on with ill-disguised contempt.

For this intimate group all hell erupted the moment Scott

burst through. In his all-black attire with ski cap pulled firmly down to his eyes he made an immediate and frightening impression. But it was the Beretta brandished in his right hand that caught everyone's attention. He discharged one round into the ceiling, showering the floor with plasterwork and causing one of the suits to dive for cover. 'Stay where you are, everybody,' he roared, the gun swivelling from side to side as he searched desperately for his target. 'One stupid move and your heads are full of holes.' His heart was pounding and his mouth was dry despite the shouts of bravado and he had to control his shaking hands. Out of the corner of an eye he saw the barmaid reach for a phone and he squeezed off another round over her head, shattering the glass behind.

Shards and splinters crashed from the wall just as Higgins kicked his way into the room, handgun pointing directly at the first face he saw. He took in the scene in seconds. 'He's not here. Out the back, go out the back,' he yelled as he let loose two quick rounds to keep the audience on heightened fear. The black-meshed beauty was now cowering in a corner, shouting something unintelligible, while her client was spreadeagled on the floor, both arms out fully and head face down. The second suit just sat on the couch, ashen-faced and shaking, flakes of plasterwork like dandruff on his shoulders. The barmaid had disappeared behind the counter and the once cosy lounge resembled a war zone, with shattered glass, walls and ceiling raked with gunfire. From outside came the unmistakable clamour of sirens, frantic shouts and muffled explosions.

Nick Ferguson didn't really know what was going on. The Scouse thug had both nostrils full of cocaine and was in post-orgasmic bliss when the black shape of Scott Nolan loomed.

Ferguson was naked under a red silk sheet, his clothes scattered to one side of the cubicle in which he lay with an olive-skinned Eastern beauty also spaced out on drugs. She moaned and crooned and played with her hair, oblivious to the chaos around her. Ferguson was sprawled on his back, both legs splayed wide, head resting on soft pillows, a crumpled silver foil with powder traces still gripped between two fingers. Despite the commotion he continued to stare at the ceiling, his bloodshot eyes rolling in their sockets. 'What the fuck's goin' on, squire?' The slurred speech exaggerated his thick Liverpool accent even further. 'Is somebody throwin' a party?' He didn't see the auto-injector in Scott's hands, nor sense the wide arc as light caught its glinting steel tip. He didn't feel the needle enter his bony buttocks but within thirty seconds his body began to shake and quiver, his muscles rippled and he effectively lost all strength.

Scott's ears rang as another round was discharged from a few feet behind and he turned to see the shape of Mark Higgins, dancing agitatedly from foot to foot. 'C'me on for fuck's sake. Get him out of here.'

The detective's voice was shrill and suddenly Scott realised how vulnerable they were, stuck on an upstairs level with only rickety stairs for exit. For the first time he could hear the clamour from the car park and the noise spurred him on. 'You're stronger,' he shouted. 'Wrap him in the sheet and carry him. I'll go in front and take the head off anyone who gets in the way.' Even in the gloom Scott could sense Higgins's uncertainty, then the detective grabbed the red silk sheet and rolled the limp body of Nick Ferguson twice until he was covered. The olive-skinned girl just curled up in a naked ball, her mind still lost in whatever world her drug-soaked brain had carried her.

Grunting and cursing from the effort, Higgins managed to manoeuvre the limp body of Ferguson on to his left shoulder, then kick his way back into the front bar. It was deserted and the only sound came from desperate stumbling on the stairwell leading to street level. 'Go, go,' he shouted and Scott flicked fallen debris away with his foot to clear a path. Behind, Higgins was struggling under the weight of his latest hostage, panting in laboured gasps of breath. 'Fuck it, fuck it,' he spluttered, 'keep going for Christ's sake.'

They reached the top of the narrow staircase in time to see the halfway point blocked by the broad-shouldered frame of one of the club bouncers. In the light his features became clear, buzz-cut ginger hair, bulbous nose, pock-marked skin and an astonished expression as he suddenly realised what was coming at him. Scott sensed him reach inside a side pocket and pointed his Beretta straight ahead. 'Back off, I'm warning you. Keep going and don't turn away from me or you're dead meat.' He felt Higgins behind and switched the Beretta from his left to his right hand as the bouncer hesitated.

'Shoot the bastard,' roared Higgins and Scott fired one round into the cracked and badly painted ceiling. The bouncer almost fell down the rest of the steps as he scrambled frantically for safety.

They paused only for seconds at the ground-floor entrance; enough to allow Scott to squint round both corners and check they weren't falling into a hostile waiting party. But the car park was heaving with activity as patrons fought to rescue their vehicles from the inferno that now filled one corner. Black plumes of smoke billowed across the forecourt, obscuring vision and adding to the confusion. In the distance Scott could see the flashing lights of rescue services, hear the wail of sirens and sense the pandemonium. 'Let's go,' he shouted over his shoulder and stood back, handgun at the ready, to allow Higgins forward. Thirty seconds later a side panel of the transit was slid open and Higgins rolled on to the mattress, dragging the dead weight of Ferguson beside him. By now Scott was in the driver's seat and gunning the engine alive. As confused customers of the Blackcastle Arms bumped into each other in their haste to escape in the frenzied exodus, Scott tried edging the transit outwards but found his way blocked by a line of stalled vehicles. Horns blared and curses filled the air as drivers stood at the side of their cars trying to see a way past the obstruction. The mood of vicious bad temper was palpable and for a brief moment Scott was at a loss to decide how to escape. Then one of the bouncers appeared at his side window, dragging at the door handle, his face twisted in fury and mouthing obscenities.

Seconds later the hawk-faced heavyweight appeared at the passenger side and succeeded in pulling open the door. 'You fucking bastar—' Suddenly he found Higgins's 9mm Walther almost inside his mouth and fell backwards, rolling along the ground to put distance between him and the gun. Immediately Higgins spun, took careful aim through the driver's side and squeezed off a single round that cracked through the toughened glass. Now the van was free and the line of cars in front melted as Scott deliberately crashed into one after another until he cleared a run along the edge of the pub and finally found a makeshift exit by racing over flowerbeds and smashing through a wooden fence. Then the transit was on an adjacent playing field and bumping its way towards a side road and safety. But watching from a short distance behind, a swarthy male in all-leather gear and protective helmet revved the engine of a high-powered motorbike and set off after them.

They took the main road eastwards from Blackcastle towards Dublin city centre, running against the flow of commuter traffic and making good speed. Scott switched lanes and overtook on the inside, oblivious to the angry horns being sounded in his wake. He reckoned they were about thirty minutes from police HQ and their interrogation chamber. Nick Ferguson was already spaced out and was also considerably older than the first two dealers they'd lifted, so the potential for adverse drug interactions was a real possibility and Scott didn't want the Liverpool thug suffering some dangerous side effects. Not only would his loss negate their promises to the Justice Minister and Police Commissioner, but they would also lose whatever information Ferguson might spill.

'How's he doing?' Scott shouted. Outside, the two-lane highway was running without hindrance and the transit was being given plenty of freedom as it lurched from right to left, depending on how the spaces ahead opened up.

'He's out cold.' Higgins was on his knees at the rear and keeping a close watch on traffic behind.

'But he's breathing? He's not blue or frothing at the mouth?'

Higgins rolled the now comatose drug dealer on to his back and briefly inspected his naked body. 'I'm no doctor but he doesn't look great. His colour's a ghastly grey.'

'Jesus,' muttered Scott and put his foot down hard on the accelerator, surging the transit forward. He cut across lanes again, overtaking on the wrong side and causing another blast of angry road rage. 'Change places. You drive and I'll keep an eye on Ferguson. We can't afford to lose him.' He glanced out of his left side mirror and noticed the single headlight of a motorbike weaving through the lines of vehicles. The light disappeared briefly, then reappeared on the inner lane. It was gaining and the way it was being driven worried Scott. 'I think we're being followed.'

Higgins was leaning over the prostrate body of Nick Ferguson, trying to decide if the dealer was alive or not. The chest cage wasn't moving as deeply as he considered normal and there was little body movement. Now he switched attention immediately, crawling to the rear tinted window. 'Where?'

Suddenly the side of the van was raked by gunfire, bullets pinging off panelling and puncturing large holes into the bodywork.

'Get down, get down,' yelled Higgins as he crawled on his belly towards the front cab.

Scott swerved the transit wildly across the highway, bumping into a lorry and forcing it against the median strip barrier. A cascade of sparks flashed into the air as metal screeched against metal. Horns on all sides started blaring and vehicles in front pulled to one side to escape the outrageous driving they could see in their rear-vision mirrors. Another salvo shattered the passenger side window and raked the ceiling of the cab, forcing Higgins backwards. He grabbed his handgun and slid open a side panel no more than inches, enough to see out. The motorbike was swerving in and out of traffic, the cyclist making sure he wasn't an easy target. Higgins saw a flash of steel and immediately rolled away as another spit of automatic gunfire punctured holes in the bodywork. Scott tried keeping one eye on the road ahead and the other on the single headlight trailing them. He spotted a car and trailer ahead, the driver obviously oblivious to the shoot-out coming hard on his tail lights. Scott swerved sharply to the inside lane, forcing a Volkswagen off the road and on to the grass verge, then accelerated hard until he was just ahead of the car and trailer. With no indication he pulled out in front, causing the driver to jam on his brakes. The trailer swayed dangerously, criss-crossing two lanes and effectively blocking any movement. In his side mirror Scott could see the motorcyclist forced well across the highway and momentarily distracted. 'Now,' yelled Scott, 'he's coming up on the other side.'

Higgins rolled across the cabin, one foot inadvertently kicking Ferguson in the face. He dragged open the right sliding door and grabbed the side frame for support. About twenty feet away and gaining, the motorcyclist was trying to cross lanes again and Higgins could see him struggle to control his bike as he took aim. Higgins steadied himself and pointed his handgun carefully, then squeezed off three rounds. He saw sparks as one hit wheel metal, then the motorbike spun wildly out of control and ended up skidding along the tarmac, its driver thrown out of harm's way on to the median strip. Higgins slammed the side door shut and slumped down on the mattress, all the adrenalin drained from his body. He was sweating heavily and his breathing was laboured as he wiped his forehead with the edge of a sleeve. 'Scott,' he barked over the traffic din, 'get off this road and find somewhere to park. There's no way we can go back to HQ. Every squad car in the city must be looking for us by now.' He inspected the bullet-scarred van, light glinting through the holes punched into the framework. 'We can't go back to base, our cover will be blown.'

Finally they pulled into a quiet sidetrack along the south city quays, beside a major construction site. The area was deserted with only street lights throwing shadows along furrowed trails. Tall cranes towered over half-built shells and somewhere in the depths a solitary oil lamp glowed weakly.

Cement mixers and yellow earth movers lay idle behind chain-link fencing and a warning sign advised guard dogs protected the zone. Higgins jumped out of the back door and lit up a cigarette, drawing hungrily on the tobacco as he surveyed the damage to the transit. Scott was inside, checking Ferguson. He had to rely on the weak interior light but could see the narcotics dealer was barely alive; his breathing was shallow and his conscious state zero. Scott squinted at his watch in the gloom, desperately trying to decide what was happening. The auto-injector drug should have cleared Ferguson's system and he should have been coming round and protesting like the other two before him. But his laboured grunts and lack of response suggested he was actually in a coma.

'What do you think?' Higgins was looking anxiously over Scott's shoulder.

'I don't know. This isn't in the army handbook but I'd say the injection has shot his brain to bits.'

Higgins glanced up and down the darkened building site. Apart from the flapping of plastic sheeting nothing stirred. In the distance the sound of police sirens and ambulance klaxons filled the night air. 'We can't stay here. Somebody's bound to get suspicious and call a squad car.'

Scott squatted on his hunkers, deep in thought. Ferguson's suppressed consciousness had to be from the combination of drugs in his system. Cocaine, alcohol probably, cannabis also, he reckoned. Maybe, Scott prayed desperately, maybe he's just spaced out and it'll take time for the narcotic cocktail to leave his bloodstream. He rummaged frantically in a small leather bag at the back of the van and produced a syringe, needle and vial. This had better work or we're in deep shit.

'I'm outa here,' muttered Higgins, eyeing the needle as he

slunk off into the shadows and lit another cigarette.

Scott pushed his glasses firmly back on his nose and tried to read the instructions for the ampoule. The interior light barely gave enough energy but after three minutes he decided he had the gist of the details. He quickly snapped the top off the ampoule and drew up the clear colourless liquid, then injected it into a fleshy vein in Nick Ferguson's left arm.

'What are you giving him?' Higgins called from a respectable distance. From his shadowy retreat he could just about make out the movements in the back of the transit. He wanted to know what was going on, though not necessarily see.

'Narcostate. It's used for drug-induced coma.' Scott slapped Ferguson's face sharply, then ran knuckles along his exposed breastbone. There was no response. Now the dealer's eyes were inspected, but the pupils were fixed and dilated, a sign of possible brain-death. Scott's heart began to race and he cursed out loud. For the first time he sensed their covert mission was coming unstuck.

Higgins leaned inside the van. 'He's not coming round?'

Scott shook his head. Perspiration was trickling down the side of his face and the ski cap was itching his scalp. He pulled it off and scratched vigorously, suddenly touching a trace of wet blood along the hairline. 'I didn't feel a thing.' He pointed out the flesh wound, a half-inch of seared skin along the crown of his head. He turned the ski cap round and round until he found the entry hole. 'Jesus, that was close.'

But Higgins wasn't listening; he was staring intently at the prostrate body of Nick Ferguson, still naked underneath the red silk sheet that covered him when was lifted from the Westside brothel. 'Scott, take a walk for a minute and clear your head. This kind of heavy stuff can be hard to handle unless you're used to it.'

Scott tried to get a fix on Higgins through the gloom but found the detective avoiding eye contact. Something niggled in his brain, warning him not to move. His professional training alerted him that Ferguson was in a critical state and needed urgent medical attention. But how were they to transport him across the city in their shot-up transit without being stopped and interrogated? Their cover would be blown immediately, the whole mission exposed. He turned to inspect his scalp wound in a side mirror when a single shot rang out and the back of Ferguson's head exploded like a ripe melon.

20

Wad'ye mean he's dead?

Somebody took him out. He was found near a building site along the quays with a bullet in the back of his head. Derek McCann was breaking the news to Jay Davis.

Jesus Christ. Davis's voice was incredulous.

The place is in uproar. There's gangs hunting in packs, street kids getting their kneecaps blown off, dealers running for their lives. It's a nightmare.

Jesus Christ.

Would you quit saying that? I'm looking for something sensible out of you.

Back off, Derek; Dublin's your scene. I just supply the goods. You have enough heavies to keep on top. Shoot two or three as an example, then smash up a few houses. Let them know you're in charge.

I've already started. Two of my lads torched a city centre club. There was a new crowd working out of it making inroads on my territory. I just needed an excuse to lay into them.

Good move. Don't let any bastard feel they can get one over you.

Pause.

Are you still there?

I'm thinking.

Well, hurry up. I'm stuck inside a phone box and it's freezing.

This worries me. Sean Kennedy is a mad, gimpy bastard and I hate to think what he'd do if he hears of any cock-ups. Are you sure this isn't a police job?

I made a lot of enquiries. I have a contact in the drug squad but he has nothing to offer. He told me the van used in the raid was found about a mile away, burned to a useless shell.

Pay him double for the next month and tell him to stay alert. You've got to keep on top of this until the deal goes through.

Are we on target?

Everything's fine. My cargo is loaded for shipment and Kennedy's Bangkok deal is in transit. Keep your head down and we'll both be very rich.

Fucking great.

Click.

The airless room in the basement of government buildings went silent. This was the second time the tape had been played and each of the four gathered there had a transcript of the conversation in front of him. Finally the Police Commissioner Peter Cunningham spoke: 'We got a positive ID on Nick Ferguson's driving companion three days ago and had him followed. His name is Derek McCann, another unknown up until now. We put a tap on his home and business phones but one of the surveillance team spotted him using a public booth and we managed to get a wire on that before he made the call. Also, McCann buys in stolen mobile phones and uses them for internal calls. We're putting together a batch with a computer chip in each that allows us to listen in and follow movements. At the moment I'm trying to work out how to get them to him without raising suspicion.' He suddenly looked directly at Mark Higgins. 'Why did you kill Ferguson?'

'He was already brain-dead and beyond resuscitation.' Higgins fixed on the law enforcement officer. His eyes were steel, his jaw muscles tight. 'Scott wanted to drop him at the nearest hospital but I couldn't see the point. A bullet in the back of the head made it look like gangland hostilities. Anything else and I felt our mission would have been blown wide open.'

The room went silent again. To the left of Higgins he sensed Scott shifting uncomfortably in his chair. Across the chipped Formica table two astonished and outraged faces stared at him.

Cunningham turned towards Scott. 'And what were you doing at the time? Checking his blood pressure?'

Scott opened his mouth to respond but Higgins cut across immediately. 'He's dead, end of story. We now know who's the main player in the drug scene and we know he's expecting a major shipment. More important, we know he's dealing with someone called Sean Kennedy who has a weak leg and arranged a drug deal in Bangkok. Cue in the intelligence we received from police there and this has to be the man who murdered my sister and tried to kill Mr Power. From my perspective wasting scum like Ferguson for that sort of information was a good day's work.'

The Police Commissioner leaned both elbows on the table and rested his chin on his knuckles. His eyes flashed again at Higgins. 'Shooting unconscious men in the back of the head wasn't in your police training manual, was it?'

'I've broadened my horizons recently, Commissioner. You'd be surprised what I'm capable of. Scott's already told me how our death certificates read so I've decided the two of us are no more than cannon fodder in this exercise. If it works out, that's great. But if it goes belly-up the state will make sure no one ever learns the truth.'

Harry Power and the Commissioner exchanged fleeting glances, while Scott sat sideways in his seat to inspect his brother-in-law. His expression reflected his support. I'm right behind you, you mad bastard. He now butted in, determined not to lose an inch in the argument. This crisis was not anticipated but he and Higgins had already agreed a damage limitation strategy. 'We discussed at the beginning that this mission wasn't going to be easy. You tried talking me out of it because of the risks and dangers involved. We got lucky with the first two dealers; everything went to plan and we gathered a lot of new information. But I don't think any of us really thought this could keep going without hitches. We have Charlie Fegan in psychiatric care and Nick Ferguson dead. He was the jinx waiting to happen. But our biggest catch is waiting in the wings. The man who shot Laura and two of your colleagues is in on this and even his own business partners don't trust him. While we don't know where he is at this moment we're still a damned sight closer to catching him than we were six weeks ago.'

Cunningham glanced across at his Justice Minister but Power was following the conversation like a spectator at a tennis match. His eyes swivelled from one speaker to the other. 'Dr Nolan, maybe your personal grief has clouded your judgement.' Cunningham's glare pierced Scott like white-hot steel. 'Shooting an unarmed and defenceless man is murder. No matter what criminal record Ferguson had, he was still entitled to medical attention and a fair trial if he survived.'

Scott held firm. As far as he was concerned this was crunch time. He and Higgins had made considerable inroads on the Irish narcotic scene, uncovering vital information on the emerging barons and their jostling for power. And while he was still sick and shocked at Higgins's action three days earlier, he was eventually convinced of the logic behind the decision to blow Ferguson's brains out. Sure, Higgins had behaved like a common hit man, the sort of thug he always detested. But they weren't working in normal circumstances and certainly not leading normal lives. They were undercover agents on a covert mission among the criminal underworld where anything goes. 'With respect, Commissioner, Higgins and I put our lives on the line when we lifted Ferguson. We were shot at and I took a hit to the scalp. Our transit was riddled with holes by the time we managed to escape. Now if you're trying to make me feel guilty because some Liverpool drug dealer is lying on an autopsy table and not me, then think again. Before I left Chicago my army contact made one telling comment: "When the bullets start flying some people don't duck quick enough." Well, this time I did. But next time I may not move fast enough. Shooting Ferguson was a brutal but necessary tactical decision. Now the real battle begins. Whoever Sean Kennedy is, he's obviously a mean, vicious bastard. So we'd better get our heads round more potential casualties before we catch him.'

Now Higgins got a chance to explain his side of the debacle. His mood was subdued but equally defiant as he faced the most senior law officer in the land. 'With respect, we're going over old ground here. I remember a stand-up argument in this very room not so very long ago where I challenged Scott. I didn't think he had the bottle for this type of operation and if it was to go ahead I wasn't prepared to carry any passengers. But we agreed on his strategy of scouring the sewers to see the rats in action. And when you sink that low, you sometimes have to forget the rule book to get above ground again.'

He now turned to Power, his voice hardening. 'You told us your life was in tatters, that your family felt under constant threat and you could hardly see a future in this country. And you agreed to the covert mission Scott and I have been working on ever since. But you didn't tell either of us about the exit strategy, the government fall-back ploy to explain our deaths if everything screwed up. Well, sir, let me tell you something man to man. We're within a hair's breadth of catching the bastard who tried to kill you. All we need is a little more time and some luck. But if our tactics don't suit, maybe we'd better pull out and let someone else take over. I hope they've balls of steel because this Sean Kennedy character just isn't going to walk up to us with his hands in the air.'

The room went silent again. Cunningham stared down at the table while Power seemed to crumple into his chair. His once large frame now barely filled the seat, so much weight had he lost. Worry fault lines coursed along his face, like dry ravines after a flash flood. He scanned the transcript of the telephone call, flicking quickly through the pages. 'What about the contact close to the drug squad he mentioned. Any idea who he's talking about?'

'Not yet but Christ help him when I do,' said Cunningham. 'Currently I have ten experienced and trusted officers working on the periphery of this operation. They're getting pretty pissed off being kept in the dark but I've told them we're about to make a significant move soon. They'll hold tight for a little longer.'

Power sighed deeply, linking and unlinking his large hands. 'Any idea who Jay is and where he was speaking from?'

'The call was tracked to a mobile phone in the south of Spain. It's untraceable after that. I have no idea who Jay is.'

'So where do we go from here?'

Higgins cut in. 'The first part of this mission is over. There's no point in trying to lift more criminals and interrogating them when sedated. We now know the name of the assassin who shot all round him six weeks ago. What we don't know is where he and his partner operate out of, so we can't move on them yet. If we alert Spanish police and the main port authorities there we might just catch both whenever the cargoes are unloaded. My gut feeling says no to that strategy. There are too many middlemen and possible leaks, and we could end up missing out on the whole consortium. Also, we would lose out to Spanish authorities in any criminal trial; they'd want first bite. And they could give us grief with extradition requests. I say we let this run to its final conclusion and hope we can catch the whole rotten shower when they land their haul.'

Power's eyebrows arched in a silent question towards the Police Commissioner.

Cunningham shuffled the paperwork in front of him to keep his hands occupied. Then he loosened a top button on his shirt and ran a finger round his collar for relief. He still looked troubled, the evening's revelations obviously disturbing him greatly.

Scott watched, heart racing as he waited for the verdict. Here I am again, putting my life on hold and in the hands of this policeman. I'm fed up to the back teeth with his attitude. I wonder how the widows and families of the murdered bodyguards are feeling tonight? What if they heard these arguments? What would they want? Hell, they'd be baying for blood. And they wouldn't be scanning the rule book for ways to haul the bastards in. Like me, they'd be reaching for the jugular.

Finally Cunningham spoke, his voice determined and firm. 'I'll order a search in the passport office for every Sean Kennedy registered. We might get a lead there, as this is definitely an Irish outfit based outside the country. I'm sure he's got a dozen sets of false travel and business documents but he might have made an application for a permit here at some stage in his own name. Also I agree with Higgins. We could jeopardise the operation by involving other agencies. Let's keep a close watch on McCann, listen and follow but no intervention. This haul has to reach here through some port and then be collected. That's when we'll move.' He turned deliberately towards Higgins, his face a mask of barely controlled anger. 'And I don't want a shooting match. You're not the only one with scores to settle.'

In the corridor afterwards, Peter Cunningham took aside Harry Power. 'This has got out of hand.'

Power grimaced. 'I know. I knew they were both determined to see this operation through but I didn't think they'd actually start shooting the prisoners.'

'If anyone finds out we'll fry. What Higgins did is a flagrant abuse of basic human rights.'

Power leaned against the wall, one knee bent slightly. The zone was deserted and silent, with only an occasional light glowing. 'So what do we do?'

'Whatever happens, we can't let these mavericks bring the government to its knees. Nolan's role is over, he's no longer useful. I'll think of a way to phase him out. Higgins is a different problem altogether. He knows too much and is in this up to his neck. Leave it with me, I'll think of something to cut them out of the action.'

21

Sean Kennedy was on his third Heineken when Jay Davis walked into the Hoost Bar in the Jordaan area of Amsterdam. It was a small, intimate pub with dark wooden floors, smoke-stained counter and stools with old church pew seats arranged in facing clusters for patrons. Over the years pocket knives had carved initials and hearts and snakes and daggers, and part of the attraction of the establishment was inspecting the names and dates, and wondering where the artists were now. There was one public phone at the end of the counter and it was through this line that Kennedy and Davis kept in touch. The arrangement was Kennedy called in for a beer every second day at three and waited until three thirty. If Davis wanted to make contact he'd ring around three fifteen and the conversation would be in short staccato sentences. We need to meet. Where and when? See you. The Hoost was also a convenient rendezvous with only one front entrance and a rear exit on to a side street that could be accessed quickly via the toilets. Kennedy particularly liked the bar because he could scrutinise the customers and study their movements. Were they in for a quiet drink, or maybe on an intelligence-gathering mission? Like Davis, he was becoming increasingly concerned about personal security. The delivery date for their consignments to hit the docks in Rotterdam was now only six days away.

Kennedy continued reading that day's edition of the London *Times*, ignoring the giggles and cooing of a young couple a few feet away. Apart from them, the pub was empty, with the only sound coming from a radio tortured with static interference and broadcasting a soccer match. The bull-necked barman was glued to the set, a cigarette hanging out of one corner of his mouth. He coughed repeatedly, then cleared his throat and spat into gauze before wiping his sweating brow with the same tissue. When the interference on the radio became too much he fiddled with the dials but rarely succeeded in getting any better reception. Kennedy knew him from old. If Ajax was playing, often the Dubliner had to reach over the counter and grab his own bottle of Heineken, dropping a handful of Euros into a cup beside the glass rack.

At that moment Kennedy's attention was focused on an article on page three dealing with street violence in Dublin. According to *The Times*'s report the Irish capital was experiencing a surge in drug-related crime, after a lull following the assassination attempt on the Justice Minister. NEW MOBSTERS SCRAMBLE FOR TERRITORY ran the accompanying headline. Kennedy finished the piece, drained his glass and massaged his cramping leg. Out of the corner of an eye he watched as Davis pretended to scan the bar, shrug and walk out again.

Jordaan had its own distinctive charm that Kennedy liked, narrow streets, concealed courtyards, bookshops, second-hand stores, boutiques and bakeries. He often spent hours strolling the cobbled lanes and alleyways, browsing and playing mind games as to what he might buy when he finally had his fortune made. That day he had no time for such distractions and five minutes later he and Davis were sitting on a bench along the Prinsengracht canal, watching the traffic and admiring the pretty young things on bicycles hurrying past. It was 4 April and the Dutch capital was warm and sunny, its winter drabness replaced by a splendour of spring bulbs flopping from gable window boxes and decorating the many houseboats along the river. Davis was breaking a bread roll to feed pigeons while the thicker crumbs were tossed towards a cluster of ducks squawking near a barge moored behind them.

'There's something going on in Dublin.' Davis was staring ahead, as if the man beside him were a total stranger.

'So I've been reading.' Kennedy stretched back on the bench and sprawled his legs out fully. A pigeon ducked its head towards one of his feet but he shooed it away with a flick of grey Adidas. 'I suppose new heads are surfacing to carve out their own territory.'

Davis followed an especially curvaceous dark girl in hip-hugging denim and short top. She had deep-red gloss to exaggerate her full lips and wide silver earrings that bounced with each step. He didn't speak until this diversion had disappeared from sight. 'No, there's something else bubbling under the surface and I don't like what I'm hearing.'

Now Kennedy turned towards Davis, his eyes narrowed to questioning slits. 'What?'

Davis kept looking ahead. 'I'm not sure if McCann is telling me the whole story or pumping it up for effect.'

'But?'

'A couple of drug kids disappeared off the streets and then were found totally spaced out minus their earnings.'

Kennedy studied the streetscape again. A postman in blue overalls and grey tunic top stopped to deliver mail to a houseboat behind and Kennedy idly followed him with his eyes. The postman engaged in conversation with the boat owner, an old and grizzled man who was working on an easel propped up on the prow. The painting was inspected, then the old man made a wide sweep with his hands and the art critic nodded sombrely, as if suddenly seeing everything for the first time. Minutes later he was off again, weaving between parked cars along the canal side. 'Still sounds like rival gangs having a go at one another.'

Davis rubbed his hands together to dust off the last of the crumbs. The pigeons sensed their meal was over and moved further away. Then, nearby, a large truck blasted its horn and the birds took to the air, grey feathers falling from flapping wings. 'I dunno. Someone took out Nick Ferguson.'

Kennedy was almost on top of Davis. 'Took him out? You mean he's dead?'

'Stone cold by now. I spoke with McCann and he says Ferguson was drugged and lifted from some whorehouse. Hours later he was discovered with a bullet in the back of his head.'

Now Kennedy looked agitated. 'So how is McCann going to get the money for the deal? Wasn't Ferguson in on this?'

'There's no problem about the money. Half of Liverpool is crawling over McCann to get a piece of the action. If anything, he could make a nice little profit by jacking up the price. It's not the money; it's the fucking warfare breaking out. I can't help thinking someone's stirring the pot.'

'Who? Most of the big dealers are in gaol or fled after the clampdown. I thought we'd cleared out the opposition.'

'We have. And from what I hear there's no single player prepared to take on McCann, just a lot of Mickey Mouse wankers jumping on the bandwagon. But where there's demand there'll always be suppliers.'

Kennedy shielded his eyes from the sun where it reflected from a window on the opposite side of the street. A cloud moved across and the glinting light disappeared. 'That's not really our problem, Jay. We take the risks to bring the goods to the market place; it's up to McCann to distribute. I just want my cut of the profits, then I'm off and I'm not coming back for a very long time. There's too many involved in this now, too many mouths with loose tongues. There's a fucking bounty on my head throughout Europe as it is, so I'm not taking too many chances from here on. If Derek McCann has problems in Dublin then let Derek McCann sort them out. If he wants to stay top of the heap, he's going to have to crack a few skulls. But I'm not doing it for him.'

Davis went into a lull, watching the lines of vehicles crawl along the narrow roads that fringed the canal. Almost on the minute he would feign some movement that allowed him check behind and to each side. Kennedy watched on out of the corner of an eye, faintly amused at the other man's paranoia. The sooner I'm free of this bastard the better, he thought, as Davis stood up and stretched, and did a full-circle surveillance. Seemingly satisfied, he sat down again. 'We need to protect our own interests.'

'Meaning what?'

'Change of plan.'

'Meaning what?'

'We move the goods by another route. We keep McCann

in the dark and let him think he's going to collect at the port docks as arranged. If anyone's pulling a fast one that's where they're going to strike.'

Kennedy thought this over for a minute while he studied the buildings opposite. Through an open window on a high terrace with ornate gables the sound of a piano drifted over the background traffic hum. The soothing tones were in stark contrast to the confusion in the Irishman's seething brain. Is Davis trying to pull a fast one here, or is he genuine in his concern? Certainly the newspaper report he'd just read suggested considerable turmoil in the Dublin underworld, with scores being settled and a new breed of young Turks squaring up to take on the establishment. McCann might have made it to the top, but could he stay there? Still, he thought, that's his problem. But are he and Davis plotting something behind my back? He suddenly realised he was becoming as suspicious as the man sitting on the bench beside him. Jesus, the sooner we get this deal over with the better. My nerves are on edge. 'Mebbe you're right,' he said finally. 'Whoever had the bottle to wipe Nick Ferguson won't be afraid of McCann. There has to be a link, somebody must have blabbed and now the word's probably out on the street that McCann is waiting for a big one.'

'That's what I think too,' said Davis. 'My big worry is some undercover police operation. McCann swears that's not a runner but we can't afford to take the risk. We could sit tight on the goods and hold off delivery until we're absolutely sure he's on top of everything.'

Kennedy shook his head resolutely at this. 'There's a lot of very tough men expecting considerable cash transfers as soon as we unload their cargo. If we don't move we don't get paid and if we don't get paid we can't settle up with our suppliers.

I'm not flying back to Bangkok to tell Toby Wurschanda he'll have to wait for his cut. If he doesn't see his bank account considerably enriched within twenty-four hours of his shipment hitting Rotterdam he'll come looking for us. And he won't ask questions, it'll be our balls on a plate and then where's the money? There's too much resting on the timescale, Jay.'

Davis scuffed his highly polished leathers against the earth, deep in thought. For a while both men studied their surroundings until the strengthening breeze began to chill. Kennedy glanced behind him and watched the elderly painter beginning to pack away his brushes and easel as the light faded. He wanted to get away from Davis, his distrust of the man so intense he could barely stand his company any longer. But he knew he was intimately linked to the ex-cop until the deal was completed. Neither could swing the complete package without the other, Davis having the Miami contact and Kennedy in deep with Toby Wurschanda. Until McCann paid up both men were going to have to live with one another.

'I've already told McCann the container will be on Dublin docks on the morning of 8 April,' said Davis. 'But I warned him to allow a day or two extra in case of delays. I have a different plan, but he doesn't know. It'll all come together on the tenth.'

Meanwhile, back in a wet and cold Dublin, Detective Alan Daly was pissed off and cursing his luck as he stood in the grandeur of Fitzroy Square, close to the city centre. Daly jealously admired the magnificent red-brick terraces with their carefully maintained front gardens protected by black wrought-iron railings. He paced the grass, noting the array of expensive cars parked inside white lines clearly marked for residents. Mercedeses, BMWs, Audis, Saabs, now the latest model Lexus, black and gleaming despite the raindrops bouncing off its waxed bodywork. There's no doubt about it, Daly fumed, the rich do live in a different world and there's not much chance of me getting into it on my wages.

Daly was in his early thirties and had been a member of the Irish police for twelve years, progressing through its ranks. But he was young and ambitious, and fretted at the slow pace of promotion opportunities. And that day he considered the job in hand beneath his capabilities, something a junior officer should have been doing. He, along with at least thirty colleagues, had landed the unenviable task of checking the Sean or John Kennedys, aged twenty-five to forty, who had applied for a passport over the previous twenty years. A separate group was scouring records for requests made through overseas embassies. Daly had been allocated one hundred files exactly and he'd been able to sift through the majority by telephone. Slowly and tediously he eliminated the many Seans and Johns not fitting the description of the one Sean Kennedy he'd been told to look out for. Some had emigrated and were now living in Australia, New Zealand, North America, Canada, Britain or any other corner of the globe where the Irish diaspora had settled. These would be checked out locally for possible ID. Now Daly's main concern was the Sean or John Kennedy, aged around late twenties or early thirties, who might still be living in the country or whose family might know where he was. He had a photofit image and description to work from and knew the man being sought was probably the assassin who had attempted to murder Justice Minister Harry Power. So while Daly was depressed with his lack of success so far and generally fed up with the whole mission, he persevered, knowing any breakthrough could lift him into hero status among his peers.

Over the previous forty-eight hours Daly had worked the phones, walked the streets, called on local police intelligence and asked neighbours. He'd found at least twelve Sean or John Kennedys who fitted the profile but one by one had been able to eliminate or at least reduce the suspicion index until he was left with eight. One of these was a Sean Kennedy whose passport details showed he had once lived in Fitzroy Square. Which was why Daly was standing outside number thirty-four and inspecting the three-storey red-brick house protected by black railings. Do the Kennedys still live here? he wondered. It had just turned two o'clock in the afternoon and grey clouds throwing down intermittent torrents of rain obscured the Dublin skyline. Since nine that morning it had drizzled from time to time, then there had been an hour's break where the cloud cover disintegrated and a patch of blue struggled to be seen. However, at noon more rain was carried in from the west and the showers intensified to an almost continuous downpour, blocking drains and lapping over pavements. Daly, a tall, thin man with curly locks growing over his ears, sheltered under an umbrella and scrutinised the property with a professional eye. He especially noted the imposing granite stairwell running from the front door to a narrow gate abutting the roadside. But fixed securely to the black wrought iron was a new lock, its shiny brass out of character with the rest of the railings. And the lock was bulky, chubby and strong. The first thing that crossed Daly's mind was how ridiculous this was as any would-be intruder could easily vault the small railings.

The detective then took twenty steps backwards, skirting a Honda CRV off-road vehicle and kicking at its tyres out of spite. He studied the property again, for the first time noticing new CCTV cameras trained to cover every possible angle. And mounted on side walls were sophisticated intruder halogen lights, the fittings holding them also as yet untouched by the elements. He made a note of the security company whose alarm box was fastened underneath the eaves, then slowly walked up and down the road, trying to see how many other houses had resorted to similar intensive precautions. Fifty minutes later, after a full screen of the four terraces, he decided number thirty-four was unusually security minded. And while Daly walked he contacted local HQ and asked had there been any reports of burglary, muggings or violent attacks by these residents? By the time he'd completed the full loop the information feedback was perplexing. No, there hadn't been any complaints; Fitzroy was a quiet and exclusive area marshalled by an effective neighbourhood watch scheme. Residents liaised regularly with community law enforcement officers and indeed, it was considered one of the safest in Dublin, an oasis of calm in an often violent city.

Now Alan Daly was intrigued. Despite hunger gnawing at his belly after a hasty snack lunch, he strolled into the gardens at the centre of the terraces and continued to scrutinise number thirty-four. At one point he saw a curtain on the second level move slightly and felt sure he saw a face look out, then quickly withdraw. He called HQ and asked for a phone number. The line was ex-directory. He forced his authority and soon had the number but it rang out without reply. This is getting fucking ridiculous, he cursed as he risked his manhood swinging a leg over the wrought-iron railings. He eased himself into the front garden, walked up the granite stairwell and rang the doorbell. There was no reply. He knocked politely on the door. Still there was no reply. Now he hammered it aggressively in case his call might not be reaching the upper floors. But no one answered. And still the rain came down in stair rods, splashing over his boots and soaking the bottom edge of his trousers. It added little to Daly's mounting irritation.

There's security conscious and there's evasion and whoever's upstairs is avoiding me. And I'm not coming back here so you'd better open up. He was about to skirt the side windows when he noticed a black Jaguar pull up four houses to his left. The car was a classic version, all sleek lines with old-fashioned bends and curves, and hinged windscreen wipers. Daly fell in love with it immediately but was more interested in the elderly gentleman who slowly and painfully climbed out, closed the driver's door and locked it carefully. Then he shuffled as fast as his elderly limbs would allow towards his own property. The detective hopped back over the wrought-iron railings and gave chase.

The driver of the Jaguar was in his seventies, with silver-grey hair carefully combed and parted. He wore well-pressed slacks under a cream-coloured cashmere roll-neck and damp but solid brown brogues. Like the house he lived in, with its antiques and delicate vases and shipping-scene paintings, he reeked of old money. 'Mr Harvey Rowe is my name,' he began, 'though I'm retired now.' Daly was sitting in his front living room, one eye looking out of the window in case there was any activity around thirty-four. 'Used to work as a cardiac surgeon until I developed Parkinson's disease and had to pack it in. Can't have a surgeon with shaky hands snipping away at heart muscle, can we?' No, agreed Daly immediately, shuddering at the thought. He glanced around the room as Rowe went off to the kitchen to make tea. In the far corner a black baby grand piano held a collection of silver-framed photographs, with more on the mantelpiece of an Adam-style fireplace. A pile of logs was stacked on both sides of the empty grate. More seascapes in oil and watercolour cluttered the walls but other than the whistle of a kettle coming to the boil the grand house was as quiet as a tomb.

Initially, Rowe had been suspicious when Daly hailed him at his front door and the retired surgeon insisted on inspecting the police badge and then confirming ID through the local police station. Satisfied, his attitude changed from hostile distrust to welcoming companion. Daly sensed Rowe lived on his own and was probably glad of any form of conversation. And police work usually fascinated the innocent, so much so that officers were often swamped with information from overzealous citizens. Now, as Daly squeezed uncomfortably into a sofa that was lumpy and smelt of must, he tried to focus his questioning. He didn't want to alienate the doctor and wondered if the residents of Fitzroy stuck together, like some old boys' network. Maybe he'll resent my intrustion and tell me to bugger off.

But he was wrong; Harvey Rowe was more than happy to help. 'Norman's a funny sort of a man.' The retired surgeon had a sad voice, almost depressed as if he knew his own life was running to its final span and he wasn't much pushed about clinging on. 'Can't say I'm overly friendly as he keeps to himself. As far as I know his only daughter still lives there.' Rowe inspected the ceiling briefly. 'Anna, that's her name. She must be in her thirties now as she was about the same age as one of my girls and she's thirty-two.' A weak and shaky hand went to his chin and his eyes searched the space in front of him. 'Or maybe thirty-three. Not that it matters a damn, I'm sorry. You're not interested in my family.'

Daly forced a weak smile and sipped his equally weak tea. He secretly urged Rowe to hurry up. 'Isn't there a boy? Sean or John?' Daly made the question sound as innocent as asking the dog's name.

Rowe sipped his tea thoughtfully and for the first time Daly realised they were drinking from delicate china set with an exquisite floral design. He put his cup down carefully, desperate not to rattle the crockery.

'Indeed, there is a boy called Sean. Or rather there *was*.' Now Rowe sounded hesitant, as if imparting some family secret. 'But he left home after his mother died.'

'Oh? What happened?' Daly could feel damp creeping into his feet and he repeatedly curled his toes in his boots for warmth.

'Very sad, really. Poor woman was found dead at the foot of the stairs. It was the boy who discovered her body, which must have been very traumatic for him. From all accounts she'd been drinking and taking pills, and must have lost her balance and toppled right to the bottom. This house is built in the same style and if you look on your way out you'll notice how steep and long the staircase is. I was away at the time and only heard about it a week or so later. According to my late wife the poor woman's neck was broken.'

'Oh dear.' Daly felt he had to mutter some words of condolence and sympathy, both for the late Mrs Kennedy and also the surgeon's wife. 'That must have been very upsetting for the family.'

'Very,' agreed Rowe, 'especially as Sean kept telling everyone his mother didn't take pills and rarely drank anything other than a glass of sherry. He wasn't very old at the time, maybe fifteen or sixteen. But he certainly railed against the world. My wife said he blamed Norman for his mother's death. He wouldn't say why exactly but I do remember some rather unpleasant mutterings and accusations.'

Daly risked another sip of tea. This time he held the cup with both hands and set it back on its saucer with great care. Outside, the evening was getting darker and big plops of rain bounced off the windows. An ambulance klaxon sounded somewhere close, then disappeared into the distance and Rowe listened to it with a wistful look in his eyes, as if he were longing to get back into action. 'Then he just took off.'

'What? Left the country?'

'Yes. Only mid teens, yet off he went. To the best of my knowledge he's never been back. I bumped into Norman one Sunday after church.' Rowe pulled a face. 'He's a lay minister and sticks to the clergy as if he's going to be nominated for sainthood some day. I can't abide that sort of mock piety, can you?'

Daly replied with emphatic disgust. 'You were going to say something there, about bumping into him after church. Did he mention anything about Sean?'

Rowe placed his cup down carefully and wiped a drip that was threatening to spill from his nose. His rheumy eyes were bloodshot and tired, and Daly wondered how far to push the questioning. 'Yes. Told me Sean was involved in construction and more or less running his own company. Making a fortune, he crowed. Making an absolute fortune.' The handkerchief disappeared into a side pocket. 'Bloody liar, of course. A week earlier he'd told one of the other members of the congregation Sean was in Australia and working on a sheep station. I don't know what happened in that house when Mrs Kennedy died but it must have been significant for a boy that young to flee the country and never return. And for his father to lie in his teeth as to his whereabouts. If you ask me' – the surgeon's voice trailed off and Daly almost screamed for him to continue – 'I'd say he killed himself and Norman's too ashamed to admit it. Doesn't go down well among church members that sort of thing. Suicide is still a mortal sin in the eyes of our more fundamentalist Catholics.'

Daly wasn't sure whether his pulse was racing from hunger or the excitement of a possible discovery. But he felt his guts knot, his chest palpate and his instincts sharpen. He kept the conversation rolling as casually as he could. 'You wouldn't happen to know why he's put in an expensive and sophisticated alarm system? I had a look at most of the properties along this square and none of the others seem as preoccupied with security.'

Rowe put down his cup and poured another mouthful of tea. Daly declined, not wanting to prolong the conversation with unnecessary niceties. The surgeon took a sip, grimaced and added a level teaspoon of sugar. He stirred the tea with a bone-handled teaspoon, his eyes focused on the movement of the liquid. Suddenly he stopped and looked directly at Daly, so severely that the detective almost jumped. 'Because Norman Kennedy is a prize bastard' – the words were spat with venom – 'and it wouldn't surprise me if he got somebody's back up. Anna, that's his daughter, is fond of dogs. Small breeds like Pekinese and Jack Russells and Corgis, you know what I mean. Easy to manage and not a handful. Well, a month or so ago somebody snatched whatever pet she owned at the time and beheaded it.'

'Jesus Christ.' Daly couldn't contain his surprise.

'That's what I said too when I heard. And whoever did it left the stump stuck on the front railings. Absolutely ghastly for the girl and I believe she was distraught for days. But who in God's name would do such a thing?'

Daly shook his head, genuinely at a loss.

Rowe leaned forward in his chair, his voice lowered to

conspiratorial tone. 'Someone wanting to get one back on old Norman, that's what I think. Anna's a simple sort of a girl who wouldn't harm a fly and I can't see her gathering too many enemies. But that Norman, he's a different fish altogether. My wife never liked him and she was a good judge of character. If Norman Kennedy needs to surround himself with CCTV cameras and fancy alarms it can only mean he's afraid of someone.'

The front door of number thirty-four Fitzroy Square was reluctantly opened about half an hour later. Alan Daly had hammered the wood, rapped the knocker and rung the bell repeatedly for almost ten minutes before Norman Kennedy finally started undoing the bolts on the inside. 'Yes, what do you want?' The tone was less than welcoming and immediately annoyed the detective.

'I'd like to speak to you about your son, Sean.' And from the startled look of fear that flashed across the older man's face, Daly sensed he'd hit paydirt.

22

Derek McCann inspected the eight men slouched in various positions opposite and felt a shiver of fear run up and down his spine. Four were his own crew and he knew them to be dangerous, callous thugs and well able to handle themselves. That's why he paid them top rates, took care of their hardware needs and insisted on checking alibis and exit strategies. And he visited their families, talking to wives and girlfriends, often slipping them bundles of cash to keep up living standards and making sure any children were well looked after. They were his men and he was determined to protect them, socially and financially. Equally, he was aware they drank and gambled the considerable sums he lavished on them and knew that probably none had a spare Euro within a week of being paid. But that was their business and he was wise enough not to interfere. McCann ran a tight ship, employing only a small number of carefully selected and trusted helpers to keep the wheels of his business interests running. If he said take out that new street dealer on the north side he was confident the hit would be carried out with minimum fuss and maximum ruthlessness, usually a single shot to the back of the head, and the body dumped along some lonely road on the city outskirts. It was simple and effective terrorisation, and guaranteed his position at the top of the pile. His quartet he knew familiarly by their first names, Paddy, Dekko, Anto and Luke. Paddy had torched the city centre club McCann was so worked up about days before; Dekko had at least three recent killings to his name; Anto and Luke worked as a team, intimidating and breaking legs when intimidation and breaking legs were deemed necessary. Good young lads, McCann considered. You knew where you stood with these kids.

Then he glanced at the four unknowns foisted on him from Liverpool by the late Nick Ferguson's brother, Billy. Billy Ferguson was now officially the Scouse half of the incoming drug deal and also on a serious revenge mission for his brother's killers. What worried McCann was that Billy, a fatter and meaner version of Nick, had considerably less brainpower but more bottled-up aggression. Which was just what he did not want. On the other hand he was becoming useful now the Dublin underworld had gone from simmer to overflow mode with a rash of violent scuffles over territory and clients. But when McCann's men went in search of the two mystery assassins who'd kidnapped and killed Nick Ferguson these aspiring dealers and suppliers retreated to their communities and lay low again. Secretly McCann was securing his turf and letting these other scum know who was now running the narcotics trade in Ireland.

And the Liverpool connection would soon have another and more devious role to play for the supermarket and off-licence owner. More than anyone else, McCann feared Sean

Kennedy. He'd been lied to by the young Dubliner, and convincingly too. McCann did not trust Kennedy and secretly decided to arrange his demise. Jay Davis he could work with, Davis at least spoke the same language and was rational. He was a businessman with some degree of social etiquette. But Kennedy was a ruthless psychopath who often killed on impulse. McCann was on the verge of becoming an extraordinarily wealthy man but despite surrounding himself with a small army of henchmen he still felt insecure.

Which was why he told Billy Ferguson that it was Sean Kennedy who'd taken out his brother. 'I can't be one hundred per cent sure on this, Billy,' he confided over a beer in the Green Man, one of two pubs in the late and unlamented Nick Ferguson's stable of assets. 'But I've made a lot of enquiries. People I trust tell me Kennedy heard Nick wasn't going to pay up and the bastard got his revenge in first.'

Billy Ferguson studied the other man's face, scowling in a bitter rage. 'I'm still gutted about our Nick, Derek. Gutted, I am. He was me only brother. You give me the word and I'll rip this Kennedy bastard apart with me own bare hands.' To emphasise the point, Billy held up two shovel-like fists, scarred and dimpled from previous brawls.

'Do nothing just yet,' advised the wily McCann. 'Keep this information to yourself; there are too many mouths who have Kennedy's ear. But when I say go, be ready to move. And be quick and careful, for this is the meanest bastard I've ever come across.'

Billy allowed a smile that showed off extraordinarily poor dental hygiene. 'He hasn't worked in Liverpool, then, has he? If he wants mean he should try taking on some of our touts.'

Liverpool, thought McCann at that moment, is Disneyworld compared with Dublin.

Now, as he surveyed the eight men about to set out on another mission of violence and intimidation, McCann was feeling somewhat less concerned. He'd gathered them together in a warehouse attached to one of his supermarkets and the gang members leaned or squatted or sprawled on crates of Coca-Cola, Pepsi and Red Bull. The large storage area was cold and its halogen lights threw shadows along the service aisles. All around were sealed boxes of foodstuffs, packages of tinned fruit, ceiling-high cartons of confectionery. One of the Liverpool crew had already helped himself to six KitKat bars and a can of Fanta, pulled aggressively from their protective wrappings. McCann let it go. What were a few Euros to a potential multimillionaire? This, he thought, is the most dangerous crowd I've ever employed. By the end of today the streets will know who's in charge of this city. He listened cautiously as the rumble of a heavy goods delivery lorry came closer and stopped. Then, as it reversed towards a distant parking lot and out of harm's way, McCann passed over a separate mobile phone to each man complete with a slip of paper advising a PIN number. 'These are clean,' he said, 'I picked them up last night. Keep in contact and let me know what's happening. Use them today only and then dump them. I'll provide another batch for the next mission.'

Five minutes later he heard the loud roar of high-powered motorbike engines being revved, followed by the scorch of tires on gravel as his angels of death took off. McCann waited until the whine of the engines disappeared into the distance before slipping into a side office to pour a stiff drink. Jesus, there's going to be a lot of blood spilled. He picked up one of his requisitioned mobile phones and called home, checking how his wife and children were keeping. Then he sent a text advising Jay Davis of his new mobile number. About three miles away at the city police HQ, his every word was being listened to and recorded by a twenty-four-hour monitoring detective detail.

In Amsterdam Sean Kennedy was preparing his own farewell and, as he packed his few belongings into a small suitcase, the Irishman was feeling particularly aggrieved. Candy, his German lover, had fled the red light district where she'd worked for so long. There hadn't been a word to her protector, not as much as an inkling that she was thinking along these lines or that he might catch up with her somewhere else in the city. He tackled their landlord, Even van Bronken, but the shaven-headed Dutch pimp could offer no information, other than that Candy had done a midnight flit three days previously owing him two months' rent. Kennedy didn't believe the whippet-like van Bronken, sensing the property owner was looking for an extra cash settlement. Equally, Kennedy didn't want van Bronken giving him grief now that he was so close to shipment day. So Kennedy peeled off the required back rent in fifty Euro bundles and stuck them in his landlord's jacket pocket. 'Keep her room free for a week or so, will you? She might come back.'

Van Bronken smiled a liar's smile. 'Sure, I'll hold on as long as I can. But demand is high and good tenants aren't that easy to come by.'

Two days later there was a tall Moroccan girl flaunting her ebony ass in the window where once Candy's very attractive buttocks had held sway. For Kennedy Candy's was the ultimate betrayal and final insult. She was only a whore anyway, a bitch who would sell her body to anyone. You're on your own now, Sean. And that's the way it should be. Trust no one.

* * *

'When can I speak to Daddy?'

'Not for some time yet, Anna. He's still talking with one of our officers.'

Anna Kennedy sighed loudly, pouted and slumped back into the hard plastic and steel chair she'd been sitting in for the past hour. It was four thirty in the afternoon of 5 April, and Anna and her father Norman had been detained for questioning since the previous night when Detective Alan Daly made the most significant breakthrough in the hunt for the man who'd attempted to assassinate Ireland's Justice Minister at the beginning of February. Initially lied to, abused and refused entry, Daly finally persuaded Norman Kennedy of the folly of his ways when he started calling up reinforcements at the still barred front door of thirty-four Fitzroy Square. 'Don't draw attention to us,' pleaded the elderly banker as he started undoing security chains and restraining bolts. 'This is a nice area and I wouldn't want the neighbours to think there's a disturbance going on.'

But two hours later Mark Higgins was pacing the floors of the grand three-storey red-brick, inspecting the elaborate security wiring and fine-tuned internal sensors. He'd already had a quick tour of the outside alarm systems and agreed with his colleague the attention to detail was unusual in such a safe zone. And while Norman Kennedy kept up the deceit for another hour and a half, Higgins finally found what he was looking for after a heart-to-heart discussion with thirty-six-year-old Anna, the only family member still residing in the house. In a quiet room near the front, where wide bay windows overlooked the darkness of the magnificent park outside, Anna Kennedy related some of the family history. The fights and squabbles between father and son, the increasingly futile attempts by her mother to mediate, and the final alienation between Norman and Sean. Then the tragic fall, her mother found by Sean at the bottom of the stairs. She recalled vividly her younger brother's plaintive and heart-broken cries, and she told how she'd wanted to go and comfort him. But Norman had held her back, warning her that the boy was too distraught and needed professional help. So Anna had returned to her room and spent the night listening to an ambulance klaxon and police sirens, and the front door opening and banging closed repeatedly. And much later poor Sean had returned home, sobbing uncontrollably, broken like a reed. And when he'd collapsed into his bedroom he was left there to grieve alone.

Now a female police officer entered the interrogation room and smiled briefly at Anna, before sitting on the opposite side of the rickety desk separating them. The minder slipped outside and into a viewing room where Higgins, and Police Commissioner Peter Cunningham were already waiting. Through concealed glass the group could see Anna Kennedy's face and movements, hear her voice. Every word was being recorded.

'Anna, my name's Sheila. I'm one of the detectives here.' Sheila had deliberately dressed down for the interview, wearing navy tracksuit bottoms, Adidas trainers and a sky-blue open-necked T-shirt. She had short, reddish-blonde hair and wore no cosmetics. Her demeanour suggested a confidante, someone Anna could share her secrets with.

'Hi, Sheila.'

Sheila smiled encouragingly across the table. 'I've been speaking to your father,' she lied, 'and he's told me everything.'

'Everything?' Anna's voice lifted an octave.

Sheila grimaced slightly. 'Yes, no holds barred.'

'Did he tell you that Sean almost strangled him, only I

stuck a knife in his leg to stop him? Did he say why Sean was so angry? I mean, did he go into every detail?'

'Yes, everything.' Sheila was an accomplished liar, her head nodding to emphasise each deceit.

Now Anna seemed to crumple in the chair, her embarrassment obvious. She was a tall girl, maybe an inch or two below six feet, and dressed in a plain linen dress with low-heeled shoes that set off the outfit nicely. If it weren't for the fact that she was in the bowels of a police station she could easily have been mistaken as on her way to a dinner date. Her dark hair was dyed free of early grey streaks and pulled into a long tress, which was held in a clasp at the side of her neck. She looked pretty but frightened and her voice reflected that fear, halting and subdued, almost a half-whisper.

'Anna.' Sheila's voice softened slightly and she leaned across the desk separating them. 'Did you know it was Sean who tried to kill our Justice Minister in February?'

Anna's head shot up and her features changed dramatically. Now she looked like a startled rabbit. 'Oh no, Sean would never do that. He'd certainly kill my father if he had the chance, but I can't believe he'd get involved in attacking the Justice Minister. How could you say such a thing?'

How's it goin'?

A-one. We're moving the containers off the docks at Rotterdam tomorrow morning.

Fucking great.

Everything should be with you in four days.

Good man, Jay. I'll do business with you any day.

How about yourself, Derek? I'm hearing all sort of shit on the TV about open warfare in Dublin.

Just taking care of business. Nothing more than you

advised. Cracked a few heads, broke a few legs. Threw a bit of petrol about.

Good man. That'll put out the right vibes. Anything further on Nick Ferguson?

Nah. But you should see the crowd who've moved in from Liverpool.

Tough nuts?

Tough? Jay, these guys are fucking looney tunes. They think we're simple Paddies and want to take over the whole show. They're desperate to kill half the city just to let everyone know who's in town.

Let them have their fun. When the goods are in your lap they can either follow orders or swallow lead.

That's what I'm planning. There may have to be more blood spilled to clear the air.

Then clear the air, Derek. You've taken the risks, you've paid the up-front fees. This is your operation; they're just hanging on to your coat-tails.

Exactly.

In a few days you can start distributing round the country and calling in the IOUs. You'll be a very rich man.

Fucking great.

Any other problems?

Nah, nothing I can't sort myself.

Good.

Oh, one thing, Jay. Will Kennedy be with you?

Pause.

Why do you ask that?

Just wondering. I don't want to get on the wrong side of him if he's in a bad mood.

Forget Kennedy, Derek. He'll be with me all right. But I think he's too young to be handling all this money, don't you?

Could go to his head, Jay.
Exactly. And we wouldn't want that. Not with his record.
So we'll both keep an eye on him.
To be on the safe side, Derek. To be on the safe side.

Mark Higgins and Scott Nolan listened to the tapes at Garda HQ. Beside them sat an exhausted-looking Peter Cunningham and a more upbeat Harry Power. The Commissioner was briefing everyone on the rapid escalation of developments over the previous twenty-four hours, including the details of thirty-four Fitzroy Square. He then set out the next stage of the police dragnet closing in on Sean Kennedy, his partner Jay and the McCann gang. Mutual agreement suggested they were dealing with possibly the largest shipment ever to be smuggled into Ireland.

Power spoke first. 'What does that tape mean in practical terms?'

Cunningham read from a fax in front of him. 'Over the last twenty-four hours there have been eight fatal gangland shootings, nine reports of violent assaults on known small-time dealers and eighteen separate petrol bomb attacks on houses throughout the greater Dublin area. There were another seven petrol bomb incidents in major provincial towns. Almost certainly these are related to and probably carried out by McCann's henchmen.'

Scott Nolan leaned back in his chair, heart beating and hands sweating. 'Things are certainly coming to a head, aren't they?'

No one spoke for about a minute, then Mark Higgins said what everyone was thinking. 'Yeah. And there seems to be a queue waiting for our friend Kennedy.'

23

At three o'clock on the morning of 7 April Scott Nolan was planning his final revenge tactics. The Dublin he'd moved to was now a major European capital while Ireland, driven by an educated and challenging population, boasted an economic growth rate the envy of other countries. It had also shaken off the oppressive shackles of centuries of Roman Catholic domination but where once a slice of income might have been reserved for the clergy, now consumerism ruled. It was Mercedeses, BMWs and Porsches that drew admiring glances, second homes and overseas investments boasted of, trophy wives secured. And as night follows day, with such sudden wealth came corruption, followed by the drug dealers, the men and women offering mind-altering pharmacology to those who craved such an experience. Heroin had plagued the capital in the eighties but was mainly confined to inner city and low-income territories. Now there were narcotics of choice for every age and economic group. Cocaine for those earning too much, amphetamines for the kids and still plenty of heroin for the serious addicts. The suppliers ran ruthless organisations, using violent and often murderous practices to secure their profits and anyone standing in the way or getting too close to the action risked a bullet in the head. Which was why Scott's personal standards and morals had also taken a hit. He'd used secret US army compounds to gather information, been involved in three kidnappings and a summary execution.

Now, as he lay in his bed in the small downtown apartment, he realised he didn't give a damn. He could find no tug at his conscience for anything that had happened since he'd downed his stethoscope for a 9mm Beretta. He wanted to destroy Sean Kennedy and was unashamed at this emotion. The intense desire to see Laura's murderer face to face before emptying a magazine of bullets into the assassin was overwhelming. But he also recognised there was a queue lining up to take Kennedy out so he was determined to be at the head of the posse. He ran a hand along the third growth of stubble forcing its way through on his shaven head and sensed static electricity. The charge was like the energy in his body; even the slightest tip could unleash a lightning bolt of pure venom.

Around the same time and five miles away, Mark Higgins sat at the kitchen table in his house, nursing his fifth glass of Jameson whiskey. There still was no firm word from the Police Commissioner as to where their target was. Upstairs, his wife and children slept at peace, blissfully unaware that on the table where they ate breakfast Higgins was greasing and checking the bolts and magazines of his Walther pistol and Uzi sub-machine gun. He had four boxes of live ammunition that he was breaking up into smaller clips, making them easier to carry and reload. He lit a Silk Cut and smoked it to the filter before grinding the glowing end into an ashtray. Cunningham has it in for me, he decided. Killing Nick Ferguson was necessary but I know he doesn't see it that way. When this mission is over I'll be pulled out of active service and given some desk job. He tapped at the packet of cigarettes until he realised there were none left, then scrunched the cardboard in his right fist and held it until his grip ached. I won't go easily, he promised, I know too much. And I won't go until I've seen Sean Kennedy's blood on the street. Revenge, oh sweet revenge.

In the affluent suburb of south Dublin where the murder and mayhem first began, Harry Power tossed and turned in his bed.

'What's wrong?' His wife, Jane, was facing him across the gloom.

'Nothing,' he lied.

'You're lying.'

'It's nothing, really. Go to sleep.'

Jane reached across and forced her husband to look towards her. In the shadows she could just about make out his features. 'Harry, I know you like the back of my hand. Something's going on. What is it?'

Power slumped heavily on to his back and fixed his gaze firmly on the ceiling. For almost two minutes he said nothing, the silence as ominous as an approaching thunderstorm. 'We know who he is.'

'Who is? What are you talking about?' Jane was now almost on top of her husband, her voice cracking with worry.

'The killer. We know his name and where he comes from. But we don't know where he is.'

'Oh my God.' Jane Power fell back into the bed, her body

shaking so much that her husband had to hold her tight for comfort.

'And he's coming back.'

'What?' Jane struggled out of her husband's grasp and sat bolt upright, one hand gripping her throat as if she'd felt an icy hand close in.

So Power related the latest developments, how they'd uncovered Sean Kennedy's identity, the telephone calls from Dublin to Spain, the drug cargo a lot of people were waiting on, including the police. 'We have a plan. This time he won't get away.'

'How can you be so sure? My God, I'll have to send the children away for safety.' There was nothing but doubt and despair in Jane's voice.

'Because even if we don't get him, his gang members will. Kennedy has made a lot of enemies who want to settle old scores. It'll be a rush to see who claims his head.'

Derek McCann watched dawn break over the Dublin skyline from the comfort of his new Mercedes. He was parked along the seafront near the inner city suburb of Ringsend, with views across the River Liffey and Dublin port. It was a bright, crisp morning, with clear skies and a magnificent orange sunrise. Outside, the river traffic moved apace, with large P&O container ships easing their way to the quayside to be tied up and eventually unloaded. Small craft were anchored well away from the main shipping lanes, their bright sails and flags fluttering in the weak breeze. Seagulls squawked and swooped, snatching at anything edible floating on the current. Only the early shift of delivery vans and container lorries ghosted along the deserted roads, an occasional car and taxi caught up in their slipstream.

McCann turned the heater up slightly for comfort and to clear the windscreen. A few hundred yards away, on one of the piers he could now see so clearly, a shipment of narcotics would soon be landed. His shipment, the consignment he would pay a fortune for, which would eventually make him a very wealthy man. Everything seemed to be in place, the plan trickling along nicely and coming to a final conclusion. I wonder who took out Nick Ferguson. A roll of ugly mugshots filtered through his brain and he mentally ticked them off one by one. He couldn't find a suitable prime suspect but quietly gloated that he was on top of the pile now. He flicked on the radio, half listened to an early news bulletin and stabbed the button off again. A milk float trundled by, cruising at about five miles an hour, while a young lad in white overalls ran alongside, occasionally stopping to offload a heavily wrapped pack of litre cartons. He gunned the Mercedes engine alive and edged it slowly on to the road, heading towards the city centre. As he cruised along the Eastlink bridge connecting the north and south of the city at its most easterly part he glanced again at the busy docks.

24

Jay Davis spotted the *Gypsy* trawler around ten on the morning of 7 April. It was a forty-metre-beam fishing boat, with maroon-coloured forward tripod gripping pulleys and heavily greased steel ropes. The boat bristled with aerials, navigation and communication devices, and at the stern a large winch held rolls and rolls of wound-up nets. There was a wheelhouse with one cracked window, on top of which a cluster of halogens could flood a thirty-yard circle of light. The hull was painted blue with red trim but the colours were faded and flaking from years at sea in inclement conditions, and rust was eating into the safety rails at the bow and lifesavers bolted to the deck. A dull and partly ripped Irish tricolour identified its country of origin, while the letters HOWTH showed which port she sailed from. The Howth promontory was a substantial headland connected to Dublin by a narrow stretch of coastline. At its north face were a village and harbour, the town nestling on a hillside with quaint terraced houses lining tight streets where one badly parked car could cause traffic standstill. It boasted a cluster of pubs and restaurants, and a few decent hotels but the focus was the port, a deep-water course that sheltered a small fleet that anchored there year round. The village was a tightly knit community from where generations of families had headed into the waters around the Irish coast and beyond to earn their living. Dotted along the seafront was a group of fish processors, packers and suppliers, and cheek by jowl with these traditional craft were the expensive yachts of those rich or fanatic sailors who took to the waves at any opportunity to pit their wits and skill against the elements.

Davis recognised *Gypsy*'s potential immediately. The boat was berthed at the dockside of Bergen's Boat Repairs, a Rotterdam yard specialising in trawler maintenance. Two young men wearing cloth caps sat idly on the oil-stained deck staring sullenly into the middle distance, occasionally glancing up at the quayside where a tall, red-haired, red-bearded man squeezed into a too small Aran knit sweater was having an agitated discussion. Davis watched from a respectable distance, his attention apparently fixed on a sleek-lined and expensive-looking yacht anchored in deep water about fifty yards away. There, a single crewman was scrubbing and hosing down the woodwork, whistling out of tune and oblivious to the heated exchanges on the dockside. The red-haired man stomped away and snapped a mobile phone into action, then barked angrily down the line. The phone was killed and a waiting game began. Red-hair jumped down into the *Gypsy*, and he and his partners went into a huddle, every now and then throwing murderous glares towards the quay. The boatyard owner, a tall, thin man with receding hairline called Dijken, now sat on a beer barrel, his body language suggesting total indifference to the rage going on beneath. Dijken had earlier tipped off Davis about problems he was having with an Irish boat, and the drug dealer sauntered further along and lit a cigar, drawing on it slowly as he weighed up the situation. Then he heard a mobile phone ring and risked a glance towards *Gypsy*, noting the agitated and increasingly desperate gestures of the red-haired skipper. The air suddenly filled with a string of oaths, all of which Davis recognised clearly.

Dijken stood up and shouted something but the background din of oxyacetylene welding and rivets being drilled swamped the words and Davis couldn't make out what was said. Minutes later the Irish crew was left alone as the man from Bergen's vanished into a Portakabin some fifty yards to the left. His face suddenly appeared at a window, telephone pressed to ear, and a prolonged but unheard conversation continued while he assessed the problem outside. Every now and then his expression switched from sour to solemn to annoyed and back to sour. Even though he was five hundred Euros richer from his exchange with Davis, it was obvious he wasn't enjoying the confrontation. Davis waited for about ten minutes, observing both sides and trying to decide when to make his move.

'Hi, there. Can I have a word?' He stood on the edge of the berth; for once pleased he was dressed casually in denims, sweater and Nike trainers. For this discussion he didn't want immediately to look like an expensively attired drug dealer.

Red-hair squinted up at him quizzically, bloodshot eyes scrutinising the stranger staring down. 'What'd ye want?' The tone was belligerent and challenging: who are you and what business is it of yours, butting in here?

'Just a word. I won't take up much of your time.'

Red-hair glanced towards his two crewmen but they shrugged their shoulders and sat back down on the deck, as if resigned to being stuck there for ever.

'Are you in trouble?' Davis asked after first learning that he was dealing with Dan Patterson, skipper and owner of the *Gypsy*.

Introductions over, Patterson had relaxed slightly when he realised he was dealing with a fellow countryman. 'Big time.' His voice was now a throaty gravel rasp and for the first time Davis could see close up the fisherman's worn features, thick broken veins, purple nose and chapped lips. He clutched and unclutched his mobile phone, passing it from one meaty hand to the other.

'What happened?' They were above the berth but far enough away from any listening ears.

'The bloody engine gave up on us about thirty miles off Waddeneilanden. We were well off course, looking for sole and plaice but the seas are so overfished ye have to go further nowadays to find any decent stock. There was a storm brewing and we were stranded, so I had to call for a tug into harbour. Then we found the engine had packed it in altogether and needed replacing.'

'Sounds expensive.' Davis hadn't a clue about fishing or boat repairs but felt obliged to make an appropriate comment.

'Bloody expensive. Twenty thousand for the tug and another sixty thousand to fit a new engine. So I'm down eighty thousand and minus four crew who quit two days ago to make their own way back to Dublin.'

'That's certainly a lot of money.' Davis was studying the other man, trying to gauge how desperate he was. A pungent smell of diesel fumes mixed with fish oils clung to his clothes and Davis had to avert his head for relief. 'But sure you've got the boat as collateral. It must be worth a fortune.'

'These bastards won't let me move her out until they're paid,' snapped Patterson, his eyes darting angrily around the yard as if he might grab someone by the throat, given the slightest provocation. 'And the bank manager won't shift on my overdraft. I've been pleading with him for the past three days but they're throwing up debts left, right and centre. He says I'm too high a risk for this amount of money. If he pays out he wants to repossess the boat.'

'What the hell would he do with a boat?' Davis was beginning to see both sides of the story and could visualise the finances being calculated by some city accountant in a downtown Dublin office. Probably a thirty-year-old who dined out regularly and never wondered how the fish ever reached his plate. A Euro and cents man whose mindset was unlikely to grasp anything other than the bottom line of a balance sheet. If the sums didn't add up, no financial rescue would get clearance. Equally, Davis knew the Irish trawling industry was going through lean times with overfishing of stocks and heavy competition from Spanish and Nordic boats. It was becoming increasingly difficult to make a living off the sea, let alone earn serious money. More and more were quitting the business and there was a surplus of traditional trawlers up for sale. So repossessing the *Gypsy* wasn't a commercially wise decision for the bank. Equally, throwing good money after bad made even less sense. It was indeed, thought Davis happily, a difficult situation all round.

Patterson spat on the ground, an act of despair as much as anything else. He started punching numbers into his mobile phone again, but stopped halfway through, sighing deeply. He cursed angrily into his beard and began to make his way back to his rusty craft.

'Maybe I can help.' Davis stopped him in his tracks and Patterson turned back slowly, suspicion etched deeply into his narrowed eyes.

'How?'

'Let's go for a walk.' Davis beckoned the skipper along the pier and away from the *Gypsy* and her watching crew. 'There's something I want to talk over with you and it's better we do this on our own.' He glanced at his watch, noting it was closing in on noon. He knew Sean Kennedy was overseeing the unloading of two containers of furniture in a remote industrial estate about eight miles south of Rotterdam. One was from Colombia via Miami, the second from Thailand via Laos and Cambodia. By late afternoon the drug consignment would have been set apart from the wood and made ready for separate transfer. Both sets of furniture would then be repacked into a forty-foot P&O steel container for shipping the next morning, arriving early at Dublin port on 10 April. The time factor was now becoming critical, the margins for error dangerously tight. McCann was anxiously waiting to claim his goods. Once satisfied, he would release considerable funds, which in turn would allow Davis and Kennedy to pay off their suppliers, and hold on to a hefty profit. But they had yet to get the narcotics to McCann, even if the route chosen wasn't what he was expecting.

Davis and Patterson walked in silence for about a hundred yards, the fisherman still swearing into his barbed-wire beard. All around was the business of boat repairs, workers in green heavy-duty overalls swarming over yachts, trawlers and tugs. Rotting wood was being pulled up, steel struts strengthened, sails replaced. The weak sun cast shadows in some corners, yet glinted off the motionless waters of the harbour. In the distance someone was testing a foghorn, its deep boom out of place in the clear visibility. They had reached the end of the jetty when Davis made his offer. 'How about I pay off the boatyard? I could transfer eighty thousand into their account within an hour.' Patterson stood rock still; listening intently but his face twisted as if he had just bitten into something bitter. Davis sensed the other man knew what was coming. 'And I can give you one hundred thousand Euros in cash to pay off your men and still make it home with money in your pocket.'

'And what do I have to do?'

Davis threw an arm round the skipper's shoulders and drew him closer. 'Deliver some goods for me.'

By eleven o'clock on the evening of 7 April a canary-yellow P&O container of teak furniture was being swung from dock to ship at the Rotterdam ECT Maasvlakke pier. Two hours later a three-hundred-kilogram mixed cargo of heroin, cocaine and amphetamines was being packed into ten-gallon barrel drums usually filled with freshly caught fish. The drugs were carefully wrapped in four layers of protective plastic, then covered with ice to create some semblance of a successful trawl of the North Sea. Sean Kennedy squeezed into a corner of the engine room and wrapped a blanket round himself. To his left were empty pallets of fish trays, to his right a jumble of safety lights, life jackets and coiled ropes. He anchored himself so he could see everything above and below deck. Inside the waistband of his denims he carried two handguns, both fully loaded, with spare magazine clips at the ready. He'd let his hair grow long again and now fashioned it into a ponytail at the back, held together with a thick elastic band.

'Don't do anything stupid, Dan,' Jay Davis warned as the

crew cast off and began testing the power of the new engine. The two men were above the berth, caught in the glare of harbour floodlights. 'My friend Sean has a dangerous reputation. Leave him alone and he won't bother you. But give him any cause for alarm and he could get nasty.'

Patterson stared at Davis through the dazzle of the light. 'I'll not say a word to him.'

'That would be wise.'

'And where will ye be?'

'Waiting on the harbour at Howth for your arrival. I'm flying out first thing tomorrow morning. By the time you've tied up I'll have a truck ready and if you and your men move fast we could be out of your hair within an hour. At least this way you get to keep your boat and hold on to some money. And I promise you'll never hear from us again.'

'I bloody well hope not.' Patterson jumped on to the *Gypsy*, sliding unsteadily along the deck. Then he straightened up and looked briefly towards Davis before disappearing into the wheelhouse. Davis watched as the lights of the trawler edged slowly along the harbour. He heard the engine rev loudly as the boat picked up speed in deeper waters.

25

For the covert team assembled to intercept and arrest the main players in the anticipated massive drug smuggling racket 8 and 9 April were tense days. Scott Nolan and Mark Higgins stuck close to one another, both suspicious of possible underhand tactics from the Police Commissioner to freeze them out of the final act. They met in the afternoon of the ninth in the car park of the Berkley Court Hotel in the Dublin four district; a central rendezvous that would allow them to spring into action should anything significant break. All surveillance and intelligence was being filtered through Garda HQ, where a four-man unit listened in and reported on any activity involving the Irish side of the operation. Higgins was going through cigarettes at the rate of ten an hour and Scott insisted on every window in their unmarked car being wound down to give him some relief from the fumes.

'Anything happening? I can't help but feel I'm being frozen out of the action.' Scott was polishing his glasses on the end of one of his black T-shirts, now back in his undertaker's assistant look and a stark contrast to the smartly dressed suits going in and out of the five-star hotel. Well-fed red-faced accountants mingled with equally prosperous-looking clients, and there was much shaking of hands and slapping of backs. The clientele were the successes of the flourishing Irish economy while the two men in the smoke-filled Saab were on the periphery of society, maverick custodians of the law.

'Very little. McCann is under twenty-four-hour watch and there are listening devices and telephone bugs all around his house and offices. He's being very cagey, though. No telephone calls, no heavies visiting or signs of unusual activity. He spent yesterday and most of today clearing out a storage shed at one of his supermarkets. Now that might just be for commercial goods.'

'Or?'

'Or he's risking everything by taking the shipment straight to his own front door. If we catch him with the goods on the premises he can hardly plead mistaken delivery.'

'What about his warehouse out in the country?' The Clonart yard had been tracked within days of McCann being identified as Nick Ferguson's partner.

'There's an armed unit staking the site round the clock. I still think that's where the cargo's going to be offloaded. It's remote and secure, with quick access to the main motorway. He could break the consignment into smaller deals and move them around the country within twelve hours.'

A sleek silver Lexus SUV pulled up alongside and a group of business types climbed out, two Caucasian and two oriental. There was an initial confusion about etiquette but eventually the group found a compromise and made their way slowly into the hotel, trying to communicate through a mixture of hand signs and broken English. It was an unseasonably warm spring day, with clear blue skies and enough heat in the sun to allow shirt-sleeves, and as Scott watched these normal transactions of life he wished himself back in a situation where he would feel comfortable, more at ease. As it was he was uptight, edgy and jumpy. And the bulge of his Beretta kept sticking uncomfortably into his waist, a constant reminder of the dangers that still lay ahead. 'So what do we do?'

Higgins lit a fresh Silk Cut from the glowing butt of another. He knew he shouldn't be passing classified information to Scott, strictly their work was completed. But the two had taken risks and been down some shady alleys and Higgins now took a secret delight in going against his boss and involving Scott. 'We sit tight and wait.' He inhaled deeply, picked at a flake of tobacco stuck to his tongue and turned to his partner. When he spoke again, Scott was taken aback at the hatred and unashamed aggression in his stare. 'Very soon, Scott, you and I are going to come face to face with Sean Kennedy. Make sure you get your head round that before the shooting starts.'

Suddenly for Scott the pressure of the Beretta didn't seem so uncomfortable any more.

Three miles away Derek McCann was issuing final orders to the regular staff at his main supermarket storage and distribution warehouse. In broken shifts over the previous twenty-four hours they'd slaved to move pallets of foods and groceries, soft drinks and confectionary, fresh fruit and boxes of vegetables. Now, just after three in the afternoon, their boss was handing over two hundred Euros in bonus payments to each for their efforts. They thanked him politely and melted into the surrounding streets to spend their new-found wealth, wondering out loud why they'd had to change so much to create extra space. Did anyone know of a new range of goods coming in? No, nothing he's mentioned. But the money was burning in their pockets and soon McCann's storage problems crept to the back of their minds.

Now McCann surveyed the situation, mentally deciding how to break up the furniture and where to store the narcotics. He didn't want it inside his premises for any longer than necessary and had already made arrangements for a squad of couriers to call and collect their orders after midnight the next day. But right then he was satisfied. Create a diversion, he'd decided. If there's someone waiting in the wings they're going to get their fingers burnt. Billy Ferguson will deal with that potential. He and his Liverpool hard-men were ready and prepared for the big day. And for the first time ever in his criminal career McCann had armed himself with a handgun. If Jay Davis doesn't get Kennedy, Billy Ferguson will. But even if both of them fail I'll blow the bastard's brains out myself. And anyone else who gets in my way. This is crunch time and I'm taking no prisoners, there's too much riding on this deal.

Jay Davis arrived at Dublin airport on a flight from Amsterdam at five that afternoon. He was travelling on a false passport, and carrying false documents and matching driving licence. He booked himself into a hotel close by and spent an hour negotiating the hire of a Toyota open-backed truck, which he would pick up at seven the next morning for return later that evening. He agreed the overpriced costs and caught a taxi to the rental yard, paying the delighted owner in cash with another significant sum for security. It was a builders' depot that rented a wide range of equipment including cement mixers, small diggers, ladders and hoists. And there was a good choice of trucks and trailers, all suitably dented and dirty and inconspicuous. Davis was quietly delighted with the one chosen for him. It had a gearshift with minimal instrumentation and could easily accommodate the load he'd seen packed into the *Gypsy* at the Rotterdam repair yard. It also looked as if it hadn't been cleaned for a year, with dirt and grime and concrete dust in every corner, so thick in places that its blue panelling was almost totally obscured. Perfect, he decided.

He returned to his hotel and demanded a table by the window for dinner. He dined well but without any alcohol, careful to keep a clear head. That night he didn't sleep, tossing and turning as the climax to months of planning approached. Even when he dozed the images were of briefcases bulging with dollar bills, a palatial mansion in the south of Spain, with marbled floors, deep expensive couches and even more expensive paintings. Then these fantasies moved to the more familiar territory of fine wines, oak-aged brandies and scantily clad young women. It even included the perverse excitement of putting one over on his ex police colleagues.

On the Irish Sea and just entering St George's Channel, the *Gypsy* trawler was making good time in almost calm conditions. There was a slight swell but nothing that the newly refurbished boat couldn't handle. Dan Patterson had taken time out to sleep, leaving one of his crew at the wheel to navigate and maintain their chosen course. Since they'd left port at Rotterdam the three men had kept a sensible distance from their passenger, barely exchanging one word with him. Not that Sean Kennedy was in a talkative mood anyway. This was the final homecoming and his senses were on high alert with an intense tingle of excitement mixed with apprehension. He passed the time planning the hours ahead.

26

10 April, 10 a.m.

The temporary incident room at Garda Headquarters was silent. Four detectives, two male and two female, swung idly in swivel chairs, gossiping in subdued tones. Each wore a single headphone with mouthpiece, and was connected to a battery of listening devices and undercover lookouts positioned at Dublin port and Derek McCann's house and warehouse. At the remote Clonart storage yard in County Meath a separate heavily armed anti-terrorist unit was hidden deep in the surrounding undergrowth. They watched and waited, checking in every fifteen minutes, and it soon became obvious by the exchanges that the six officers were getting pretty bored. On one wall a large map of Dublin and its surrounding counties was displayed, with colour-coded pins marking areas of possible confrontation. Squeezed into one corner of the room were Mark Higgins, Harry Power and Peter Cunningham. Scott Nolan had been deliberately marginalised from this stage of the investigation, the Commissioner considering him a potential risk rather than an asset. So while the main action was focused at HQ, Scott simmered in his downtown apartment, waiting desperately for a call from his brother-in-law.

Cunningham looked tense and drawn, his body language reflecting the emotions of the main players in the room. They knew there was a mole in the force and a leak now could destroy the careful planning and possibly collapse the set-up. With the final day of reckoning upon them, each was acutely aware of the risks involved in the next stage. Might McCann have conceived a different strategy? Would Sean Kennedy, the one they so desperately wanted to detain, turn up as the telephone intercepts suggested or would the assassin outsmart them? After all, this was the man who almost murdered the Justice Minister in broad daylight and managed to escape the subsequent police dragnet. Kennedy was the main target, followed closely by the consignment of drugs, and the rest of the gang involved in its importation and distribution. If everything went to plan it would be a massive coup for the police and a huge morale boost. Also, it would strike a crippling blow against organised crime in the city and beyond. Equally, if things went belly-up the consequences could be ruinous.

Higgins was forced to smoke at a window in the outside corridor and darted back and forth, each time anxiously questioning the listeners: 'Anything?' Four heads shook and Higgins fretted for about five minutes before risking another cancer stick. Power tried making small talk but everyone was so uptight that after a few embarrassing stops and starts he abandoned his attempts and continued to stare at the wall speakers, willing something to crackle through. Cunningham left at regular intervals to deal with other pressing matters but touched base repeatedly during these forced absences. Finally the silence was broken.

Is that you, Derek?

Yeah.

Checkin' in, squire.

Where are you, Billy?

At the P&O terminal. The driver's just hooking up the container.

What's it look like?

Wadd'ye mean? It's a big yellow steel container with all sorts of writing on the back. Weight and volume and all that shit. What's it matter?

It matters a lot, Billy; we don't want to take the wrong one. Check the bottom right-hand corner at the back. There should be six numbers that look as if they're recently sprayed.

Pause.

Yeah, yer right. Eight, nought, four, two, two, nine.

That's it, Billy. You've got the right one. See you later.

OK, squire. Keep in touch.

Cunningham immediately spoke with a two-man unit covering the docks, ordering them to follow Ferguson. He then double checked with harbour police who had a speedboat berthed close to the freight pier. They were able to give a positive ID on which container the Liverpool thug was hovering around. Thirty minutes later a static distorted voice confirmed the steel trunk was being driven away by an articulated lorry with a Rads Haulage logo on the front. This information was then passed to the unmarked squad car and a police helicopter whirring in the skies above the city.

Higgins immediately studied the wall map. 'Where is

McCann now?' There was a quick interchange between look-outs and control, and everyone in the room heard the response. McCann was at his own storage depot two miles south of the River Liffey and in the exact direction to where Billy Ferguson was headed. Then the wall speakers crackled into life again.

Derek?

Is that you, Jay?

Yeah.

Ah Jesus, that's brilliant. Where are you?

Close enough.

Are you calling over?

Not yet. Has your container arrived?

It's on its way.

Any problems?

None so far. I have two lads at the docks keeping an eye out but everything's going smoothly. I was worried someone might make a move on us down there.

Call me when your container arrives.

OK.

The operation room exploded into activity, with Higgins already halfway out of the door. 'They're going to meet at McCann's warehouse. That's why he cleared it out; he's storing the goods there.' Higgins patted the handgun snapped to his waist. 'Let's go.'

But Cunningham brought this impetuous move to a sudden and unexpected halt. 'Stop right there, you're going nowhere.'

Higgins's jaw dropped. 'What the hell are you talking about?'

Power buried his head in his hands while the four police listeners kept their eyes firmly forward. 'I'm not having a bloodbath while you settle your own personal score.'

Cunningham had drawn himself to his full six foot plus, towering over the detective. 'I have armed and experienced officers ready at every potential flashpoint. I want these men taken alive and brought before the courts. I'm not risking a shoot out with you involved.'

Higgins stood at the doorway completely taken aback, his edgy, taut features had now collapsed to a bloodless mask of total shock. Then he looked straight at Power. 'You knew about this, didn't you? You've been dangling me like a puppet for weeks.' He leaned down into the Justice Minister's averted face. 'Haven't you?'

Power grimaced and left the room.

11.55 a.m.

The *Gypsy* was within sight of Howth harbour, ploughing through calm seas on a bright and cloudless day. The sun was to the left and still rising, and there was some warmth in the air, even out on the ocean. Pleasure craft sailed past, ahoying and waving at the fishing boat but there were few acknowledgements. Dan Patterson and his stony-faced crew kept their attention fixed firmly on the granite walls of the beckoning inlet ahead. The journey had been uneventful, with Sean Kennedy keeping well away from them and they in turn making sure not to disturb the unwelcome passenger. But Patterson and his men knew the next hour or so would be the most dangerous part of the trip. If they could offload their cargo without raising suspicion and get Kennedy and his partner away, they could breathe a sigh of relief and get back to normal life. They would still have their boat, be free of debt and have a few extra Euros to enjoy. It was a risky business but the benefits were too attractive to pass up.

Kennedy finally left the darkness of the hold and stood beside the wheelhouse, inspecting the vista. To his right was Ireland's Eye, an uninhabited island with a few sheep grazing on its grassy slopes. To his left were the suburbs of south Dublin and behind them the gentle curves of the Wicklow Mountains. On the waters other trawlers churned away from the coastline, sounding their foghorns as a salute to the incoming *Gypsy*, and Patterson gave a short blast every now and then to make things seem as routine as possible. They were now less than three hundred yards from the north pier and Kennedy could just about make out a solitary figure at the very end of the quay. He borrowed a pair of binoculars and squinted through them, adjusting for the rise and fall of the boat and the unfamiliar lenses. Finally he picked out Jay Davis, wearing what seemed like green oilskins. Beside him on the dock was a pick-up truck.

12.30 p.m.

Higgins was convulsed with fury. He sat on his seat in the corner of the makeshift operations room, his body shaking and his face white. One hand kept reaching for his handgun, then retreating at the last minute. He cursed himself for trusting Cunningham and Power. Those bastards have had me in their sights for some time. They only wanted Scott and me for the dirty work. Once they had the intelligence, they started running the show behind our backs. He fumbled in his pocket for a cigarette but only found a crumpled empty packet. He swore violently and flung it into a corner, then pulled out his cellphone and jabbed at the numbers.

12.45 p.m.

The *Gypsy* was pulled against the granite wall at the end of the north pier of Howth harbour and Davis was grinning from ear to ear as he caught Kennedy's eye. 'Did you get seasick?'

Kennedy shook his head. 'I'm stinking of fish but apart from that there are no problems.'

Suddenly Dan Patterson edged himself out of the wheelhouse. 'We can't unload here.' Davis quickly glanced around as if there were some unexpected danger he hadn't spotted. But the dock was deserted and the nearest activity was about five hundred yards away on the main street of Howth village as people went about their daily tasks. 'This inlet is always kept clear,' Patterson shouted. 'The middle harbour is for yachts and small craft, and the west pier is where fishing trawlers bring their catch ashore. This looks too suspicious so I'll take her to the far side.' A meaty hand pointed in the general direction, and when Davis and Kennedy looked across the water they immediately understood what Patterson was suggesting. The north inlet was empty apart from a few boats held fast to the quayside. The middle pier was almost full with yachts and speedboats, their bright sails flapping in the weak breeze. Over a thick dividing wall was the west pier and here most of the Howth fleet was tied up. Their large masts and bulky hulls stood in stark contrast to the sleek pleasure craft in between. 'Drive to the very end of that quay,' Patterson shouted as he began teasing the boat away from the wall, 'and I'll meet you over there in ten minutes.' Davis was into the pick-up within seconds and soon reversing back towards the main road. Kennedy kept watch as the *Gypsy*'s engines growled again, one hand gripping tightly to a rope stretching from mast to prow.

In the middle of the west pier Kevin Quinn, manager and owner of Quinn Fish Packers and Processors, watched the boat's every move. Fifty-year-old Quinn had kept the first-floor window of his offices open to enjoy the beautiful day and sea views. Sunlight glinted off the almost pond-like waters in the harbour and there was a general air of laziness in the air. Few boats had put out to sea that morning and most were berthed no more than twenty yards from his business. Quinn's company was one of four that dealt directly with Howth fishermen, buying catches as they were offloaded and selling them on to the major supermarkets, shops and restaurants within the greater Dublin area. He'd been in the business for over twenty years, and now knew most of the trawler skippers and their boats. And he'd learned about *Gypsy*'s difficulties when one of its crew arrived back from Rotterdam two days previously. The same man told him about the engine snarl, the tug to port and the wrangle over money. Now Quinn was puzzled to see *Gypsy* back in Howth. Dan Patterson was one of the more shady characters in the industry and everyone would be more than interested to learn how he'd managed to make it home considering his poor finances. The salt air and sunshine became too tempting and Quinn decided to take a break and nose around the boat as it berthed. He slipped his mobile phone into a side pocket and put the landlines on answering mode. Downstairs, where he employed three to sift orders and arrange deliveries, he explained he'd be out of the office for about twenty minutes.

12.55 p.m.

Scott Nolan was at breaking point.

Mark Higgins had called to warn him of the speed of developments and how both were now effectively blocked out of the final hours of the operation. 'They don't want us in on this, Scott. To them we're nothing more than dangerous mavericks.' With Higgins's cellphone still on and held chest high, back in his apartment Scott listened to the interchanges at the incident room. A forty-foot canary-yellow steel container with the letters P&O prominently displayed on both sides was now resting outside Derek McCann's store and already his henchmen were shifting pallets of furniture. Unknown to McCann, these activities were being monitored from a nearby tower block by four undercover detectives using long-range lenses. An extra ten armed officers wearing bulletproof vests had been drafted closer to the action. At present everyone was assuming the container held the drug consignment. And equally, everyone was assuming Davis and Kennedy couldn't be far away, probably awaiting confirmation of a successful connection before showing up.

In the outside corridor an agitated Higgins could take it no more and barked into the mouthpiece, 'Get yourself up here immediately, Scott. I'll meet you outside the front barrier.' He took a quick drag on his thirtieth cigarette of the day. 'And make sure you come armed and ready.'

1.10 p.m.

Kevin Quinn was puzzled. He was standing over the *Gypsy* where she had berthed at the most extreme end of the west pier. The trawler was lying low in the water, suggesting there was a small catch below decks. Not a significant haul but by the waterline markings something was on the boat other than her crew. And Dan Patterson was pointedly ignoring him, despite Quinn's repeated attempts to engage him in conversation. The skipper kept fiddling with ropes and pulleys, and directing his two-man team to get on with the sort of menial tasks usually reserved for slow days when nothing was happening at sea. Quinn had never seen him fuss like this after a long journey. No, usually the fiery red-haired skipper would be up on the quayside, cursing and swearing and ordering everyone around, and shouting abuse at any slackers. But whatever was on board Patterson was showing no urgency to move it. And something else concerned Quinn. Standing beside the wheelhouse was a tall, long-blond-haired man in his late twenties or early thirties. He was staring straight at Quinn with a look that both intimidated and unsettled. Quinn had watched him move around the trawler, immediately sensing how out of place he looked. His hands were smooth rather than calloused, his face pale and not weather-beaten. And he was oblivious to the maintenance activities going on. That's no fisherman, Quinn quickly concluded.

'Bugger off, Quinn,' Patterson finally barked from an opening near the engine room. 'Have you no fucking work to do?'

Quinn spun on his heel and strode back to his office, deep in thought. Then he spotted a builder's lorry parked nearby with its engine running and the driver watching him closely.

'Since when did Dan Patterson start landing his catches on to a Toyota pick-up?' he asked one of his female employees when he reached his offices again. All he got back was a baffled frown.

1.25 p.m.

Derek McCann was a heavy-set man with ample waistline and receding hair. The only exercise he did was pouring shots of whiskey and counting the takings at the end of each day. So he stood to one side as Paddy, Dekko, Anto and Luke toiled to move the delicate and exquisitely carved teak wood from the P&O trailer. There were sets of dining-room tables and chairs, outside furniture including recliners and sunshades. On another group of pallets came solid and substantial-looking beds with matching side tables. All were top quality, with exquisite attention to detail in the carvings and brass fittings. McCann calculated he could sell the lot to a dealer he knew for close on one hundred thousand Euros. Not that he needed the money, for deep inside the yellow container now being empited he knew there would be a large recess containing his drug order. That's where the millions would come from. He had a half-grin on his face as he watched the wood being jammed into the corners of his store. Then, from deep inside the steel container he heard a shout and hurried to the edge, squinting into the gloom.

'Did you find it?' His voice echoed off the metal walls.

'Yeah,' replied Anto, a whippet of a youth who could wriggle into the tightest of spaces. 'Bloody big hole between two loads of furniture. You'd really need to be lookin' to find it.'

'Brilliant.' McCann was so excited he clapped his hands with glee.

'Hang on, boss.' Anto's voice was less than enthusiastic. 'There's fuck all inside.'

1.40 p.m.

'Hello, is that the Garda station?' Kevin Quinn was convinced something suspicious was going on right under his nose outside. 'Look, I may be wasting your time but . . .' And he related his observations of the activity around the *Gypsy*, describing the very unusual-looking fisherman and the other dubious character waiting in a Toyota pick-up covered in builders' dust. 'I mean,' he finished, 'I've never heard of anyone taking fresh fish away in such a filthy truck.' Then he hung up, satisfied he'd done the right thing and already planning how to explain his legitimate concerns to Dan Patterson if there turned out to be an innocent explanation. He busied himself with paperwork, before making a number of calls to regular customers, taking orders and advising of deliveries. He gradually became aware of a strong smell of fish in the room and turned to find Sean Kennedy staring straight at him. 'Who were you talking to?'

The phone slipped out of Quinn's grasp and crashed on to the desk. His mouth went suddenly dry and he felt his legs turn to jelly. The man in front was scaring the hell out of him with his narrowed eyes and taut, vicious face. 'J-ju-just my clients,' he stammered.

'Anyone else?' The voice was as menacing as the gaze.

'N-n-no. No one. I was just talking to clients, I swear to God.'

'Good. That's very wise.' Then a single shot echoed round the office and Kevin Quinn's left eye disappeared in a bloody mess of jelly and bone.

27

1.45 p.m.

Mark Higgins was about to flee the incident room when he caught the final exchanges over the wall speakers.

Where's the cargo, Jay?

I'm bringing it straight to you.

Don't fuck with me, Jay. I'm staring at a big empty container that was full of furniture up to half an hour ago. And I didn't order furniture, Jay. If I wanted furniture I would have shopped locally. Now where's that fucking shipment?

Everything's in the back of a pick-up. I wasn't happy with what I was hearing coming out of Dublin so we decided to use a different route. As long as you're ready we'll have it with you in an hour.

Where are you?

Howth.

What the hell are you doing in Howth?

You ask too many questions, Derek. Everything's being

loaded up here. As we're talking I can see Sean doing a final count. Now where do you want to meet?

Bring it to my supermarket yard.

Is it secure?

Billy Ferguson is beside me, listening to every word. I have four of my men and there's another four of his. That's enough manpower to wage a small war so don't worry about security, just get here before everyone loses it completely.

Give me an hour.

I've started counting.

We'll be there.

With Kennedy?

With Kennedy.

Did you hear that Billy? Your friend Sean Kennedy's on his way.

Click. The line went dead.

Higgins listened to the exchange open-mouthed. A lot could happen in one hour. If someone made a wrong move, or if Billy Ferguson and McCann started a shooting match, the main players could easily go to ground. He pored over the wall map, his fingers shaking with nervous tension. There were three roads leading out of Howth and if they could be sealed off, his main targets would be trapped like rats. He grabbed a telephone and within minutes was speaking with the duty officer at Howth police station. Fifteen minutes later he pulled Scott Nolan into the passenger seat of his Saab and gunned the engine alive. 'The Commissioner can do whatever the hell he wants with McCann and Ferguson,' he snarled as he rounded a bend halfway up on the pavement. 'As far as you and I are concerned it's now open season on the other two.'

2 p.m.

Sean Kennedy and Jay Davis elected to take the most direct route into Dublin; along the same road Davis had earlier brought the Toyota truck into Howth. As they drove, both men could hardly contain their excitement. Dressed like a couple of casual labourers and steering a filthy pick-up, they were carrying the most significant illicit drug shipment ever brought into Ireland. They had *actually* pulled it off. Months of meticulous planning combined with the careful nurturing of top contacts in the narcotics underworld had produced a cargo worth many millions. And it was less than a few feet behind them, hidden underneath thick tarpaulin. They were laughing and congratulating one another when they rounded a corner and suddenly found themselves in a traffic jam. In the distance they could see a policeman at the head of the queue, leaning into the driver's side of a car. 'He's probably checking insurance discs,' Davis suggested, his fingers drumming on the steering wheel. 'And little does he know the biggest heist ever is going to glide past him in a few minutes.'

He grinned smugly at Kennedy but was surprised to see his partner frowning. 'There are three squad cars up there. It's not worth the risk. Let's go another way.'

Davis reacted immediately and edged the Toyota into a U-turn. 'We'll take the scenic route,' he sniggered. 'May as well enjoy the view.'

But Kennedy's elation was fast fading. Why were there three squad cars? 'Put your boot down,' he snapped. 'If we don't offload with McCann within an hour there'll be war.'

Davis touched the accelerator until they reached forty miles an hour in a twenty speed limit. The centre of Howth village loomed ahead.

2.35 p.m.

Mark Higgins broke every red light, overtook on the wrong side of the road and even risked instant death by speeding round two blind bends. He bullied his way through the city centre with siren screaming and lights flashing. And Scott Nolan held up an Uzi sub-machine gun so that everyone could see this was no ordinary police chase. They ignored the Police Commissioner's frantic shouts over the intercom for them to back off and zigzagged through yet another stalled line of traffic. At the seaside suburb of Clontarf, which was halfway through the frenzied journey, Higgins spun the steering wheel dangerously and his Saab skidded for about twenty yards before he corrected the line. He paused for no more than twenty seconds to collect his wits before he was off again, now pushing the speedometer past eighty miles an hour. Out of the passenger window Scott could see a blur of people as they stopped and stared, fingers pointing, heads nodding together. Now the car was past the city limits and in less congested territory, and over the link to base they learned that police in Howth had sealed off the village. Also, they had a definite sighting of the Toyota truck. And yes, they were aware the suspects were armed and dangerous.

2.55 p.m.

The focal point of the Howth headland was its village and harbour, both at its northern side. The promontory sat proudly on its own after a curve of territory linking it to the Dublin coastline. It also had a significant hill with light-house and views of Dublin Bay and the Irish Sea. A warren of roads and winding tracks criss-crossed the locale, many interlinking and others ending in a cul-de-sac. There were only three routes leading out of the peninsula and the scenic track, as Jay Davis had jokingly described the narrowest trail, was now blocked. Sean Kennedy leaned out of the passenger side door, anxiously scanning the setting. Ahead a large yellow JCB squatted in the middle of the thoroughfare and a cluster of enraged drivers stood at the sides of their vehicles, gesticulating and shouting as if curses alone would move the machine. 'Take the village road,' barked Kennedy, trying to control his growing sense of unease.

'What the hell's going on?' Davis was half standing in the cab, trying to see past the JCB.

'I dunno and we don't have time to find out. Shift it.'

It took almost five minutes to reverse the Toyota.

3.05 p.m.

A police helicopter now hovered overhead, its two-man crew diverted to the seaport as soon as news broke of the drug shipment being landed. From their vantage point they watched Higgins's Saab round the highest part of the Howth promontory and race along the narrow winding roads leading to the town centre and harbour. The pilot held position until he saw it finally skid to a halt beside a heavily manned police intercept. Three squad cars straddled the throughfare at different sites, effectively preventing any ramming exercise that might be attempted. Officers in bright yellow flak jackets could be seen crouched at strategic points, allowing good views of all movements coming at them from the village. Satisfied, the pilot banked to the left and closed in on the port area.

3.10 p.m.

Billy Ferguson stared at his watch, by now convinced Derek McCann was double crossing him. The one-hour deadline promised by Jay Davis had come and gone, and still there was no sign of this huge deal he'd been involved in since his brother had been murdered. 'Where's yer mate, Derek? He said he'd be here in an hour and it's well past that.' McCann fished inside his pocket and dialled up on his mobile. Combined with Davis's no-show, Ferguson's ugly features and intimidating attitude were annoying him greatly. The number rang out after three minutes and McCann's forehead creased into a deep frown. He redialled, one eye on Ferguson watching the Scouse's reactions while his other hand eased his handgun free. The number rang out again. 'Well?' Ferguson was almost in his face with a twisted and menacingly offensive scowl. He poked McCann in the midriff. 'Where's yer fuckin' mate?'

At that moment McCann's patience snapped and he turned the phone towards Ferguson, momentarily confusing the other man. 'The number's engaged.' Ferguson took one step back to get a better look at the small mobile screen. 'Yer a lyin' bast—' It was the last insult Ferguson ever started as McCann emptied six rounds of copper-tipped bullets into his chest.

His impetuous move was the signal for the armed response unit to break cover and there was sustained gunfire in the area for almost ten minutes.

3.25 p.m.

Sean Kennedy spotted the roadblock first. He leaned out of the passenger side window, his ponytail flicking as he desperately tried to see a way round the situation. Jay Davis was revving the engine but going nowhere as the pick-up sat stalled in yet another line of cars. 'What the fuck's going on?' Davis's voice was shrill and edgy, and for the first time Kennedy sensed his partner was losing control. He jumped out through the side door and limped a few yards ahead to get a better view. In the background he could hear the steady drone of a helicopter and he swivelled three hundred and sixty degrees to track its position. But while he could hear the engine he couldn't see the chopper and decided to dodge between the queue of vehicles and get closer to the barricade. It was about fifty yards ahead and now he could clearly make out a significant armed police presence.

He hurried back and climbed into the passenger side. 'Turn for fuck's sake,' he shouted and drew his handgun.

Davis was now shaking from head to toe. 'What's happening?'

Kennedy kept his gaze firmly ahead as he eased a fresh magazine into his Heckler & Koch. 'They're on to us. Shift this thing or we're dead.' In his panic Davis reversed so fast the pick-up crashed into a green Ford Focus and from behind came a string of oaths. Davis then shot the truck forward and finally managed to create enough space to swing into the opposite lane and turn towards Howth village.

The enraged face of a young woman suddenly appeared at Kennedy's side window, her hands gripping the sill. 'Stop, stop this minute,' she shouted angrily. Kennedy brought the full force of the butt of his handgun on to her fingers and she howled in pain and let go.

The road back into the village was narrow and winding, and Davis was having difficulty holding the steering wheel. He grated the gears, causing the truck to kangaroo jump and bounce Kennedy's head off the roof. 'Drive the fucking thing properly,' Kennedy roared but when he looked across he knew immediately Davis had lost it. The once suave and self-confident womaniser was now a wreck. His hands shook, perspiration poured off his brow and his lower jaw trembled.

The pick-up reached a tight bend and Davis tried to drop to a lower gear for better control but succeeded only in stalling the engine. 'Fuck it, fuck it,' he screamed at the dashboard. The truck remained defiantly fixed on the corner, refusing to start. 'Get out and push.' Davis was desperate as he feverishly dragged at the controls to find second gear. He glanced sideways, only to find a Heckler & Koch pointing straight at him and there wasn't one word spoken before Kennedy squeezed the trigger.

3.45 p.m.

Scott Nolan and Mark Higgins were the only two from the armed unit who pushed through the roadblock and started running towards the stalled pick-up. Ahead they could hear the screams and frightened cries of drivers and passengers stuck in the line, saw others jump from their vehicles and dive to the ground, some crawling for better cover. 'You go left, I'll take the right,' shouted Higgins and immediately the two split up.

Almost on cue the police helicopter droned overhead, the deafening swirl of its blades adding to the drama but also drowning out verbal communication. Scott saw Higgins point in one direction, then indicate he was heading towards the truck. He also noticed Higgins was carrying an Uzi sub-machine gun.

3.55 p.m.

The only thoughts in Sean Kennedy's head were self-preservation and evasion. He was still a young man and while he had been responsible for the early deaths of many over the years he was determined not to join their ranks. Equally, he was resolute about escaping arrest. There was no way he would face the ignominy of the courts and then rot for the rest of his life in some stinking Irish gaol. Those dual fears now drove him along the narrow and winding side streets of the village of Howth.

He jammed his handgun into the waistband of his denims and pulled his T-shirt over it, limping as fast as his weak leg would allow. The sun was sinking into the west, casting long shadows in the lanes and alleyways and the area was almost deserted, with only an occasional soul going about business, oblivious to the unfolding events nearby. Kennedy reached the top street and paused briefly. Through gaps in steep tracks leading to the harbour side he could see large crowds gathered, held back by policemen in yellow flak jackets. I can't go down there, he decided. There's only one way out and that's along the forest trail at the edge of town. Memories of childhood days exploring the popular port flooded back and he tried desperately to clear his mind. He heard a scuffling behind and dropped to the ground, rolling to one side and coming up with handgun at the ready. But it was only a dog pawing at a discarded refuse sack. Now Kennedy's heart pounded so much he could hear the pulse in his ears. With the sun no longer throwing warmth, the afternoon had become cool, yet the assassin was sweating, his face red from exertion. His ponytail was dank and ragged and he pulled strands of wet hair away from his face to see more clearly. Keep moving, you've got to keep going.

4.05 p.m.

Scott Nolan was lost. He'd never visited Howth before and was unfamiliar with its terrain. He'd split from Mark Higgins about fifty yards from the stalled pick-up and now was racing along the top roads of the village to get a better view of the streets below. Almost unbelievably, there were people walking around as if nothing were amiss, while others stood at their doorways looking up and down, faces a mixture of puzzlement and concern. The drone of the helicopter as it swept over the area was unusual and one or two necks craned to stare upwards. Round bend after bend Scott rushed, up steep steps and cobbled pathways. This time his handgun was drawn and he was aching to use it. I know you're close, Kennedy, I can almost smell you. Come out and show me your face. But the effort misted his lenses and he had to stop and wipe the glasses on the end of his black T-shirt. He paused briefly to listen and felt perspiration trickle along his chest and hairline. Quickly he tugged his shirt free and ran the front along his head. When he put his glasses back on the street was deserted.

4.20 p.m.

The young woman never knew what hit her. Sean Kennedy spotted her wheeling a buggy with a sleeping child along the top road and followed. She was in her late twenties, he calculated, short red hair and freckled face giving her a classical Celtic look. She was in brown corduroy slacks and white roll-neck sweater, and completely preoccupied with the baby. Every now and then she would lean over and check the tiny figure before pressing ahead. In a side basket clipped to the push handlebars were groceries and Kennedy guessed she had bought something perishable and was in a hurry to get home. The woman finally paused at a terrace of mock-Georgian houses and opened the front door of one at the end of the row. She was shuffling the buggy inside when Kennedy made his move. A scream stuck in her throat as his right fist hit her left cheek with such force she dropped like a stone. And through the commotion the child slept soundly.

Kennedy was now inside the house, the buggy in the hallway, his victim dragged into a front room. Through a back kitchen window he had a commanding view of the harbour and seafront, and could see even more people milling about than before. There's no escape through that mob. Then he squinted to one side as he spotted the police helicopter swoop over the top end of the town, its engines so loud the child in the buggy stirred, yawned and stuck a finger in his mouth before falling back to sleep. Kennedy breathed a sigh of relief. He followed the chopper as it circled the area, now diving so low that nearby telegraph lines shook from the downdraught of the blades. I've got to get out of here. They'll start searching the houses soon. He tried desperately to clear his brain, forcing silent questions he had to answer. Where am I? At the top end of the village. Where's the forest trail? At the top end. But where at the top end? He tried to imagine the last time he and Anna had chased one another along these same streets, she disappearing and escaping his frantic searches, finally reappearing about a mile outside the town limits. Where did she go? Think man, think. Which way did she go to hide?

He stepped over the unconscious body lying on the floor and squinted out through the window. To his right there was nothing but new housing developments and these confused him. But to his left, back along the road he'd taken, he was sure he could make out a row of stone steps leading to a grassy hillside. That's it, he almost shouted out loud. That's the track.

4.30 p.m.

Mark Higgins was exhausted and panting and sweating, and cursing his addiction to cigarettes. He'd sprinted along the side streets and back roads of the small town, knocking on doors and rushing through pubs and hotels. But there was no sign of Sean Kennedy. At the stalled pick-up he'd seen the body of Jay Davis, though the dead man's facial features were barely recognisable. Now he was concerned about his brother-in-law's safety. If Scott confronted Kennedy he knew who'd be standing at the end of the shoot-out. He leaned against a squad car with its crackling intercom liaising with HQ and the police helicopter. Within a minute he learned there was still no firm sighting of the suspect and that Scott was at the highest point of the village. Since many of the side streets leading to the top roads were too narrow for vehicles Higgins set off on foot.

4.35 p.m.

Sean Kennedy feverishly cut at his ponytail with a pair of kitchen scissors and soon had trimmed his locks to a pudding bowl style. Rummaging through an upstairs wardrobe he found a navy-blue beret, fresh white shirt and beige V-neck sweater. When he finally left the house, pushing the sleeping baby in the buggy, he looked like any proud father out for a stroll. His Heckler & Koch was underneath a nappy change bag in the side basket, completely hidden from anyone passing. Ahead he could see the stone steps he reckoned would lead him to freedom. Even though his leg ached, an adrenalin rush gave him renewed strength. Just keep your head up and check the baby every now and then like you saw his mother do. Don't rush; this is a stroll with your son. When you finally get to the far side of the woodland trail you'll be past the roadblocks. Then walk the buggy for another few hundred yards or so and hijack the first car you see. By the time these bastards have figured out what's happened you'll be miles away. He was no more than twenty paces from the steps when he saw a tall, rather gaunt man emerge from a side street. It's OK. Try to relax, it's not a crime to take your child out for a walk. He glanced to his left and noticed a long, steep, winding row of steps running for at least thirty yards downhill.

4.37 p.m.

Scott Nolan wasn't sure what to do. He'd been out of communication with everyone involved in the chase and didn't know whether Kennedy had been detained elsewhere. But the continuous sweep of the police helicopter suggested the hunt was still on, which was why he continued to scour every back alley and side street at the top end of town. His Beretta was jammed under his trouser belt to free his hands but he was beginning to lose heart; there was no sign of the man he so desperately wanted to confront. Now he was almost at the end of what he'd decided would be the last passageway he'd climb that day. He was in shade and a few feet in front bright light beckoned. He paused to catch his breath and was certain he heard footsteps ahead. He stepped into the upper road and saw a young man in his late twenties or early thirties pushing a buggy. Through his fogged-up lenses he could just about discern the man's physique, he was slim, with a narrow face, tight lips and hooded eyes. But he didn't look like a man on the run, rather like any father out for a walk with his baby in a buggy.

4.38 p.m.

Sean Kennedy had studied Scott Nolan for many weeks when he scouted his targets for the attacks on 10 February. He knew every wrinkle on the doctor's face, every hair on his bedraggled head. And, according to media reports he'd read, Nolan had fled Dublin for his native Chicago at the beginning of March. Yet there was something disturbingly familiar about the man now staring at him. The hairstyle was bad beyond description and nothing like the mess he'd seen so often. And the doctor had been better fed whereas this character looked almost emaciated. But there was something about the slight stoop, the mannerisms with the spectacles, the body language. And now Kennedy could see the bulge of a pistol in the stranger's belt. He slipped his right hand into the side basket until he felt the comforting steel of his Heckler & Koch.

4.39 p.m.

Their eyes locked and in that split second Scott Nolan knew he'd found Sean Kennedy. He reached for his Beretta.

Fuck it, it *is* him. By now Kennedy had his handgun drawn and pointed straight at Scott. An amused smile flitted as he watched the doctor struggle to engage the firing mechanism of his pistol. He grabbed hold of the buggy and pushed it violently towards the long, winding, stepped lane. Suddenly the child awoke and piercing screams of terror filled the air as the buggy bounced off cobblestones until it reached the top of the path. Inside, the toddler had wriggled free and now was almost falling out. One more roll of the wheels and he would be pitched head first to his death down a steep row of steel and concrete steps.

4.40 p.m.

Instinct took over as Scott dived to his right, managing to grip one of the wheels. The buggy was still unsteady from the thrashing of the distraught child and Scott rolled twice on the ground to get a better hold. He was dragging the stroller backwards when he felt a sting in his right shoulder, followed by the unmistakable sound of bullets pinging against stone as a series of rounds missed him by inches. He pulled the wriggling boy closer to his body and rolled again so he could protect him from the onslaught. Then the alleyway filled with gunfire and Scott closed his eyes and prayed.

4.42 p.m.

He wasn't dead. His right shoulder ached like hell and felt wet and sticky, and as the infant bucked and screamed he felt darts of pain that took his breath away. But he would not let go, it was too dangerous. He risked a glance backwards and saw Mark Higgins standing over a limp and blood-stained body, his Uzi pointing downwards. Then he took aim again and the air filled with the spit of automatic gunfire.

Higgins rushed to Scott, dragging the now speechless child from his arms. Little hands flailed helplessly and the toddler's face was white with shock and fear. Scott rolled on to his back, groaning with pain. A strange darkness closed in as he sensed Higgins kneel beside him. 'You just couldn't stop being a doctor, could you? You are one mad, mad bastard.'

From somewhere distant came the welcoming sound of sirens and ambulance klaxons, and through his intense discomfort Scott managed to twist his head and glance back up the street. 'It was Kennedy, wasn't it?'

Higgins pulled off his sweater, quickly rolled it into a ball and rested Scott's head on it. 'Yes, there's no question about that.'

Scott felt cold and clammy, his body drained, and he desperately wanted to sleep. 'We finally got him then, didn't we?' His words were almost a whisper.

'Stay quiet and save your strength.'

Now came hurried footsteps, and yells and angry roars and urgent voices barking orders. And as a blackness washed over him, Scott wondered would these be the last sounds he would ever hear. He opened his eyes but found the world blurred.

28

One year later.

Scott Nolan sat perched on a high stool at the bar of the Brehon Pub in the Near North district of Chicago. The Brehon was the last traditional corner saloon in the city, frequented as much by tourists as regulars and Scott was nursing his second draught beer from one of the establishment's famous frosted glasses. He had one eye on that day's *Tribune*, the other on the door. The first two pages of the broadsheet were filled with the latest outrages from city and country, drive-by shootings in the Southside, corruption in City Hall, sex scandals in Washington. As Scott scanned the headlines he concluded little had changed in its reporting over the years. Chicago continued to have the highest homicide rate in North America, City Hall still seemed to produce a steady line of officials on the take and in Washington politicians just couldn't keep their hands off pretty interns. It was creeping up on five in the afternoon and outside the temperature was stuck at two degrees below zero, as it had been since daybreak.

It had been a long winter in the mid-West with heavy snowstorms throughout January and February. The snow had turned to slush by early March but another severe freeze at the beginning of April caused transport chaos and restricted movement throughout Illinois. Earlier Scott had taken a cab from the University area but traffic snarls and road closures delayed him nearly an hour. Still, when he entered the bar and looked around there was no sign of his guest so he consoled himself with a drink. A wall clock now chimed five exactly and he was engrossed in an article on page three when he heard a familiar complaining voice beside him.

'Jesus, what a bloody ice-box of a city. How the hell does anyone live here?'

Scott looked up at Mark Higgins, grinning when he saw his purple nose and flaming cheeks. Frost was clinging to his eyebrows and lashes, even to the lapels of his overcoat and gloves.

'And nice to see you too,' he said, secretly delighting in Higgins's whinge. 'Would you like a chilled beer?'

Higgins's eyes rolled in his head. 'I'm so cold all I want is a hot water bottle.'

Scott shook his head with mock dismay. 'Sorry, no can do. Around here real men never let a snow flurry get in the way of a drink.'

'Snow flurry my arse,' growled Higgins as he struggled out of his coat and scarf and thick woollen beret. He smoothed his hair into shape and dragged a high stool closer, his gaze taking in the range of bottles available behind the bar. Then he flagged the bartender. 'I think I'll have a whiskey to put fire in my belly.' They waited in silence until the tumbler was set down and Higgins took a generous mouthful, rolling the amber liquid around his tongue before swallowing. He sighed with content and glanced quickly around the room. Apart from Scott and himself there were three separate groups gathered in distant corners, their conversation and occasional laughter mercifully drowning out some televised political debate. Finally both men shook hands, Scott noticing the firmness of Higgins's grip and sensing the warmth and camaraderie behind the gesture.

'How's the shoulder holding up?' Mark Higgins's jet-black hair had greyed significantly since Scott saw him last, at the end of his bed in a military hospital two weeks after the Howth shoot out. Next day Scott was stretchered onto a US special services aircraft and flown directly to an army medical facility outside Washington. There he spent another month while doctors and physiotherapists struggled to repair his right shoulder. But Sean Kennedy had left his mark and when Scott was eventually discharged he had only fifty per cent movement in the joint. Since then there had been no communication between the two despite Scott's many attempts to get in touch.

'Stiff and sore, especially in this sort of weather. But it's no big deal considering . . .' He let the rest of the sentence hang in the air. 'How are things in Dublin?'

Higgins shrugged and sipped on his whiskey. 'Same as usual, cold and wet. The fat cats get fatter while the rest of us struggle to get by.'

Scott played an imaginary violin. 'Your story breaks my heart.'

Higgins grinned and waved for another round, wriggling on the chair for comfort. Then he inspected his one time partner. 'Good to see you've put on a bit of weight and tidied up your hair. And trendy glasses at last. You could walk the streets without scaring the locals. What are you up to these days?'

Scott ignored the question. 'I tried calling you.'

Higgins passed a ten-dollar note across as the drinks arrived. 'I know.'

'So why the wall of silence?'

'Government policy. I was under virtual house arrest after you were flown out. All contact was strictly forbidden. My home phone was tapped, my cell phone monitored and I was followed everywhere. I didn't even feel safe in the toilet. Cunningham insisted I take six moths paid leave while he decided what to do with me.'

Scott inspected Higgins's face closely. There were wrinkles now that he didn't remember before with deeper crows' feet and tightness around the mouth suggesting a man who'd been under a lot of pressure. Even the muscular frame seemed slacker. 'That can't have been easy to take.'

'It lasted six weeks.'

'Then what?'

'He dragged me in again. Spanish police gave us a tip off about an Irish gang operating out of Alicante planning to ship cocaine through Dublin airport.' He took another sip of whiskey, pulled a face and then turned to Scott. Now he was smiling and the wrinkles disappeared for a moment. 'So I went undercover again.'

Scott shook his head. 'You are one mad bastard.'

Higgins burst out laughing, so loud the other customers turned to look. 'Now that's a phrase I recall from some time ago.'

Scott frowned as the memory flooded back. Higgins had used those same words as he lay wounded on a bloodstained road in the village of Howth. Ten yards away was the bullet-ridden body of Sean Kennedy, the man who had destroyed so many lives. Was it really a year ago? Now Higgins was staring straight at him. 'I heard you're working at some academic position. Why didn't you go back to being a real doctor?'

Scott mulled this over. He took a long draught of beer before replying, wondering how to phrase his answer. For the past seven months he'd been a research fellow at the University of Chicago medical centre. 'I'm not the same man, Mark. What happened in Ireland shook me to the core. I never knew I was capable of such intense hatred and loathing that I'd be prepared to kill. It wasn't in my nature and went against everything I'd been trained to do as a doctor. I'm supposed to heal the sick, not blow their brains out. But Kennedy unleashed a side of my personality I didn't know existed and I didn't much like it. So I decided to go into research. That way I can ease my mind back to some degree of normality without the emotional pressure of dealing with sick children every day.'

Higgins's expression reflected his puzzlement. 'But you were so crash hot Laura never stopped boasting.' His voice changed as he tried to mimic. 'Scott's one of the top paediatric liver specialists in the world. He could have had a job in any top institution but he chose to come here.'

At the mention of Laura's name Scott turned away. He was hoping they wouldn't drag her into the conversation but immediately realised how foolish that notion was. Laura's death was the catalyst for all that happened afterwards. The pain and anguish of her loss, then the bitter arguments with Higgins when he tormented Scott for being alive while his sister was in her grave. It was only after some of the most dangerous moments of their undercover work that both gradually came to respect each other's identity and feelings. 'Yeah, well maybe Laura read me wrong.'

Higgins leaned to one side to catch Scott's attention. 'No

she didn't. Sure I called you some choice names and it took me a long time to get over her murder. But you put your life and career on the line to find her killer when most would have disappeared on the next flight. And maybe you think you're no hero with this research post but when we took out Kennedy we probably saved a lot of lives down the line. He had a track record that shocked even me.'

Scott switched tack and changed the conversation. Going over old ground was too painful, the emotions still raw. 'What brings you to Chicago?'

Higgins checked he couldn't be overheard. 'The Irish Government extradited one of this city's more notorious criminals. He was hiding out in Dublin over the past two years before being tracked. Four of us flew him first class across the Atlantic and straight into the arms of the local cops. It's the only time I've seen so many men refuse free drink. The downside is we go back steerage and pay for every damn thing.' The dregs of the whiskey disappeared in one gulp and Higgins inspected his watch. It was closing in on six o'clock. 'Did it take you long to get here?'

'Over an hour. The traffic's worse than Dublin and that's saying something.'

Higgins started pulling his coat back on. 'I better get going. There's a briefing at seven and the way the roads look it's going to take some time to get there.' Now the scarf was being wrapped around his neck, the woollen beret dragged over his ears. His eyes suddenly caught Scott's disappointed stare. 'Any girl friends?' he asked. 'Are you having a social life?'

Scott shrugged and swirled the beer around his glass. 'I've been dating someone for a few months.'

'Don't sound so defensive,' growled Higgins. 'Everybody

has to pick up the pieces again. Last October Harry Power moved to Brussels to head up a EU task force on organised crime. Then in January my beloved police chief retired on a Friday only to open his own personal security company on a Monday. Life goes on.'

'And what about you?'

'What about me? I'm a survivor. Knock me down and I'll bounce back. And you have to bounce back too otherwise I may as well have let Kennedy finish you off. You're a doctor, you should know all about the grieving process.'

Scott shook his head in mock disbelief. 'Am I hearing correctly? Are you offering me therapy?'

Higgins tucked his scarf closer to his throat and grinned widely. 'We've come a long way, Scott. Twelve months ago I'd have knocked your head off given half a chance. Now I'm buying you beer in your own hometown. Life's funny, isn't it?'

Both men were on their feet and facing one another. Their eyes locked briefly and a thousand unspoken words rushed through Scott's brain. He half extended his right hand, turning slightly to protect his shoulder. 'Take care of yourself.' The words were mumbled. 'And keep in touch this time. I'd like to hear what's going on in Dublin.'

Mark Higgins took a deep breath, held it and then let it out slowly. Scott could see his one time partner was trying to protect his tough man image. But slowly the cracks appeared and the crow's feet deepened around his eyes. He stomped his feet and bear hugged himself a few times. 'A stranger could easily get lost around here, couldn't he?' Higgins's voice was full of exaggerated concern.

'Absolutely.'

'Especially in this sort of weather.'

'It's real cold and dark outside,' Scott agreed as he turned to the bartender and ordered another round.

'And this briefing will probably only be a waste of good drinking time.' Higgins started dragging his coat and scarf off.

'I wouldn't fritter one minute there if I were you.' Scott watched as the coat was laid to one side. 'Reunions like this don't come around too often.'

'Damned right.' Higgins dragged his high stool closer to the counter and leaned on one elbow, grinning from ear to ear. 'Did I ever show you how to use a Sterling sub-machine gun?'

Scott groaned out loud. 'No more hardware lessons, please. I don't want to go there again.' The drinks were set down and another ten-dollar bill flashed. 'Cheers,' they toasted and two glasses clinked loudly.

Scott took a quick gulp and cleared his throat. 'Now then, did I ever tell you how to give an injection without leaving a mark on the skin?'

Higgins spluttered so much he had to wipe good whiskey off his chin. He scowled at Scott. 'No you bloody well didn't.'

Scott's face creased in fake surprise. 'Really? Every undercover agent should know that trick.'

'I don't wanna hear.' Higgins had both hands over his ears.

Scott motioned to the bartender again. 'Could we see the counter menu please? I think this could turn out to be a long night.'